I0772745

The Growing Darkness

Book I

The God Killers Trilogy

Written By:

Sean D Gregory

Cover Art Hand Painted by Libby Musacchio

Content Editing: Steven Moore - Condor Publishing
Line Editor: RB Michaels - Writer's Journey Services
Copy Editor: Laura Thompson - Writer's Journey Services
Map Design: RB Michaels - Writer's Journey Services

First Edition Printed 2024 in Hardcover, Paperback, and eBook

For more information, visit: www.sean-gregory.com

Dedication

To Aunt Bobi and Nate. Every day still hurts.
But this story helped.
You are not alone

;

Tal
Kerakot
Breakridge
Pall
Tehsket
Hericot
Valley View
N
W
E
S
Gal-Daro
Valley of Cusk
Coraside Bay
Old Towne
Gotar Springs
King's Regal Highway
Rogue's Pointe
Valshannon
Rhine Woods
of
Rhinestar
Gal Danang
Hildabrestand
Charger's Wharf
Winding Run
Rankin Lake
Brine Riverhyre
Killinshire
Dresdin
Renshmere
Arelo
Cliffport
THE FIVE REALMS
OF CONISHANT

The
Growing
Darkness

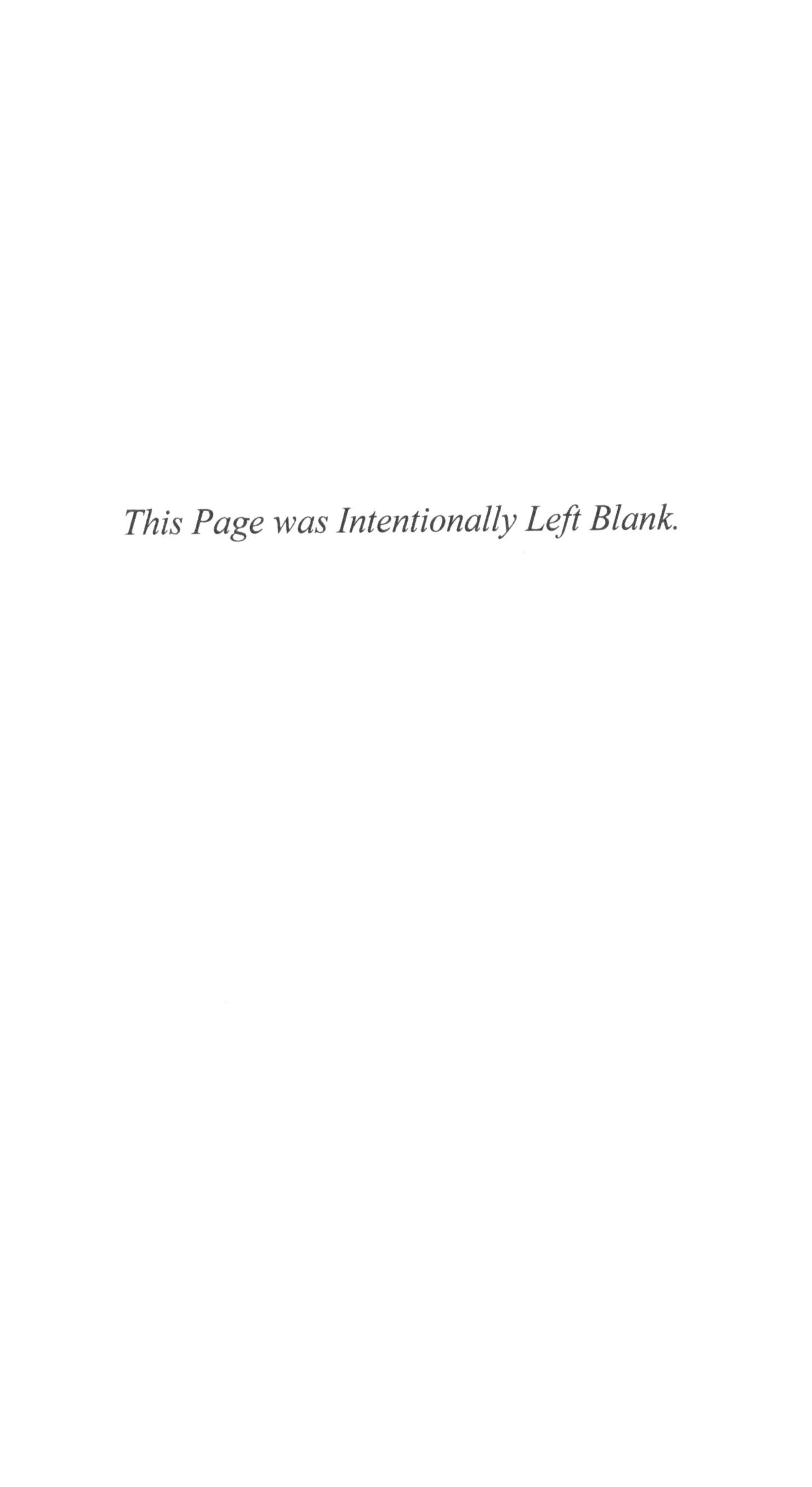
This Page was Intentionally Left Blank.

Prologue

Shamna paced the back wall of the chamber perched at the top of the Tower of Tunisia as six sets of eyes tracked her path—most in mild amusement. Her ears and cheeks flushed bright crimson as her blood pressure increased with her temper. The once-controlled simmer erupted through her delicate mask of cool assurance.

"Fools! All of you! I'm trying to prevent the destruction of everything we've spent millennia building!" she screamed.

Six bemused faces stared at her. All except Nadur, of course. Without a glance in her direction, her husband remained distracted, writing in his research log. The fool should be supporting her. Instead, he sits there scribbling away; his obsessive focus directed on those damned netherstacks.

Focus on the problem at hand! she screamed in her head.

After all, he was part of the problem. Unbelievers grew in increased numbers—quiet pockets of the faithless sprouted throughout the Five Realms. Her spies had already infiltrated one group. She knew there were others.

She glared at her husband.

I should divorce you the way I did Hakaka so many ages ago, she thought.

After thirty thousand years, she expected growth toward maturity would be a foregone conclusion. Eight millennia of marriage later, however, Nadur still behaved like a man-child, caught up in whatever study or experiment he thought was most pressing at the time. He was supposed to be her ally, the one she could count on to support her in this discussion. She watched him, teeth clenched, as he scribbled into that insufferable notepad he carried everywhere.

Great Eight, my ass, she thought. *We are still little more than spoiled children fighting over petty differences. Maybe I should not put so much energy into keeping the monsters locked away.*

They held this annual Council gathering for thirty millennia to maintain their connection to one another. Sure, there'd been a few Great Wars—all brought on by her ex-husband—but they'd always worked together. This time was different.

Once a hallmark of their collaboration, the Council had devolved over the past few decades into primitive egos protecting individual turf. She couldn't believe, after all of their efforts, she was ready to go her own way, exhausted by the burden of fruitless compromise and inaction. A storm loomed on the near horizon of time and threatened to destroy all they'd accomplished. She could feel dark forces pressing on them—some defined, others unclear.

Today's session, already many hours long, culminated after days of relentless politics. Shamna's final conclusion: the gods of Conishant could not reach a unified decision. All week, the raging sea of turning tides ebbed and flowed as alliances formed, fell apart, and were replaced.

She slammed her hands against the grand oval table that stretched before her. No one flinched. Those who understood the problem glared across the wooden span at those too petty to consider they might be wrong. She'd only swayed two her way. Most of the others remained unconvinced.

One was yet to chime in.

The ascent to godhood hadn't changed any of them for the better. They'd been made worse. Self-absorbed and less unified, the lust for power drove them now.

Nadur sat in his usual spot to the left of the empty chair reserved for Juu, the Father of the Great Eight. Juu, who was conspicuously absent from the Council meeting for so long that no one bothered to mention him. Juu, who led their ascension to godhood, had become reclusive, growing in neither power nor influence. Juu, who for centuries contributed no power to the pool of energy used to contain many of Conishant's dangers. Even his location remained unknown until he showed up in their sphere, unannounced, with some odd demand.

No matter, the Father of the Gods was unnecessary in this assembly. If they included him, it was out of nostalgic reverence—a sentiment universally lost over the last thousand years.

To Nadur's left, Krikhi sat fixated on her scaled skin, which she'd evolved after several thousand years of ex-experimentation. The multi-jeweled skin of the Queen of the Korund reflected the multitude of candles suspended from above and cast prismatic images onto surfaces—flashes of ruby reds, emerald greens, blue sapphires, and jade bounced around the room as she drummed her fingers.

Morze, who always positioned herself to Krikhi's left, leaned away from the corundum-covered woman who had once been her closest ally. Her gills expanded and closed as she breathed within the orb of water she'd kept encircled around her head. The shimmering mass was yet another distraction. Shamna wished the woman would just hang up the act. She didn't know who Morze thought she fooled with her "this is me" story. Still, the woman insisted on the show. She sat back, her bare webbed feet crossed and propped on the table. Over her palm hovered another liquid orb, much smaller than the one around her head—her incessant fidget toy extracted from the moist mountain air.

"Are you bored, Morze?" Hakaka asked from the other side of the room. His signature wry smirk made Shamna's skin crawl.

Morze looked across the table at the bird-nosed man and rolled her eyes.

"Yes. Aren't you?" Morze said. "Must we continue this stupid conversation? Everyone here knows you won't reduce your contribution to the barrier, Shamna," she said as she watched the raging woman pace the room. "And you, my dear vengeful Hakaka, will start another war no matter what happens here this week. You always do. It's been what, three hundred years?" She dismissed the small water ball with the wave of her hand, and it evaporated into the air. "I say bring it on. Let's cull some of the chaff out of the population."

Hakaka smiled, his sharp teeth bared. "I welcome the bloodshed."

What did I ever see in you? Shamna wondered for the millionth time.

"Sister," came a soft voice. Shamna turned to Ezra, always more concerned with her appearance than contributions of value. Her golden hair shone with a radiant light, like thousands of tiny filaments illuminated from inside her dense skull, their light a halo around her smooth black skin. Even after thirty thousand years, the woman was radiant in her beauty—and incredibly vain. "I understand your concerns, but Hakaka has assured us there will not be another Great War." Ezra looked at Morze, "Despite what some of us say."

Morze shrugged in indifference.

"And you believe him," Quietius mused, a statement, not a question. "Really, Ezra, I think all this sunshine has gone to your head. You've spent so much time as the Sun Goddess I think it fried your brain."

"Eat shit, Quietius," Ezra spat. "Don't you have some dead folks to trick into paying for a ride to the other side? You are such a fraud."

The Lord of the Final Slumber drummed his fingers on the table, steady beats echoing in the chamber. His deep-set eyes looked tired. Eternity weighed on him. Shamna had thought so for several decades, but the last two years seemed somehow worse.

"No, Quietius is right," Fildeus said, her tone a soft command. She shifted in her chair next to Hakaka, beautiful furs conforming to her muscular body. Hakaka turned toward her, expectant.

"What assurance is your word, Hak?" she asked him.

Shamna winced at Fildeus' use of the familiar. She'd never understood the friendship between the Goddess of the Hunt and the God of War. Fildeus believed in the value of life and the sacrifice life made to beget more life. Hakaka only cared for conquest and bloodshed.

"Why, whatever do you mean, Huntress?" Hakaka asked. "I intend to keep my side of the agreement."

"Hah!" Shamna barked. "You've never kept your word! Three Great Wars! Three! You always start them. I can smell the lust on you." She walked around the table and stood over Hakaka as he spun his chair to face her. "You promised then, too. Your track record stinks."

"I know you think I still harbor ill will toward you and Nadur, darling, but that's ancient history." He stood to face her, his beaked nose so close to hers she could make out the pores. "Don't flatter yourself. I haven't loved you in so long a thousand generations have passed." He turned to Nadur. "Besides, you seem to prefer dorks over real power."

"Hey!" Nadur said, leaning forward on an elbow, his finger aimed at Hakaka, "watch your tone with my wife. I beat you then. I'll do it again. Last I checked, you were oh and three."

"Oh, that got your attention, husband?" Shamna replied, exasperated.

"I only need to win once," Hakaka taunted. "You have to win every time."

Nadur leaned back in his chair and crossed his arms.

"I haven't lost any power. My following has grown at twice the rate yours has. You are no longer the heavyweight in this bout. If you want to start another war, I'm fine with it. I'll take you on, one on one."

Hakaka smiled at Nadur, his sharp teeth elongating as he did.

Ezra interrupted the face-off and asked, "Are we ready for a vote yet?"

"Not unless Krikhi wants to weigh in," Fildeus said.

All eyes turned to the precious stone-scaled Goddess of the Korund. She looked at everyone, startled by the attention.

"Don't look at me. You already know I am here as an advisor only. I promised neutrality and will not violate my promise."

"No, Krikhi, you pick a side this time," Shamna demand-ed. "You've profited from neutrality for too long."

Krikhi stood up. "I don't answer to you. Feel free to stop buying the weapons of my people at any time, honey." She turned to the members still seated. "I'm heading home. This has been a waste of time, as usual." Without another word, Krikhi walked out the chamber door, her eight-foot-tall frame ducking under the arches as she went.

"Well, it's settled then. Without Krikhi to validate the vote, we have to wait 'til next year," Morze said. "I'll go back to my waters. The seas need to be tended to."

Murmurs across the group seconded her sentiment, and one by one, the Gods of Conishant left the chamber, their moods dark.

Three minutes later, Hakaka and Shamna stood alone in the chamber. They eyed each other before Shamna walked to the large double-doors to ensure the others were out of earshot. Satisfied, she turned back to Hakaka.

"Do you think they suspect?" she asked.

"No. Are you sure this is the way you want to play it?" Hakaka queried, his tone softer.

"It's the only way to protect what we've built," she said.

"You'd pay such a heavy price over this?" he asked as he approached her.

"Love requires tough choices." Tears formed in Shamna's eyes.

"You truly love these mortals," he said. He stood before her and placed a hand on each of her shoulders. "I know I've been a pain in the ass the last twenty millennia, but I do still love you."

She nodded. "We know what happens if we don't protect them from themselves," she replied. She raised her eyes to meet Hakaka's. "And your love costs too much, I'm afraid."

His face soured at her harsh words, and she regretted them immediately. But too many years passed, and truth was truth. Besides, she loved her husband, man-child or not. And Hakaka is a hothead. Unstable.

He bowed his head, kissed her forehead, and turned to the door. As he opened it, he stopped. Without looking at her, he spoke softly, pain in his voice.

"I will do this for you," he said. "But this is it. Next time, it will be war."

He walked through the door, closing it as he left.

Shamna let out an unsteady breath. She knew she played a dangerous game. If Hakaka figured out her plans, he'd definitely start another war. Should the others figure out she worked with Hakaka behind the scenes, they'd never trust her again and pull their support for the barriers, leaving it all to her and weakening her powers further.

She resisted the urge to burst into tears as she weighed the consequences of success. The consequences of failure were worse. She knew she might regret the decision someday, but the cost of inaction was too great. Besides, the decision was made. For the good of Conishant, some sacrifices were required, no matter how painful. Thirty thousand years had removed much of her compassion, albeit not entirely. In another thirty thousand years, the memory of the coming events would be lost to time, of which she had plenty.

She worried about how the decision would impact her husband. She hated to admit it to Nadur, but she now knew he was right. The netherstacks were a problem. An existential crisis. If she admitted to him this fact, however, he'd pressure her to take his specific brand of action. Action she knew would be insufficient. Her dear husband refused to look away from physical science and step into social science. The real problem was atheism. The solution was far more complex than his mind could handle. Besides, he was too soft to ever agree to her plan. She needed Hakaka and his easy willingness to sacrifice blood.

She only hoped it worked.

The Growing Darkness

Chapter One

Journal Entry: 1

Dear Whoever,

If you are reading this, it's very likely I'm already dead.

It wouldn't surprise me if that were the case. Between my own attempts and the many attempts of others, I am astounded I've lived this long.

As my first entry into these pages, I am addressing it to you, the finder of this journal, because I fully expect, based on my life thus far, for my death to come violently, when I am alone, and not peacefully surrounded by friends.

And I have no family.

I only hope my death was a long, drawn-out battle—a glorious story told in song for generations. Though I doubt it will be. A different discussion for some other time. If you read this, you'll soon discern why.

Either way, holding this journal in your hands leaves only two possibilities.

Possibility one: I misplaced this jumbled mess of thoughts.

Which wouldn't be a surprise to anyone. I tend to misplace stuff over time. In that case, please take this to Mistras' Tavern in Winding Run, south of Valshannon. Give it to Cali. She'll know what to do with it. Tell her Shen said she owes you a pint of Rhinestab's best ale as a thank you.

Possibility two: I'm afraid I am, in fact, dead—a likely scenario and of little shock to anyone. In this case, you stumbled onto my rotting corpse and looted my body, as is your right. I only ask you to please be kind to whatever reputation I left behind. That reputation is all I ever had in this life, regardless of the manner of my death.

And if you happen to be the one who took my life, well, congratulations. You managed to accomplish the goal that hundreds of would-be killers before you attempted and failed. Whoever you are, I hope you at least have some wounds to remember me by.

By the way, the valuable items are my weapons. I'd be shocked if you found any Realm Notes or coins. But whatever you find, take them, especially the blades. Better sold or put to good use than remanded to obscurity to rust away in perpetuity. They are made of Korund steel and forged by Brinker.

Inside these pages, I've poured my soul. Every joyous, embarrassing, hopeful, frightened, dark, and broken thought since my fifty-third birthday is recorded for who knows what reason.

How funny would it be if this is the only entry when you stumble onto it? Imagine I decide to record my innermost thoughts in an attempt to find peace with myself, only to die after the first entry. Or set this damn journal down somewhere and forget where I left it.

Talk about karmic irony, if that even exists.

But I digress.

Part of me hopes it helps me understand myself. It's as honest an attempt at truthfulness as I can summon. Hopefully, my honesty won't cause too much psychological damage to you or me.

You'd be surprised how difficult I find internal honesty.

It's a key insight into understanding me. I'm the king of lying to myself.

If, as you begin this journey, I come across brooding at times, it's because I tend to get trapped in my thoughts. I spend a lot of time there.

Because, mostly, I am, for all intents and purposes, broken.

Avenge Sevenfold

"Today you meet Quietius, *Harbinger*."

The arrogant venom in the last word triggers involuntary reflexes, and my jaw tightens. My gums ache from the insufferable habit and I force my jaw to relax. Generally, I find delight in the confidence of my opponents. But his arrogance, unsubstantiated by evidence, would engage my worst traits on a good day.

Today is not a good day.

I'd resist the primal urges he's spawned, but then he coupled misplaced arrogance with the revelation he'd discovered my identity. That discovery alone sealed his fate. But none of this matters. He and his companion mage made my shit-list yesterday. They just hadn't reached the conclusion themselves yet.

"You probably should have kept that bit to yourself," I say.

The mage remains silent, his confidence shaken a moment ago when I interrupted spell with a fist to his mouth. His warrior pal isn't reading the queues, however. The fighter before me should reconsider his plan. Yet, here he stands, sword unsheathed, feet set in a rudimentary combat stance, proclaiming his success as inevitable. He overestimates his abilities and underestimates how little my own death frightens me, which is to say, it doesn't.

The elusive nature of Quietius, Lord of the Final Slumber, still stands as the most significant source of my never-ending ire.

That's the crux of my life. An endless series of ne'er-do-wells who fail to achieve the ultimate prize and deliver me the peace in death that is missing in life.

Like every delusional miscreant who proceeded him, this prick will fail.

The insufferable irony is my own arrogance outweighs my thirst for death. I'd welcome my death, but I'm unwilling to stand here and let this fool run his sword through me. I still have my pride.

If only he understood that mere hours ago I peacefully ventured on the pilgrimage to my final resting place.

Then I found the bodies.

Peaceful acceptance of death faded in a storm of visceral anger. Fueled by images of heinous deeds committed by these two mercenaries, my plans changed.

It's personal.

"If you intended to get my attention, you succeeded," I say to the man with his sword aimed at my chest.

"Good," he replies.

"No. Not good. Not good that you know my identity either," I whisper loud enough for both bounty hunters to hear. Only two people carry the secret of my identity. To the rest of the world, "The Harbinger" is a ghost, an enigma—a shadow of stories retold by those I rescue. Never by my opponents. They aren't afforded the opportunity to tell their tale.

I don't see how these two figured it out. But since these bounty hunters did, they should know better than to square off. Either they are stupid, or they've overestimated themselves. Too bad for them.

"You will die today," the swordsman says as I dodge his blade, which misses wide.

His grunts of effort annoy the hell out of me—evidence he lacks finesse—and skill.

"Wow," I taunt, "I thought I was the talkative one. Do you always talk this much?"

The muscles in his jaw bulge as he clenches his teeth and jabs the tip of his blade at my chest. Sloppy and undisciplined, he should reconsider his attempt to collect a bounty he'll never live to see. This fight is a waste of my time and boredom stacks atop my rage. I dodge his attacks with near superhuman speed and pause a foot away from him when he completes his strike. I drive my heel into his leg from behind, which buckles his knee. A high-pitched grunt escapes his lips. He stumbles forward, and his momentum drives the sword tip into the ground.

I can't play my usual games. His partner is the greater threat. Without ceremony, I punch the mercenary's neck, twisting my hips for power, and release the blade hidden in my bracer. The blackened

Korund steel pierces his skull and exits his throat. I watch as his body collapses face-first into the road, his sword still stuck in the ground, the only grave marker he'll receive.

Blood drips from the blade as I stand over his corpse, and I can't help but wonder, for the thousandth time, if this is all I am. There's little time for me to follow that trail of thought. While the man dying at my feet is no longer a threat, the voice behind me, speaking a prayer, is. The soft sound of mumbled words returns me to the immediate.

The mage once again weaves his spell behind me.

I spin on the balls of my feet to face the source of the voice. As expected, the mage extends a periapt of the Goddess Shamna in a tight grip, the symbol toward me. His tan robes billow in the slight breeze. A familiar cadence in his voice carries on his breath. One I've heard too many times before—a prayer to Shamna.

Well, the Goddess of Luck won't hear this prayer completed any time soon. My boots make no sound in the dirt road as my body rotates, and my arm launches toward the mage. My fingers spread to release a throwing knife into the air. His prayer changes to a gasp, the spell interrupted. My speed always has a dampening effect on my enemies. I could clear the ten-foot gap between us instantly if I wanted. Instead, I choose the thrown knife.

I never miss.

The small, Korund steel blade flies true and pierces the hand holding the periapt—his sole connection to Shamna's supposed blessings. The mage's face, wrinkled with age, contorts in pain. The stone emblem of his faith falls to the ground, the soft dirt of the road muting its impact. His prayerful words transform into a scream. The incomplete prayer dies in the wind, and remnants of manifested energy evaporate into a ripple of air between us. I smile once again, with a wink this time.

"That's twice you tried to cast a spell on me. I warned you the first time not to try again. Shamna's ears won't hear your prayers before my blade pierces your skull now," I say.

"You really are him!" the mage cries.

I try to repress the sigh, but it escapes anyway. The mage reconciles reality with the realization the rumors are true. The person he and his deceased partner chose to hunt is a monster. It doesn't matter how many times I see the look on my victim's face or hear the fear in their voice. My reaction is always the same.

Sorrow.

Once more, I ponder whether this is the entirety of my life. Does this moment encompass the sum total of who I am? Again, I consider whether the world would be better off without me.

"Please don't kill me!" he cries. "I beg mercy!"

It's wasted breath. My earlier discovery of Farmer Tillion's body at the gate to his own property solidified my course. The poor man drowned while standing at his gate, repair tools scattered, and water pooled in his mouth. It wasn't hard to figure out what caused it. He was nowhere near a water source. Only magic can do that. Similarly, only blades cause the carnage I discovered a few moments later when I hurried to the farmhouse to inform his wife.

I choke back my guilt, remembering the sight of her bleeding to death, her eyes locked on their children, already dead with their throats slit, their bodies still warm.

I snapped. One minute, I was sad. The next enraged.

The Tillions were good and kind people. They never turned me away when I needed food, water, or a comfortable place to sleep in a bad storm. The sight of them broke me. I don't have many friends. Those I do have, I cherish.

Now I have fewer.

Enraged, I searched for the trail left behind by the killers. Anger and guilt grew hotter, pressure building inside like a volcano as I followed their trail. Promises were made on the journey. Promises to the dead. For a full day, I followed these two as the pressure grew, each step I gained on the perpetrators adding more fuel. They didn't even bother to hide their tracks. The trail led me right to these purveyors of death, one of which no longer breathes. The other soon to join him.

He has the audacity to beg for mercy?

"Mercy? Like the mercy you showed the Tillions?"

The mage points to the dead mercenary. "It wasn't me. He did it. I… I… I told him not to! I begged him!"

"Even if I believed you, it would have been better for you to have died trying to stop him than still be alive here," I snarl and step closer.

He backs away, the hand with the knife still stuck held close to his chest. Tears stream down his face as I scoop up his stone talisman and study it. Its intricate symbol, engraved onto a rare stone, illustrates stylized dice called *Shamna Rocks* with the Teshket symbol for twenty-three underneath—lucky twenty-three. The exquisiteness testifies to this mage's success.

"Nice piece," I say. "Not so lucky now, are you? A mercenary mage with a stone like this doesn't strike me as the reluctant murderer type."

I look up at him and witness his mask of remorse transform into a sneer as he drops the facade. My reputation precedes me. He knows who I am. He knows he's already dead. The words of another prayer start to flow from his lips as he reaches into a pocket with his uninjured hand. I don't waste time with conversation or thoughts.

With speed no one can explain, including me, I lunge and cover the ten-foot gap between us. Before the mage can blink, I stand toe-to-toe with him, the blade on my other bracer at full extension. I've never known the source of my speed, but it's as instinctual to me as breathing. To my enemies, it's only slightly more shocking than the complete silence of my motions.

Not for the first time, I ponder whether I'm an actual ghost.

His flesh offers no resistance to my blade as I pin his hand inside his pocket. The blade severs the bones and tendons, lodging into his hip. The ferocity of my advance stuns him as my blade pierces not one but two places of his body.

He screams again, and hatred burns in his eyes. I'll take the hatred as long as it stops his mouth.

"How?" he asks through tears and gritted teeth.

"Don't ask me," I reply.

He wants to know the secret of my speed. Even if I knew, I wouldn't say. As far back as I can remember, I moved this way—fast and silent.

I bring my other blade to his eye, let the tip hover there momentarily, and observe him with mild curiosity. His focus on the point is steadfast. His body trembles in horror. But he is still defiant. I like his spirit. Too bad for him; I like the Tillions more.

"How about I just give you the tip?" I jest.

"I curse the day you were born," he spits.

"You aren't the first," I reply. My soul weeps. If only he knew how often I agree with the sentiment.

"They'll find you," he hisses.

"They always do," I reply and drive the blade through his eye. The tip protrudes through the back of his skull.

As his lifeless body collapses, the anger that drove me to this point fades, replaced by guilt over the fate of the Tillions. With a heavy sigh, I chastise myself for not questioning these hunters about the senseless murders. I always react too quickly. My habits are too ingrained.

They'll find you.

I'm curious who the mage meant by "they." These two explicitly hunted me down. How they tracked me to the Tillions will weigh on me.

The Tillions are dead because of me.

Is this all I am?

Deep down, I know the answer to the question.

I am a blight on the world.

I am death.

Guilt ravages my sleep. Dawn passes and the waking world includes thoughts I'd rather not face. Thoughts of the Tillions. If not for me, they'd still be alive. It doesn't matter how irrational the thoughts are. I'm who those bounty hunters sought.

I've wandered the entirety of the Rhinestab for thirty-five years. As a result, anyone and everyone could be an ally. For this reason, my very existence puts everyone at risk to those who seek their fortune by collecting the substantial bounty on my head.

Hence my identity is a tightly held secret.

I squeeze my eyes tighter. But the amber glow persists, and Ezra, the Goddess of Light, peeks her head through small gaps in the canopy of tree leaves above where I sleep. I resist the light that glows through my eyelids. But it's no use. She beat me again.

Yesterday's events hang like the muggy, swampy dampness of the Seething Bellows around Rankin Lake. I can't take it anymore. The memory of the scent of the children's blood sends me into a hopeless spiral. I hoped to be in a better mood today, but I knew last night it would be hopeless. As I feared, the words of the murderous mage invaded my sleep. They taunted me with evolving dreams as images shifted into disjointed scenes of non-realities. No matter the world my mind created, *he* would arrive—and wound me with those words.

"I curse the day you were born."

My ears ring with a tinnitus-fueled echo—audible signs of the trauma the mage's words caused. Sleep did little to improve my mood. I'm a bit salty at the bitch in the sky right now. Realistically, I know it's misdirected anger, but it's morning, so I couldn't care less who my frustration is directed toward. I'm not much for the early hours, anyway. I hate them. So, my dreams probably have less impact on my mood than my own charming personality does.

I *really* hate mornings.

This one in particular. Number fifteen thousand eight hundred and ninety. So many, and yet, my ability to handle them hasn't improved. They still suck.

I try not to think about it, but too much time has passed. Am I that old? Fifty was hard, but fifty-three is somehow more frightening. The proximity to sixty compared to forty seems unfair. It's not as unjust as thirty-five, though. Has it been thirty-five cycles of seasons? Thirty-five years of repeating the Gothically decorated tapestry of a life filled with "why me?"

Wow. Thirty-five years to the day.

I try hard not to think about *that* day, but it raises its venomous head. I thought it would have gotten easier by now, but it hasn't. I push the memory deep into the lockbox of compart-mentalization and ignore it. I prefer to stuff it down rather than lie to myself about it in a stupid attempt to protect my psyche. Better to ignore past sins. Of the moments that shaped me, that one's the most influential.

Yet, I wouldn't change my choices if afforded the opportunity.

Still, I can trace my obsession over my own death to a particular singularity. Thoughts of death meander like a worm burrowing through the tainted soil of my cerebral cortex. I mull over my own death. I don't *want* to obsess over it, but I resign myself to the process. It looks like today is a good day to die. Everybody dies eventually. It's life in a nutshell. Mine just seems to be evasive.

Not today. Today is the day.

I shake my thoughts away with the wave of a hand and consider a trip to the Great Rankin River and jumping in. Its fast, nearly unswimmable current and roaring rapids would do a decent job ending all this. Even if I manage to survive the swim, there are dangers in the river that will make me wish I hadn't jumped in. I chide myself over the thought. Drowning doesn't sound like a pleasant way to go.

But then again, a peaceful death isn't in the cards for me anyway.

Maybe I'm crazy, but I guess yesterday's plan is back on.

There's a voice deep inside me that screams it's not my fault. But every time I try to hold on to it, voices from the past come back at me with vicious regularity.

"What do you expect? He's just like his father."

"That one is just not right."

"Why can't you be less of a burden?"

"All you're good for is thievery and murder."

I wrestle with these thoughts as voices from my past slam into my psyche. The mental gymnastics exhaust me. My mind simultaneously assumes the role of protector and destroyer the discordant thoughts wage their endless war. Two imaginary pugilists step toe-to-toe, and neither gains supremacy over the other.

No wonder I'm fatigued.

This, whatever this is, wasn't part of my plan.

Come to think of it, I never had much of a plan—for anything. My days flow by as I make spontaneous decisions, hoping that tomorrow will either be better or won't happen.

There's nothing to be done about it. Yesterday's tomorrow is now today. The futile attempt to ignore the glow through my eyelids is an epic failure. It's pointless to resist, so I stop. Sleep is finished.

I sit up and extract my journal from my pack. At least I can write. My pen works furiously as scratches on parchment fill the gaps in morning activity around me.

Overhead, the tiny vestiges of light illuminate the floating dust in the air; long, slender beams of warmth shift with the leaves that move in the slight breeze. The motion of the leaves reminds me of thousands of little hands waving "Hi!"

Cheerful bastards. It's too early for cheer. What I need is coffee. In fact, I'd kill for coffee. No, that's not true. I would, however, sell sexual favors for a cup of coffee right now. I should have taken coffee from the Tillion's farm before I left.

Sadness grips me at the thought of them lying there, lives wasted for no good reason.

All around me, the forest's day walkers come to life, and momentarily, they pull me from the gloom of my internal monologue. I listen as I ponder what to put in the journal. Thoughts of roving bands of healers come to mind. Absently, my hand wanders down to the knives at my waist, and their well-sharpened edges scratch the clouds from memories. Those sharp edges coincide with matching scars carried inside and out, harsh reminders of past failures.

I run my finger along the edge of one. Its sharp blade feels good against my skin. It comforts me.

I let out a heavy sigh. The last attempt to end it all failed. I have to remind myself I'm glad it did. I remember how fun the day after turned out to be. That was a rather good day. Tamrin and I crossed paths unexpectedly and chose to travel together for a while. I smile at the memory of what turned into one hell of an adventure. Days like that get me through days like yesterday.

My bladder cries out with pressure but I'm still too lazy to move. I stare up at small glimpses of dawn's light through the leaves.

To my right, a large bush rustles, which distracts my thoughts. A sense of elation washes over me as I close my eyes and wait. It's an old game I play. A fantasy forms, and I imagine a vicious monster draws near and stalks me as its prey. I pretend it brings a death where I can't control the outcome.

My expectations are low, however. Odd fantasies never play out in reality.

Since the day I escaped the guild, I've roamed this world without a single attack while asleep. As someone who rarely sleeps in sheltered bliss, I've left ample opportunity for such an attack. People are attacked in their sleep all the time.

Why not me?

Random encounters, surprise attacks by would-be assassins, and the plethora of nighttime predators cycle through memory, but never has one occurred while I slept. Only once has an encounter happened while I was vulnerable, but I was awake—damn healers.

I've prayed for death, but no prayer of mine was ever answered.

The gods either aren't capable, they aren't there, or worse… they're cruel.

More rustling leaves pull my thoughts back again. Whatever it is, it's closer but barely louder. Disappointed, I shift into quiet meditation and focus on my breathing to center myself with techniques the old monks taught me.

The rustling stops, and a critter lets out a light squeak.

I ignore the creature and listen to my heartbeats. Both hearts beat in a triple beat, representing the only clock I use to gauge the ticking of time.

Bump-bump-bump.

They distract my meditation with the unanswered question of my genetic anomaly. I've never met another person with two hearts. Side by side, I feel a pair of alternating war drums in my chest. Two hearts, one for each personality. I don't know why I try. Meditation never works. It's short-lived as boredom sets in rather quickly.

Bump-bump-bump.

Bump-bump-bump.

Bump-bump-bump.

I turn and take a one-eyed peek at my little visitor.

"Well, I gave you a chance to attack," I say to a bakru who sits, staring at me, hunched on his hindquarters, a walnut perched in its front paws.

I find bakru mildly amusing with their jackrabbit ears, squirrel-like tails, and front paws. But those raccoon stripes across their eyes, making them look like bandits, are too much. Such an odd mix of features makes me think the other three species must be related somehow. It's like some mad mage combined the three creatures and set them loose on the world.

"I don't suppose you're rabid and ready to strike?"

He offers no reaction.

"You wouldn't happen to be a vampire bakru, would you? No, you wouldn't be. Ezra would have fried you already..."

He squeaks his indecipherable bakru chatter, accompanied by nose twitches and tail flicks, his walnut poised, bandit eyes locked on mine.

"Clearly, I don't speak bakru," I reply. The bakru's lack of response tells me he doesn't speak my tongue either, or else this bakru is rude.

Clearly not rabid, the bakru holds his walnut and sits frozen like he's carved from wood.

"You gonna throw that nut at me?" I ask.

The show down continues a moment longer before I finally let out another heavy sigh and twist to face him. I'm not surprised the little monster doesn't move. He remains unphased by my question, choosing to sit with his walnut between his paws, sniffing the air. This little one doesn't see me as a threat.

I'm not surprised. Animals always seem to act like I am part of the landscape.

"You do know that I'm not above hunting?" I have half a mind to skin this guy for breakfast. But I won't. It's like he knows I won't. Odd.

Bakru doesn't react.

"Listen, I am kind of in a hurry here. If you plan on attacking, get it over with or get gone." He stares blankly. "Fine. Just sit there. Stare away. But, for the record, it is rude to stare."

Another sniff, followed by another light squeak.

"Go on. Git." I shoo him away.

He doesn't even react. His sniffs are followed by a curious tilt of the head. I think he understands me.

Resigning myself to his outright disrespect for my privacy, I continue our conversation. It occurs to me I'm referring to the critter as *he*. But I don't see the naughty bits as "Bakru" (its name now) sits and stares, holding his nut. Bakru and I continue our conversation for what feels like hours. I even pull a bite of jerky out of my pouch and eat while Bakru stares, nose wrinkling. Eventually, it gets brazen, comes over, and puts a gentle paw on my knee.

"Well, hello there. That's a first," I say.

Bakru sniffs the air around my jerky and makes a face as if what I have is unnatural. I offer the critter some, which it sniffs again and politely declines by sitting back on its haunches. It picks up its walnut and turns it around in its hands.

We continue this way for a while when a more obtrusive sound startles us both.

A terrified scream pierces the conversation between me and Bakru.

Bakru drops the walnut in fright and bolts to the nearest tree in full flight mode while he chatters at me like the disturbance is somehow my fault. I watch as the tail disappears around a clump of leaves, and branches bounce in response to Bakru's agility.

Gone.

"Coward," I say to Bakru.

I hop up and look to the south, the direction of the scream. It was definitely not an animal. It definitely sounded female.

Damn the gods… all eight of them.

Another more strangled scream comes from the same direction as the first. It's not far. The sounds are too clear to be far. I recognize the screams as someone in a particular kind of trouble. I tuck my journal, the small bottle of ink, and my pen into their protected spots, grab my cloak and my small pack, and take off in full sprint through the RhineWoods toward the sounds.

"Why am I doing this?" I mumble aloud.

But I know why. I can't help it.

One of my many compulsive behaviors.

Memories of my mother's voice resonate, *"Be an asset, not a liability."*

In an effort not to be a liability, I do the only thing I know how to do.

I help.

The Growing Darkness

24

Chapter Two

Journal Entry: 2

What if I told you I feel worthless?

What if I admitted to everyone that I'm driven by an incessant need to help? Helping is the only way I can cope.

Would you think less of me? Would my insecurities make you dislike me? It's a fear I have. Every action I take is an effort to convince everyone, including myself, that I'm not worthless. I do have value. But it makes me feel like a fraud. Desperate for approval. Helping for my own satisfaction and not because it's what an average person would do.

My life adds no value.

I help so I feel like my life has purpose.

But it's exhausting. It costs me.

Hell, my brand of help often costs somebody else, too. I only have one talent.

But what else is there? It has become compulsive.

Frankly, it's my most annoying trait... to me anyway.

I helped a Brain Devourer once. You know, those giant multi-limbed creatures that look like a brain-shaped spider? Or some sort of weird fleshy footstool with funny bumps on it? Detects the intellect of its prey, leaps onto your head, and devours the brain right out of your skull. I hear it's a horrible way to die.

The sucker should have wanted to kill me. I must be vapid or dumb as a turnip for it not to pick up on me. Yet, there I stood, Brain Devourer and me, and it didn't seem to register me. Maybe it assumed I wasn't too bright and clearly not fit for consumption.

I thought it was kinda rude, honestly.

I probably should have killed it for the insult.

That's not a good example, though. I was having a bad day, so I had an ulterior motive for helping that sucker. Maybe it knew what I wanted and found greater pleasure in torturing me.

I'm tired of thinking, so this will be all for now.

Sean Gregory

The Insufferable Compulsion of Helping

Wild thoughts run through my mind as I charge through the dense clusters of oaks and maples into who knows what. The familiar burning through my body stings as I push myself faster. It's painful but bearable.

Not five minutes ago, thoughts of my own death consumed me, and now I rush to the rescue of a stranger. As I barrel through the brush, I dodge trunks and roots while I maintain a small portion of cognizance on the landscape. The RhineWoods loves to disorient its visitors.

This portion of the RhineWoods is the most beautiful. The trees are healthy, the ground firm, and the soil rich in forest matter. I spend a lot of time here, and as a result, navigating the forest is easy— at least in the immediate area. A thousand yards west of me is the only part of the RhineWoods I avoid.

I cast a cautious glimpse westward to ensure I don't drift too far to my right. In the distance, even in the early morning light, I can see the black fog of death ooze along the forest floor. The lone netherstack, its tall, slender, stony spire, spews its dark cloud. I glance at it as it sits right where I want it. Far enough away, its deadly emissions won't touch me. That's one way I'd prefer not to die.

The sounds of a struggle grow louder not far ahead.

"Damn," I curse.

Of course, the disturbance is farther to my right than I'd like instead of directly ahead. The gods hate me. I adjust my path toward those sounds—and the netherstack.

The staccato rhythm of intermittent shadow and light in my vision disorients me as I run at breakneck speed through the trees, but I'm used to it. Conspicuous silence brought on by that first scream presses on my eardrums. The combination of audio and visual effects feels surreal. Life in the forest is frozen—typical animal behavior when danger presents itself.

I guess I have a date with Quietius, the God of Death, after all.

Alert and ready, I scan my environment while I weave through the maze of trees, distorted vision notwithstanding.

As I draw closer, I discern other sounds among the screams. Grunts and mocking taunts, in the baritone of male voices, reverberate against the trees. Combined with the woman's scream, I assume the worst. Malice-laced laughter breaks out and sends a chill down my spine. It's not the first time I've stumbled onto a scene like the one I expect to find.

If I believed in gods, I'd think maybe this was a plan or fate. But it's all random luck. Rotten random luck at times, but luck, nonetheless. At least I'm not afraid to die. One advantage of my obsession with my own passing is it liberates me. Death has no hold on me. I can take risks others won't—sometimes foolishly. A distant memory of a Brain Devourer enters my mind.

Ahead, a thick patch of brush grows beyond a felled tree, rotted with time.

Like your soul.

"Shut up, brain," I say to no one.

The sounds come from beyond the tall line of brush. The manic laughter echoes over all other noise. My skin crawls in aversion. I push my pace, my muscles tightened in preparation to fire a surge, as my body-tingles transition from discomfort to mild pain. I leap over the large log, using it to gain height and clear the thick patch of branches and leaves, somersaulting with flair, and land in a small glen.

I should have cried "Tada!" or something.

Disappointed, I realize my stylish entrance went unnoticed. Everyone's backs are to me, except for a struggling woman who's a bit preoccupied with survival. I slump my shoulders, unfulfilled by the lack of attention.

I lose myself briefly and admire the clearing I somehow never knew existed. If not for the violent activity, I'd take more time to bask in the discovery. This part of the Rhine Woods is too close to the netherstack for my comfort, so I'm not shocked I've never been here. Besides, this isn't a birthday party for me. I push the thoughts aside and focus on the matter at hand.

Three men tower over a fourth, cheering him on as he struggles with a woman on the ground. Two men have short swords drawn, and the third carries a thin club, its tip resting in the dirt. Their filthy stench of male musk pollutes the newly discovered space's otherwise natural beauty and serenity—the rank odor is like offal rotting in the sun.

Damn them for this. If I'd discovered this place alone, it would be a new favored spot. Now, it's forever tainted.

There's no friendliness in their intent. Bile rises in my throat at the horrible thought. The fuse on my temper reaches its inevitable terminus, and my body flashes hotter.

I'm usually hard on myself when I lose my temper, but in this case, I feel justified.

"She's a feisty one," one of them says.

"I like a good fight," says another.

By the sound of the third one's laugh, the one with the club, he's barely intelligent enough to remember to breathe. Ten feet from them, another man lies unconscious, blood oozing from a gash on his head. I note how similar he looks to the woman who struggles. I glance at the bandit's club and see the signs of fresh blood.

The fourth bandit grapples with the woman. A large hand pins hers to the ground over her head. Near her hand rests a small dagger. At least she's not giving up without a fight. With his free hand, he works to lift her dress. She is valiant, but she is losing steam and she's incredibly outmatched. Fights don't last long, and this one has lasted longer than most, from the looks of it.

I'm not surprised they didn't hear my arrival. Long ago I accepted the nature of my eternally silent motions will go forever unexplained. I just wish these sons-of-bitches knew I stood a mere two yards behind them. For my own ego.

No one knows I am here.

Well, I know.

But they don't.

My disjointed thoughts allow me to linger while they take the last of the fight out of their victim. Her body goes limp; she's exhausted.

Then her eyes lock with mine.

I recognize that fatigue.

The men laugh.

I hold a finger to my lips as I release the pressure of explosive energy pent up inside with a flurry of motion. Muscles contract and release in rapid succession. My insides burn with the usual discomfort associated with the speed of my actions. The small fire set ablaze inside tingles every cell of my body, igniting some engine I've never understood. The sensation fueled by this need to punish threatens to overwhelm my senses.

Nobody ever wants to be on the receiving end of my venom. I push the shame I feel over my temper back down to the deepest parts of my mind, memories of my mother's anger threatening to overwhelm me. I need this anger. It feeds me.

"Now you lay there while I give you a special treat," the bastard holding her down says.

"Give it to her good," says the second one.

That's my queue. The fire is under control, and my hands move fast.

The world around me slows down from my perspective. With well-practiced, fluid, precise motions, my hands fly. I don't have to look at my belt. My tools are always in the same place. Muscle memory is ingrained to the point of boredom. My hands flick like a Shamna Rocks dealer as three knives travel through the air faster than my bakru friend bolts up trees.

All fly true.

All embed themselves into the bases of three skulls, effectively ending the lives of three foul-smelling bandits, and three bodies simply fall to the ground.

Sadly, their deaths didn't kill the smell. Their stench saturates the air. I wrinkle my face in disgust. A secret code must require bandits to smell like a fermented dung heap. I fight the bakru trail within my mind, and I force myself to reign my thoughts in.

The loud thuds of their bodies against the ground announce to the almost-rapist I've arrived on the scene. Not that this waste of oxygen knows it's me, per se. But this man knows someone's here and that his companions' laughter has ceased. The raucous encouragement vanished in the face of the danger that lurked behind.

Just in case he's daft, I cough conspicuously.

It doesn't take him long. He pauses his efforts, one hand desperately trying to work his trousers, and slowly turns his head in my direction. His face contorted with anger as he recognized the body on the ground with its mouth wide, eyes unseeing. The expressions on his and the dead guy's faces are worth the delay in my plans.

I find joy in the little things, so a light snicker escapes my lips.

He doesn't take long to look back, and we make eye contact. I squat down, wave, and give him my best smile.

"Whatcha got there?" I ask as if he's a toddler.

I'm surprised by the speed with which he spins off the woman and skillfully drags her to her feet. He positions her between us as he turns to face me. The display of strength, speed, and agility is impressive. He handles her like a rag doll.

"Oh!" I say. "You're spry."

My adrenaline surges and elation bursts through my ex-pression at the presence of a challenge. Both hearts quicken at the possibility this guy is skilled.

"Let's find out how good you are," I taunt.

Before I engage, the current situation requires an adjustment. My preferred method toward resolution of my dilemma is to antagonize this dung pile of a human—get him to willingly do what I want—fluster him a bit.

"Are you seriously using a woman as a shield?" I raise my hands, palms up. "C'mon, man. Hiding behind a woman? Are you afraid?"

Call this a personality flaw. I could easily kill this guy where he stands, with no risk to the hostage, but it's not how I like to work. Besides, the hostage is an unpredictable variable, which places her in greater danger than I'd like. Her presence impedes my ability to partake in one of my few joys—I like to play with my food.

"Well, it seems you've decided today is a good day to die," I say.

He doesn't speak. He just glares at me, eyes narrowed.

His woman-shaped shield stands between us as his gaze alternates between me and his three dead friends. She struggles to break free, but the goon holds her fast. I raise a soothing hand and place a finger on my lips. She stops, her brow furrowed. Sometimes, snapping someone out of their fear or panic is as simple as throwing a little confusion their way—a cognitive reset.

"It'll be alright," I say to her.

I have no intention of being flippant with her life. Quite the opposite. I take calculated risks to get what I want. As long as she's calm, I have a chance to convince this asshole to let her go.

Right now, I want her free of his grasp. I can see his pea-sized brain work through mental calculations while his eyes bounce back and forth a few times. He can't understand how his companions are dead when I'm the only other person standing here. His eyes wander around the forest.

I wiggle a finger in his direction. "Oh yes, I can see comprehension of what happened here eludes you."

He and the woman in his grasp look confused by that one. But the fear in his eyes gratifies me more than the dumbfounded look on their faces.

"Tell your friends to come out where I can see them," he demands.

I bow and gesture my arm out in a flourish.

"Yoohoo!" I yell into the woods. I look back at him and pout with my lower lip. "Oh no. Looks like it's just me. Seems I'm the one tasked with disposing of the garbage." I flick my hands at his dead cohorts. "You're welcome. It was nothing, really. I don't mind the work. They were in the way, don't you think? I'll be nice and not charge you for the service."

In moments like this, I enjoy a little dramatic pause and a monologue. It fulfills my childish need to feel heard. Since I don't like to burden my friends with it, I tend to torture my enemies instead.

"Who the hell are you?" he asks.

"Who the hell am I?" I ask, pointing at my own chest. "That's a common question. One I rarely answer." I shrug. "Today, however, might be your lucky day. You struck a chord in me. Call it a byproduct of the emotional musings I wrote in my journal this morning. So, I'll entertain the question."

I tap my chin in honest contemplation.

"Here's the problem. I don't know the answer. Don't get me wrong, I know my name and where I came from, but I don't know if I actually know myself. For all the time I spend up here inside this busted cranium," I say, tapping my temple, "this question is a question I always ask myself. But I always feel it to be a frivolous pursuit. Too deep for this moment." I point to him. "I think you'd agree, no?"

I stare at the ground, scuffing the dirt and leaves with my toe.

"Come to think of it, now doesn't seem like an appropriate moment, especially not with the likes of you. It's self-indulgent for me to discuss myself at this particular place and time. Besides, you're too daft to understand anyway. Waxing philosophical with you seems a waste of my energy and decidedly unfair to the young woman who has apparently enamored you with her wily charms." I point to the still, petrified woman held tight in his grip. "I'd rather be flippant. Let's say who I am is…" I pause, "well… I'm the purveyor of options. Of which you have three, I think."

I count on my fingers.

"Yup, three." I hold up four fingers.

I watch him fight to gather his wits… and courage. Sometimes, it's difficult to tell if they realize I'm a consummate smartass or if they think I'm just dumb… or crazy.

"Yeah?" He sneers. A crack in his voice betrays his attempt at courage. "What are they?"

He knows I'm playing with him. I shake my head. "You are smarter than that, surely."

I point to his friends' bodies while I maintain eye contact with him. His eyes follow my finger. He squeezes the woman's throat in a threat toward me, and her eyes bulge from the pressure.

"Ugh, seriously?" I say.

I wince at how whiny that sounded. The nature of a younger sibling is hard to break. Memories of my older brother's tendency to torment the piss out of me for fun, however, elicits a brief smile from me. I wave it away.

"You're pissing me off," I say. "You don't want me to over-react. I guess it goes along with my temper, which, considering the great inconveniences the so-called gods have managed to heap onto me the last two days, is growing more difficult to control by the minute. But I'll manage, if only so I can keep my wits about me."

He squeezes her tighter.

"Careful, now," I say. "Don't let this friendly banter fool you into the mistaken belief that hurting this lady further will help you. The way I see it, your options are simple, albeit fairly limited. We can stand here forever, locked in this stimulating conversation, until one of us gets tired..." I let it trail off.

He blinks at me, uncertain.

I continue.

"Now, normally, I like that option because I am well rested, have nowhere important to be, and well, in about three hours, your hands will grow tired, then she'll grow tired, and then you'll be fighting to keep her in control, watching me, while you watch her. Meanwhile, she's watching me the whole time, shifting her feet from exhaustion, and well, that's a lot of tasks for you to track. The entire time, I'll stand here and clean my nails while you decide. All because I have no intention of watching either one of you watch me watch you. Then again, I have to pee. I mean, you did interrupt my morning routine with all the racket."

I flip my hand at him, dismissive.

"No matter. I'll pee myself. It wouldn't be the first time. You need a break? You two seem to have been at it for a while. Or did you wake up a few moments ago, too? Did a genie answer your wish and 'poof,' a lovely woman and her escort landed in your lap?"

I look at him with mild curiosity. "Wait. That's not what happened, is it?"

He groans, my jokes far from entertaining him.

"No, I imagine you were on your little voyage to dimwit town to meet some other dimwit friends and stumbled upon this serene locale where these two camped. Target of opportunity, right? Probably been up a few hours? Needed some entertainment after a long hike through the RhineWoods? All those steps made you work up an appetite for destruction, didn't they? Which means I am not the one who could possibly have burned up some of their reserves. How's your morale right now? Mine's fine. Then again, three fourths of my party didn't die while I was unaware. I'd really hate to be one of your friends."

More mental calculations force his brow to crinkle, and resignation comes with a decision.

"Good, you aren't as slow as I suspected. Your next option is to let her go and walk away."

I watch the machinations of his mind play out on his face as he considers this option, and I can see he wants it. Who wouldn't? He started with a raiding party four times the size it is now. Yet, here he stands, alone, and his men didn't put up much of a fight.

They didn't put up any fight, come to think of it.

It's at this time that typical bad-guy behavior dictates the negotiation of a truce. I'm also still angry and ravaged with guilt over the hand I played in yesterday's events, so I might have considered it. But the Sun Goddess pissed me off today, a strong enough annoyance to mute any sense of mercy I might carry.

The would-be rapist is still using this woman as a shield. He's royally pissed me off too.

"Ugh, oh," I say, embarrassed.

I can't hold it anymore. My bladder is about to explode. I curse aloud, fully aware that I should have taken care of business before I arrived. I raise my finger, indicating I need a moment, and sidestep to a tree. I slide behind it and lean out to keep the pair in sight, a slight smirk on my face as I do.

The woman's eyes narrow as she rolls her eyes. Considering her current situation and where she is emotionally, I'm impressed at her resilience. She has the presence of mind to display her displeasure through her distress. It's not the first time a woman has given me that look, and it's a sign of her strength. I nod at her and mouth it will be alright as I untie my pants and relieve my bladder, careful not to flash myself like some pervert.

The comical looks on both their faces force me to stifle a laugh. I find my actions kind of funny, but admittedly, I feel bad for the woman. She wants no more than for this display of toxic masculinity and tomfoolery to end so she can be on her way to safety somewhere. But I can't hold my water anymore, and I don't like the feeling of wet clothes. Not to mention, the smelly bandits make me realize I don't want to smell like piss, either.

Unfortunately, I pee on my own boot a little. What can I say?

I need to keep my eyes on this guy.

"Dammit. I peed on my boot." I let out a heavy sigh.

Safely tucking my stuff away, I tie my pants back snugly, maintaining eye contact with my new bandit friend the entire time. The awkwardness is exquisite, and I fight the urge to giggle at my inappropriate behavior.

Tamrin's voice echoes, *"You were born on the inappropriate side of the line."*

He's not wrong.

The bandit's gaze bounces around the glen as he considers his options. I imagine he probably thinks I am too crazy to mess with.

He's not wrong in that thought, either.

I did give him a pretty tawdry expression while I held my manhood. But I have no intention of letting him walk away. It's a ruse. I want the fight. The look of indecision on his face drives me insane, so I decide for him.

"Of course, you have to hope I don't throw a knife in your back as you walk away like I did your friends here. Oh yeah, it wasn't in their backs. No matter. Either way, that's the gamble you took when you decided on this path."

That settled it. Muscles tighten in the bandit's cheeks as he steels himself against my verbal assault.

"Yeah, ya know what?" he says. "I see yer game here. I ain't afraid of some blow-hard who sneak attacked my boys. Let's see how you fare when you can't sneak up on your victims. What's the third choice, smartass?"

I'm elated.

Familiar insecurities return over imagined judgment the world would pass on me if I said these thoughts aloud. At best, I'd be viewed as a sadist. At worst, no better than those I kill. Maybe I am no better than them. I'm a sadist to the sadistic, though. I believe in giving back what's given out. Give kindness, and I will return kindness. Show mercy, and I'll extend all the mercy at my disposal. Give fear, pain, suffering?

I will return such evil back tenfold.

I have little to give of value outside of justice.

My bandit here has shown no mercy, compassion, or remorse.

So, he shall receive none in return.

My reputation is built on that.

"Let her go, and we fight. Unless you're a coward. Then you can stay hidden behind her 'til you collapse, and I slit your throat while you sleep. If we fight, then you have a chance. You win, she's yours. I win, she's free."

A moment of guilt hits me as her eyes grow wide.

"Don't worry," I say to her. "I'll win. This guy only picks on those he thinks he can beat."

I study my nails as I curl my fingers to inspect the dirt caked under them. I'm bored of this already, and my nails are too long. I haven't chewed them off in a while. Not my preferred method anyway. I need a manicure, I think. Or at least a good nail brush.

"Or I could kill her," he snarls, "and then you."

My eyes remain on my nails while my other hand snaps to my belt. My last throwing-knife flies toward the bandit in a blur. It buzzes his ear and embeds into a tree behind him. A clump of his hair falls onto his elbow. His eyes glisten with shock when I look up. He touches his ear and winces from the sting. I caught the edge, which left behind a nice little laceration on the ridge.

"And that I did without a glance. Next one won't be as friendly," I say. "Now you'll want to reconsider your last comment. You hurt the lady, then I have no reason to end this quickly. As long as she is alive, I have every reason to show you mercy. If she dies, I will kill you slowly. I will take my time." I use my other hand to dig at the dirt under my nails. It bothers me.

"Maybe I'll peel your skin while you're conscious. I've never done it, but I hear there's a certain gratification, like peeling a sunburn, only bloodier. Then I'll look you in the eyes while I slowly disembowel your skinless body. It won't be pleasant, but I'll sleep fine afterward. As you beg for death, I'll tie you to the tree behind you and tell you stories. I have a lot of 'em. Fifty-three years I've walked this continent. I've been to many places, participated in many activities, and had so many adventures. Could take days, or even weeks, to get through every story."

My grin spreads ear to ear.

"You'll die in pain and of boredom."

I celebrate quietly as I free the last bit of dirt from my fingernail. One down, nine to go. I pause as a musky stench wafts up to my nose and realize I might be the stinky one. I thought it was the bandits, but I'm not sure. I sniff my armpits and wince.

It's me.

"Gross," I whisper.

My brain crackles with admonishment for my inability to remain undistracted, and I re-establish my focus on the bandit and the girl.

"Now, I'd take the offer for a fair fight. It's your only chance to survive and raid another day."

"And how do I know you won't just kill me when I release her?" he asks, the crack in his voice gone. I look up from my nails.

My lip curls on one side, and I point a finger at his face. "You're a fighter. It's my sincerest hope you are as good as you think you are so I can finally get some rest."

Confusion. The doomed always look confused.

The woman looks confused. No surprise either. I frequently baffle women.

I let out a heavy sigh. I am so, so tired.

"Let's get on with it, shall we?" I say.

As much as I wanted to curl up and die last night and this morning, it's good I didn't. This poor woman and her wounded comrade need rescue. No one else is available for the job. It's lucky for them I was close. It's ever more apparent that my only hope for peace is someday, someone like this guy is as good as they seem to think they are.

Today isn't such a good day to die anymore, though.

I breathe a sigh of relief as the bandit throws the woman to the side. He's rough. It makes my skin crawl. I fight to control the newest shiver of rage that threatens to push me too quickly. She breaks her fall with her hands and lets out a painful grunt. I give the guy the middle finger.

"That wasn't nice," I growl.

"Enough talk," he spits.

I planned to make this quick. Now, it's gonna be a long day for this guy. He could have simply let her go. But no, he had to throw her aside like a useless toy. I clench my fists.

As she tries to collect herself, a portion of her dress falls away and reveals a rather attractive thigh. My natural instincts involuntarily trigger a glance her way, and she glares up at me. Her soft white skin shimmers with odd smudges of stardust in places. I immediately recognize it as an expensive body makeup worn by wealthy women. I don't see it often. Only the most affluent women use it, covering their entire body in makeup. She only has little mismatched streaks here and there. It looks like it's been wearing off for a while.

Wherever she is from, it's not deep in the dangerous RhineWoods. I don't know why she's here, but she's far away from home. Based on her clothes, hair, and eyes, my guess is Teshket.

Her blue eyes plead at me, tears pooling at the bottom, streaks evident in the dirt on her cheeks. Her twig-filled, silvery-blonde hair, tangled and mussed, covers half her face. But I still notice she is beautiful. She has the tenacity and wherewithal to follow my gaze and defiantly yanks her dress closed.

Blood rushes to my face as we lock eyes, and I recognize that I've been staring. I hide my embarrassment with an awkward smile that only makes her cower from me more.

I immediately look away, knowing I look like just another lust-filled hunter. I make a mental note to apologize to her later. She's more of a curiosity to me. Still, even though she's dirty as hell, I can see she is pretty.

I shake my head. She's a person, not an object. Free and soon-to-be safe. I redirect my attention back to the bandit and away from her to eliminate any further discomfort my presence causes.

Just as well because the bandit pulls out two short swords and smiles a wicked grin.

"You picked the wrong one to leave alive," he says. His wide, toothless grin is lovely to see. I'm intrigued.

"Lose your teeth in a bet?" I taunt.

He growls.

I bow in mock appreciation again and wait for him to attack. It's hard to admit, but I enjoy fighting a willing opponent. I love to see the look on their face when I don't jump right into the fray. I imagine the internal dialog is similar to "What is this guy up to?" Or maybe it's "Should I make the first move?" But I stand still, no weapons evident, take no defensive stance, and feign a lack of interest. In this case, I wait, my cloak hanging loosely in one hand. I'm in no hurry. The outcome is already predetermined.

He flips his blades around in a figure-eight pattern. With a final flourish, he flicks them forward, their tips pointed at me. I watch as he pivots on his rear foot.

It astounds me that people do that. I often wonder why it's never occurred to them that the dazzling display of their weapons is pedantic. It is as if some random kata at the start of a fight should intimidate everyone. It's an annoying habit. Now I hate the guy even more, which I didn't think was possible. It's showy, unprofessional grandstanding to get the crowd excited. Flash over substance.

Maybe he thinks he impressed the girl?

"Seriously!" I exclaim. I mock him. "Look at me! I can spin my swords! Watch me flip my knives and juggle them! Oh, check out this windmill with my bo-staff! What's next? You gonna spin in a circle and release an arrow? Waive your hands, make animal claws, and do spin kicks at me?"

This guy's a prick, and I feel like making his ego suffer. Too bad for him. I've never lost a fight. Ever. I think about that. If I were a professional sports fighter, my record would break records.

"In hundreds of fights, how often do you think I've spun my weapons or made animal noises?" I ask him. "I'll tell you. Zero. Never... have... I... ever. There's no need. I don't mind telling you by doing so, you've told me your exact fighting style. I already know more about what you will do than you do. Thanks for the heads up, dumbass!"

That riled him up. I guess I am fighting for sport now. I watch as the pressure on his back leg increases, and minute muscle twitches signal his coming attack.

Step one. Don't project intent. Step two. Don't make the obvious opening move. Step three. If you see me…run.

His initial charge closes the gap in less time than it takes me to blink, which catches me by surprise.

"Whoa!" I exclaim with excitement.

The two swords move with almost blinding speed in precise

slashes. First, his right-hand sword swipes at my neck, its trajectory diagonal toward my hip. I slip away with minimal effort and observe his form as he spins the sword's grip and draws his left sword overtop, the sharp blade aimed for the other side of my neck. It's the windmill pattern he attempted to intimidate me with.

I don't have the heart to repeat how obvious his style is. Better to demonstrate through live education.

The right blade reverses to a sideways strike across my abdomen. I can almost do the count for him. His blades travel with precision—perfect lines, but too specific. He glides through well-practiced routines in rapid succession. But they are precisely that—routines. Shoulder to hip, hip to shoulder, across the belly, crotch to head, neck to bicep, thigh to hip. He targets a major artery with each attempt— femoral, brachial, carotid—alternating based on his position. He directs his strikes with confidence, aimed at targets where his blades have the greatest opportunity to inflict maximum damage.

He intends this to be a short fight. Anyone else would struggle against this man. He is not used to losing, and his confidence is well-placed. He's about to have a bad day, though.

I critique him as he strikes.

"Shouldn't have moved so much," I say.

"Shut up and fight," he growls.

"Oh, that was well executed," I offer. "Nope, that's too soon," I continue as I step out of the way.

His blades slice clean lines through the air.

"Too bad the air isn't your enemy, or it would be suffering right now," I jest.

His only response is another flurry of sharp metal.

"Word of advice? You should probably learn how to strike without preparing the next move with such obvious intent," I taunt as his feet alter their pattern. "*That* was a very nice transition!" I exclaim.

I'll say this for him, he's fast. Incredibly so. The masterful demonstration triggers another adrenaline surge. This warrior moves with impressive speed, and the tightness of his routine is near maximum efficiency.

We'll be a while. Good. I needed exercise.

It's hard to express the energy my unworthy opponent

expends because I expend so little in this dance. His breaths are well-timed, although I can follow the rhythm and match it to the cadence of his strikes.

Just my luck, he's a mouth breather.

I wrinkle my nose as the stench from his agape orifice wafts into my face. His feet rustle the ground as he shifts his position while I wave the foul air away.

With a smile, I offer encouragement. "Oh, ball change, quick step on the footwork. Smooth."

He mixes and matches his katas; his adjustments are fluid and spontaneous. His attempts at unpredictability would work against most opponents. He's still alive for good reason. His confidence is well-earned.

Too bad he ran into me today.

I dodge, step, and dance out of the path of his blades. My head, shoulders, and torso bob and weave in constant motion, never planned, always on the fly. My footwork patterns force him to make uncertain decisions, never sure where I'll move next. With controlled and easy motions, like soft breezes in a meadow, I steer him away from the woman with subtle intent. He's too focused on the attack to realize I lead this dance. I control the position of our bodies. I lead him where I want him, all while making him believe he's in control.

His footwork is impressive. There were four step changes, two rhythm changes, and a couple of feigned stumbles. He attempts a spinning attack, an extended pirouette with both blades, the only real sign that he isn't as good as he could be. It's too bad he won't be able to learn to remove his mistakes from his repertoire later.

His footwork truly is wonderful, though. My footwork is better.

A blade passes my head during a particularly close dodge, which elicits a giggle from my lips. My nearly imperceptible motions risk a close shave, but it's better to have him close. I'm impressed with his stamina, considering there's been little rest between now and however long he struggled with the girl. This fight is already several minutes longer than most, and we still dodge each other at a strenuous cadence.

His sword draws a little too close, and the sound of air moves in time with his blade inches from my shoulder. Still, he hasn't managed to land a single blow.

The near miss boosts his confidence, so he modifies his attack. His strikes inch closer. This guy's a learner. I recognize I've fallen into a complacent pattern and make minute adjustments to my steps. His eyes narrow, acknowledging the change.

I shake my head with a smile, my appreciation for the discipline it took to get him here evident. He's good.

He sends a foot toward my knee.

"Nice!" I encourage. He's more than fancy katas; he's well-rounded and experienced!

Another involuntary giggle escapes my lips. I enjoy myself and can't hold it in. I rarely receive the opportunity to fight someone of his caliber. It's good to stretch my skills. He's keeping me sharp and on my toes. I'll give him that.

He takes my giggle as an insult, I guess, because he spins a foot sweep at me and almost connects. More importantly, it angers him enough that he loses himself and presses harder.

I slow down my dodges imperceptibly to give him a boost. My muscles are warmed up and limbered nicely now. I need the cardio, so I don't want this to end too soon. It takes a lot to get two hearts beating fast. Keeping them strong takes much more work for me than for someone with only one.

He pauses and, with a curious look, steps back, swords held at the ready. His breathing is controlled but heavy. It's hard to believe, but he thinks he is still better than me, even though I haven't pulled a weapon yet. His eyes roam my body, looking for the weapon he knows I must have, and clearly wonders what game I play.

It's that moment when my opponent contemplates whether his efforts match mine. The villain asks himself whether he can surrender and live. He contemplates the questions best asked the moment my knife flew past his earlobe.

If he'd remembered who roamed the RhineWoods with the uncanny knack to show up unannounced, he could have avoided this situation.

I am sure he asks it of himself now.

My internal conflict is different. Yesterday's emotions return.

Every villain with the unfortunate luck to stand before me causes this internal drama at some point. They question whether they are about to fall victim to the tales told around taverns, bonfires, and in bards' songs throughout the Five Realms. Meanwhile, I worry that my only value is vengeance.

I'm almost famous, or infamous, rather. There are many names for me. Too many for me to list off. I am a rumor, a ghost, a fairy tale, or whatever cliché one prefers.

I watch his thoughts play out on his face. The wrinkles in his forehead and the narrow gap in his eyelids are visual clues that his mind is at work. Finally, it dawns that I'm toying with him, and he fears I am the legend. I'm relieved we've reached this point. I wasn't sure my attention span would allow me to keep up the ruse much longer. Although skilled, he knows many fighters out there are better than he is.

"This is somehow different, isn't it?" I ask him.

He doesn't respond. Once again, my opponent knows he's bitten off a whole lot more than he can chew.

Still, this knucklehead thinks he can take me.

Is it hubris?

This is the moment I dread the most. It's the worst. I've encountered this too often. Skilled fighters suffer delusions of grandeur. They believe they can take me down. I wouldn't mind if this one did. But I never get my hopes up.

This fight continues until one of us dies. It's inevitable now. The only other certainty is it won't be me.

One look at the woman on the ground, wild panic in her eyes, reminds me of the stakes, stakes that aren't mine to pay. She is counting on me. I know this scoundrel's intent with her. I glance at her comrade, who won't live long without attention.

"Times up," I say with no emotion.

I gave him a chance to prove himself, a chance to survive. I offered him the opportunity to bring death, to save his own life, to prove himself worthy.

He failed.

"You shouldn't have stopped to think," I continue.

"What?"

"You were almost there. Your last blade strike came close. But now it's time for you to go." I indicate to the woman and drop my cloak. "My lady friend here has waited long enough for you to leave. You should know by now: 'No' means 'Never'."

He rages at the verbal jab and lunges at me, a much faster flurry of blades. Desperation pushes him to his absolute limits. He realizes it's now or never and devotes his entire well of energy to this fight. Hyper-aware that without a killing blow, his life is forfeit.

The bandit's blades come the same as before, only faster. Furious metal sings in the air as it passes. His speed is fast enough to force me to pick up my pace. If only he knew how long I could keep this up. But it's time to end this. As I dodge him, I carefully roll up my sleeves. It takes little effort to concentrate on both actions. I bob my head and shoulders, twist my hips from his blades, and roll up my sleeves. I hardly look at him and direct my focus on my task between his blade swipes. He hasn't realized how much I hold back.

A blade slices the air toward my head, and rather than dodge the attack, I opt to cross my arms in the path of the sharpened edge. His blade catches between the metal shields of my bracers. For the first time, he hears metal on metal. I twist my body and press his blade away as I step to his outside. He stumbles but maintains his grip and slides free from me.

He lunges again, and his blades clash with my armored forearms again. Gal-Danang's craftsmanship easily withstands the blows of his lesser-quality swords. Little sparks fly off at each impact as pieces of his sword are edged away. Each blocked attack dulls his blades a little further.

Revealing my armor usually elicits a reaction. Not this guy. His poise is further testimony to his skill and focus. It enrages him further. The song of metal on metal is always the first sign I am armed, and he didn't even flinch. My forearms come up faster than he can land his blows, so I slow them down, impeding his strokes at the precise moment he commits to the arc.

I am impressed with his stamina.

But it's not enough. It will never be enough.

His blades come down and hit my bracers again. They come up and hit my bracers. With each strike, I apply more pressure to my countermoves. He kicks at my leg. I lift my knee and block his kick. The crack of his shin against the leg bracer hidden there is almost as loud as his grunt. He grimaces in pain and develops a slight limp in his footwork.

"I know that hurt," I taunt.

His swings grow wild. He strikes with manic energy fueled by fear and a desire to live. The sheer force of my blocks leaves his defensive positions wide open. His arms recoil farther back than he intends. Fatigue sets in as the lactic acid in his muscles builds. His form turns sloppy, his breathing ragged. Sweat pours down his face, which I'm sure stings his eyes. We've fought now for nearly ten minutes.

The smallest twinges of sweat break out along my hairline, hardly noticeable. Mild signs of effort, barely a nuisance to me.

That's got to be disheartening. I wouldn't know. I've never experienced what this guy is experiencing right now.

He gives a final, desperate series of swipes, each one an attempt to strike a killing blow. He's run out of energy. I can see the defeat weigh him down. I've prolonged his suffering enough.

I'm not cruel. I'll taunt my adversaries and make them pay for their crimes, but I try not to be intentionally cruel.

Pity wells within me. Bone-weary fatigue overcomes all who engage against me. I know that fatigue.

His shoulders slump, his feet slip every couple of steps, and his swings weaken with each impact. He's spent. He wants this to be over. His well-earned and hard-won confidence is my first victim, and seeds of doubt blossom into fear. He wants to run but knows his chance passed.

It's time to move him to acceptance. I step deeper into his space after a ferocious block pushes his arm behind his hips and twists his body open. I am inside his elbows before he can recover, too close for him to strike. Fear clouds his face.

That's when my blade slips between his ribs.

He never sees the metal come for him. One minute, I block blows empty-handed, and a scant heartbeat later, my blade slides from the bracer on my left arm and enters through his ribcage, piercing his right lung.

His eyes go wider as I pull him close and stare into them. He doesn't want to die.

"Please," he begs.

I shake my head. They always beg when it's over.

I don't smile. I don't sneer. I offer this warrior a death where he is not alone. I offer to be there as he takes his last breath. While I have no honor for his actions before this fight, he fought well. I will give him that courtesy. An honorable end to his battle.

I place my right hand against his other side, and the spring-loaded bracer launches the blade hidden there into his left lung. A soft wheeze comes out of the wound.

Slowly, I pull my hands away, the hidden blades covered in his blood slip from between his ribs. His arms slump as his swords fall to the ground. He looks down, grasps his side, and then pleads back at me.

"You're real," he barely whispers, with no air in his lungs to do more.

"Unfortunately, yes," I say.
It's the last words he hears as he collapses and drowns in his own blood.

The Growing Darkness

Chapter Three

Journal Entry:14

I'm a horrible person.

Whatever my reputation is, it's deserved. As I think about this, the familiar pangs of self-recrimination assault me.

But I can't change it. The Tillions are dead. It doesn't matter if I caused it unintentionally. I brought death to their door.

As a result, my anger got the best of me, and I did, in fact, commit murder.

It makes me think of Mistras, Cali, Kara, Tam, and the few other friends scattered in the Five Realms. Will I bring death to their doors as well?

Will it get out that the man with the most enormous bounty on his head ever recorded is friends with those I care about?
Only two know I am that legend, "The Harbinger of Death."

Well, that was true. But the list more than doubled in a single day.

Just one more way, I am a burden to those around me. The events surrounding the Tillions lend perfect evidence to that. How, in the name of all creation, does a bounty hunter cross paths, randomly, with their target?

I almost missed it. Had the mercenary never asked the question, I would never have realized the men were looking for me. I would have assumed they were bandits who chose the Tillions as easy targets.

I'm the reason my friends are dead.

Life has already been cruel, so what's a little more handed my way?

Sometimes, I wish I could cut this woeful streak out of me.

Instead, I cut the cancer out of humankind.

Sean Gregory

The Girl

The fire inside subsides, the tingle subsides into the never-ending mild vibrations to which I'm accustomed. Standing in these woods, looking down at the four dead men, I shake my head and wonder, for the hundredth time or more, what possible purpose I serve. Everyone is better off if I stay away.

A gentle breeze draws my attention away from the coppery smell of blood around me. I return my focus to the present. Oaks and maples surround me in an almost circular pattern as their branches creak slightly.

I look toward the overhead view of the sky through the large gap between the trees. A small cluster of clouds slowly journeys across the gap. Their edges shift in whatever causes them to evolve up there. I don't get a lot of sky views in RhineWoods. I'll have to remember this place.

Motion behind me draws my thoughts from the clouds to events closer to the ground. The crunch of twigs and leaves layer over a soft sob and invade my thoughts.

Oh, right, the girl.

My soul aches for the disheveled woman driving her heels in a desperate attempt to escape me. Tears streak the dirt from her cheeks, her face frozen in horror. I recognize the signs of shock. She doesn't realize it, but her back presses against a giant oak at the clearing's edge.

It's hard for me to understand that level of fright because I've never suffered it—but it's not hard to have empathy. For all my faults, lack of empathy is not one of them.

Her lips quiver as she struggles to escape. Her feet slip against the soft earth. Tracks dig more deeply with each thrust. Her palms take minor scrapes as she pushes them down on the exposed tree roots in a useless effort to flee.

She can push all day; the oak won't budge.

The scratch on her face and bruise on her cheek tells me she took some hits. I need to calm her down. My blood boils again, my cheeks flush and a scowl forms, which must register on my face because she digs harder and tears flow heavier.

I don't judge her for it. It's not her fault. She's just survived an intense nightmare. Compassion and some sign I won't hurt her like I did the four men that lie dead on the ground is what she needs.

Man, those guys stink up this otherwise beautiful place.

I hold both hands up, open palms, and squat to be at eye level without approaching her.

"Hey, hey, hey. It's okay. You're safe now," I say. "I will not hurt you."

I make no move to touch her. It's better to stay here and let her come to her senses independently. I can be as patient as she needs. It's not like I don't have spare time. My destination isn't far, and I don't need to be there 'til tonight.

Besides, she does not need another dirty man touching her. The rivers of tears from her eyes slow as her gaze shifts from me to her now-dead assailant, then back to me.

"I'd like to apologize for how I looked at you when you fell. It was wrong," I say softly. I trace a figure-eight with my finger into one of the footprints in the dirt.

She still doesn't speak, but I can sense her eyes on me.

A sigh escapes my lips, the pressure valve of anger for her and shame at my behavior toward her release. I close my eyes slowly and count to ten. Far too often, I stumble upon one human committing horrible atrocities to another. How frequently have I sat like this, waiting for the rescued victim to calm down enough to realize I would not harm them?

Too many. It makes me hate and have compassion for people at the same time. I remain still, eyes closed, forearms resting on my thighs, hands relaxed and open.

She seems to have let some tension go when I open my eyes.

Progress.

She's taking the risk that I am honest and sincere.

"Did they...?" I let it trail off. I don't even want to say the words.

She shakes her head slowly and wipes tears from her eyes. A mild groan comes from my left. I turn and look. It's her companion, or at least I assume he is. He seems to be waking from his unconscious state. At least he isn't dead. She should find relief in that.

I turn back to her and realize her companion's groan did more for her than my attempts to calm her.

I remain squatted and offer my hand, barely close enough so she can reach if she wants, but not so close as to intimidate her. She looks up and nods. More progress. She accepts my support, and we rise.

"You'll be right as rain in time," I say as she pulls her hair out of her face, straightens her dress, and uses the heels of her hands to push away the last of her tears. Her body shivers slightly as she takes a deep breath through her nose and lets it out through her mouth, a heavy sigh on the wind.

"Thank you," she says quietly. I shrug, indifferent. Most people would have done the same as me. They just don't do it with as much panache.

Ugh. Get over yourself, man.

While I practice internal flagellation for my high-minded self-admiration, she hurries over to her companion. I step to the side and keep my distance as best I can. Four dead bodies and a wounded man take up most of the space, so keeping a distance is relative.

She reaches the "not-bandit" and collapses to the ground next to him.

"Jesmir," she whispers. Her hand touches his face in a tender caress. His eyes flicker slightly and close back shut. She glances around, then points to a well-designed pack a few feet away, some of its contents scattered about, and looks at me.

"Hand me my bag."

I tilt my head to the side, curious at how her tone changed from timid pleas to confident commands. The sudden shift in how she carries herself surprises me. She is far from helpless. I wonder if she is one of those people who shifts into triage mode in the face of a crisis. It's good. It means I don't have to babysit her. It also means she's tough. I can appreciate that. Her coping mechanism is taking command of the situation and solving problems she can solve. I can respect that, even though I tend toward oppositional defiance.

I suspend my inherent nature and do as she commands.

Unsure of whether the contents that fell out are what she is after, I gather the scattered pieces of her life and put them in the pack before I take them to her. She thanks me and rummages through the contents. When she retrieves her hand from the bag, it holds a small clay jar with a sealed lid. I recognize the symbol on the lid immediately. It's the Talisman of Ezra, Goddess of Life, or The Sun Goddess, or as I always refer to her, "the blasted bitch that burns my eyes."

The girl opens the lid, swipes her fingers into it, and removes some brown paste. Setting the jar on the ground, she carefully parts her comrade's hair. I assume his name is Jesmir. She applies the paste to the wound on his head with a tender touch.

Then she prays.

Damn it. I knew it when I saw the symbol.

She's a Healer.

I hate healers. They are the most zealous of the religious folk in any of the temples of the gods. I fight to keep my comments to myself. She's been through enough.

Commanding or not, however, I refuse to sit through this. I have no use for prayers. Besides, where there are bandits, there's loot. As she prays, I decide to scavenge the bodies of the assailants. Might as well do it now. I already planned to, anyway.

Bandits come in basically two flavors: prosperous and not-so-successful. It's a dumb joke, but it is true. It's not even that enlightening of a thought. I'm distracting myself from prayer, so I dwell on it for a minute.

I don't expect much from this group. Their stench offends my olfactory glands. Or is that still me? It could be me. I sniff my armpits again, in case it's me. I confirm I stink, but this particular stench isn't mine. It's them. They must be from the second category of bandits. There's no chance these guys bathed since the last war, one hundred and fifty years ago.

I'd sacrifice a limb for more successful bandits. They tend not to smell when only dead for less than a day. Releasing their souls to the other side didn't improve their funk, either. Their offal is gross.

I'm worried one of them soiled themselves. I hope not. That

would be awful—funny—but awful. I'll avoid private areas while I search. I do not want to find more than I bargained for.

I scavenge the first three, and my gag reflex responds in retaliation. As expected, I don't find much in the first three bandits' pockets or coin purses other than a couple pieces of copper. Literally, two. I extract my knives from the base of their skulls and clean them on their clothes. Well, not clean… but at least not covered in blood and gray matter anymore.

I work my way to the fourth. His blank stare signals his life has long faded. He looks peaceful, except for those two holes in his sides. I envy his peace.

I ponder what in life causes people like him to resort to banditry. His skills were impressive. He could have been a soldier, a mercenary, a bodyguard, or a professional fighter. Of the hundreds of fights I have been in, he's in the top ten percent. His alternate options were plentiful, and any one of them would have been better than this life. Why go this way? Is he inherently evil?

My hypocrisy has no limits.

Karma says he gets peace, and I don't. I spit on him. That pisses me off.

I'd close his lids and cover his eyes with copper pieces for his journey with Quietius, except he is a rapist, and I'm down to one copper. Well, three, now. He can negotiate his own way across the river of souls. He's lucky I'm resisting the urge to piss on his body. But seeing as I already cared for that immediate need, I opted to spit on him again.

Then again, I still might piss on him. I can be pretty petty.

A thorough search of his belongings reveals a well-crafted knife. Almost as good as mine, but not Gal-Danang quality. Good enough to sell later, maybe get a good meal and some drink out of it. But the real find is the purse hidden inside his waistband. I have to admit. I'm stunned. It's hefty.

"Clearly, you defy the rule, you smelly bastard," I say.

Rules are made to be broken anyway.

The substantial weight of the bag thumps my palm as I heft it. The distinct sounds of coins and the rustle of paper come from inside. It's the paper that surprises me. Only the wealthiest tend to have paper money. This guy's carrying enough paper money to feed a large village of families for an entire winter season.

"My, my. You either hit a mother lode of a raid, or you have some savvy spending habits," I whisper to the dead man.

The purse is stuffed with twelve Realm Notes, each worth a thousand gold coins. But these aren't any Realm Notes. These are Haabrestand Realm Notes. I don't know much about economics, but Haabrestand is the current standard for all of Conishant. While not the wealthiest of the Five Realms, their economy is the most stable.

The notes make me think of Tamrin. I picture the light-skinned man in his furs and am excited to see him tonight.

Returning my thought to the purse, I stare at the bandit's face. This guy stumbled onto a major haul somewhere. Whoever this group raided was wealthy, either a merchant or nobility.

Ballsy.

Further investigation of the contents reveals another fourteen copper coins (not Haabrestand), six silver coins, a ring with a signet I do not recognize (looks important), a folded note, and a couple of well-cut emeralds. All in all, it's a hell of a day, like hitting lucky twenty-three on the Shamna Rocks.

I pull the copper and three silver coins, the note, and the signet ring and slip them into my purse. There could be a reward for the signet ring. I'll hold onto that for now. I tie the bandit's purse shut and walk back to the girl. She sits cross-legged, with her hands resting, palms up on her knees, clearly still in prayer. In a patient effort not to disturb her, I watch.

She opens one eye and peeks at me.

"I'm done praying," she says. "I'm just centering myself."

I squat next to her. She is recovering quickly. Quicker than I expected.

"Are you hurt?"

She shakes her head as she closes her open eye. I observe her sleeping companion.

"How is he?"

She doesn't open her eyes but says, "My prayer will be answered. Ezra always answers my prayers. He will be fine. Just needs some time."

I plop down on the ground and wait. Clearly a woman of faith, I'm inclined to think her foolish, but whatever. Using a healing paste and claiming a prayer is the cure is like saying you're clean because you dressed after you bathed. It's silly fairy tales the devout tell themselves to make sense of their world. I guess some people need a crutch.

She takes a deep breath, holds it for what seems like forever, and then lets it out slowly. When she finishes, she opens her eyes, and her body relaxes.

"Thank you for saving my brother and me," she says.

I nod an acknowledgment in her direction with the tip of my head. I've never been comfortable with gratitude.

"I do what needs done. Nothing more," I say.

Her inquisitive look is one I am used to. In response, I toss the bandit's purse on the ground at her feet.

"There's at least twelve thousand gold in there, in Haabrestand Realm Notes, and a couple of gems," I say. "I have no use for it. You might as well take it."

She blinks at me, her face a mix of shock and confusion.

I ignore the look. It has become such a common reaction to me it doesn't even phase me anymore. I don't have any desire for wealth. Wealth only serves to make one reliant on comfort. Get too comfortable, and suddenly, you begin to rely on it. Then you'll do whatever it takes to keep it. Wealth frightens me. I have known very few good wealthy people. I don't think I'd be one. Best I avoid it.

She shakes her head at me and picks up the purse.

"Who are you?" she asks.

"Nobody you'd care to know," I say. It sounds as cliché in my head as it does out loud. But I am a walking cliché. The words are accurate enough.

My gaze fades off into the distance while I consider which direction to head. I lost my sense of direction during the fight. I contort my torso to glance backward in search of my entry point.

"What's wrong?" she asks.

"I've never been in this clearing before. I lost my bearings."

She points to a gap in trees behind me.

"Oh yeah, thanks,"

I point to the opposite side of the glen and remind myself I'm headed to Winding Run. Lucky for her, this was close to "on the way."

"I'm Jesma," she says.

Her kindness toward me calms me down. I recognize she is lost and out of her element. But something about her doesn't feel right. I can't put my finger on it. Whatever it is, though, it's not my problem. I did what I came to do. I helped her. As much as I'd like to help her more, what comes next is not a role I am comfortable with. Companionship is not my strength.

"Pleasure, Jesma. That's Jesmir, your brother, then?" I say and point to the still sleeping but no longer unconscious man. I don't offer my name.

"Yes," she says. She is cautious. "We are on our way to Valshannon and slept here last night. We were preparing to leave when those men found us."

"Lucky for you, I happened to be close by," I say.

Her face flushes with memory, and her eyes start to well up. She composes herself quickly. That's my queue. I'm not a good shoulder to cry on, either. I am barely comfortable with my own emotions.

"Well," I say, "safe travels." I stand to leave.

"Where are you headed?" she asks. There's a hopeful plea evident in the words. That same hope appears on her face.

I hate that look.

No. No. No. My path lies the other way, I tell myself.

While I would like to help, I have somewhere to be later tonight. I'm not in a hurry, but Valshannon is a day's travel in the wrong direction. Two if I account for the backtracking I'll have to do. I helped. That's what I do. I am not an escort, bodyguard, or travel guide. She wants me to accept the job, but I'm expected in Winding Run.

"Not Valshannon," I say softly. A wave of guilt washes over me, but I push it aside.

Her disappointment is evident. Her eyes fall to the coin purse, then rise to me. She considers offering me money but recognizes the futility of that approach.

"Nice to meet you, Jesma," I say. "Stay to the road the rest of your journey?" I point east. "It's a mile that way." I point toward the now hidden netherstack. "Under no circumstance should you go that way. The RhineWoods is not a place for the two of you. Crossing the Great Rankin is nearly impossible except by the main roads. If you get to the road, you have enough in the purse to hire transport. The King's Regal Highway has a lot of merchants who'll be willing to give a ride for a fee. Just don't go flashing money around. Use the silver. I left some in there."

She looks frightened but nods. With that, I am off to Winding Run. As I cross the threshold of trees, another twinge of guilt hits me.

At least by not traveling with her, I won't be a liability, though.

That's what I tell myself anyway. It's a defense mechanism. I murdered four men in front of her. I'd start to feel judgment from her in short order.

I exit the clearing and make it about twenty paces when my melodramatic exit is interrupted by a nagging thought. I left my last knife stuck in a tree. With the grace of a clown, I turn back, avoid eye contact with the woman in the glen, and retrieve the knife. Before I leave the clearing, I hear a small voice.

"Please," she whispers.

I ignore the plea and don't look back.

The Growing Darkness

Chapter Four

Journal Entry:21

It's quite impressive that I am still alive despite my best efforts. Sometimes it pisses me off. Sometimes, I'm grateful. Depends on the moment.

Last year, a caravan of healers did me dirty. I think that's what you call it——a caravan. Let's just say it was more than one because one wasn't more than necessary anyway?

Overkill... no, over heal... over save?

Whatever.

Anyway, a caravan of healers showed up in the middle of a remote desert as I was on my way to blissful oblivion. I had accepted Death. Quietius had drawn near, and I was fine with it. But the healers showed up instead.

"Lucky we found you when we did," the head priest said.

"Lucky for whom?" I snarled.

They didn't realize how lucky they were I am not an indiscriminate murderer.

The adjective there matters. Anyway...

Those self-righteous jackwagons healed me without asking me first. And, since I didn't ask them to, I didn't thank them. I wasn't grateful this time. I was rather upset, honestly. I was at peace for the first time in a long time.

How, in the name of the Great Eight Gods, did a caravan of Shamna's healers, dressed in those stupid wood pulp pants and those flower wreaths on their heads, just happen to be on a pilgrimage in the desert?

They had the audacity to ask for a donation.

I gave them a suggestion instead.

Using one finger from each hand.

The only pleasure I got from the experience was I offended them. The leader even offered to open the wounds back up for me. I laughed at his humor. It was a good comeback. One I deserved.

I told them to pound sand. Which they did. Literally. They went right back to their march through the desert. I am snickering, even now, at the memory. They only did what they thought was right. Timing is everything.

I'm not a fan of healers anyway. Never have been. Masking science with faith. It amazes me that people think healers' pastes are more about prayer and faith than medicine. Healers and their damn hypocritical oaths. Yes, I'm aware that's not the word. Don't care.

"Do no harm."

What about the harm you did me? Thanks to them and their uninvited healing, hours of contemplation and guilt followed. I wasn't pleased. Not in the moment, anyway. I already carry an incredible amount of guilt that these thoughts exist. I'm in no way blind to the

harm I would cause to those who love me should I succeed.
                    Sometimes, it's too hard to stop myself.
    Sometimes, living frightens me.
    What if I'm never okay?
    Wouldn't everyone be better off without the weight of me?
    Sometimes, it's as if I've learned nothing.

Annoyances

Images of the rescued girl and her brother occupy my mind as I travel south.

"Damn it, I guess I could have taken them to the King's Regal Highway," I mumble to myself. It wouldn't have cost me much to assist them. A couple of hours to escort them to the highway wouldn't have killed me.

Deep down, however, the obligation to go further would have weighed on me. My motivation for leaving the pair to fend for themselves was driven by my desire to avoid the burden of responsibility for the pair's continued safety. It's been almost nine months since I've seen my best friend. My primary concern is to keep my promise to meet him; otherwise, I might have deviated from my path and escorted the siblings to Valshannon.

My stomach grumbles as I traipse through the trees. I haven't eaten since yesterday morning. I check my pack for any remnants of jerky. It's the tenth time I've searched.

"Don't know what you thought you'd find in there," I grumble.

I'm famished. Killing six people in two days takes a lot of energy. My stomach aches from the emptiness. I'll be useless to myself or anyone else without some food.

Rationalizing through the fog of my hunger, it dawns on me I'm not far from one of my favorite hunting spots. Ezra's achieved her zenith, so I have a good handle on time. I have leeway to hunt for food and maybe find some edible roots or mushrooms on the way.

Or to have helped those lost souls find their way safely to the highway.

"Oh, shut up," I tell my conscience.

Serenity Creek is only about a mile south of me. I smile at that. I'm rather proud of the name since I'm the one who named it. Most people simply refer to it as "the creek," but over the last few years,

"Serenity Creek" has started to stick. "The creek" doesn't do justice to how this place soothes me. It's not on any map, though it does see many visitors. It's one of the few plentiful fishing spots in one of the only safe places in the southern RhineWoods. It offers other tastier, non-fish options.

I reach Serenity Creek by mid-afternoon to no small amount of disappointment. Louder than necessary, voices echo off the trees and slowly flowing water. Lost in thought over the two out-of-place siblings, it doesn't even register I hear voices until I walk into the small collection of people.

"Oh," I say, startled. I chastise myself for my lack of awareness.

A tall, slender woman rises from a squat at the creek's bank and turns toward me. Her thin, lanky body peers through a sheer silk nightgown, her skeletal form evident through the backlit material. Long dark hair accentuates her pallor. Her dark brown eyes scan me from head to heel and back.

The others, dressed similarly and equally as lanky, seem not to notice my presence as they remain squatted at the water's edge. Eventually, they turn to look at me, almost in unison. A chill runs down my spine, the spooky timing almost choreographed.

"Hello there," the woman says.

"Ugh, hi," I say. I glance upstream and downstream and then point upstream. "I don't mean to interrupt. I'll just head that way a bit."

I turn to leave, but she steps into my path and holds up a hand at waist height.

"You don't have to. All are welcome to join us here," the priestess says, her tone warm. But the whole scene gives me the creeps.

I resist rudeness, but I'm not interested in friendliness. A gathering of smiles, radiant with bright eyes, mirth, and kindness, aim toward me like weapons of hidden danger.

I resist another shiver.

As I take in the scene, I notice they each wear necklaces and recognize the periapts of Nadur, God of Nature. I hang my head and groan.

"What's the matter?" she says as she steps closer. I hold up my hand to stop her.

"Nothing is the matter," I reply. "But I'm not the guy you proselytize."

She looks to her friends and then back to me, her brow furrowed.

"Proselytize?" she questions. "What makes you think we want to convert you?"

I indicate her periapt with my hand and then swing my arm, encompassing the others with the gesture.

"Are you not priests of Nadur?" I ask.

She smiles, and her eyes sparkle. "We are, yes. But that doesn't mean we intend to turn you away from your god."

I laugh out loud at that. The rest of the group stares at me with curiosity. I recognize my rude behavior is based on implicit bias toward religious zealots.

"I'm sorry," I say. "My experience with priests is different. But turning me away from any god you could never do."

"Oh?" she says as she tilts her head. "You follow more than one?"

I fight down my inclination to laugh again, resulting in a strained smirk that causes her to raise an eyebrow. I hold up a hand in apology as I fight to exercise self-control. Members of the group shift to my right and I sense they are working to flank me.

"I'd appreciate it if you didn't stand behind me," I warn. The motion stops as the woman before me glances at her companions. I sidestep to keep everyone in view. The other members of her party exchange furtive glances. That raises my suspicions. My hands twitch to release blades, my nerves on edge.

"We mean no harm," the leader says, holding her hand up to the rest, commanding them to remain still. "We are priests of Nadur. That is true. We're on a pilgrimage in preparation for Winter Solstice. He tasks us to pass his blessings onto the creek and the Rhine Woods."

"You speak to him, then?" I ask.

"Well, yes, in our own way," she replies.

I nod, my suspicions not allayed.

"Well, I will leave you to it, then," I reply.

"Won't you come sit with us and allow us to pass a blessing to you?" she says.

"Let me stop you right there," I say. "Keep your blessings to yourself. I have no need of them."

"Oh? You must have a strong relationship with your patron to need no blessings," she says.

I laugh until tears form. "Lady, I am my own patron."

The others gasp at the blasphemous comment.

"You?" she asks, surprised. Her fearful expression confuses me until she says, "I'm sorry." She starts to bow as she asks, "Are you one of the Great Eight?" The crack in her voice as she bows her head is only slightly less funny than the sudden prostration of her companions. All six of them start to kneel.

I laugh harder, almost too slow to reply, "Stop! I'm no more a god than any of those phonies!"

Her fear instantly flashes to anger.

"We mean you no harm, but do not test our faith with blasphemy," she says. Her tone hardens, and her hand clutches her periapt. I'm triggered by the behavior and cast my eyes toward the group. Each of their hands clasps the stone emblems that hang from their necks. My laughter stopped as quickly as it started.

"You don't want to do that," I warn.

"You dare blaspheme the Great Eight?" she asks.

"Sister, the Great Eight is a fantasy. They either don't care or don't have the power you think they do."

She tilts her head at that. "You have no patron?" she questions, shocked by the realization.

"I have none. Nor will I. Save your message for someone that might give a shit."

"May I ask why you turn your back on the ones who provide life for us and protect us from all manner of danger?" one of the others asks, the tone innocent.

I turn and look at her. "I can't stop you from asking. But it's none of your business. I keep my own council." I turn back to the woman who clearly leads this pack of zealots. "If you don't mind, I would like to be on my way."

"As you wish," she says. She steps to the side, extends her

arm, and allows me to pass. I nod and continue my walk.

"I will pray for you, stranger," she says. "We all will."

"Save your prayers for someone who wants them. I'm perfectly fine without them," I reply and continue to walk upstream. Behind me, I can hear them talking among themselves.

"I've heard rumors of these atheists, but I've never met one before," says a soft voice.

"They are an abomination," says the leader.

"Who do you think he is?" asks a third voice.

"I don't know," the leader replies.

"You don't think he's…" the question dies out.

"Hush," the woman hisses.

An uneasy silence settles behind me, and I'm grateful. It's short-lived, however, as a loud voice rings out.

"Harbinger!"

I flinch at the name but don't look back. It cuts me deep into my core. My throat tightens as a rush of emotions threatens to overwhelm me. I choke them back.

"I hate that goddamn name," I whisper to myself and continue to walk. I refuse to acknowledge the callout or to even look back.

Perched in the crook of an oak tree's trunk and one of its larger branches, I listen for my prey. The sounds of wildlife reverberate around me. I take solace in the sound, thankful it is only animals, insects, and creaking trees in the breeze. I worried the priests planned to follow me and try to continue the conversation. But they didn't.

The order of life pulsates with its natural rhythm all around me. To my right and below me, Serenity Creek babbles along. I stare at the water from my perch. Its surface reflects small shafts of the waning late afternoon light. A few fish swim by, living the life of fish. I call it Serenity Creek, but it's just a stream. There's enough water flow for small fish and ground game to drink freely, but not so much that it drowns out the noises I need to hear. It's a lullaby for a great nap if I wasn't so hungry.

I could nab a fish and be done, but I'm in a mood. I smirk as my patience pays off. A honk sounds out below me and to the right.

It's an exercise in self-control as my excitement builds. Only one meal will satisfy this craving, and I'm a slave to my cravings. A short time passes when I see the slow-moving display of colors contrasting the greens, browns, blacks, and oranges of the Rhine Woods. Transfixed, I watch long, wispy feathers rise from the back and spread in an incredible display. The peacock honks again, trying to attract a mate.

Part of me feels bad for the guy, but the feeling passes as my stomach rumbles and my mouth salivates. I don't waste time. With a quick flick of my wrist, my knife finds its mark, and thirty minutes later, the strong scent of stewed peacock rises over a modest fire.

I add the last of my salt and a few mushrooms I foraged and sit staring at the water as it slowly passes by. I consider the previous two days and the progression of events. A twinge of sorrow grips me as I remember the Tillions. I choke back a sob and once again wonder why the world is so cruel.

The aroma of my stew returns me to the moment, and I force myself to focus on it rather than the images of the Tillions. I lift the lid from the pot, and steam rises to meet my face. So much better than the stench of the bandits earlier.

A picture of the siblings, Jesma and Jesmir, comes to mind, and I drift back into my thoughts. I'm unsettled. There should be a sense of satisfaction for my good deed. But my soul aches. Familiar doubts about my character bubble to the surface as guilt threatens to consume me for leaving them to fend for themselves.

It doesn't help that my one valuable skill is one I can't even brag about without sounding like a villain. The pull into depression whispers at my conscience and causes me to sink into myself.

Nagging questions form. Why would they decide to leave the relative safety of the patrolled roads to sleep in the Rhine-Woods? Where are they from? Why are they headed to Valshannon? Neither their appearance nor demeanor screamed hardened traveler.

What drove them this way? How can they not know deviating off the road is dangerous? This is Rhinestab, after all. The woods, the plains, hell, and even the rivers are known to be hazardous. In my mind, I see the whole of the Rhine Woods: Spiderlyche country to the northeast, River Gnomes in the Great Rankin, the netherstack to the northwest, peppered with bandits, zealots, and a notorious resident known as The Harbinger.

What were they thinking? No one ever camps in the woods of Rhinestab. Except me, of course.

Well, at least now they have enough money to find safe passage to Valshannon. Maybe they can hire some bodyguards. The progression of thought recalls to mind the bandits' loot. I reach into my purse and dump its contents onto the ground. Sifting through, I set the few coins to the side. What's left is the folding knife, the ring, and a folded piece of paper. Upon further inspection, I notice remnants of a wax seal.

"Hmm, what's this then?" I say. "Let's see what you have to offer."

I unfold the paper and find an elegant script written inside. The penmanship is perfect, clearly from someone of some importance and education. But it's written in the language of Killinshire. I am not fluent, but I recognize a few of the words.

Three words stand out to me, "Valshannon," the Killin-shire word for "contact," and the number twelve. The rest might as well be invisible because I don't know what it says.

"Interesting."

I set the paper aside and look at the knife. Unremarkable, it's worth enough to pay for ink or a pint of ale and not much more. I set it with the note and the coins and focus on the ring. It has a signet on it. There is a familiarity about it; I probably should recognize it, but I struggle to place it. The best I can tell is it's a Teshket family signet because of the dragon on it, but I couldn't tell who it would be. There are too many Teshket Royals to track, and I haven't spent more than ten days there since I left at eighteen. Teshket is little more than a distant bad dream to me now.

I return to the note and pick it up, holding the ring and note side by side. A Teshket signet and a Killinshire note. A bandit with twelve Haabrestand Realm Notes. What could it mean? Thankfully, I know someone who can read and speak Killinspeak, and they just happen to own the finest tavern in Rhinestab. That tavern happens to be my destination.

I return the contents to my purse and pull out my journal. I'm almost out of ink, so I must be selective on what to put down. Hopefully, Mistras will have some for sale.

I ponder the note and why a lowly bandit holds a Teshket signet, a note in Killinspeak, and twelve Haabrestand Realm notes in the middle of Rhinestab.

It doesn't make sense.

The Growing Darkness

Chapter Five

Journal Entry:24

I actually enjoy people, especially my friends. How I live my life and how I feel about socializing are not in tune with one another. But what choice do I have? Death follows me wherever I go. I'm used to death; I'm not even afraid of it anymore. Some would say I am a bringer of death.

Not Quietius, God of Death. Be cool if I was, right? Maybe I wouldn't think like this. You'd think we'd even perhaps be associates. But we aren't. While the Lord of the Final Slumber and I cross paths often enough, he never takes me.

Most days, I'm grateful for it. But some days, I wish the bastard would.

On those days, I think he's a dick.

I'm so, so tired.

No... tired doesn't do it justice. I'm exhausted.

What I feel is a bone-weary, muscle-aching, pervasive fatigue. It's deep, like an un-scratchable itch that sits just underneath the kneecap. You feel it but can't locate it, so you scratch and dig deep between the tendons and bones, pushing your fingers as hard as possible. It's like some small entity crawls around, tickling you from inside. Maybe you grasp the kneecap and move it around, pressing it down into the joint as you do.

But it doesn't work to cure the itch.

It's an odd sensation of discomfort without a remedy that doesn't involve a knife and some bloodletting. Luckily, that itch eventually goes away.

The fatigue never does. It leeches life from me.

Most of the time, I can suppress it, bury it deep, find a source of joy, and persevere. Sometimes, it overwhelms me.

Sean Gregory

Change of Plans

There's a big part of me that is grateful those bandits interrupted my suicidal plans. I'd honestly forgotten about this promised visit.

Now, new copper coins burn a hole and beg me to spend them. After a relatively long hike through the RhineWoods to reach the southern part of the King's Regal Highway, the craving for a good buzz grows.

I'm thirsty, and water hasn't cut it. I want a pint. I haven't had a good drink in so long that I'm hyper-focused on getting to Winding Run, where a good pint and a good friend wait. As I come around a bend in the King's Regal Highway, the faint glow of streetlamps appears, illuminating the dark road and the forward edges of the trees in warm yellow.

All around me, the nocturnal members of nature fill the air with sounds of life. The road is quiet, with occasional stragglers heading home or toward the tavern few and far between. But I can hear the sound of music and merriment ahead.

My destination is just past the first bridge over Winding Creek, not far into the town of Winding Run. A name given to this small village for the way the creek crisscrosses its way back and forth through the town.

Home to barely two hundred people, the small village runs a straight line on the highway. The main drag runs straight as the edge on my Korund steel blades. I can see from one end of town to the other, even at night. Every couple hundred feet, the creek crosses the highway like a snake wrapping around a tree trunk. The road crosses over the creek five times, each spanned by a stone bridge wide enough for three carriages to cross. Patches of bright green moss glisten in the soft yellow light from the gas lamps that flank the bridges every ten feet. The mixture of green moss, gray stone, and yellow light paints a quintessential land of peaceful bliss.

Winding Run is the common halfway point for travelers making the journey between Valshannon, about a two-day ride to the north, and Dresdin, a two-day ride to the south. It takes as many as four days to travel by foot to either place from here. Taking the path through the RhineWoods adds many more days.

The thought triggers another image of the siblings. Why wouldn't they choose to come here and hire transport to Valshannon? Maybe they're running from some danger. A twinge of guilt pokes my conscience because of my mother's incessant drumming of her "be an asset" missive. I feel bad for leaving them, but two fights in two days don't have me in a good head space.

"Be an asset, not a liability," my mother would say.

"They aren't my problem anymore," I tell myself, not wanting to head down that bakru trail.

Why can't I stop thinking about them?

This hyper-fixation needs a distraction only booze can offer.

My feet move on their own volition, and I approach Mistras' Tavern. Softly illuminated signs on buildings on either side of the highway mark the small shops that line the road in between the series of bridges. Flickering gas lamps, fed by the natural gas well underground, cast dancing shadows on the entire stretch of the town. The saddlery, one of the most sought-after places in Rhinestab and the second-largest building in the village, is clearly visible at the end of the main road—even in the relative darkness of mid-evening.

Thriving on the revenue created by trade and the convenient proximity to the southern halfway point along King's Regal Highway, the town's wealth is legendary. Winding Run boasts the highest per capita income in Rhinestab outside of Valshannon, which has the largest economy. Financial resources in Winding Run are limitless. There isn't a citizen in this town who suffers from poverty, and that's by design. Businesses here are strictly protected monopolies.

Common perception says this establishment is the best Rhinestab has to offer. It is sometimes universally accepted as accurate, like Mistras' Tavern. Mistras' is my favorite place in all of Rhinestab. Not just because I have personal ties to the owner.

Mistras' is the largest building in Winding Run by at least half as much as the Saddlery. Standing outside the large three-story structure with thirty rooms for rent and its strong, dark, perfect temperature ale, I am as close to feeling at home as I can get.

A sense of home soothes me as I stare at the tavern entry. "I'm so looking forward to this," I say out loud.

"I hope you aren't here to cause trouble," a female voice taunts from behind. I turn slowly to address the source. Three well-armed fighters, their faces illuminated by the light emitted from the tavern, stand ready to accost me. Their blackened light armor identifies them as WinRun Guardians—another famous fixture of this renowned village. Flickering light of the gas lamps glistens against the polished armor.

Nearly a third of the population of Winding Run serves as a Guardian, paid for by the high taxes enacted on those who travel through town, so their presence doesn't surprise me.

They don't tolerate loitering, vagabonds, or troublemakers.

I'm all three, depending on who is asked.

"I don't cause trouble. I am trouble," I reply, lacing the comment with sarcastic disrespect.

The leader, a woman about a head shorter than me, her armor slightly better cared for than her two sidekicks, steps up to me. A thin, dark red sash across her shoulder marks her as a Captain. Her two short swords crossed at her waist identify her as someone used to getting her way. She steps forward and pokes me in the chest with her armored finger.

"Ow!" I say.

With a voice as hard as gravel, she snarls at me. "You have a smart mouth for someone dressed in such tattered clothes." I peak over her head at the two guards behind her. They cast awkward sideways glances at each other before looking back down at the Captain glaring at me.

"Last I checked, poverty wasn't a crime," I say.

"Last I checked, this isn't a homeless camp," she replies. "How about I take you into the station and strip search you for stolen goods?"

"Poor means thief to you?" I ask, narrowing my eyes.

The two younger guards fidget, and their armor creaks in the background of the noise from the tavern behind me. I notice the fear of inexperience in their eyes.

"No," she replies. "Thief means thief, and you look like a thief to me."

I clench my fists and snort. "I've never known Winding Run to be unfriendly to travelers."

"Travelers are welcome," she says. "Vagabonds are not. Do I need to remove you from here by force?"

"You wanna dance?" I threaten while I flex my pecks.

The men behind her grab the hilts of their very short swords and draw them out. I incline my head to them, and she holds up a hand to stop them.

"I've got this miscreant handled, boys," she says. They set their swords back into the scabbards, but their hands remain on the hilts.

"You might want to call off your dogs," I say. "Kids get hurt when they play too rough with wild animals."

"And you may want to rethink the claim you aren't a thief," she replies, squaring her shoulders.

I lean in and whisper loud enough for the others to hear, "Stealing your heart does not make me a thief. Did you dress sexy for me? Or do you treat all visitors with such a feisty welcome?"

She looks at her armor and back at me quizzically, then punches me in the shoulder. I'm not sure if the force was accidental or on purpose. Still, the impact causes my torso to turn more than either of us expected, my leg kicks out behind me to maintain balance. At least, that's what I tell myself, judging by the look on her face.

"Owwww," I say slowly, in a hoarse whisper. "Really?" I whine.

"I thought you weren't going to show your face around here again," she says to me, her tone harsh though she smiles.

The two guards exchange confused glances with each other.

"What would give you that idea?"

"You still owe me two copper, mister," she says and places a hand on her hip.

"You still think I owe you? Kara! You lost that bet," I say.

She turns to one of the other guards, a much younger man with a thin early mustache. He looks like he might still be in puberty. She leans back toward him and lightly taps him with her hand. Both young men relax as they realize she's toying with me.

"You believe this guy?" she says. "Makes a bet, loses, and skips town before he pays it." She looks back at me. "Now, what kind of person does that?"

"A thief," the young guard says.

She looks at me with a grin and says, "See, they catch on quick."

I laugh. "I'm not a thief. I'm a scoundrel. There's a difference." I raise my arms, palms up. "Wanna arrest me? Take me back to the station?" I say, leaning forward. "Tell me what a naughty boy I am?" I wink.

"You seriously want to go there? Before you walk in that door?" she says, lifting her chin up to the entry into Mistras'. She holds out her hand. "Pay up, sucker."

I look down at the ground and draw a line with my foot in the dirt.

"Well, as I recall, you didn't win," I reply. "This was the line, and you never made it across," I retort. "Wanna try again, short stack?"

Her face turns red. "The hell I didn't! I had a witness!"

"And I had two. Cali," I say, holding up a finger, "and your buddy? What the hell was his name…" I start to question, holding up a second.

"Rivas," she offers, conceding with a sigh.

"Riiiight. Cali and Rivas both said the opposite," I reply.

"Cali had a crush on you, so she doesn't count," she responds. "And, it turns out," she says through the side of her mouth, "Rivas was half blind. We had to remove him from the Guard. So, he doesn't count either." She leans on her back leg and crosses her arms. "By my count, it's Kara one, Shen zero."

She puts her gloved hand out again.

With a sarcastic grin, she points at me. "Pay me what you owe, thief."

I point a finger at her face. "I'm not paying a debt I didn't know I owed, especially on the word of a cheat. Now, unless you plan to arrest me, the answer is no. But," I offer, "will you settle for a pint?"

I turn, holding out my elbow like a gentleman.

She waves me off. "Bah! You know my brother lets me drink for free, you deadbeat."

"How about a different form of payment??"

Her sly grin almost stings. "Ha! I'd rather have the money!"

"Now that's hurtful," I say.

"Boot fits."

We stare at each other and laugh. I step forward, and we grab each other in an embrace.

"Where the hell have you been?" she asks, finally showing she's genuinely glad to see me.

"Around."

"You've been avoiding my brother," she accuses.

"Well, yeah, probably," I admit, "but not on purpose."

She looks up and down the street and then waves me on. "Well, go on. If you haven't passed out by the time I'm off, I'll come get that pint from you."

I nod as she looks at me up and down.

"Undressing me with your eyes?"

She snorts. "You look like shit, you know?"

"I know," I reply.

"It's good to see you, lover. Stay out of trouble," she admonishes.

"That, I guess, depends on your brother," I say, unable to hide my nervos.

"Oh, he's still pissed at you."

I swallow hard.

She taps the side of her nose and points at me before she waves her team on and heads up toward the saddlery. I watch as the little patrol makes its way up the road, stopping to talk to other travelers and packs of roaming guardians.

I climb the short stairs to the large porch, stretching the entire building facade. Luckily, I'm good friends with Mistras, the owner of this beautiful tavern. We go back a long time. If there isn't a room, he'll let me stay in the kitchen on a cot if I drink too much—which I intend to do tonight.

He always has a room for me.

Well, unless he truly is still mad at me. I feel the butterflies of nerves and almost don't go in. But then I remember Tamrin should be inside, and this rare social evening is exactly what I need to clear my mind. Mistras will have to get over it.

I hope.

While I prefer to be alone most of the time, this inner monologue is sometimes too heavy. Reclusive as I am, I do enjoy taverns. When I drink, I want crowds. Drinking doesn't stop thinking, but a few ales enjoyed with people do. While drunk, lively discussions tend to get me out of my head.

Besides, it's been some time since I caught up on news around Rhinestab. A tavern is a perfect place for that. After a few drinks, some laughs, and a conversation with total strangers and fellow travelers, I'll be up to date before the evening ends. The best insight is found between the lines of exaggerated tales from drunken mouths.

The music coming from inside the tavern, a mix of stringed instruments and soft drums, lures me in. I love this place. The dark, well-seasoned, polished wood reflects the lanterns hanging around the outer wall and inner pillars. People mill about on the catwalks of the second and third floors. Some run in and out of the rooms, bouncing between dwellings in a never-ending sea of light debauchery.

The forty-plus tables and the twenty-seat bar are filled to capacity. Along the outer walls, a variety of folks stand, leaning against the courtesy shelf installed for standing-room-only nights like tonight. Everyone has drinks in hand, and the place is filled with chatter and laughter.

This is my kind of place.

I spot Mistras' daughter, Cali, behind the bar. She's grown since I last saw her over a year ago. Her dark hair, short stature, and deep green eyes give her a childlike look that betrays her recent ascension to womanhood. She always reminded me of an old friend I had when I was younger.

Memories, long since shoved into a dark corner, come rushing back. I stuff them back into their box and wave to Cali. She waves back, her face ignited with surprised joy.

I sidle up to the end of the bar and relax. She'll swing by when she finishes her list of customers ahead in line. I watch her laugh and joke with the various patrons at the bar. She grew up beautifully. Cali's natural friendliness welcomes all manner of folks. Armed with quick banter and a charming smile, she disarms even the saltiest people.

Her laugh breaks out over the din of voices at a quip she heard while grabbing two small glasses and pouring hard liquor into each. She passes them to a guest with one hand, deftly snagging up coins with the other.

I love Winding Run. Mistras' is the flagship of the friendliest place in Rhinestab. They welcome all races, religions, and travelers from anywhere. Even Killinfolk can find a warm welcome here.

As long as it's a short visit. Winding Run is legendary for its selectivity in who can move into town, citizenship requiring a seven-year service with the Guardians if you weren't born here. Guardian status requires an apprenticeship with one of the businesses in town, a position that has become more of a challenge to land due to a steady supply of recruits.

Even local-born must serve three years with the Guardians to stay. That's how Winding Run remains safe. The leadership here keeps its reputation high and its population small.

No amount of money can buy your way in. Only skilled tradesfolk of new and significant value currently non-existent in Winding Run are invited to stay, and it is by invitation only.

I've never been asked to stay, nor would I if asked.

I can't take my eyes off Cali. Memories of a three-year-old toddler caught in the hands of hired bandits in the RhineWoods, nearly a full day from town, run through my mind. I was a regular at Mistras' by then. I recognized his daughter as soon as I saw her. When I confronted the kidnappers, they attacked. Less than a minute later, they were dead, and I carried the girl home. The kidnapping was an effort to get Mistras to sell his tavern.

Mistras has called me "friend" ever since, and it's become a reality over the last twenty years.

I think back to how incidental the moment was to my journey. Life's funny that way. One minute, you perform some mundane task; the next, you've added a whole new dimension to your life. I have been close to the two of them for a long time.

They treat me well here.

Cali walks toward me, grabs a mug from behind the bar, and dunks it in one of the oak barrels beneath the shelves. She smiles as she sets it before me. A frothy foam spills down the side. They know what I like.

"Shamna's luck! It's been a while, Uncle Shen," she says.

She leans over the bar and kisses my cheek. She's particularly bubbly today, and that's saying something for this happy-go-lucky girl I've known since she was in pigtails.

"Hi, Cali, you look well," I say, genuinely pleased to see her snatch the mug.

"Well, I oughta. I got married last month!" She exclaims loudly. A chorus of cheers throughout the bar rings out.

"No way!" I shout back. Then, after a pause, "Wait, why wasn't I invited?"

She smacks my shoulder. "Because you never come around," she snaps. "Pop was pretty sore about it. He has some words for you. We expected you months ago."

I clench and bare my teeth in appropriate chagrin. "That's fair."

Her eyes drift toward her belly and back to me, and she holds a finger to her lips. I blink in astonishment. It seems like just yesterday she was running around this tavern, a sprite little schoolkid.

Now she is a wife and about to be a mother?

"I only told father this morning."

"Who's the lucky husband?" I ask her.

"The butcher's son, Bansly."

I raise an eyebrow. Cali laughs. She knows exactly why.

I have known Cali since she was little when she dreamed of marrying a fairy prince and becoming Fae. The last time I saw her wasn't that long ago, compared to lifespans. So, this news is revelatory. Bansly is decidedly not Fae.

I mean, she didn't stand a chance of marrying a Fae. Her father would have begged me to kill whichever Fae had ensnared her as soon as it happened.

Fae-Human relationships? That's always disastrous.

For the human.

Thankfully, I can take worrying about Cali off my to-do list. She is safe from her childhood fantasies.

"So, no Fae?" I tease.

She laughs, the memories of our discussions over her childhood obsessions returning, and shrugs. "You know father would never have allowed that. Besides, Bansly is so handsome." Her eyes sparkle with the kind of joy I envy.

"I'm happy for you, Cali," I say as I watch the ale settle in the mug. "And I'm sorry I missed your nuptials."

"Me too," she says, her eyes sparkle as she leans on the bar and watches the mug with me. I rest on my elbows and lock eyes with her over the top of the mug.

"You look happy," I say softly.

"I am," she smiles, closing her eyes briefly. When she looks at me again, she frowns and stands up suddenly.

"Where have you been?"

I sit up and smile. "The usual."

"It's been almost three full seasons this time," she says. "You know father's still mad at you? And not because you weren't at the wedding. Though I'm sure you'll hear about that." She tilts her head at me. "Is that why you haven't come around?"

I look back at the ale, not wanting to have this discussion with her.

"Still, huh?" I say.

"Well, when Daddy saw Tam and realized today was the day you two were coming, he got a bit testy," she says with a smirk.

I wave a hand. "Tell pops to get over it."

"Not before he punches you. He said that's to be your birthday present," Cali replies, singing the words. "I gotta get back," she says. "Drink up, and I'll get you another."

I watch as she runs along the bar, serving with a smile.

I'd be a liar if I didn't admit most ales are tasty. It's rare to find one that's not palatable. But some are absolute standouts. Some, like the one sitting before me, benefit from a person who loves their craft. Mistras loves to make good ales. This one is my favorite. It's rich, smooth, and nutty, with notes of cocoa and the heavenly maltiness I love. The chorus of flavors is the closest I'll ever experience to heaven if such a place existed.

I pick up my mug and look around the tavern. A thin layer of smoke rises to the third-floor ceiling as a scattering of patrons smoke their pipes. The room is filled with the sweet, spicy aroma of pipe smoke. I am not a big smoker myself, but I love the smell and occasionally will toke on one. It's a full-on party in here.

A group in the center breaks out in song, and a large portion of the tavern turns and joins in. A pressure change in the air exerts its presence over my personal space. Without looking, I can identify every aspect of the intrusion. In my peripheral vision, I see a mountain of a man standing next to me, covered in several furs. I try not to smile and pretend I don't know he's there. Easily a whole foot and a half taller than me and probably twice my weight. He's hard to ignore. He rocks back and forth between his toes and heels, causing his braided beard with a Talisman of Fildeus, Goddess of the Hunt, to swing in and out of my vision.

I can't pretend, and I can't keep the smile off my face. So, I turn and look at the lug.

He smiles a big toothy grin at me. His slightly tanned nose and cheeks shine in the flickering light framed by his long, curly brown hair and beard. He's grayer than the last time I saw him. While his hair shows signs of age, his youthful grin never changes.

"Well, slap my ass and call me a donkey!" he booms. "You made it!"

Before I can get a word out, the big guy grabs me and hugs me with a giant bear hug. Ale spills from my mug as his musky scent overwhelms the delightful smell of the pipe smoke. I'd say I couldn't breathe from the hug, but, unfortunately, that's not true. I'm getting a total whiff of Tamrin Saltar, tracker and trapper extraordinaire.

My favorite person and my best friend.

"You can let me go now," I mumble into a mouth full of wolf fur.

He laughs and puts me down. A few people are watching the

exchange, but not many notice it. He leans down to speak, and I use the opportunity to grab hold of his beard and pull his head closer.

His eyes get wide.

"How many times do I have to tell you, Tam, not to draw attention to me?"

I let go before anyone notices. The chagrined look tells me I might have hurt Tamrin's feelings. But he gets my point and leans in again.

"Aww, Shen, I'm sorry. I just get excited when I see you. I wasn't sure you'd show up today." He winks. "Especially to-day."

"That was yesterday," I say.

"I know."

He never forgets my birthday. He is my best friend. My true friend. As much as I allow him to be, that is.

I feel guilty for pulling his beard. I shouldn't have. But the big guy, as smart and observant as he is, is too gregarious for his own good. Or at least for mine. I smile with shrug and offer an apology for the beard pull. He waves it off, and just like that, we're friends again. He smiles, turns to Cali, who just set two new pints on the bar for us, and hands one to me. We clink mugs, and he puts his big arm around my shoulder as we join the chorus.

It's the fight song from the third great war—a Rhinestab tavern staple. A fine choice, as long as you aren't from Killinshire.

I've got no wind
I've got no sail
I've got no coin
To purchase ale
'Tis been too long
This thirst I wale
I'll pay you back in labor

Been many weeks
Since I drank
My mouth is dry
My breath be stank

Sean Gregory

I'd much prefer
My lips be dank
Your darkest ale I favor

Run, run, it's all for fun!
I'll live by the sword
And I'll die by one
I'll give my life
Till the battle's won
And I won't return 'til the job is done!

I left my home
For Killinshire
I left my love
To start the fire
It's been too long
For her desire
I fear she's with my neighbor

If I should find
When I return
My love has left
A fate I earned
My heart be broke
The lesson learned
It's only ale I should savor!

Run, run, it's all for fun!
I'll live by the sword
And I'll die by one
I'll give my life
Till the battle's won
And I won't return 'til the job is done!

Run, Run, it's all for one!
To die by the sword
When you live by one
We drink for the glory
We drink for the fun
And for friends, we lost at Hizeron!

Tavern songs fill me with joy, and I join in with gusto. For the briefest moments, a good song offers me a chance to feel less like an outsider. When the song finishes, my burly pal squeezes me while we clank and drain our mugs.

"Damn good to see you," he says, the smell of ale heavy on his breath. "Let's grab another!" he yells and winks, turning us both back to the bar. I smirk at his outlandish behavior.

"Barkeep!" he yells to Cali. His voice booms but doesn't overpower the general noise of the room. She looks at us and waves at Tam, her smile more immense than earlier, if possible.

Cali's father, who has entered from the kitchen, looks over at us and beams when he sees Tam, then scowls when he sees me. His dark hair, dark beard, and loping gate are as familiar to me as Tam's booming voice. Tam takes my mug from me and hands both to Mistras. I smile and shrug sheepishly in the hopes that Mistras will just let the past go.

"Two more, my friend," Tam says, "each! We're getting drunk tonight!"

It's a fair statement. I intend to tie one on, and there's no better drinking companion than Tamrin. Unless you wish not to draw attention to yourself. When Tamrin is around, everyone has a good time.

Mistras stands with his arms crossed. "How about one more, and you tell your friend here to get lost," he says to Tam, nodding at me.

"Aww, c'mon, Mistras, can't you let it go?" I say.

"Let it go!" Mistras exclaims. He looks at me and points a finger. "You betrayed me."

I hold up both hands. "No. No. That's not how I remember it. Besides, Kara's a big girl, and we were drunk. I won't apologize for behaving like an adult."

"No, you seduced her."

Tam starts laughing and reaches across the bar to put a hand on Mistras' shoulder.

"Oh no, we both saw how it went down. Kara practically dragged him back to her bed. You can't blame our boy here for succumbing to her. If I was inclined, I would have done the same," Tam says.

Mistras glares at Tamrin.

I give Mistras a contrite look, place a hand on my hearts, and offer an apology. "I'm sorry I had sexual congress with your sister."

He looks at me, blood rushing to his face, and tries to speak but stutters over his words. We laugh as he collects himself, takes a deep breath, and shakes his head.

"You're a bastard, Shen," he says.

"Hey, my parents knew each other," I say.

"Well," he replies and points a finger at me, "it better not happen again."

He places two new mugs on the bar, and Cali comes over with a large plate of roasted potatoes, carrots, and a whole roasted chicken.

"I can't promise that," I say under my breath as I hold the mug to my mouth. Tam spits ale on the bar. "Besides," I continue, "Chocolate's hard for a girl to resist, and she was so happy the next day."

Mistras explodes, "You son-of-a-bitch!"

Tam bursts out laughing, and I smile at Mistras, who can't help but hang his head. I see his shoulders shake, and I know I have him.

Mistras offers his hand to the big man, who grabs it and pulls him half over the bar in a bear hug. I lightly bang my head on the bar.

"Mistras!" the big guy exclaims.

"Tamrin," Mistras mumbles into Tam's furs, "so glad to see you both." Tamrin releases our friend, who then says, "Keep your money tonight. It's on me."

Mistras walks to the other end of the bar. He leans into his daughter and points to the two of us while talking in her ear. She peeks over, nods, finishes serving the patron where she stands, and heads over to us. We watch, tongues licking our lips, as she grabs two mugs in each hand and fills them.

"Tam!" she exclaims as she leans over the bar to give him a kiss.

"And how is the new bride?" he asks.

"Happy and eating for two now," she says, winking as she sets two more ales on the bar. Tam's laugh is boisterous and thunders through the room. I can feel a few eyes on us, so I look around. Nothing strikes me, and I turn back to my conversation.

I reach into my purse and drop a copper coin on the bar, as does Tamrin.

She waves her hands, shooing our coins away. We pick them up and toss them across the bar to the open coinbox against the wall. She gives us a dirty look, and we both shrug. Tamrin holds his pint to me in toast.

I pick mine up and clank it against his.

"It's good to see your face again, Friend. Happy birthday," he says.

"I've missed you, Brother," I say, and we both down our ales.

Now, I'm no lightweight. I can hold my liquor pretty well, but never let it be said Mistras serves swill in his tavern. He prides himself in his brew-master skills and makes his drink strong. His price is higher than most, but his ale is one of the best in the land. Worth every damn copper piece.

Thus, I find myself, a few hours later, eight pints in, deep in conversation with Tamrin and more than a little drunk. The big man and I belted out songs, laughed at several jokes, and exchanged many new stories, mine carefully selected and under-exaggerated. Tamrin knows everything about me but is unaware I am the legendary vigilante.

Only Mistras and Cali know my identity as the Harbinger, and I live in constant fear someone will discover their knowledge and use it against me. Their knowledge is a natural by-product of how we became friends. They guard my secret closely, even from my best friend.

Sometimes I feel bad about that. But some secrets are easy to justify.

Too often, assassins come after me, putting the people I care about at risk. So, even with my friends, I am extra cautious. It's the hazard of the existence I live. The fewer people carrying the burden, the better their lives are, and the more accessible mine is.

Hence, when sharing stories with Tamrin, I play down my exploits.

The tavern is quiet now. Few patrons remain, some finishing their last drink at the bar and the small group speaking calmly in the corner at the table.

The group at the table bothers me. I noticed them during the last round of songs and felt the strangest feeling of familiarity. They never joined in the singing and revelry throughout the evening, and their drinking pace was slow. They never glanced in my direction, so I thought nothing of it. Now, it's conspicuous in the relative quiet of the nearly empty tavern. It could be the ale, but they rub me the wrong way.

I do my best to pay attention to them while not losing focus on Tam, who is finishing a story.

"…so, he jumps up on the table, performs the worst dance I have ever seen, steps on the plate, sending it flying, as he pretends to slip and fall on his back. The commotion distracted the guard enough that I knocked him out unseen. It gave me enough time to snag the crate and sneak out the back." The big man roars in laughter. "Best silver I ever spent watching those thieves scrambling to get out of the way of all the stuff he spilled! I returned the crate to its rightful owner. Meanwhile, that poor drunk made haste out the door."

I laugh with him and raise my last mug up to him. We clink too hard, sending ale over the sides, shrug at the spray of ale that splashes on the bar, and down the last of our ale. We're definitely drunk.

"The funniest part of that story is you doing anything unseen!" I laugh.

"It's true!" he exclaims, holding one hand on his heart and one in the air.

I shake my head and stare at the bottom of my empty mug. Looking at Tam, I force a "boo-boo" lip.

"Ah, damn. All gone."

He shows me his empty mug and frowns.

Cali comes over and drops a key on the bar next to me.

"Your room key," she says, smiling. I slur a "thank you" to her and slide over two more coppers. She takes them, grabs my wrist, and flips my hand over with a smile. She drops the coins back into my palm before she rolls my fingers closed and then looks at Tamrin.

"If these find their way into my lockbox, I swear, I will fill your bed with bakru shit."

I gulp.

"She would," Tam mumbles.

"You need a room, Tam?"

"Oh no. I am staying in the camps tonight. The whole party leaves early. Those kids ain't gonna find themselves, you know." His "s's" slurred to "shh".

I look at him curiously.

"What kids?" I ask.

He looks around and says, "I'm with the bounty party. Looking for some siblings who stole an item of considerable value and murdered three guards in the process. Took place in Dresdin. They needed a tracker who knew the RhineWoods. I was in Dresdin selling some of the newer furs I bagged. They hired me two days ago. We tracked the two through the southern RhineWoods here to Winding Run. Picking up the trail again in the morning."

"Bounty party?" I ask.

The big guy looks at me. "See the table behind me?" he asks. He eyes the table that has been giving me the creeps. They are barely paying attention to us again.

I nod.

"They're the employers. Apparently, that gray-haired fella is a world-class Bounty Hunter. I've never heard of him, but everyone he's hired seems to know him well. Goes by the name Brandin Casfold. You ever heard of him?"

I shake my head.

"We could use you if you're free," he says, his face registering a new idea.

"No. Not interested," I say, shaking my head. The room spins when I do.

Tamrin shrugs. We sit quietly for a while. My body tingles, and I feel like I'm on a boat. Clapping Tamrin on the shoulder, I smile at him. He's a little blurry, but I blink it away. The big guy yawns and slides off the barstool.

"I gotta go to bed," he slurs. "Early reveille."

He gives me a hug.

"Happy birthday, Pal."

"Thanks."

"Good night," he says. I watch as he leaves and nods to the table on his way out. They don't even acknowledge him.

The older man at the table watches Tam leave and turn directly toward me. Our eyes meet, and I am sure I recognize him. He studies me, brow furrowed. My brain tickles with a memory, but I'm too drunk to think clearly. The fine lines, clean stitching, and well-pressed nature of his attire tell me this guy's a man accustomed to getting what he wants. The battle scar and scowl on his face suggest he's willing to use violence to get it. He seems familiar, but I struggle to place him. Either way, I don't like the look of him.

He leans over to one of his companions and whispers in the woman's ear. She glances at me and nods. The scar-faced man rises and heads my way. I'm not opposed to the idea, but I don't like how my skin tingles when I look at him. If he knows me, I'm at a distinct disadvantage. Better to play coy. I return to the bar, searching my memory banks for his face, but come up empty. There's an inkling of a memory, but I can't connect to it.

It'll keep me up tonight. I just know it.

Cali comes up to me. "You two goofballs done for the night?" she asks.

I ask for a mug of water, and she dunks one in the barrel.

I take a big swig and let my head hang heavy, playing more drunk than I am. Although, I am pretty wasted at the moment. Drunk enough, I don't want another ale.

Drawing a blank, I lose myself in a memory search when the old man from the table sits in the seat Tamrin previously vacated. I down the rest of my water and pretend not to notice.

"Do I know you?" he says, his voice rough.

His voice finally breaks the mental logjam. A tidal wave of memories floods back. It takes inordinate restraint not to spin around and jam a blade into the source. Even drunk, I maintain my composure, though it's difficult.

How could I not recognize him? The only person in the world I want to kill more than this guy is myself.

Such is the dichotomy of my existence.

Maybe another reason I haven't succeeded in killing myself is the small list of essential actions I'm compelled to close out. Maybe fate doesn't care one bit about my desire for death until that list is complete. As far as fate is concerned, I have work to do. The opportunity to kill Captain Brogen of the Dark Guard of Killinshire just presented itself.

Brogen is as ruthless as they come. Usually, I'd know him by sight. I can't believe his crappy disguise is enough to throw me off. Then again, he is almost seventy-five years old, and though he looks fantastic for his age, his dark skin barely has a wrinkle. I haven't seen him for nearly thirty years, and the only noticeable difference is the scar.

But his bird-beak face should have been a dead giveaway.

Judging by his expression, he may know who I am. I pretend to be intimidated and turn back to the bar, mumbling gibberish.

He taps my shoulder. With a slow turn, I squint at him. Intense eyes regard my face while he assesses me. If he doesn't recognize me by now, his memory will come up blank. Though we've crossed paths more than once, each instance was brief. They weren't "moments" for him like they were for me, and most times, I was in the crowd.

His gray Killinshire-style military haircut makes his head appear pointy. His goatee is neatly trimmed and shaped to a fine point in the center, and his long hawk-like nose only makes it look worse. Hardened killer or not, I fight to suppress a laugh.

His presence here concerns me. He never leaves Killinshire. He shouldn't be anywhere near here. I can't imagine his purpose, but whatever it is, it can't be good.

"I asked you a question, sir. Do I know you?"

"I don't think so," I slur. "You look too wealthy to be one of my friends." I turn back to my empty mug and then reach into my pocket, pretending it's empty, and pull out some pocket lint and a loose button. I pick through it as if I am looking for some coins.

"Damn it," I slur.

I look at Cali and pretend to try and fail at a whistle. She looks over, surprised to see I have a new companion. She plays it cool. I'll give her that.

"Haven't you had enough?" she says, walking up to us. She's people smart. It's why she is so good at what she does, and she knows when I'm up to tricks.

I hand over my button and pocket lint.

"Can I get one more?"

Brogen watches me closely. Thankfully, he's drawing the conclusion he's misjudged me. To me, at least, it appears the ruse is working. I sincerely hope it is. He slaps a copper coin on the counter and nods to Cali.

"Give him another," he commands.

"Thank you, mister," I say and offer my hand. "Name's Brandin." My slurring is getting a little worse, partly by design and partly because I'm drunk. He accepts my hand, and I let my hand stay limp—barely firm enough to match my callouses, less a little for drunkenness.

"Well, that is odd," he says. "So is mine."

I nod and point a sloppy finger at him, "Well then, pleased to meet me."

It takes every ounce of self-control I can muster to fight the urge to stab him in the throat. An image of him, eyes wide, mouth agape, my blade sticking out the back of his neck, almost causes a smile to break out on my face.

Reckless as I am, I briefly consider instigating a fight with the man. It would be a great way to go out. As drunk as I am, I'd only get the one shot, but I could rid the world of this ruthless jerk right here. I'm a good fighter when drunk. For most of my twenties, I lived among drunk monks in the northernmost mountains of Teshket at the Temple of the Drunk Fists. I spent the better part of six years continuously drunk, whether in deep meditation, in study, or in combat. It's why my tolerance toward booze is so high, although that has been decreasing as I age. I'm not a lightweight, but I am in a weight class lower than I used to be, in the drunken sense.

There's a good chance I've exceeded my weight class right now. As a result, he could beat me. I could die right here. All I have to do is throw the first blade.

But then there's Cali and Mistras. Hard rule. No fighting in the Tavern. The guards will haul me in, and there's no fine—just two years of hard labor. They'll come in with the full contingent. It's a case of *overwhelming force* to keep the peace. I'm good, but I can't fight thirty at once.

And then there is the Bounty.

I have a sneaking suspicion I know who Tamrin's siblings are. The thought has been nagging me since he said it, and if I am right, well, that's bad. If Captain Brogen and the Dark Guard are after the siblings, they are in real trouble.

He's an evil man.

This raises doubt over the validity of any story told to Tamrin that would get him to agree. Tamrin doesn't work with bad people. Except for me, that is.

But first, if he has plans for the siblings I rescued, I'd find great pleasure in ruining those plans. I'm also very interested in what they did that brought this sinister monster out of his domain, traveling incognito to hunt them down.

Change of plans. Looks like I'm heading to Valshannon anyway.

I down the ale that this lump of basilisk crap bought me.

One good thing?

I'm drunker than I thought. I slam the mug on the counter much harder than I intended. Then, turning to thank the vile bastard, I puke on the Captain of the Dark Guard.

It's one of my finest moments.

I'm actually proud of this one.

I slip off my stool and pass out on the floor, smiling.

Chapter Six

Journal Entry:26

In the quiet moments, when my belly is full or I'm too comfortable, or too safe, my self-hatred goes hyperactive. It's then I realize how little I offer those around me. I'm a burden to them. To my friends especially. Overwhelmed by a sense of neediness, my thoughts become cloudy. In the moments where I can rationalize, I can see the absurd nature of these thoughts. But Tam, Mistras, and Cali have their own lives. I have no life. Who am I to burden them with the weight of me?

I want what they have, but I'm no good to anyone in this state. I can fake it for a time, but then the real me emerges.

It's weird putting these thoughts down. This whole exercise is self-indulgent.

But a part of me feels better doing so. Even if it puts me in a bad light, I must remember why I am doing this.

I want to understand myself better. I'm hoping I am not the terrible person I think I am. Sometimes, the only driver that keeps me on the side of right is this twisted moral code I have.

So many times, I yearn to be near friends, to experience a

sense of belonging. Instead, I drift through the realms, occasionally reconnecting with old friends, staying long enough to catch up, have a few laughs, and then leave before I overstay my welcome.

Guilt torments me.

"I've stayed away too long."

"I come around too often."

"I've overstayed my welcome."

"I left too soon."

These thoughts tear at me, nipping at my brain, continuous internal jabs that no one ever said but I hear all the time.

The idea that I might burden others with these thoughts, the heaviness of my presence, makes me uncomfortable. Honestly, what do I say to people when they are talking about their lives, plans, or what they do when all I give in return are stories of death and loneliness?

I can't imagine why they let me stick around.

It must be my charming personality.

Sean Gregory

Disappointments and Backtracking

The sound of rustling stirs me from my sleep. From the sensations on the private parts of my body from the sheets against my skin, I know I'm naked. The muffled sounds of the activity of dining guests getting an early start echo through my door from below. Dawn has arrived, and Mistras' guests are already busy about their day.

I don't know how I got here, but I am grateful. Rubbing my eyes, I look across the room to the shuffling noise that woke me and see Mistras there, his back to me, quietly placing a pile of folded clothes on a wooden chair in the corner.

"You put one on last night, mate," he says, a twinkle in his voice as he turns to face me. "I hope you enjoyed your birthday. Shame you passed out before Cali could give you the cake she made for you."

My mouth is dry as cotton.

"Water's there next to you," he says.

"We good?" I ask, my voice hoarse.

He snorts, and I grin, happy my soirée with his sister is behind us. He points to the scars on my wrists. Mistras knows me almost as well as Tamrin. In some ways, he knows me better.

"Couple of new ones since the last time I saw you." His sorrowful expression causes a wave of guilt. I'm causing him stress with my presence. It hurts to know that.

I reach for the large tankard of water and drink it down. While dehydrated, I'm amazed, as usual, I'm not hungover—another testament to Mistras' skills.

"Don't start," I say defensively. I don't know what else to say.

He raises his hands in surrender. "I accepted you for who you are long ago, mate. But I'm allowed to pray to Shamna for your safekeeping."

He lumbers over in his lazy gate, feet pointing out as he walks. I always thought he walked funny. I look at my wrists. Lines of scars mark the days when despair got the better of me. Six, to be exact.

"Well, stop, would ya? I don't think I can die. Every at-tempt has failed," I say.

His gratuitous grunt ends the conversation as he places his hand on my shoulder. I twist my shoulder from his touch. He sighs and points at my clothes.

"Cali washed your clothes for you. Probably needed it before you covered yourself and that other guy in puke." He giggles. "Defi-nitely needed it after. That guy wanted to tear you apart. Thankfully we do a good job of posting the law here. He showed restraint."

Mistras leans into me. "But it took him some effort." He shakes his head with a smile.

"Yeah, had more of your ale than I planned," I say, standing, ready to move to the waste room down the hall.

"You gonna walk out there like that?" he asks.

I look down at my naked body.

"Well, I guess not, no," I say, and grab the blanket from the bed, wrapping myself in it.

"Hey, come find me when you're ready to head out. I have a favor to ask."

"Will do."

I leave my room, peeking over the railing to the gathering hall below, and scan for Tam. Along the inward-facing walkway, most of the rooms are closed. A few of the cleaning staff carry new bed sheets, dropping them on the floor at the doors to empty rooms. Above me on the third-floor landing, a young couple giggles quietly, lost in their party of two.

From my room, dead center on the second floor, I can see Cali gathering empty plates and bowls from tables. She looks up and smiles at me, and I offer a half-wave in return. Not for the first time, I wonder if the position of my room is more for Mistras to keep an eye on me than for my convenience. He always puts me in this room. It strikes me as odd that it's always available.

Makes me wonder if he always keeps it empty when I am not here.

Burden.

Mistras follows as I head to the waste room, going his way

down the stairs to the main level when we reach that point. My room is equidistant from the four corners where the waste rooms are located on my floor.

I never cease to marvel at the unique technology in Winding Run. Their toilet system is one such invention.

Every building has at least one. The tavern has ten. Pipes run from the creek right under the waste seat and are fed by the creek. Inside the seat, water rushes by, taking waste out of the building continuously—no need for piss pots, bed pans, or waste buckets. The wastewater flows to a main pipe into a massive waste building at the southernmost end of the town, where the waste is extracted and converted into the richest fertilizer in the Five Realms, the water returning to the creek no worse than how it left. According to Mistras, it's cleaner than when it left the creek.

In a three-story place like Mistras', upstream paddle wheels run the water through an aqueduct system that spans the buildings. Fresh water flows through an elevated clay pipe network, ending in roof-mounted reservoirs.

I'd hate to see what happened to this town if the creek ever dried up.

The modern marvel is unique in the world and attracts visitors from everywhere. The treatment building is in permanent lockdown, and the process is a closely guarded secret. It's another part of Winding Run's industry and generates significant communal revenue. What fertilizer is not consumed in the year is sold at auction on the last growing day of the season and is a big celebration for the town.

I conclude my business and head back to my room to dress. As I put on my bracers and knife belt, I notice how clean the blades are. Cali went the total distance for me. I need to remember to thank her.

I peek out the window to the rear of my room. The view out of town toward the main campgrounds is emptier than it was last night. Many of the temporary population had already departed to wherever they were headed. I wonder how many were from the bounty party Tamrin was hired by?

Early morning oranges and pinks paint the sky, complemented by rich blues and purples, adding depth to the clouds and providing extra texture to nature's canvas. I am up before the sun appears.

My thoughts drift to Tamrin and Brogen, and I wonder if I'm too late to catch my friend. My concerns over Tam accepting a job from the likes of Brogen nag at me. There's more to the story. It's hard to believe Tam doesn't know who he works for.

I scan the crowd below again. I recognize most of the faces as locals preparing for their day. The few I don't know are clearly not Tam—either dark-skinned like me, too small, or both. I assume he's already headed out. Likely, Brogen's gone too.

A slight adrenal surge washes over me, and a sudden sense of urgency triggers my body to take action. My plan to speak with Tamrin and learn why he is working for Brogen can't happen if the big guy is on the road already. The butcher of Killinshire is on the hunt, and I have no idea how far behind them I am. I'm also unsure who he chases, but I have an idea.

Whatever plans he has, they aren't for anyone's benefit but Killinshire's. Ruining those plans would offer immeasurable pleasure. I hate the man. If Jesma and her brother are the targets, thwarting his plans to capture them is as good a way to spend the day as any. I have to reach them before their pursuers do.

Time to figure out where Tam and Brogen are and, if they left, which direction they headed. I'm confident the siblings are the target of Brogen's efforts. I could be wrong. Regardless, the guilt over leaving them alone in the RhineWoods weighs on me. Whether Brogen is after them or not, helping them is on my list of priorities. But if it is them, I can kill two bakru with a single blade.

If I'm right, Brogen's team will set out for Valshannon. If so, the logical choice is the main road. A hard ride by horseback would get them to the largest city in the Five Realms before Ezra slipped into her slumber. But I know Tam. He'll investigate the trailheads into the woods and locate the siblings' tracks, which, by my count, are four days old. Not many can track a four-day-old trail.

Tam can. Tamrin is one of the best trackers alive. If there is a trail to find, he'll find it.

Why did the bounty party stop here, though? If they are tracking Jesma and Jesmir, why leave a warm trail and stay the night here?

They wouldn't.

Unless they knew precisely where their prey was headed. Then they could take their time, send and advance par…

Shamna be damned!

I dash down the grand stairway, four steps at a time, drawing looks from around the dining area. Neither Cali nor Mistras are in sight, so I take my liberty and head through the swinging doors to the kitchen. As rarely as I come by, they still give me some leeway. I ignore the big sign carved with "No Patrons Beyond This Point Ever, Yes This Means YOU!" which is clearly not meant for me.

Actually, it is, but it's a running joke between us, and even if it wasn't, this is more important than the sanctity of the kitchen.

"Damn it, Shen!" I hear as I storm through the door, slamming it into the shelves hidden on the other side.

"Mistras!" I almost yell as I shove the note I'd forgotten about until this moment into his hand. "What does this say?"

My tone makes it clear the importance. Mistras gives me a perplexed glance and wipes his hands on a towel that hangs from his belt. He unfolds the note, reads it, and snaps his eyes to me.

"Where'd you get this?"

"Please," I say, pointing. "What does it say?"

He translates it aloud. "We've identified the emissary. Twins en route to Valshannon. Intercept before they arrive. Meet at The Dead Eye Pub on Swill Street. If you cannot intercept, signal emissary and replace with our agent. You'll find twelve Realm Notes enclosed as payment. We are in pursuit with the tracker."

My suspicions confirmed, I swallowed the catch in my throat.

"Have you seen a young couple in the last couple of days? Siblings, and if this note is what I think, likely twins. Blond hair, blue eyes, boy and a girl?"

"Why?" he asks. Based on his tone, I know my assumptions were accurate.

"I'm not playing games, and I'm not asking lightly."

"Shen, what is it about these two that everyone is looking for them? Don't give me the 'they murdered my kid' line that bird-faced man you put yesterday's lunch all over tried to sell me this morning. Tam's helping him track these two down. I couldn't lie to Tamrin, but I also didn't like the look of the other guy."

"I'm so gonna ruin Brogen's day," I mumble, giddy at the thought.

"Brogen?" Mistras questions.

"Yeah, Brogen."

"*The* Brogen?" he cries.

"Shh!" I reply, trying to keep him calm. "Mistras, I swear I don't know what is happening or why that animal is looking for those two. But yeah, my vomit buddy from last night was Captain Brogen."

Mistras' mouth falls agape, and he stumbles over his words. I place my hand on his arm to calm him down.

"It's okay. What happened?"

"That was Brogen?" Mistras pauses. "Oh, Shen, those kids were scared. I knew they were running from some danger, but Brogen is more than just some danger."

I relay the events of the previous morning, as many details as I can remember.

"Not good," he mumbles.

"What did you tell them?" I ask.

He grimaces. "Not much. I told him the two were here for the night and left the next morning, early." He takes a deep breath. "The young man asked about the dangers of RhineWoods and if it was safe to travel. I told him it wasn't safe but that it was the easiest way to stay unseen. They asked if many people traveled that way, and I told them only people looking to remain hidden or those seeking a death wish."

"Do you know what direction they went?"

"North, through the north-western trailhead. I told them that anyone traveling through that mess was better off on the western side of the highway. I'm sure they went that way."

"That's where I was. I am pretty sure these twins that Brogen is after are the two I saved. The girl mentioned she was headed to Valshannon. This note was in the possession of their attackers."

He nodded. "They were headed to Valshannon. To meet someone. Like the note says."

I take a deep breath. Mistras rereads the note.

Mistras grabs both of my shoulders, his expression tense.

"They have no intention of taking them alive. Brogen said

they would ride hard to intercept them at the Rankin. Shen, he spoke in Killinspeak. They didn't know I understood them."

"Lucky for you. On both counts," I say.

"No, that's not the point." He swallows. "Brogen was talking as they left. He told his companions, 'People die in the RhineWoods all the time.' I don't think Tam knows. I tried to get a moment with him before they headed out, but it happened too fast." He wrings his hands together. "Honestly, I planned to ask you to head out after him and tell him. That favor I mentioned."

"How long ago did they head out?" I ask.

"Two hours ago, at most."

I groan. "I have to move."

This is one of those moments where I'm relieved my suicide attempts haven't succeeded. Tam would never forgive himself over this one. What helps me get through a day is having an important task to complete. I become consumed with the goal, and I'm focused on another thought for a time, an important one. It requires my full attention.

Like now.

I must reach Tam and those kids before anyone else does.

There's a deadline here, but I have no clue what that is. 'Fast as possible' may not be fast enough, but it's all I have control over. Time is a luxury I do not have. At best, I have a day to reach them. Likely, much less.

I have no clue how fast Brogen's team is moving, but I imagine they went by horseback on the highway. If I were them, I'd split my party in two and send one tracking through RhineWoods, the other on an intercept course along the road before the fleeing siblings reach Valshannon. I doubt the pair made much progress, with one hurt and neither skilled at navigation nor survival.

They're running scared. The induced stress level will consume a lot of energy. I last saw them almost a full day ago. My relaxed pace yesterday, accounting for the time I spent hunting and resting, ate up several hours. At my best pace, I can return to where I left them before midday. If I head out now. No chance they are moving at better than a quarter of my fastest pace. That would put them less than another half day's journey out.

I can catch them by nightfall.

I desperately hope they ignored my advice and remained in the RhineWoods. This is one of those rare moments where sticking to the King's Regal Highway is the worst idea.

Unless they managed to get a ride from someone.

But there's the note. Whoever those siblings intend to meet is also in danger. That someone might not be *their* someone. According to the letter Mistras' interpreted for me, this emissary can be replaced with an agent. In that case, it's a reasonable assumption that the siblings have no idea who the emissary is.

They're walking into a trap.

Before I backtrack through the woods in haste, I seek out a few of the WinRun Guardians to gather intel. Three quick conversations later, I'm no more equipped with helpful information than after speaking with Mistras. Ready to give up and plow headlong onto the trailhead, I spot Kara. She smiles when she sees me until she notices my dour expression.

"What's wrong?" she asks.

"Tam left already, and I need to find him."

"He left hours ago."

"You see which way he went?"

She points northwest, confirming what I already knew. I chastise myself for wasting time.

"He headed out alone or with a group?"

"This morning? With just him and one from his group from yesterday."

"Yesterday?"

"Yeah. Tam arrived with that group of 'merchants' yesterday. Merchants, my ass. I know mercenaries when I see them. Some of them were Killinfolk. What are you messed up in, Shen?"

"I'm not messed up in anything," I reply, feigning innocence. "I need to find Tam and give him a message from your brother."

"I've seen you naked. I can tell when you're up to no good.

What is it?"

"I think Tam's messed up in some trouble and doesn't know it. I'm trying to catch up and warn him."

"Much better." She turns and points up the King's Regal Highway. "Most of the party tore outta here up the highway on horseback. Made quite a racket." She turns back toward the trailhead. "Tam and one other bloke headed up the trailhead about two and a half hours ago."

"Was any of them an ugly fellow with a scar?"

"Yeah. Dark skin pointy beard, looks like a hawk?"

I nod.

"He went with the horses. Seemed to be the leader, actually."

Brogen.

I can catch Tamrin easier than I can horses. Tam's a fast tracker, but he'll be slowed by the stale trail, and I'm much quicker than he is and unlike him, I know the first place he's headed. I create an action plan on the fly. Catch Tamrin, tell him who he is working for (or beat him senseless for working for Brogen), eliminate the other party, if necessary, and catch the twins.

"Give me ten minutes. I can get us horses, and we'll ride out with you," Kara says.

I shake my head. "Kara, trust me, I will be faster on foot through the Rhine Woods," I say.

She gives me a skeptical look and starts to argue, but I shake my head and put a hand on her shoulder. "I have to go," I say.

"Well, don't stay away so long next time. I'd like a re-match."

"Oh no. I'm not making any more bets with you."

"That's not the rematch I'm talking about, stud," she says while showing her tongue.

"It's a date," I say with a smirk.

I kiss her cheek for fun and break through the woods without another word.

"Mistras is gonna murder you someday," she calls after me, but I'm already to the trailhead by the time she says the last word.

Within minutes, I'm backtracking my steps from yesterday to get to where I last saw the siblings. A sense of responsibility for their safety replaces the guilt over leaving them yesterday. It's impossible for me to believe they deserve the fate that hunts them.

Shamna be damned. Luck, schmuck.

It's possible Jesma and Jesmir are villains. If so, I missed it because I was too busy preventing another villain from harming them. I have an annoying habit of rushing into situations unaware, for sure.

But some details in Tam's story don't add up. Whatever Brogen's reasons are, I know enough about him and saw enough in the girl's character to understand the math doesn't add up. I'm not letting her fall into his hands, regardless. She could have murdered his only child, but I'd still refuse to let him get his hands on her.

Brogen's only child should be murdered if he's anything like his father. If that story is true, I might just buy her a pint and call it a day.

Besides, even if I want to, which I don't, my conscience won't let me walk away again. I was already feeling guilty about leaving the girl and her brother to their fate in the RhineWoods. At least now I can redeem that. Either way, I must know. I can't *know* if I don't get to them first.

Thankfully, I have knowledge Brogen doesn't.

Their exact last known location.

Equally, thankfully, I have peafowl jerky and a few pieces of cake Cali gave me as I ran around like a chicken with its head cut off chasing down information.

Mistras watched me leave, wringing his shop towel in dismay. The poor guy feels guilty about what little information he gave. He made the right choice. Better to offer a piece of the truth with omission than to outright lie. Harder to detect.

Brogen is a killer. He'd find joy in laying waste to Winding Run to get what he wants. Fortunately, Winding Run isn't in Killinshire, or he would have out of spite. Whatever he is after, he will work covertly. Anything else would restart the hostilities between

Rhinestab, Teshket, and Killinshire.

The atrocities of Hizeron would pale compared to a fourth Great War. We've become more efficient in the abilities of war technologies across the Five Realms, and the acceleration of magic in the world has been unprecedented over the last two decades. Everyone wants to prevent a fourth war. I don't think the world would survive it.

I sprint through the woods, the surrounding trees blurring in my vision. I can feel the furnace in my core fire hotter, and I wince at the unexpected intensity of the pain. While the pain has always intensified with increased speed, this time, my body burns hotter than I can ever remember. My clothes chafe my skin, and it dawns on me I'm running faster than I've ever run. I'm unsure how long I can maintain the pace. But my ego won't let me slow down, so I push through.

With my fresh tracks from yesterday blazoned over the forest floor, I have no issues following my own trail, even at this pace. My knowledge of the RhineWoods rivals anyone's, especially within thirty miles of King's Regal Highway in both directions.

Clarity provides a path to action.

I have enough to go on, and I'm making good time. The highway is at least a half mile to the east, a fact that reduces my chances of discovery. Hopefully, the bounty party will stay on the highway 'til the river and has no plan to intercept the siblings in the woods somewhere. If the latter, I have no idea when they might enter the woods, but I have a guess.

The King's Royal Highway runs a circuitous route through RhineWoods. Even with Brogen on horseback, I can reach the river at about the same time as him. There's a chance I'll catch them first if the siblings stay away from the highway. I hope I reach them before they reach the river.

Up ahead, I spot the clearing where I last left Jesma and her brother. I hide in the shadows as I approach the perimeter, listening for motion. A large boot print catches my eye. It's fresh. Its size allows only one conclusion. Tam's been here already. I check the pattern and confirm it's his.

"We really have spent too much time together, buddy," I mumble.

Satisfied, I continue on. The clearing is less than fifty yards ahead.

I'm pleased with myself and the progress I've made. Until I remember the bodies.

Damn. Gonna be hard to explain to Tam when he sees me following him. There are too many clues the Harbinger was part of the events in the clearing. Seeing me will raise questions I don't want to answer. My paranoia is getting the better of me, but I can't fight it.

I squat in the stillness of the woods, listening for sounds. A few birds chirp overhead. An argument between squirrels and bakru echoes in the distance, likely fighting over territory. Based on the absence of any out-of-place sounds, I deduce that I am alone.

The boot prints continue in the direction I expect. Ahead, the larger boot prints intersect with the tracks of a lighter, more petite set of prints. Tam is good. Seeing his print was a stroke of luck. As big as he is, he's light on his feet. His companion is nearly as good. Well-placed steps dot the area, indicating signs of traffic about ten feet behind and to my left.

Further investigation reveals two other sets of faint footprints, much smaller and left by individuals less skilled at hiding their tracks. One is significantly smaller and feminine. They are a day or two older than the other prints.

I spot a broken sapling, and from the state of the sap seeping and wilted leaves, the damage occurred within the last couple of hours. I've made better time than I thought. They aren't too far ahead of me.

The Great Rankin River is fewer than a couple hours' travel for me from here and a little over twice that for Tamrin. It's also where the siblings would likely, albeit ignorantly, choose to rest. The closest crossing to here would be the Crags, though few would see it as ideal. I need to reach them before they foolishly attempt such a task.

Time is my enemy. Should Tam catch the siblings first, st least he will ensure no harm befalls his quarry while in his charge. He'll insist they are delivered, unharmed, to a magistrate. But his travel partner may have other plans. If Brogen's team meets up with them, Tamrin, though outnumbered, will not go down without a fight.

I must get to him first.

I've gained time on the big man. But I've already been moving for three hours, and my muscles scream from the exertion. I've never run so fast for so long before.

Boot prints from too many sources cross over one another. Two days of activity from eight individuals left a chaotic mess of clues. But Tam's and a smaller set, which I assume to be his companion, are the only ones made within the last few hours.

Tam and his colleague were thorough. Tam even found my tracks where I exited yesterday. I spot the massive imprint of his feet at the base of the tree from which I retrieved my knife previously. The pattern is deep in the toes.

He squatted here and inspected the direction my prints went before returning to the glen.

They spent some time looking around. Time enough, I may have gained precious moments. I have no trouble locating their route toward the Rankin. Tam's partner, who is less careful with his tracks, is easier to follow.

Their trail intersects where the siblings' tracks exit. Confident the trackers found the direction the fleeing twins headed, I follow.

Tam's tracks begin to grow more prominent. He found what he needed and no longer cares to hide his presence—the evidence in this glen was sufficient. A small set of feet accompanied by larger prints, closer together, one boot dragging provides a beckon.

Damn. The twins can't get far if the brother is still in rough shape. Tamrin will catch them quickly. He'll pick up the pace now that he knows one of them is injured. Tam's making good time, and the twins have less than a day's head start. I must catch him before he catches them.

Formulating a plan while charging forward toward so many unknowns is difficult, but I've watched Tam track. Once he's confident of his prey, he moves swiftly. I don't know how he does it, but he always attributes success to his faith in Fildeus.

"I don't know, Shen," he would say. "I just see the tracks."

I don't have that luxury. It takes concentrated effort for me to follow the tracks. This time, I'm not sure exactly where I'm headed, so I can't run as fast as before. I'm not sure I could keep up that pace much longer, anyway.

I can't shake this guilt for leaving Jesma helpless. I can only blame it on the stress of seeing the Tillions, my guilt for my role in their deaths, and my worry about Tam. Stress, guilt, and worry are not healthy mindsets. I have no time for any of them.

Time is not on my side, but speed is. I know Jesma and Jesmir travel north. I know their final destination, and I know the RhineWoods better than any person alive. My best tools are my familiarity with these woods and my knowledge of human nature.

At worst, the twins are less than half a day ahead of me. Maybe four hours. Tamrin is hot on their trail and will catch them in half the time it took them to get wherever they are. At best, I have two hours to catch up.

I'd bet I only have one.

The unknown variable of Brogen and his team is my only genuine concern. Where and when they will enter the woods for the cut-off is out of my control, and that is the actual time-pressure element. Based on my progress, Brogen and crew have likely reached the intersection of the King's Regal Highway and the Great Rankin River by now. If I were Brogen, I wouldn't hesitate to leave the horses tied at the edge of the road and head into the RhineWoods to intercept. I might split the team in two to cover both the north and south banks. Eight in number, they can spread out in the search and can risk pace and noise.

Jesma and Jesmir are all but trapped, and they can't cry for help.

Even if they could, there is no one to rescue them.

No one but me.

My silent steps snap twigs and crunch leaves as I run as fast as I dare, tracking two parties headed in the same direction. I formulate a plan for what to tell Tam when I catch him. I wouldn't put it past Brogen to mock up a lie to convince a guy like Tamrin that his work was for a just cause. Tam wouldn't take the job unless they convinced him it was just. My question, where Tam is concerned, is whether he knows he's working for Brogen. That bugs me.

"Why, Tam?" I mumble.

I reason out the truth, dousing the heat of my ire. While it's difficult for me to imagine Tam doesn't know who he works for, I know him. He'd never purposefully choose to work for the most no-torious man in the Five Realms.

A dull roar echoes in the distance through the massive trunks surrounding me. The Great Rankin River is not far ahead. I recognize I'm near the worst of the rapids. Damn it if the siblings didn't manage to find The Crags. In Jesmir's condition, I hope they wouldn't attempt to cross there. It's a solid bet they turned to the highway once they saw the river.

The Crags are easy to cross for someone like Tamrin or me, who are endowed with some agility. It wouldn't be the first choice for someone with a hitch in their step. If they try to cross there, they won't realize the danger 'til they're well into the effort. At that point, they'll be trapped if they lack the skills to navigate the final third of The Crags.

Especially if the River Gnomes see them.

The Great Rankin flows too fast to traverse. Any attempt to cross takes more skill than the average swimmer can muster. It's too wide to swim. I'm better and faster than most swimmers, and I've never dared try to swim it.

I wouldn't unless I wanted to die that day. Then, maybe.

Another worry emerges. The siblings likely don't know about the River Gnomes. Those sneaky bastards are always a threat. Trigger one of the River Gnomes' little traps, and they're as good as gone.

Unless they attempted to cross and drowned.

Either my charges have crossed safely (not likely), been cap-tured by River Gnomes (good chance), drowned trying to cross the river (in which case I'll never find them), are already captured (plau-sible), or wait at the riverbank providing an opportunity for me to ar-rive before anyone else (Shamna Rocks time).

Shamna, give me that elusive *twenty-three*!

The Growing Darkness

Chapter Seven

Journal Entry:31

The gods, if they are authentic, seem to spend a lot of time inflicting suffering on us. It's why I despise them. In case I haven't pointed that out already. The level of cruelty malevolently meted out to us mere mortals in no small measure malignantly macerates our souls.

Sometimes, I like to wax poetic. It's a stupid self-indulgence.

Do you, finder of this account of my life, think that by lifting your voice in prayer, an unseen entity will hear those words and find you important enough to be answered?

Assume they are real and all-powerful. Would they not be consumed with their own greatness and find us beneath them?

I've never come across a single believer who has ever spoken with or met a god.

I most certainly never received an answer to a prayer or witnessed one smidgen of evidence hinting at their existence that science couldn't explain.

But I'm routinely asked to trust the same gods who allow so much suffering to continue despite their supposed power to cure it.

No way these gods, whether Ezra, Shamna, Quietius, Krikhi, or any of the others, are worthy of my worship.

Sometimes, I think I feel this way because their inaction is worse than my actions. Sometimes, I fear I chose to help in the manner I do because I secretly find pleasure in causing suffering.

I don't. There is no joy in it. Excessive cruelty is not an activity I deliberately participate in. But sometimes I can't help myself.

Is my moral code little more than a thin veil to hide my hubris?

Am I just a psychopath exerting my dominance over weaker people using self-righteous justification to hide the brutal truth? Am I no better than the gods who wield unbalanced power over humankind?

When I stumble across evil propensities in another, I actively seek to extinguish that flame. I use my innate talents to subdue those lacking moral character. In some cases, my actions indicate a willingness to cause suffering. Cold, ruthless action painted my rescue of the twins. It wasn't until I saw the terror in Jesma's eyes that I realized how monstrous I must appear.

Sometimes, I get so vengefully angry I feel it's my duty to deliver a similar punishment to perpetrators of such cruelty.

It's most assuredly self-righteous. I see that.

And hypocritical.

Oh, look, another trait I dislike about myself. Shocker.

Well, it's written in indelible ink now. No turning back from the truth.

When I say I help, I guess what I mean is I help myself to self-indulgent expressions of power and dominance. I solve immediate problems with my own non-katas and run away before the burden of facing other people's perceptions of me or, worse, before they can burden me with requests for the help they really need. Help I have no desire to provide.

Wait. Do I avoid people because I find them a burden?

Am I the asshole?

That would be unfortunate.

Just writing this down hurts.

Gnomes, Fishbowls, and Favors

The mystical anomaly known as the Great Rankin River defies logic. Mages have studied its currents and trekked its banks for centuries, some say millennia. Unique in the world, or so I have been told (the world is a big place), there is nothing in modern discussion more perplexing or more debated.

I take this sentiment with a grain of salt. I've never left the Five Realms or crossed the four great seas. Since I've never been on any sea, never been off Conishant, and haven't seen all of Gal-Danang, Teshket, Haabrestand, or Killinshire, I accept the validity of the claim but wouldn't argue if someone disagreed.

This river flows uphill. Literally, no one can explain it. Water flows from some deep well far below Rankin Lake to the east in Haabrestand.

Standing here, the uphill flow is imperceptible. But the Great Rankin flows against the laws of physics and moves uphill. From my current position, the terrain is flat, at least to the eye. However, follow it long enough to the west, and the flow will demonstrate its uniqueness as it *climbs* the hills leading to Sanctum Mountain. Once there, water climbs a three-hundred-foot vertical wall of rock called the Bird Song Waterrise.

The risers, so-called because they aren't falling, disappear on a high plateau and into Sanctum Mountain through a cave at the top. It almost looks like the mountain is sucking the river dry into its great giant maw.

This massive, broad, fast-flowing, mystical marvel of a river is also home to the most annoying of creatures, the River Gnomes.

River Gnomes, annoying little devils who stay hidden in the Great Rankin River, only reveal themselves right before they take their victims. No one knows where they come from. No one knows where they go. No one who has been taken has returned to tell tales of their society, where they live, etc. No one speaks their language.

No one knows what they eat.

Many say Cuska are the last great mystery of humankind. I disagree. Nobody wants anything to do with Cuska, so they'll remain that way. I contend if nobody is interested in solving the mystery of Cuska, they aren't a mystery.

Merely thinking about Cuska sends a shiver down my spine. I'd rather encounter a River Gnome.

Everyone assumes the mystic nature of the river and the gnomes are related. But nobody has ever provided evidence to support the claim. It doesn't stop the arguments. Honestly, I would love to know.

Others say the God of Time hides there. I've never met a follower of Grankin, and I don't know anyone who has. I'm certain he's made up.

Such is the mystery of the Great Rankin River. Heated debates, fervent study, dubious unsubstantiated rumors, and the undeniable visual proof that the river is flowing uphill. That's all we know.

I'm unaware of any captured River Gnomes. I'm unaware of anyone speaking to a River Gnome. As far as I am aware, I'm the only person who has ever seen one and walked away, and I never talk about it. I don't want the notoriety. No one knows anything about them except this: don't fall into their traps. Unsuspecting travelers go missing all the time here as they try to cross the river, walk along the river, or sleep by the river. River Gnome traps are clever—very, very, clever… or so I've been told.

See a whirlpool? Avoid it. Avoid the whirlpool? Should swim to it. Swim halfway across the river, and somehow, you'll wind up back where you started. The sneaky bastards will offer just enough progress to tire a person out so the River Gnomes can snatch you while you rest.

These are stories from supposed eyewitnesses to those who've been lost. For all I know, we might have fallen for a children's tale.

River Gnomes are infuriating little buggers, though. I've encountered them several times, always on the shore and always on the opposite side of the river from me. They never come to my side, never approach, never speak, and never try to take me for some reason. Sometimes I get sore over that. But mostly, I'm okay with it.

The roar of water crashing through The Crags lures me into the majesty of the river. Lost in the hypnotic call of nature, I forget about River Gnomes and marvel at the glistening white caps and the spray of water into the air. My spirits lift, and I almost forget why I'm here. Ezra's light plays on the mist in the air, casting a shimmering rainbow, its colorful circle hovering above the river's surface. It's difficult to believe in the dangers of the river when so much beauty exists here.

I picture the life of River Gnomes in this place, and it occurs to me I've only ever encountered the same one. Or they all look alike to me. I sound racist, but I swear it's the same guy every time I see him.

"Dammit, Shen," I admonish. "Don't get distracted."

I return to my search for Tamrin and find tracks of several feet appearing to turn upriver.

The trail is much more difficult to follow due to the mist in the air and the wetness of the mostly rocky ground. Signs of their trail are harder to find. Either they tried to cross or returned eastward to the King's Regal Highway.

If they attempt to cross, they're lost. My only chance at picking up the trail again is to think like anyone but me. "Not me" would head to the highway from here. "Me-me" would cross The Crag. But I'm also a reckless idiot, so I'll follow this path until I receive an indication to go another way.

Across the way, a small humanoid creature watches me. I immediately recognize it's a River Gnome. Not just any River Gnome— the only River Gnome I have ever encountered.

It has to be the same one.

"Great," I mumble.

His white robe flows in the soft breeze. I am always amazed at how pristine it is. Not uncommon for this guy. At least not in my experience. His face is bearded, but the beard looks like flowing water, shimmering in the reflection of Ezra's light. It's difficult to discern from this distance and through the detail-obscuring mist, but I think a goldfish swims around in his beard.

The goldfish settles it for me. It's definitely the same gnome. I'm always fascinated. I grab my own short beard in envy. He giggles.

At least it looks like a giggle; I can't hear him over the rushing water.

He can't be more than two feet tall, maybe three at most. His smile as he waves me over to his side of the river appears genuine, but I'm not falling for it. He's never done that before. Usually, he just stares at me and jumps back in the water.

Let the games begin.

I wave him over to my side in response, shaking my head at his invitation.

He waves me over to him again.

We go back and forth, and he seems to enjoy the debate over who will cave first and cross.

I'm not falling for that, I tell myself. I decide to wave the gnome off and return to my mission. Several feet ahead, I find more prints. Some of the moss on the rock has been disturbed. Hard to tell by what, though. But a companion boot print in the soft ground and relative position to each other makes me think it was a hand—a small one.

Out of the corner of my eye, motion draws my attention back across the river. My little gnome friend is still there, keeping pace with me. He keeps waving to cross. I wave back to him. I have tasks to complete and don't have time for shenanigans. He can take his shenanigans and shove them up his… never mind.

A few feet further up, a large displacement of mud on the riverbank catches my eye. The tracks lead upstream toward King's Regal Highway and right into the hands of Brogen. I squat close and inspect the small, nearly washed-away footprint. The impression lacks detail, and the downward edge is bunched in a clear mound, indicating a sideways slide. It looks like Jesma's, and it appears she lost her footing here.

Further investigation reveals a set of prints that can only be Tam's and his partner's. Most of the prints appear smudged, some overtop others. Without any context, I surmise that a fight broke out. But who? Did Tamrin start fighting the siblings? Did he and his partner actually attack them?

That's not like Tam. It almost looks like Tam was fighting his partner.

Meanwhile, the only evidence of the siblings indicates that

Jesma, still helping her brother walk, slipped into the river. I'm at a standstill. The trail ends here. I spin around slowly while the River Gnome watches me, smirking. My heart sinks as I realize all four may have fallen into the river.

Not wanting to admit defeat, I continue to search for clues. Ahead, fifty feet or so, the trail goes cold. Both sets of tracks end.

It's as if they vanished from the spot of the struggle.

I glance over to the other bank, wary of the lingering gnome. I turn back downriver to see if there are other Gnomes.

Nope, it's just this guy popping up directly across from me no matter how far I walk.

An object in his hands gives me pause. I can't tell if he's offering or showing me something. Whatever it is, it's vaguely familiar. I shrug and lift my hands.

He wants me to jump in this river and play his game.

It would be an excellent way to end my life. I might even get the answers to the mystery of the River Gnomes or finally find peace. It's not a terrible idea. A sort of 'buy one, get one free' opportunity.

I have a sneaking suspicion that my charges and quarry have fallen victim to the river and, by extension, the River Gnomes. Ezra, on the latter part of her journey for the day, is well behind the tops of the opposite bank's treetops now. The day wanes and I've lost the trail. My choices are to continue forward and run directly into the Brogen Gang or finally go for a swim.

Whatever choice I make, it's Shamna's call now. Two pairs of travelers vanished without a trace at the Great Rankin River.

The gnome beckons.

I shake my head and give him a one-finger salute with each hand.

He laughs.

I laugh… on the outside.

He holds up a finger, and I shrug. Different finger. He wants me to wait.

My excitement surprises me, curious at what new tactic he's devised.

He places the item on a flat rock, and I watch in mild amusement while he waves his arms in some intricate pattern. It looks a lot like the first kata the monks taught me.

He's another show-off. But for some reason, this time I'm entertained.

I shake my head but can't take my eyes off the spectacle.

He holds his stubby arms forward, hands together, and lifts them over his head. He never breaks eye contact. He spreads his arms apart until they stick straight out his sides. He remains like that and breaks out in a full-belly laugh. He looks like a pudgy cross.

He appears to enjoy my fascination while he watches me, expectant, one eyebrow raised. His smirk tells me he isn't done yet.

What happens next astonishes me.

Honestly, I've never seen anything like it. The river bends into an upward arc. The entire river between us rises, the flow of water climbing some invisible hill as it floats into the air, sunlight shimmering off the surface, reflecting on the trees around me.

I stare across an empty riverbed at the gnome, the air before me clear of mist and rainbows as a fifteen-foot-wide arch of water hovers overhead. The entire section of the river, from one bank to the other, flows through the air. The exposed and dry riverbed below offers a safe path to traverse quickly.

I stand, mesmerized by the majesty of the river's overhead flow, uninterrupted by its sudden change in course. The shimmering water, backlit by the late afternoon sky, traverses the invisible arch and returns down the other side, continuing toward Sanctum Mountain. Aside from the occasional drops of spray falling back to the riverbed, the gravel ground is dry. This small section of river is now a sky river.

My jaw falls agape.

I clap like an eight-year-old seeing an illusion for the first time.

"Bravo!" I yell out to him. "Bravo!"

I'm a fool for even contemplating this, but when he set the unidentified item down, it dawned on me where I had seen it. It's the same clay jar Jesma carried her potion in. The same one she used when she healed her brother. That's when I knew.

The River Gnomes nabbed the siblings.

For all I know, they snatched Tamrin, too.

I have no worries about the gnomes taking me. They never do.

Maybe that's the game they have been playing with me. I want it too much. Can't toy with the willing. Hoping this guy will talk to me and I can glean some measure of truth out of the word games he'll probably play, I step into the archway.

I admire the view and how his magic outclasses anything I've ever seen. I have no skill in magic, so it never ceases to fascinate me. While I don't believe in benevolence or even the existence of gods, I've encountered enough magic to know practitioners use faith as their tool to wield it. They grasp their periapts with fervor and hope that defies logic and reason. The most straightforward explanation to me is science. Faith is too intangible. Even when Tam does it, I want to roll my eyes.

But this guy didn't use any device of any kind. It's nice to see someone use magic without the fervent prayers and white-knuckled grip on some periapt.

I've witnessed magic in many forms, but this is a first. Tam always says endless possibilities and outcomes are limited solely by the caster's imagination. I admit to the presence of some intangibles that I don't have, like inherent ability. Still, I can't concede to the idea it comes from prayer.

Finally, I have empirical evidence that I'm right.

I have one hell of an imagination. Apparently, that isn't enough because I never imagined this. Whatever the secret to magic is, those capable keep it tight to the vest, laying it on faith. However they do it, it's a closely guarded secret, as hidden as the water purification process in Winding Run.

Thankfully, I've never required magic to do what I do, and I can rely on myself. My skills have never failed me. I've seen Tam's prayers go unanswered.

But this magic renews my fascination. As I walk under the Great Rankin River and wonder at its beauty, the light of the late afternoon sky shimmers from above. It casts dancing lines of colored light on the rocky riverbed. I can identify the currents flowing within the mass of water overhead. Turbulent subsurface waves compress and expand. Fish swim above me, but I'm dry.

It's a sight to behold. I'm mesmerized with admiration. The

sheer power of this gnome's magic captures my attention.

I shake my head in astonishment and, like a child, clap at him, safe in the knowledge he'll never take me.

He tilts his head with a smirk.

Ugh oh. That's not good.

The gnome laughs, waves, and drops his hands.

"Fuck me," I say softly.

The river crashes down on me.

I have never been hit so hard in my life.

Death hurts.

Blackness.

Eternal blackness.

So, this is death? Not what I expected.

It's disappointing. Nothing feels all that different otherwise. Any minute now, I should see some sort of light. A bit of *out-of-body* seems like it should accompany death. But my hands and feet are still here. I can feel them, move them. I can feel every inch of myself. In fact, my muscles hurt, and my head aches.

Or what I imagine would be my muscles and head.

Wait!

This doesn't make sense!

I'm still me!

Where the hell is the peaceful bliss?

My eyes are open because I feel myself blink. Yet all I see is deep blackness.

A never-ending sea of blackness.

And silence. Dead silence.

I focus my attention on the silence. The lack of sound presses against my eardrums, the steady thrum of my heartbeats, and the incessant ringing are the only evidence my ears work. It's the worst end I can imagine. If the sum total of my existence culminates into an eternity stuck in darkness accompanied by this unbearable ringing, I'll go absolutely insane. The silence is deafening... more accurately, the ringing in my ears is deafening… the silence frightens me.

I float, suspended in this vast, dark void. My arms and legs move until an unseen force tugs them back, my range of motion limited. I reach with my hands and feet to feel for any boundary of walls or ground or ceiling, but each time, that tug stops my motion. I focus on the tug and notice, finally, pressure around my wrists and ankles.

Wait, am I bound?

I thrash in a physical tantrum. I can hear myself grunt in frustration, but no other sounds exist. I pause. Soundwaves do exist here.

"Hello?" I call out.

Still silence. It's not only my grunts that I hear, however. My hands slap against my thighs and chest as I thrash about and test the strength of my restraints. The impact of my hands against my sides is accompanied by the swish of fabric against my skin. I'm simultaneously unnerved and relieved. I'm captivated by the sounds. For the first time, I can hear my own motion. I've never listened to my own actions before. The unsettled feeling transitions to curiosity.

Focus, dummy.

Okay, no sight and the only sound I get to hear is of my own damn voice and motions? I get tired of my own voice internally. This is cruel.

But I can hear my own sound, which is not at all valuable, and would be entertaining if not for everything else.

I'm in Hell. What a load of crap!

I'm severely pissed off right now. A verbal tirade explodes from my lips. The obscenities I unleash on the universe must be audible through all nine layers of this black hellscape to which I'm subjected. I threaten, I curse, and I spit vehement discontent at the universe.

In all the iterations of an afterlife or the lack thereof, this wasn't on my list. Countless nights attributed to the contemplation of the sweet ever after, the final drift into blissful unawareness, or, alternatively, my arrival into the welcome ranks of those who passed before me, and I never anticipated this. Me, stuck, alone, with no entertainment but the filth of every care, worry, and self-loathing thought! Even in death, I'm not allowed to evaporate into forever-forgotten memories.

I continue to struggle against my restraints until my heart rates elevate.

Wait, heartbeats? So maybe I am not dead?

If I'm not dead, someone will have a bad day when I get loose.

Think, damn it.

What's the last memory I have?

Running. I remember running as if my ass was on fire.

Okay, that's one memory. But where was I headed in such a hurry?

I remember trees. That's it! The RhineWoods. I blazed a trail through the RhineWoods!

Great, you have the what. Now you need the why.

I don't know. It's what I do. Nothing particularly spectacular about that epiphany.

It's not actually an epiphany, genius.

Fine. So, I ran through the RhineWoods. What was the purpose? Hunting? Had to be hunting. Was I?

Another insightful deduction. When aren't I on the hunt?

This is going nowhere.

Why was I running?

I can't remember.

I turn my head. Okay, at least that works. If I can get my hands and feet free, maybe I can find solid ground. The commands from my brain to my arms and legs seem to work. Muscles tense and relax with my mental commands.

There's an increase in soft pressure against my back, hamstrings, and buttocks. Like a chair has slid into me. The tension on my ankles and wrists increases as I fold, almost voluntarily, into what feels like a sitting position.

I'm a marionette. Lovely.

I fight against the involuntary motion but the grip on my wrists and ankles tighten, so I relax.

Yup, whatever is tied to me controls me like a puppet.

I'm dead, and this is my payment for my horribly useless life.

I'm locked in this position. Just great. Of course, now my nose itches! I try to scratch it, but the restraints prevent me from solving that problem. I twist and strain to contort my body, but I am held fast.

This is torture!

I unleash more vehement cursing into the void.

I am definitely dead.

No doubt this is Hell, and I'm doomed to suffer from a nose itch I can't scratch through eternity!

The gods are sadists!

I shake against my restraints, screaming obscenities.

After five minutes, I wear myself out and let out a dejected sigh.

Shit.

Damn it.

Quietius be damned!

Screw you, world. I tried to do good and still suffer punishment.

"Is it because I killed a bunch of bad guys?" I question aloud. "Well, if you expect an apology for that, you aren't going to get one. I won't apologize for taking out the trash."

I yank at the restraints violently again and release a guttural scream against my predicament. It merely echoes into the darkness.

"When I get loose, I'm gonna stuff someone's nuts down their throat!" I scream out loud, though there's no one to hear me.

A loud pop and a flash of light simultaneously startle the hell out of me.

My ears ring from the sound. My temples throb, worsening my headache. But the pop had an odd playfulness to it. Like a kid's entertainer sort of sound, only muted. It's not hollow. It's, I don't know, like a bubble pop.

I squint against the light. It's as if Ezra herself has come down and landed right on my nose.

"Ahhhhh!"

My eyes adjust as dark and light patterns dance around me, a shimmer like water. I squint toward a single point before me. It's beautiful, though frightening.

Okay, maybe this is the transition. I relax, relieved there's an afterlife, after all. They say, "Walk toward the light," but these damn restraints lock me in place.

Damn, but my nose still itches. There will be somebody on the other side, right?

"Can somebody scratch my nose? Please!" I yell.

"Certainly," says a scratchy, deep, soft voice. That startles me. I flinch.

I hear the voice but don't see anyone. A stubby sausage-fingered hand reaches toward me from nowhere and rubs my nose with vigor only someone who's experienced an un-scratchable itch can muster. Words to express my gratitude don't exist but I try.

"Oh, thank y…" I choke on the rest.

A lone hand, severed at the wrist floats in front of me. Not the bloody, pieces of flesh dangling, grotesque type of severed. Maybe severed is the wrong word.

Disembodied.

Misty vapor traces a line from the wrist and fades into the abyss, like the remnants of some dismembered ghost. The hand is solid enough because, well, my itch is gone. I felt the knobby, rough skin and calloused knuckles scratch the itch into oblivion.

I'd inspect my new environment, but this hand floats in front of my face. It's pretty distracting, like a gnat. It pulls away and hovers, misty tail drifting away.

"Do you like shadow puppets?" the voice says, as the hand makes funny shapes with… itself.

I can't right now. Seriously, I just can't with this guy. Is it serious? I'm tied to a chair, trapped in who knows where, while unidentified light shimmers all around me, and this jagoff wants to play games?

"Where am I?" I ask.

"Where do you think you are?" the voice says.

You have got to be kidding me.

"Dead?"

The voice booms with a jolly laugh. It's good-natured, all things considered. I might even laugh along under normal circumstances.

"No, my boy, you are most definitely not dead," the voice says.

"Boy? I'm fifty-three years old! At least I was."

This time, the laughter is raucous. Whoever this voice belongs to is sure enjoying themselves at my expense.

"You humans are so much fun. First, let me say you look much younger than fifty-three. Whatever you are doing, keep doing it. Second, what is fifty-three years in the span of time? If your time in the world were measured in drops of water, compared to a single rainfall, you wouldn't even fill a thimble. I can't even remember when I was fifty-three years old."

The voice trails off in what seems like thought.

Then it speaks as if to itself, softly, "Hmmm. How long ago was that? Has it been that many… oh yes… it has been. My, how time flies." Then louder, directed at me, "Well, no, it doesn't, actually. Fly, that is. Time is what we, or well, I, make of it."

I'm still stuck on the 'you humans' comment.

"You humans?" I ask. "Who… or what… are you?"

"You don't know?"

This guy can't be serious.

The disembodied hand is joined by another one… at least they aren't the same hand… one's a left, and one's a right. The wispy, smoky trails they leave converge toward the same general area…

OK, now we are getting somewhere… a wizard, maybe?

"Do you like my horseman?" the voice says as the hands come together and contort a shape that looks nothing like a man on a horse or a man shaped like a horse. Or anything I've seen. Just a jumble of short, fat fingers, knuckles, and hands.

This is absurd. I love a good gag, but this is untenable.

"Ugh, yeah, pretty good," I lie.

The hands drop as if to the sides of a body, floating in displeasure, suspended loosely from the end of their vapor tails.

"You didn't even look," the voice accuses.

"I did, too."

"No, you didn't."

"I looked right at you!" I yell. "Or, near you."

"No, you watched my hands. Not over there. Do you even understand the concept of shadow puppets?"

"Duh."

The invisible jailor snickers and a little nubby finger points to shimmering lines of light as waves of iridescent colors dance across a large boulder to my right. The boulder, smooth and rounded, plays the backdrop to a bright circle of light shining from my left, like a spot lantern. As I watch, the shadow of a man on a horse galloping in place appears.

I snap back to the hands and see the same knotted jumble of fingers from before.

"Oh," I say, "that is impressive." I couldn't care less if I tried.

"Tada!" The hands wave in the air in triumph. "It's taken me over a hundred years to perfect that one," the voice says. "This next one I have worked on for over ten thousand years."

I look back to the rock. This time, a dragon floats, flapping its wings. At least, it's what I would imagine a dragon to look like based on paintings I've seen. I have never seen an actual dragon. In fact, I don't know anyone who has.

I form what I hope is an appropriate expression of awe, which is the exact opposite of my mood.

"That's pretty good."

"Pretty good?" There's a twinge of disappointment there. "That's fantastic. It's flawless. Looks exactly like Primus, the first dragon."

"Ugh, yeah. It does."

The hands drop again.

"How would you know? You weren't alive sixteen thousand years ago. I'd bet the only dragon you've seen is a painting or drawing."

"Sixteen thousand years?"

Now that's a number.

The hands hang there. The voice doesn't speak.

"That's it? That's what you focus on? The time?" the voice bemoans.

"Ugh. Was there something else?" I ask.

A blubbering babble of sounds emanates from the space between the hands. "Was there something else?" the voice mocks. "I mention Primus, the first dragon, and you don't even seem impressed! I ask you, have you ever seen a dragon?"

"Well, I just did."

"What? Where!" the voice cries, excited.

I indicate with my head, "Well, on that rock over there."

The hands move back and forth as if some invisible body paces frantically. An image that is easy to create since it is accompanied by more blubbering.

"What a preposterous man, this one."

My mind drifts from the conversation and into my environment, intrigued by the light that shines on the boulder. It's source doesn't exist. Wherever I am, it's an anomaly with invisible sources of light.

I'm held in the open. That much I can discern. I'm surround by a strange, oddly featured valley. The ground cover, a mixture of large, smooth stones and drifting dirt, is unlike any place I've seen in my years of travel through the RhineWoods.

Large, bright green, loose-leaf plants swirl and sway. Grasses, taller than any I have ever seen, stretch upward toward the sky, gently bending in an undetectable breeze. The sky… well, I don't know if I can call it a sky. The surface overhead shimmers like a membrane and appears an awful lot like the underwater view of a lake's surface when deep underwater. But I'm not wet, so that can't be the answer.

A backlit shadow passes by like an odd cloud. Only this one seemed to propel itself and looked like a giant trout.

"Umm. Did a fish just swim overhead?" I ask, stunned.

"I am not inclined to answer you at this time. You appear to be daft. I introduce you to a dragon, and you don't have the decency to offer even a modicum of awe. For ten thousand years, I've worked on that shadow puppet. All I get from you, young man, is 'sixteen thousand years?'"

"But that's a giant fish!" I yell.

It's the biggest fish I've ever seen. One that could decide I'd be a snack, swim down, and eat me. I observe the smooth rocks again. The bits of dirt and sand that float by take on new meaning. A school of massive salmon—giant salmon—swims by. My mind snaps to sudden alertness.

"Oh," I whisper.

"Oh, look. Guess who finally found his wits. Figure it out, did you?" the voice asks.

"Am I underwater?" I scream. The pitch of my voice is

unflattering, but this entire situation is unflattering.

Under normal situations, I'd express genuine excitement about this, but I'm disoriented and completely lost. All I can think about is how to break free. The voice laughs again, and the wispy smoke at the end of the dismembered hands coalesces into forearms. As forearms form, the smoke travels onward, and more body parts solidify out of thin air (or water, as it may be). Biceps, shoulders, neck, chest, and finally, a head materializes.

When the show finishes, a small man, his round face immediately familiar, smiles at me. I have never seen him up close before. Usually, he's much shorter than I am, but now he stands close to my height. Yet, somehow, he still carries the same stubby appearance of a gnome.

Eyes, black as coal, surrounded by star-like sparkles, twinkle at me. It's as if the night sky came down and took up residence to replace his irises. I'm drawn to their hypnotic appearance. His gruff face, wrinkled but more weathered than old, is equally warm and frightening. His white robe and long white hair flow like they are caught in a current. His beard, long and flowy, is difficult to make out, nearly invisible in the river's water. I can neither see nor feel the water, though the evidence of its presence surrounds me.

"You are indeed! This is the bottom of the Great Rankin River," he says as if this were an everyday occurrence for me.

River Gnome. Great.

I'd be excited about this under any other circumstance. Finally, the River Gnomes nabbed me. Well, a single River Gnome, but still. But don't I have a task to do? I don't remember what, but a thought teases the back of my brain that I forgot an important assignment. Yet, here I am, tied down. I'm not happy about that. So, the moment is lost on me.

I look down and try to remember, but no memory comes to mind.

"Umm, shouldn't I have drowned about now?"

"Well, yes, most assuredly, you should have," he says. "Would that make you more comfortable if I allowed it?"

I blink. No, it wouldn't.

I shake my head vigorously.

He giggles.

"Drowning sounds like a horrible death to me. Ranks right up there with death by fire. Or boiled in oil, for that matter. I think I'm fine with whatever this is," I say.

He laughs again.

"I like you," he says.

"Umm, thanks?" I reply.

I still can't determine how I ended up here. Vague ghosts of memories, hidden behind a fog, taunt me with distant familiarity but evade even the most aggressive attempt to focus on them.

"Lost some memories?" he asks, observing me.

I fight against my restraints and grit my teeth as I answer.

"Yeah. How did I get here? Could you please let me loose? And do I know you?"

"Ah, first one question, then the other, and then, maybe, the last," he says.

I stare at him blankly.

"First, how you got here. Easy enough. I brought you here, of course."

"Well, that doesn't tell me a whole lot, now, does it?" I retort.

What is it with people? That's barely an answer.

"You do enjoy your snark, don't you?" he asks.

I offer my best smirk, never one to back down. "Don't you?"

"Hahahaha! Yes, yes. I do." He winks at me.

"Well, this has been fun and all, but you can let me go now."

He clicks his tongue. "Not yet. I will cut you loose eventually." He takes several steps to the left and turns back to me. "Eventually. We have all the time in the world, now that I think about it. Enough as far as you are concerned." He trails off, lost in thought again. "Really, we do. So much time. Where has it gone?"

I cough to draw him back to our conversation. This guy is seriously worse than me. I would never have thought it possible.

"Where was I? Oh yes. I will let you go, but before I do, I need you to agree to do a favor for me," he says.

I can feel my scowl form as my lids narrow. "So, I'm the kidnap victim and the deliverer of my own ransom. Not a good start to this relationship. What kind of favor? Is it a small favor? Or is it a favor-favor?"

He paces as he talks.

"Good way to look at it. Much like the Picaroons! I am sorry about the approach, but I need this favor from you. I'm not accustomed to trading favors, so I like your ransom approach. We'll call it a future payment for your immediate release. A task. I'd do it myself, but you see, I have responsibilities that can't go unattended here."

He stops and stares at me for a second.

"A task you are uniquely qualified for."

He returns to pacing as the goldfish swims around his head.

"I have watched you for so long. You cross The Crags, walk along the river, and run through these woods, aimlessly helping strangers. You use your magic willy-nilly. Do you find fulfillment when you help people? Does it fill you with joy?"

He comes to a stop and offers a kind smile, but the kindness is lost on me. I am, after all, held captive. At the bottom of a river, I might add. But he said magic as if I'm a mage. This guy's not as smart as he thinks he is.

"What magic?"

"Your magic, of course."

I shake my head. "You have me confused with someone else," I say. "I don't do magic. I do fists."

His expression makes me feel uncomfortable, like an animal in an experiment. His head tilted to the side, he asks, "You don't do magic?"

I shake my head, irked by the stupidity in the question.

"I see." He twirls his hand in his invisible beard. "You speak the truth, I see."

I bite my tongue.

"Interesting. I was certain…"

He picks up his pace, his feet almost gliding, and suddenly halts as if a new conclusion came to mind on some experiment.

"Does it bring you joy?" he asks again.

"What?"

"Oh, don't be obtuse."

"Yeah, sure," I say, distracted. I wish this guy would get to the point. I have questions. Like, why aren't I drowning? I look down at my hands.

Oh my.

I'm not in a chair. I'm held by grasses. Blades of river grass hold my wrists and ankles. Isn't that interesting? They aren't tight or uncomfortable, but they hold firm.

I pull against them, but they are stronger than I guessed.

"Doesn't seem like it," he says.

"Hmm," I say. I've lost interest in the conversation.

"I said it doesn't seem like you enjoy the life you lead."

"Oh, right," I reply, still focused on the restraints.

"It won't do to tug at them. River grass is quite strong, and I have no intention of harming you."

"What's your deal here?" I ask impatiently. "Are you some sort of involuntary therapist, then?"

"Ha, ha, ha. That snark. What do you like to say? How does it go? Oh, yes," he leans in and looks directly into my eyes. "You can't really be that stupid, can you?"

His perfectly straight, perfectly white teeth gleam in the water-filtered light when he smiles.

I'm kind of stunned at the comment. Do I say that a lot?

He steps back a little, eyes locked on mine. He seems to be waiting for me to speak.

Or does he wait for me to understand? Is this a test? I hate tests.

"What was the question?"

His smile widens bigger than before. "You know, I've never met someone so easily distracted. It's annoying."

"You can't be serious," I say with sincerity.

"No, no. I'm serious. You really can't stay focused without the weight of a purpose, can you? You've opened my eyes to a subject I'd like to consider someday. But back to your answer."

"You're a kidnapper and a hypocrite," I say.

He laughs. "Well, now, I guess I'm this is what it's like to hold a conversation with me." He paces some more, "I don't get many visitors. Still, how about you answer my question?"

"Whether I find joy helping people. Why wouldn't I?" I say.

My mouth runs counter to my thoughts, however. I've never

really considered this question. Does my intercession in the troubles of others fulfill me? It's the right thing to do. But do I receive some joy from it?

I can't count the number of people I've rescued. I've run rampant around Conishant for so long, it's a habit. It's compulsive. I don't bother to resist anymore. I've never been one for keeping score. I'm compelled, driven by inner turmoil. It's much like those who drink, conquer, or explore. People do what they do. How many of us get the chance to choose what we spend our lives doing?

'Does it bring you joy?'

Seems like a straightforward question. I should know the answer.

But I don't know.

I regard this gnome and his gentle eyes with suspicion. Like I'm some lab animal, he observes every action or expression I make. His insertions into my inner monologue are uninvited and make me uncomfortable. I'm tired of this game.

"What do you want?" I ask.

He doesn't answer. He simply stares at me.

I struggle to free myself again.

A pointless effort.

'Can you really be that stupid?'

Well, no, I don't think I am stupid. I don't think this gnome thinks I am, either. Maybe that's his point. That's certainly my point. I usually ask it when I think the answer is obvious. If it's obvious and the other person doesn't know, it's generally because they don't like the answer. Do I already know the answer? Do I dislike it?

I must, right?

No. I am not honest with myself.

I don't help because I gain joy from it. I already know why I help. In the countless days, weeks, months, and years spent in nomadic solitude across the Five Realms, I spend most nights in relative discomfort. I avoid people other than those I genuinely like whenever possible. I take little from anyone and give whatever I have to everyone. My small circle of friends, whom I trust, are all I can count on, and even then, I hate to take from them. But they are the people I would die for. Kill for.

Have killed for.

But I avoid annoying them by staying away. I keep my visits short, take as little from them as possible, and try to be there when they need me.

What's wrong with that? I am a burden to nobody. At least, I try not to be.

I help because it boosts my self-esteem. I'm not some benevolent do-gooder. I do it because the alternative makes me feel worse about myself.

Be an asset to the world, not a liability, like mom always said—usually when I screwed up. But her point was valid, even if the delivery was cruel. I try not to think about her. I prefer it that way. We are not walking down that bakru trail today.

Is this an involuntary therapy session? Do we discuss my parents now? What was it my dad always said?

"Make your own way in the world. Ask no one for anything." I remember that. They were the last words he said as he walked out the door, his possessions tied in a pack, never to return.

Then my brother died.

I remember when I became the man in the house after-ward—every day, a struggle to make my own way, to be an asset. I never asked for help. I shouldered the heavy lifting. I've got broad shoulders. I learned early on, I can carry the weight. As an adult, I find that anonymous service has become the easiest way to do that. But people ask a lot. They ask without asking. Helping becomes a burden. But it's my burden to bear.

A burden I never want to be on anyone else.

No. I find no joy in this life. My actions only ensure I can continue the lie that I'm not a burden on the world. It allows me the chance to believe I am at least of some value. Without it, I am just a liability.

"No, I wouldn't say joy is my reason," I answer.

Chapter Eight

Journal Entry:33

I have an unusual trait. Some might call it a skill. It would be a skill if I had control over it. I don't, so it's a trait. There's no mastery here. I don't know why this is, but it has always been true. In fact, my mom used to yell at me all the time about this. I swear it's not an exaggeration.

I make no noise when I move.

To be clear, I'm not talking about an "oh, wow, you move so quietly I can barely hear you" type of quiet.

You literally can't hear me. I can't even hear myself. But I can't control it.

It's true. I've never met another person like me in this regard. Not even in the trade guild... that is relevant, but now isn't the time. In any event, it is a strange trait and immensely useful.

It's always been this way: walking, running, jumping, crawling, or falling, regardless of whether I am in sand, on stone, in the woods, or in a structure. I could be walking on marbles or broken glass, or, well, use your imagination. It won't matter what it is; my motions will remain silent. My clothes don't even rustle when I walk. Believe me, I've tried. It's strange. I am a veritable sound vacuum when I move.

When I walk into a room unseen, it startles even the most observant people. Mom made me carry a large bell when I was a kid. Somehow, I can use a bell, a drum, or even a lute. No one understood it, and I've grown to accept it.

I had to shake that stupid bell when I came into the house and when I moved around the house.
And when I left the house.

She blew her temper if I surprised her with my sudden appearance and disappearance. Sometimes, I would scare her soul right out of her while she was making dinner or hanging laundry. More than once, dinner ended up on the dirt floor of our little house. She usually made me suffer for that. She was mean.

Hence the bell. I didn't mind because it was my protection from her wrath.

I lost the bell once. That was a bad day. At least, how I remember it, it was. She definitely shared her displeasure. Those bruises lasted for months.

I could have avoided the beating if I wanted. I'm that fast.

It's odd to be quiet and fast. I'd make a good thief. I make a good many other things. There is no honor in any of the things I'd be good at, but I digress... again.

Fools Rush In

"Well, why do you do it?"

"I naught better to do than bust the skulls of those who'd seek to harm others for their own gain. It's better than the alternative use of my skills."

"Ah, yes, the alternative use," he says. "That's what I wish to speak with you about."

I raise an eyebrow. This can't be good. My skills serve two purposes outside of how I use them. Neither of which are benevolent.

"You like to help people, and I need your help."

I don't like where this is going.

"What if I don't want to?"

His smile, this time, is less than friendly. Soul-crushing terror grips me for the first time. Admittedly, the revelation is exhilarating. It's a strange feeling, fear. I cannot think of the last time I felt it. At least not as it relates to me. This guy makes me think he can do far worse acts than just manipulate life and death.

Floating in impenetrably dark silence trapped with my thoughts comes to mind.

But, for sure, here I am, strapped to a grassy chair under the Great Rankin River, while a River Gnome interrogates me with a smile, and I am honestly utterly terrified.

His eyes. The little twinkling night skies disappear. It's as if all the stars were snuffed out instantaneously. A shiver runs through my body.

"You see, I intend to let you go," he says. "But just you."
"Huh?"

My stomach flips as a sudden unseen current drags me down-river.

Hmm. That made sense. Guess I know the answer now.

Together, he and I float down the river, me still held by grasses. My body feels weightless. I don't know how that's possible. It just is.

The current rushes us past lilies and weeds and a giant boot. I swear it was a boot. Big enough for me to sit inside. Anyway. The rocks on the riverbed become a blur beneath my feet. The sudden acceleration from stop to river-rushing speeds is exhilarating and disorienting.

As suddenly as we started, we came to a stop. My stomach flips again.

"Whoa," I whisper.

Across from me, four more tufts of grass hold four more bodies. Three of the occupants aren't familiar to me. One is so familiar I fight against my restraints in anger. Tam's eyes, wide with panic, focus on me. The hair on his furs flows in the unseen current along with his hair. He looks simultaneously panicked and relieved to see me.

"Tam! How the hell did you get here?"

A blonde woman struggles with similar restraints next to him. Next to the woman, a blond man with identical features fights to break free. He looks like he could be the woman's twin or some other close relation. At the end of the line of captives is a short man with dark hair and skin, like mine. A bruise on his right cheek looks fresh, and his right eye is nearly swollen shut. He fights against his restraints violently when we lock eyes. I don't know why. He appears angry and frightened.

I guess I can understand that.

Everyone looks terrified. It's unsettling.

The grass wrapped around their faces, blocks their mouths. They each try to speak, which is kind of difficult with mouths full of grass.

I wonder who the other three are. There's a vague familiarity with the two blond ones, but they seem like ghosts from my past.

"Still struggling with the memories?" the strange gnome asks.

I remain quiet. I'm not sure what the gnome means.

With an amused expression, he drifts into soliloquy. "Yes, interesting, the river. It flows, time flows, both continuing forever. Memories often fade with time. But here, as the river flows backward, so does time. And with it, so go memories because, as far as time is concerned, they haven't happened yet." The pudgy gnome turns back to me. "But since the memories were real, you haven't lost them.

They're merely clouded by the fog of future uncertainty. No one can know the future. Therefore, you can't know what happened that no longer has."

He seems pleased with his wordplay and continues.

"That's the way of memory. Spend too much time down here, and I'm afraid you'll completely forget who you were. I'd recommend an early exit if you can manage."

I blink at him.

Time flowing backward? How is that possible? What does he mean?

"Don't try to understand. I promise, you will have lost no time when I return you to the surface. Your memories will return with a few more added. For now, know this. Three of these people are important to you. Promise to do as I ask, and they will be returned with you."

He leans in close, his smile sinister.

"Fail to fulfill your promise, and I will not hesitate to make your life an eternity of suffering."

I swallow. Yeah, I'm that frightened.

"Deny my request, and the four of you will remain here, with me and that one." He points at the stranger at the end before he looks back at me. "Never to return. Lost, with so many others, to the Great Rankin River."

I assume he means me, Tam, and the twin blonds. It isn't clear to me why I should care about anyone but Tam, but since I have a chip on my shoulder where bullies are concerned, I do. I don't know why the last man is excluded from going free while the rest of us aren't, but I don't intend to leave anyone in this place with the crazy gnome. Whatever the game is here, I struggle to reason it out. But I do know that I need to get Tamrin free.

"Why not the one on the end? If I help you, let all of us go."

The gnome looks at me with curiosity.

"You just can't help it, can you? You do not know this man. Not of his purpose or drive. Yet, you will help him? Oh, you are an interesting fellow. If we had time, I'd set you free and have you live here so I could pick that hyperactive brain of yours. Have you not learned from past mistakes?"

It's a punch to the gut. Waves of regret wash over me again as past transgressions flood my thoughts. My head spins as I try to gather up the shattered pieces of my ego spilling around my mind like a jar of marbles. The trembling of a panic attack grips my chest, and my breath comes in short, rapid bursts. I want out of this nightmare where my words are twisted, and my past is free to haunt me. I need to move, to run away, but the damn grasses hold me firm. I grow claustrophobic.

The gnome hurries over, the stars in his eyes reappearing. The edges of my vision darken, and my skin begins to tingle. My thoughts turn over on themselves as I struggle to control my own body. I feel my cells burn as I struggle against the grasses, my motions picking up speed. Everything around me is slipping away, the dark tunnel growing deeper. My ears ring as the strange gnome's voice echoes in the distance.

An object slips over my head, and the world goes black. The air around my face changes, somehow warmer, smelling like my own breath. With each breath, the temperature of the air rises, and the sense of panic grows.

Is this how I'm going out? Asphyxiated with a bag over my head, tangled in river weeds?

I fight against my restraints.

"Easy, son," the Gnome whispers. "Just breathe. Nice slow breaths."

His voice somehow calms me, even though I'm convinced he's torturing me. But I do as he instructs, and gradually, the tingling in my skin fades, my hearts slow, and my breathing returns to normal. Light returns as the bag is removed from my head.

The gnome stands before me, a burlap bag in his hand. I glance at Tamrin, his face twisted into relaxed worry.

"Oh, I am sorry. That was unfair. Calm down, child." His hand on my shoulder is tender. "I truly am sorry. I meant no harm by that." He points at the smaller man. "This one is not your friend. This one has ill intent toward you. He will stay with me. I have need of him here. Do not risk your life, or your conscience, on him. That is all I meant."

I have no clue what he wants me to do. But, as he said, I can't help it. I help. Tam and the other two look as confused as me. At least this gnome is talking to me, and these people need my help. If it was just me, I might tell this guy to go have sex with a donkey. But it's not just me.

Dammit to Hell.

I nod. "What do you want from me?" I ask.

"Good," he says, "I will tell you. But, before I do, let's all take a ride upriver? I have something to show you."

Once again, sudden acceleration causes my stomach to flip. The trip upriver is as fast as the one down. A floating gnome and three prisoners, bound by grasses mystically rooted, slide along the riverbed. The small man with ill intent disappears into the distance, left behind to struggle against his restraints. I watch his form shrink, curious about who he is and why the gnome thinks he intends to do the rest of us harm.

A wave of nausea causes me to vomit. I watch as bile leaves my mouth and travels downstream. The gnome raises an eyebrow and pulls a rag out of nowhere to wipe my face clean.

The atmosphere of the upstream trip pushes against my body, the pressure from the river's flow resisting our motion, reminding me we are, in fact, underwater. The pressure makes sense, I guess. I've never done anything like this. I don't have a good comparison.

Eventually, our pace slows. This time, more gradually than the sudden stomach-leaping stop we made downriver. I'm grateful because I have no desire to vomit again.

As we slow, we pass the boot and the shadow puppet rock from earlier. I watch each of them as they pass. My fear subsides as my mind accepts this strange new environment, time normalizing the fantastical.

Still, my displeasure with the restraints persists, but at least they aren't uncomfortable.

Thoughts of restraints are short-lived as a flood of memories returns, mental images flashing across my mind's eye. By the look on the three faces across from me, it's a safe bet they are experiencing the same stunning return of memories.

Nothing can explain the feeling, but I rejoice over the lifted fog.

"What is happening?" I blurt

By the time we come to rest, the familiar rock falls out of sight into the past. The gnome ignores the question and points skyward.

"Here we are. This is where you entered the river," the River Gnome says.

None of us resist the instinctual urge to follow his gaze. Overhead, actual giants stare down at us, and I flinch. Awed by their sheer size, I struggle to find words. I've never seen giants, and I always assumed they were the stuff of legend. One female, dressed like a hunter, squats and points somewhere over us.

As I observe the activity above, I start to recognize some of them. It hits me. The giants aren't giants. We've been shrunk.

Giant Salmon. Giant boot. Giant grasses. I shake my head. The evidence was all around me.

I am definitely not the sharpest knife on anyone's toolbelt.

It's Brogen and his party, staring down into the river.

"Can they see us?" I ask.

"No, they aren't looking directly at us. Although, with the size of their faces, it's hard to tell," the gnome says. "Besides, my illusions disguise us. To them, we are tadpoles."

"I'll never look at tadpoles the same again," I say.

Brogen's scowl looks even worse, magnified as it is. His birdlike features are quite unattractive.

"Oh, he's definitely single," I say out loud.

The gnome snickers a bit. Tam rolls his eyes slowly. It's what he does when he's exasperated by me. I shrug at him, chagrined. The twins don't seem to find me funny.

It's clear the party above us is searching.

"They found your tracks," the gnome says. "That man is familiar. I feel like I should know him. Hmm. It'll come to me when I go to sleep. Mind if I call out to you when I remember?"

"Huh?" I reply. He ignores me.

Booming voices travel through the water, but the words are hard to distinguish. Muffled by the river water, they sound like distant thunder. First tadpoles, now thunder.

I wonder how much of the world is an illusion of perception... stop... damn brain.

"How do you know they are looking for us?" I ask.

"Well, they aren't looking for *you*, now, are they?" he corrects, pointing at me. "They are looking for *them*." He turns and looks at the siblings across from me.

"How do you know that?" I ask.

"I know everything that happens in my domain, boy," he says.

"I'm not a boy," I growl.

"Oh, but you so are. Didn't we cover this?"

I take my focus from the band of pursuers and look at the gnome, my patience at an end.

"What do you want?" I ask.

He strokes his watery beard. The goldfish pops up through his fingers, still swimming around his chin.

"They'll be here a while." He points overhead. "At least they will once they enter the river. I will slow it down and let them reach the halfway point. Oh, how the river will speed up and carry them away for a while," he says, a gleeful smile on his face.

He turns to the other three. "They'll waste some time. Quite a bit of time, to be honest. Mostly trying to remember how they got where they'll be and where they left their horses. Here's the fun part," he says, looking at me. "They'll have extra time; they are headed back in time, after all. You'll move forward at about the same rate. They won't discover what you already know 'til it's too late. Time is funny that way. Move it back far enough, and all memories are lost. Move it forward enough, and eternity is lost. In either event, one could miss some important details. How I love a mystery."

He turns back to me. "I'll take you upriver to the other side of the King's Regal Highway, as you call it." His eyes glaze over as his voice becomes distant. "I remember when that road was little more than wagon tracks through the woods. Pity."

"Yes, yes, such a pity. Life was so much less complicated back then. But now everyone's in a hurry. It'd be nice if the road went back to a trail."

He shakes his head and returns his gaze back to me.

"Oh, sorry. Where was I? Oh, yes. You will lose some daylight, but I will give you a significant head start in your journey. Distance will be your advantage. Don't squander it by dilly-dallying because time is not on your side."

He turns and looks at the other three.

"You two must hurry," he points at the siblings. "Your pursuers will not give up easily. They will lose your trail for a bit. That will cost them any time they gain once they remember why they are even in these woods."

He glances at his hands, "If they remember why they are in these woods." Looking back at the twins, he continues, "I will delay your pursuers a sufficient amount for you to get to a safe place. With the help of these two, you should be able to make up the time you have lost."

He looks at Tamrin and points a thumb at me.

"Keep an eye on this one. Make sure he doesn't do anything stupid. He will need you on this journey. Of that, I am certain."

Tamrin nods vigorously.

Back to me.

"You, there is no point in giving any instruction. You can't help yourself, can you? This is now your party. See it through, as I know you will. My payment demands are much more for you."

He leans in and whispers so only I can hear him, "Deep in Killinshire, locked away in Milslog Castle, lies a book which belongs to me. Lost long ago, it has been found and is in the hands of my enemy. I'm sure you can guess it is more than a simple book. It requires some materials before it can be opened. Materials that are easy to find once someone discovers what they are. Those materials are not important to you. The book is. I want my tome. It belongs to me. More importantly, it does not belong to the Emperor of Killinshire. In fact, his reign has been too long. Get my tome back and… well… kill the Emperor. Then return to me. With my book."

The starlight in his eyes returns. The kindness I saw before is back.

"Swear to me you will do this."

I admit I am utterly confused.

"Why are you helping us?" I ask.

"That is a question, now, isn't it? Because I like you. I have so enjoyed watching you pass by my river all these years. So fearless. So bold. So stubborn. That's good. You're gonna need all of it for the road ahead.”

A massive boot steps into the water, its toe larger than my head. I worry that we’ll be crushed. Still, the gnome navigates us around as a swirl of dirt, disturbed by the boot, dissipates in the unseen current, drifting downriver.

“Why not just drown them?” I ask. “That would make this so much easier.”

“Yes, yes. Good suggestion. I suppose it would make your life easier. But you don’t like easy, do you? Besides, there’s a story to play out. No, no. I think having your pursuers still out there will do you good.”

“You’re a sadist,” I say.

His eyes flash with anger, and his voice booms like thunder. I flinch as he speaks, “Don’t presume to know what I am, boy!”

The visage of the kind old gnome returns, the sinister demeanor evaporating as quickly as it appeared. I squint at him, wanting to push his patience, but a gut instinct tells me to hold my tongue.

“Swear to me you will do as I ask. Get these two to safety. Then go get my book.”

I want to be defiant. But I nod. What choice do I have?

He turns and looks back downriver. His face contorts.

“Good, they are crossing the river,” he says. “Time for me to go.”

He turns back to me. “One last thought. You have control. You don’t seem to know that, but you can decide when to use it and when not to.”

“Huh?” I say.

He shakes his head. “You’re not very bright, are you? Bring me my book, and I will tell you your secret.”

The roar of an oncoming flood drowns out his words as the world suddenly spins out of control. The grasses that held us release, and the river sweeps us upstream. I catch flashes of the gnome as he stands waving, his body disappearing in a spinning image. My last vision of him is two disembodied hands making hand puppets again.

"Well, this is awkward," I say.

Tamrin and I face each other on the northern shore of the river. Puddles of water form at our feet, our clothes saturated. The twins, visibly shaken, fearful, and unsure of the intent of the two strangers before them, huddle together. Physically uncomfortable and unsettled, we find ourselves on shore soaking wet. My fists clench, the act involuntary. We've barely overcome the shock of our experience at the bottom of the river. Now we find ourselves unceremoniously dumped onto the shore, our clothes clinging to us.

Confused, our glances bounce around the group in mute shock. Tamrin resembles a drowned bear, his furs matted flat and waterlogged.

Ezra slips further behind the horizon, and the RhineWoods fall into twilight while our little foursome gathers its wits. Jesma, furtive and frightened, steps behind me, her eyes on Tamrin, eying the big guy suspiciously. I fight shivers, the air cooling as nightfall approaches, but I cannot discern if it's emotional or physical.

"What just happened?" Tam asks.

"I have no idea," I reply. "That's my first abduction by River Gnomes," I smirk at Tamrin. "Not what I expected, if I'm honest."

"How did you end up here?" he asks.

I turn to Jesma, who shakes her head and defiantly addresses Tamrin. "Who are you? Why did you do that?"

"Do what? Track you?"

She inches further behind me, using me as a shield. Tamrin looks down at his giant feet, reticent.

"No," she whispers. "Why did you attack your friend?"

"Umm," he starts, his deep voice soft, "well, that wasn't my friend. I was hired to track you, not kill you. He seemed to think the 'dead' option in the 'dead or alive' was preferable. I don't kill for sport. You're wanted, not convicted."

"What are you talking about?" I ask.

Jesmir reaches for his sword, ready to fight Tamrin. His hands shake. I assume it's fear. Jesma places a hand on his arm. I offer a warning glance, and the younger man freezes.

"You're with Brogen's men," Jesmir accuses, his grip on the

sword turning his knuckles white.

"Hold up," I say.

"And who are you?" Jesmir demands.

"Jes, this is the one I told you about," Jesma whispers, a sense of relief in her voice.

Tamrin's and Jesmir's heads snap to me. Deep lines in Tamrin's forehead form as he considers Jesma's words. I imagine his thoughts and squirm under the scrutiny. Jesma, though frightened, seems comfortable with my presence. Jesmir, still tense, addresses me.

"You're our mysterious rescuer?" he asks, incredulous.

I glance at Tamrin, nervous. The big guy isn't stupid.

"Listen, we need to get moving," I say, attempting to deflect the conversation. But Tam's unrelenting scrutiny makes me squirm. "Tam and I will help you get home. Where is home?"

"Hold on." Jesmir points at Tamrin. "We're not going any-where with him. He's one of Brogen's men."

"Brogen? Brogen, who?" Tam blurts.

"Captain Brogen of The Dark Guard," I reply.

"I'm sorry? Repeat that?" he says.

"Oh, Tam, you have no clue who you've been working for, do you?" I say.

Tam looks at me curiously. "What do you mean?"

I step up to him and put a hand on his arm. "Tam 'ole buddy, you were lied to." I look at Jesma and Jesmir, "the man you were working for…"

"Brandin," he interrupts.

I shake my head, "No. Brogen. Captain Brogen."

His eyes go wide. "No. I would never work for The Dark Guard." Tamrin says to Jesmir, a deep hurt in his voice. "Listen, I was hired to track murderers and thieves," he continues. "I'm to locate you and escort you to the magistrate. The warrant I saw was legitimate. Let's get to the magistrate, and you can tell your side of the story there."

Jesma shakes her head in desperation. Her voice cracks. "We are not criminals!" she cries.

Tam holds up a hand. "That's fine. There's a magistrate in

Valshannon. We can head there."

I hold up both hands, silencing everyone.

"Tam, listen," I say. "The man you call Brandin is Brogen. He travels under false pretenses. I recognized him after you left. Mistras overheard their conversation and asked me to come after you to warn you. The bastard is after these two, and he intends to kill them."

"No, I…" He stops himself and slams his hands on his thighs. "Oh hell!" he exclaims, his deep voice echoing over the loud river. "Shen, I had no idea he wasn't who he said he was!"

I nod, "That's what I suspected."

Tam looks at the siblings. "What does he want with you two?"

"We don't know," Jesmir says. Visibly shaken, he glances at his sister. They both fight back tears.

I'm uncomfortable with crying, so I interject.

"Listen, I don't know how far downriver the gnome will send Brogen's party. I don't understand what that was either, but when Brogen's team crosses, it may be a while before they figure out where they are. It may not. We have no way of knowing what games that gnome is playing. Any minute now, your pursuers could pop up right here. Even if they don't, it will dawn on them that they missed our tracks, and they'll start heading this way. We won't know until it's too late."

I point west.

"The highway is that way. But so are they. Unless the river took them to Gal-Danang, we have no time to sit here. I suggest we get someplace safe. Make ourselves harder to track. Then we can argue over who we are and why we are here."

I turn to the siblings. "How does that sound?"

"But this guy is one of them," Jesmir cries.

"His companion was the one who tried to kill you, no?" I question.

Jesmir doesn't respond. Jesma nods, jaw clenched.

"Let me ask you this: did this man before you try to kill you? Did he give any indication he might?" I look them in the eyes. "I know I left you to fend for yourselves yesterday. Not one of my finest moments. But, if you'll trust me, I'll see you safely to Valshannon. I hate the man that chases you. I would love to see whatever he has planned fail. If you have nothing else, you have that."

I turn and start heading west toward King's Regal Highway. "And to be fair," I call over my shoulder, "I'd trust that man next to you with my life over anyone else in Conishant."

Quick footsteps follow after me, faint over the roar of the river.

"What will happen to the other man?" Jesma asks as she appears beside me.

I turn and look back at Tamrin.

"Wanna go back?" I call to him.

"No. I don't want to see that river again," Tam says.

"There you have it," I say. "Let's get a move on."

Two steps later, my chest explodes in searing hot pain, and I fall to my knees, clutching myself reflexively. I cry out, continuing downward, curling in a ball. The intensity overwhelms my senses, and I'm unable to move. It's the worst pain I've ever felt. Tears flow as I scream out.

Tam's giant hands grab hold of me.

"Shen! What's wrong?" he yells.

"I don't know!" I growl, teeth clenched. My skin burns like hot iron is pressed against it. Tam kneels beside my curled body. I cry out again, writhing in agony, ripping at my tunic. The burning spreads across my entire torso. Tears flow freely. My hands and feet turn clammy, and my limbs feel cold. I feel myself losing consciousness, unable to reason what is happening.

"Shen, what is it?" Tam's voice shakes.

I'm in too much pain to answer, vaguely aware of the activity around me.

Tam barks orders. "Grab his arms. I'll grab his feet."

My muscles contract protectively, locking my arms in place. The excruciating pain causes me to pull my knees into my arms involuntarily. Strong hands hold my ankles town, preventing the motion. Another set of hands pulls at my arms. I resist, but the collective strength overcomes my locked muscles. Tears roll down the sides of my face into my ears as the hands roll me onto my back. My muscles strain against the weight of Tamrin and Jesmir while Jesma kneels beside me and gently opens my tunic.

"Fildeus' curse!" Tamrin says.

"What is it?" I croak, my jaw locked.

"Shen, you need to open your eyes and look," Tam says.

I try, but the pain is so intense I start to hyperventilate. Shooting stars fly through my vision. My body tingles as, once again, I find myself slipping into unconsciousness. I struggle to open my eyes against the pain. It's like burning embers are buried inside my chest.

Tam speaks quietly, "Shen, it'll be all right. Stay with me, okay?"

I nod violently and force myself into the box breathing technique I learned when I was in my twenties. After four breaths, the tingling subsides. As does the pain. But there's no getting used to this sensation, so I grit my teeth and open my eyes.

The center of my chest glows bright red. Directly over my sternum, an inflamed handprint, raised and illuminated by an internal light, shines, revealing subcutaneous blood vessels.

Jesma gasps in shock.

"You've been marked," Tamrin says.

"I've been what?"

"Grankin's placed his mark on you. I've heard stories but never actually seen one. Gods mark you if they lay claim to you. It's said their mark means they can find you anywhere, anytime. I've only heard they are used to uphold a promise. To ensure you live up to the commitment you made. What did you promise?"

I shake my head. "I have never spoken to a god!"

"You just did," Jesma says.

I look at her, confused.

Tamrin gives me a wry look. "Whatever he asked of you, it must be done. You'll have no choice. He'll make you suffer if you don't."

"Who?" I cry, gritting my teeth.

"Grankin," Tamrin whispers.

"Grankin? The God of Time?" I question. "What the…" My voice fails me.

Shit.

Rotten luck. Some believe at the bottom of The Great Rankin sits… it dawns on me.

Grankin? Great Rankin? How have I never put that together before?

"Damn, this hurts," I moan.

My life sucks.

I take a few more breaths as Tamrin towers over me. From this vantage point, Tam seems like a giant. Even Jesma and Jesmir, their thinner and lighter frames, seem large from down here.

"You are one mountain of a man, Tam," I mumble.

Tam snorts a laugh and turns to the others. "Yup. He's okay.".

I'm unsure how long I've been lying here, but it's long enough.

"It's not so bad now," I say as I close my eyes, holding up a hand. "I need a minute."

"Gather your thoughts?" Tam jests. I can't help but smile, even in pain.

"Jerk."

He laughs.

"You're gonna be fine," he says and helps me stand.

"Wait, if he really is a god, then why the hell does he need me?" I ask.

"The gods do what the gods do," Tamrin replies.

"That's a convenient answer."

He slaps my back as I bend over and catch my breath, the sound announcing how much the impact stings. I wince, building up the courage to walk again. Three shadows pass as the twins and Tamrin head out along the river toward the highway. Tamrin mumbles, "Even in the face of evidence," as he passes. I right myself, take one last deep breath, and hurry to catch up, walking behind the odd party of escaped victims, the tracker hunting them, and a rescuer without a clue.

A few minutes pass before I speak. "They're just bedtime stories. Gods aren't real."

The trio of believers exchange glances, an unspoken affirmation that the collective thinks I'm insane. I know what they think. We were all there and witnessed the same events.

"Doesn't make him a god," I mumble.

I rub my burning chest as I trail behind. It doesn't help, but I can't stop myself.

"Tell that to the mark on your chest, buddy," Tamrin says, his deep laugh carrying through the woods.

I'm in too much pain to argue. The sting of two handprints is the story of my life. If looks could kill, Tamrin would spontaneously combust where he stood. I button my shirt, the cool air causing me to shiver again. I drag my feet to catch up, too tired to put much effort into the task. In the distance, the bridge over the Great Rankin River beckons us, silhouetted by the distant twilight of the western sky. We should reach it before full dark, and at this point, I want out of these woods and away from this damned river.

God of Time. Grankin, and a burning handprint. If gods are real, I intend to kill one before I die.

What the hell have I gotten myself into?

Walking the King's Regal Highway, I find my thoughts linger on the idea of fear. I don't suffer from it often and never in a fight. It's always a more emotional experience. But I'm feeling it now, and it's definitely primal.

The pain from Grankin's mark, while significantly better, pounds against my psyche. At its peak, I thought I was dying. I have no desire to die writhing in excruciating pain. Thankfully, the burning sensation is little more than a bad sunburn now. I can concentrate on more important matters, the pain reduced to an nuisance.

Questions without ready answers form.

What the hell did I just commit to? Was that indeed Grankin? When am I supposed to do this job? Do I have a timetable to meet? Where am I supposed to find this tome? How can I retrieve it? What comes first, returning the twins home safely or acquiring the tome?

"What do you think Grankin meant by 'they'll lose time'?" Jesma asks while we walk.

"I'm not sure," I reply. Another question lingers as painfully as the handprint on my chest. "It has me thinking about memories. For a moment, you weren't even a vague memory. You were more like a ghost."

She contemplates my response before speaking again. "I remember wondering who you were, and then it was like a veil was removed, and I was suddenly glad you were there. It was like I knew but didn't know." She trails off on the last word.

"It's difficult to wrap my mind around. Memories lost and regained. When they were lost, I didn't know they were lost. But when they returned..."

"You thought, 'Hey, how did I not know that'?" she interrupts. Nodding in affirmation, I reply, "Exactly."

"That still doesn't explain how they will lose time."

"Grankin controls time. He moves up and down the river as he sees fit, able to move himself and anyone with him, forward or backward in time," Jesmir chimes from behind.

"How do you mean?" I ask.

"It's easy. The river flows in the opposite direction of time but in sync with it. Swim downriver faster than the current, and you can move backward in time. Swim against the current, and you can move forward in time."

"How would you know that?" I ask incredulously.

"He's a scholar," Jesma says. "One of the brightest."

"You mean they teach you how the river works in school?" Tamrin asks.

"No. However, the concept of time and its relative relationship to position, point of view, and even speed matter. Especially speed. We learn that much. It's rooted in the methods of time magic, speed magic, and even teleportation magic," Jesmir says.

"Are you a wizard?" Tamrin asks.

Jesmir doesn't answer at first.

"He's struggling with his faith." Jesma's tender words elicit a wry smile from her brother.

"I'm not struggling with my faith," he says. "The gods don't grant me access to magic. I studied it at university to see if I could understand it and figure out why."

"Don't worry," I reply. "I don't have access to magic, and I get by just fine."

He doesn't reply. We continue on in silence for a while again, and I retreat into my head, contemplating whether I believe that Grankin could be real. It's not a trivial concern. If Jesmir is correct, there seems to be at least a little truth to the idea of "The God of Time." If he is, then that means there could be literal gods.

Have I been wrong all this time? What about that trick with the river when he trapped me? That was no small trick. It wasn't an illusion.

I shiver again. This time, it is definitely psychological. The river crashed down rather painfully. Grankin, if that is who he is, seems to like his games.

That's the telltale behavior of the so-called gods.

This thought stresses me out.

But these questions, whether benign or existential, can't overshadow the question I most don't understand. It's the one I've been avoiding. Grankin's most unsettling comment suggested I had control over something.

What, in Quietius' shadow, do I have control of? I have no control. I've been thrust into these events.

I don't even have control over my own life or death. Every attempt to take my life has been interfered with by one interruption or another. Six scars up and down my arms provide evidence of that.

We walk in silence for miles. The collective discomfort of wet clothes offers the only motivation to continue. The promise of an end to our discomfort at an inn in Valshannon beckons. Tam speaks, but I'm lost in thought, so I miss it at first.

"What's that?"

"I said I can't believe I didn't recognize him."

"Who?"

"Brogen. I had no idea he wasn't who he said he was. He wasn't the one who hired me. One of the others did. A woman." he says.

"How could you not recognize him, Tam? He's the most unattractive human in the world," I fire back.

"I've never met the man!" he growls.

I realize I'm angry and taking it out on him, but my emotions are in a frenzy. I've lashed out unfairly in frustration. My encounter with Grankin and this mark on my chest makes me think my worldview may have been shattered.

But I'm cold, wet, and angry, so I don't really care if I hurt the big guy's feelings.

"I'm sorry, Shen. I'd never deliberately take a job from the likes of that man. I'm no mercenary. You know that." He addresses the siblings. "They said you two had murdered three guards and stole an object of great value." Jesma comes to a halt. I turn to look at her while Tamrin speaks. "He also said you were fleeing to Teshket by way of Valshannon. The Mayor of Dresdin signed the warrant, complete with the mayoral seal."

Jesma and Jesmir look horrified by the accusations.

"I'd never hurt anyone who wasn't trying to hurt me or Jesma," Jesmir says in dismay. "Hell, I'm not even good at that," he mumbles.

Jesma looks at me, eyes pleading. "We did no such thing! I wouldn't hurt anyone!"

"Well, you better start," I say sarcastically.

Tamrin gives me a disapproving look. I shrug. He shakes his head and turns to the twins. Gentle eyes study the two waterlogged fugitives. Anyone with even the smallest amount of people skills can see it's no more possible the twins are cold-blooded killers than I am a priest. Whatever the reason Brogen is after these two, it's not for any criminal mischief on their part.

"Of that, I have no doubt," Tamrin says. "After stumbling across the campsite, something didn't sit well with me. I was even more sure when Kairn drew his sword and asked me to help him kill you both. You didn't behave like any violent criminals I ever met." He looks to me, "I would have never let anything happen to them 'til we arrived at the magistrate's office."

"I know," I say, touching his chest. "I'm glad to have you alongside me, as always, old friend."

His penitent grin makes me smile. Tamrin has a compassion level I lack, and I've always admired him for it.

I turn to the twins. "We've shared more than a few adventures together. Watched each other's backs in many fights. This guy here offers a level of comfort I need right now," I say. "He's loyal to a fault. Even when I'm wrong, he has my back. He'd pitch a fit, but he always stands beside me."

I smile back at him, my heart bleeding a bit.

"Let's keep moving. No sense in wasting the time we have chit-chatting here."

My thoughts drift over to Tamrin as we continue up the King's Regal Highway. The poor guy has loved me for years. He doesn't know I'm aware of his feelings. He keeps them to himself, but I noticed how he looked at me almost a decade ago. He's never outright expressed it, but I catch him sometimes and see a longing like I carried for my first love. I remember when I was younger, unrequited feelings for a girl who saw me as only a friend. I told her how I felt, and she stopped speaking to me the next day.

If Tam ever told me, I'd be kind but firm, and I'd still be his best friend.

Even though he knows we'd still be friends, he'll never say it out loud.

Exhaustion grips us. Jesma stumbles, and I catch her. Her momentum spins her until we face each other. He smile when our eyes meet sets my inside aflutter and I fight to suppress a smile of my own.

"I know what killers look like," I say to her. "You two are not that." Her cheeks flush a soft pink, and I look over her head and clear my throat. "You need a rest?"

"No, I'm fine, just didn't pick up my foot enough."

As we pick up the pace, I'm left thinking about the stain of death that lingers on killers. It's a stain that emanates from the soul— a putrid rot festering over time.

I carry that stain. The twins do not. I look at the twins in curiosity.

Satisfied that neither Tam nor I mean them harm, the twins visibly relax. Tamrin nods, and we start walking again. I push the pace. Tamrin steps up to me, and Jesma slows down to be beside her brother. Tamrin fidgets, and his movements become distracting. I can't help but think he's wrestling with guilt over blindly accepting the tracker job.

I tap his arm, seeking to get out of my own head. "You okay?"

"You killed the four men in the forest?"

I cringe, the comment catching me by surprise.

"Yeah, that was my handiwork."

"Yours are the tracks I saw leaving the clearing a half day or so back," he states, squinting at me.

Dread grips me. Tamrin's so good at reasoning evidence out. I feared this when Jesma called me out back at the river. There's a reason Brogen's team hired him, and there's no point in denying his statement. I shrug.

"What happened?"

"Bandits doing what bandits do when they find a young woman and a lone escort hiding in the woods. They picked the wrong place at the wrong time."

He nods, understanding my meaning and why I don't say more. I resist a glance back at Jesma.

"Those men got what they deserved," I say.

"Aye. That they did."

He shakes his head and points at me. I'm sure the siblings missed it, but Tamrin's no dummy. He's drawing a conclusion.

"I have questions for you," he says, his tone clear enough. "But they'll wait. Now isn't the time."

He lifts the talisman tied to his beard and kisses it. It's his periapt of Fildeus, the Wild Huntress.

"We need her help if we wish to avoid those who hunt us. Brogen's team is very serious about finding these two before they reach Teshket," he whispers.

He says another silent prayer, kisses the talisman again, and lays it gently against his chest. I'll never understand these people and their gods. My thoughts must show on my face because Tamrin stares at me with a disapproving look.

"After all that, you still doubt?" he says.

I go to rebuff him and think better of it.

"What?" he says, daring me to let loose a smart-ass comment.

"Never mind," I say. "It's just… nothing."

Magic. Grankin's power is magic, not some god power. He must be a mage.

But he didn't use a periapt like everyone else. A shiver runs down my spine. My chest stings. Doubts creep in.

"I've watched you in combat how many times? Twenty?

More?" Tam asks out of nowhere.

I shrug, "Sounds about right. Why?"

He glances back Jesmir and Jesma, a slight smirk on his face.

"You heard of The Harbinger?" he asks them.

Shit.

"The ghost of the Rhine Woods?" Jesmir asks.

Tamrin casts a sideways glance my way.

He points at me, and my hearts skip beats. I feel the prickly sensations in my body intensify. It's fight or flight, and I'm forcing myself not to flee. He's discovered the secret I've held for decades and wants me to know it. I wish he knew how much I hate that title.

"This guy is almost as good," he says.

Maybe he doesn't know! I fight my elation from showing and keep my head forward, focused on the road. Unbeknownst to my friend, he's set my mind in motion on a new obsessive thought. Several miles later, I'm still thinking about that name, and I realize Tamrin may not have let me off the hook.

I sneak a glance, and he's noticeably not looking at me. The name rings in my head repeatedly.

Harbinger.

Harbinger.

Harbinger.

Whoever created that moniker for me will get slapped if I ever meet them.

At least Tam didn't call me Quietius the Second.

I would have killed him where he stood. Slowly.

Chapter Nine

Journal Entry:34

It is my steadfast opinion a vast majority of people cause much of their own suffering despite the cruelty of their false gods.

What of the rest of the suffering that is not self-inflicted? There are those out there bent on making others suffer. I'll never understand it from their perspective. It's a level of malevolence I can't allow to go unchecked, though.

Hmm, it's hard not to see myself as a hypocrite. I do punish those I feel need to be punished.

If I were forced to give a purpose to my existence, I guess the best answer would be to meet out cruelty to the cruel, mercy to the merciful, and kindness to the kind. Doing the job the gods are supposed to do. I don't like it when one person causes another's suffering. I don't like seeing suffering. Not yours, not mine.

Why all this talk about suffering? I'm hungry... woefully so.

Interesting story... or maybe not so interesting. A while back, I tried to starve myself to death. It was punishment I delivered on myself for harming someone that didn't deserve it. It was a long time ago.

Many years ago, my choices caused someone else to suffer horribly. Not always does my interference improve lives.

I helped the wrong person. Misjudged a moment and rescued someone who should have died. Others suffered later as a result.

It sent me into a despair spiral I couldn't escape. It is one of the reasons I struggle with self-loathing. I don't think that guilt will ever leave me. It's a part of me now. I carry a lot of guilt. I've made choices I can't take back.

I honestly don't know if I deserve peace.

Chaffed Thighs, Taxis, and a Tall Tale

I'm grumpy now. We all are. We move on willpower alone. Twilight released its hold on the day, the cold darkness of night erased the last bit of color from the sky. Night settled, so the Ezra isn't heating the humid air. The resultant drop in temperature, however, leaves us shivering in our wet clothes.

A few wagons passed by, but none were large enough to hitch a ride. We've occasionally passed the slower foot traffic of travelers on the highway, but it's relatively uncrowded. If not for our soaked clothes and shear exhaustion the journey would be easy. But we are tired.

Signs we are close to Valshannon appeared a mile back. Guard towers keep this portion of the RhineWoods safe every quarter mile and provide assurance the city is near.

A young man pulling a fruit cart comes into view, and we rush to catch him and buy a few pears. I don't hesitate to bite into the ripe fruit. Juice runs down my chin. The sweet aroma and light flavor are one of my favorites. I made Tamrin pay since he took half the payment to track the twins up front. I told him it was punishment for his lack of savvy. Besides, I'm broke again.

Yet I'm still grumpy. It's everything.

My chest still stings, my clothes are soaked, the humid night prevents our clothes from drying off, and the temperature has dropped further into a constant chill. Fall is here. I shiver and my feet hurt from wet shoes and socks. My thighs are chaffed.

Every body part below the neck hurts.

Yet, gods want me to believe they are real. I'm stubborn. I'll need more than a magic trick, a little time dilation, and a handprint to convince me.

Call me cynical.

Correction, all this thinking has given me a headache.

It's official, everything hurts.

A guard calls out from the tower ahead. "Hear one and all! By order of the Council of Valshannon, any person wishing to spend the night within the safety of the walls must be inside the gates before the evening bell sounds. You have twenty minutes!"

It's the closing call. We are dangerously short on time. Valshannon closes its gates at night, and we have to hurry if we want to have the best chance of avoiding Brogen and finding a decent night's rest. Our best bet is any one of the inns inside Valshannon's walls. But to get to one of those, we need to be inside the gates before the change of guard is complete. No one gets into Valshannon at night without a writ of entry.

All we have is a set of siblings with a warrant out on them.

I hope the word hasn't reached this far north yet.

As we pass the tower, a small contingent of guards climbs down the ladder and exchanges words with a fresh troop. I watch as they fall into formation with military precision. The guard captain sounds a cadence call, and the returning troops begin their march toward Valshannon, their pace moderate.

I wave the others on and force them to stay ahead of the contingent of guards. Behind us, panicked voices and frantic footsteps ring out from travelers eager to pass the guards to avoid a night locked outside the city walls as a result of the guards making their way back to the barracks inside the city walls ahead of them. The pace makes my thighs, calves, and shins hurt. Fatigue is a liability, and we've reached our limits. Every one of us has been on the run for over eighteen hours.

Tamrin lags behind, but I'm unsure if it's tactical or he's so heavily waterlogged that he's running solely on willpower. I hear him stumble every once in a while, so I settle on tired. Jesmir does his best, but I can see he hasn't fully healed, and his gate grows clumsier as we go.

My brother, if he were alive, would say we are dragging ass.

Up ahead, the welcome glow of light illuminates a tall stone structure. The noise of human activity echoes off the trees lining the King's Regal Highway, raising our spirits slightly. A quarter mile further, the bazaar outside of the walls of Valshannon comes into view, with dark shadows against the backdrop of the gaping maw of the southern entrance to the massive city.

Vendors close shutters on their little shops or place canvases over carts of vegetables, fruits, and wares as we approach. Some have already started wheeling their carts back inside the city walls.

Valshannon, its hexagon-shaped sixty-foot-tall, forty-foot-wide stone wall, is intimidating from the outside. Six main gates, each at the center of their leg of the perfectly symmetrical city, are the only ways in and out. Another wonder of the engineering skills of Rhinestab is that each gate is a series of three iron portcullises, protected in front with large wooden doors that swing in.

These massive hand-carved doors are only the beginning of the marvel these entries into the city represent. The road begins a steady decline as we reach the entrance, running under the walls, not through. Master crafts folk of all trades worked together to build and secure these tunnels from enemies. Forty feet wide and over one hundred feet long, the main portals are a series of gates.

All traps to invaders.

As we head down the long slope underground, an ornate dragon's mouth threatens to swallow us, the first of the three portcullises protruding like teeth from the dragon's mouth. The entry is meant to inspire awe and project fear. For invading armies, it works.

Master masons, engineers, carpenters, and iron workers are in high demand in Valshannon. The largest city in the Five Realms, Valshannon boasts over one hundred thousand citizens and a thirty thousand boot garrison. It's the most defensible city ever built.

The tunnels can be filled with water or tar on command. Passing through the gates, the scale of it all only impresses or intimidates more up close.

No one knows if the city was built in the woods or if the woods grew around the city. Legend says Valshannon is over one thousand years old. In any event, the Rhine Woods create yet another obstacle for any would-be attackers. That leaves the only direct lines of attack as the main roads leading into one of the six gates. It's a naturally designed bottleneck.

Attacking armies have a hell of a time against Valshannon. Even if they could get through the first gate, the large doors above would release the hidden fluids, drowning invaders in a sudden water flood. Or worse, covered in tar only to be attacked with fire as they come out the other side.

The city engineers keep improving the design.

Valshannon has never fallen to an enemy in its thousand-year history, partly because of its location. Mostly because they constantly reinvent their defenses, staying ahead of modern siege technology.

The guards wave us in as we approach the main gates, eager to get the first gate closed. The ever-growing garrison of troops behind us echo as they enter the city gates, marching in solid formation. The shift change is nearly completed, and it's not hard to imagine that they're ready to call it a day.

"Gates closing in two minutes!" one yells.

Walking through the main gates, I look up at the pointed tips of the portcullis. They are as big around as Tam. The image of one piercing my body makes me think that would be a quick death. I imagine dying that way. Outside of the initial horror of seeing it coming, I don't think I'd mind. If it didn't kill me, or worse, completely missed, the thought of burning covered in flaming tar or drowning in dark water gives me shivers.

The intimidating entry transitions to one of the most welcoming cities in the Five Realms. At night, the town lights up like fireworks in a darkened sky. Gas lamps line the streets, while candles and lanterns light up the interior of residents' open shops and homes. Stores open well into the night to invite visitors from all over the world to shop and enjoy after the gates close. Music from buskers mixes and mingles into a delightfully confusing chorus of competing tunes as the street musicians vie for attention and tips. The orchestral onslaught of the musicians plays a chaotically entrancing tune. The shopkeepers voices an accoutrement to the musical notes as they announce sales of food and supplies, trinkets and gadgets, or potions and wards.

A priest of Shamna stands at an alley entrance, his table a jumble of coins and thrown dice, as gamblers stand around cheering each other on, tossing money on the table, trying their luck with Shamna Rocks.

Each of the six gates into Valshannon is identical. They dump visitors into one of the six Valshannon Propers, the name of the local main streets meant to separate visitors from their money. It's a well-designed concept. I can enter from any gate and find whatever I want without walking across the city.

It's so thoroughly thought out after a thousand years that most citizens of Valshannon never leave their little sector, finding all they ever need within their own neighborhoods. I'm grateful for that.

To walk clear across the city would take more than half a day. Worse still, while the first four streets run concentrically to the outer wall, the inner streets transition into a random maze specifically designed to confuse and intimidate visitors from other realms or cities.

Valshannon's governmental infrastructure is mingled in a maze of residential and financial buildings on streets with no discernible pattern through the center of the sprawling metropolis. Invading troops, if they make it past the defenses of the incredible outer wall, which is unlikely, find themselves hopelessly lost within moments, running into each other, picked off by well-hidden bowmen strategically placed throughout the inner city's layout.

Technology aside, Valshannon is Rhinestab's central hub of commerce. Currency exchange, banking, craftsmanship, and most importantly, drink.

Citizens of Valshannon are pretty proud of their drink. Mead, Cider, Ale, Wine, or Hooch, whatever a visitor's preference, Valshannon makes, sells, and exports it. The center-most street, the last of the hexagonal roads before the confusion of the governmental maze, is home to every brew house, meadery, cider house, pub, and tavern. It is made on that street if it is brewed, fermented, or distilled.

Swill Street.

I turn to Tam, "You know. Assuming an invading army did make it this far, I imagine they'd fall prey to their own vices and never make the central hub."

"Imagine being that commander," he replies. "We took the city! The hooch is ours!"

"We've conquered the city! Let's Kill the Swill!"

The thought makes me giggle.

Great, I'm so tired I'm punchy.

A popular pastime in Valshannon, called "Kill the Swill," is little more than an ambitious pub crawl whose ultimate goal is to partake in one drink at each pub and mill about the entire perimeter of Swill Street in a single night. Participants start and end at the same pub without returning to any establishment twice or try to anyway. Participants pick a starting point and go.

Everyone has tried it.

One famous Korund, Godot "The Sot," is the only one to ever make it. That was over one hundred years ago. It's a legend that can't be proven, but it lives on as motivation for everyone. There's one tavern named "Sot's Spot," reportedly his starting and ending point.

A statue of Sot holding a tankard of ale with a big drunken smile on his face welcomes all who pass. Its sole purpose is to entice passersby to spend money at the supposed legendary place of the only one to ever "Kill the Swill."

That's not where we are headed.

Unfortunately, or fortunately. Tam and I can never resist a challenge.

But we are headed to Swill Street. That is unfortunate because it's a hike. I could sleep where I stand right now.

Tamrin taps me on the shoulder.

I turn to him, and he hands me a copper coin.

"What's this?"

He points at a horse-pulled wagon.

"Taxi. I can't walk anymore." He indicates to the siblings. "Them either."

Atop the wagon sits a man in a brown cloak and a strange, wide-brimmed, bright orange hat. Three purple feathers stick out of the top like an odd peacock. Resting on his forehead are strange goggles made of leather and brass. He looks like he's on his way to a costume party.

"The chauffeur? I don't understand," I say. Tamrin shakes his head like I'm an idiot. "Why are you looking at me like that? Did I suddenly sprout three heads?"

His sigh suggests I might be stupid as he snatches the coin back and walks over to the man in the carriage. They chat as Tamrin indicates in our direction.

That confirms it. I'm dumb.

No, I'm tired.

The man in the silly-looking orange hat nods. Tamrin waves us over as he climbs into the carriage. I follow Jesma and Jesmir. Jesmir climbs up first, and I help Jesma, accidentally pressing on her backside as I do. I withdraw my hand as my cheeks flush, self-consciously biting my lower lip.

"I'm sorry," I whisper.

She smiles and says, "It's okay."

I can't tell with the dirt and the low light, but I think she blushed, too. Jesmir frowns at me as he climbs into the cab. I follow after him and do my best not to look at either of them, self-conscious over the odd sensation I feel from touching Jesma.

I catch her watching me, and we divert our eyes. More blood rushes to my cheeks as I try to settle in, feeling awkward as racy thoughts work their way into my imagination. I shove the thoughts away.

Great. I'm attracted to her. Inappropriate, Shen, in-a-propri-ate.

Tam leans over to me and says, "He'll give us a ride to the Jesting Pot Inn. That's directly across Swill Street from the Dead Eye Pub."

I let out a massive sigh of relief.

Maybe the gods are real?

I still doubt it, but I thank them anyway.

Jesma leans on her brother, struggling to keep her eyes open. I use the opportunity to sneak a glance at her, drawn to her by some unseen force. She opens her eyes, catching me in the act. I look away as she quickly shuts her eyes. My stomach does a little flip.

Definitely not appropriate.

Jesmir stares at the passing buildings and pedestrians, but I'm pretty sure he isn't seeing them.

Tamrin is glad to be off his feet.

"I could get used to this," I sigh.

He laughs.

"You've never taken a taxi?" he asks.

I shake my head.

"The thought never occurred to me." I watch the pedestrians as we pass and mumble, "To be honest, I never knew that's what these guys were. I thought they were chauffeurs for royals."

Tamrin busts out in a booming laugh, slapping me on the knee.

"Well, my friend, you need to learn to enjoy the finer things in life. Like not having to walk everywhere all the time."

"I don't walk everywhere. Sometimes I get transported by a psychotic gnome on a river of time," I say as I rub my chest.

He slaps his knee as his big laugh booms louder, startling some poor, unsuspecting pedestrians as we pass.

I won't lie. My leg stings now, too. That's three handprints on my skin. Maybe I'll start a collection.

It's different tonight.

Either I'm too tired to think, or I'm concerned I'll let down the people counting on me. I don't know exactly what I'm supposed to be doing, but here I am. Too exhausted for conversation, too tired to eat, and fed up with being wet, my routine thoughts of anger and despair are not overwhelming me at the moment.

It's quiet in this too large suite on the top floor of the Jester's Pot Inn. Two sets of strangers strip down to bare skin in an awkward silence, tired, achy, and still wet. At least the bulk of the water is gone, mitigating the need to mop up puddles from the hardwood floor. Firelight flickers around a well-decorated room. The massive, intricate fireplace pops and sizzles as shadows dance everywhere.

I find it hard not to look at Jesma as she undresses, so I turn to angle my sightline at a corner, but in the attempt, we lock eyes, catching each other's naked bodies. Once again, blood rushes to my face, and I snap my eyes to my targeted corner, frozen like a hunted animal who saw its hunter. I look around for a blanket to wrap myself in, but I'm awkward. I'm pretty sure I look like a pervert who's been caught in the act of peeping.

My heart sinks.

What the hell is wrong with you, Shen?

I grab the blanket from the back of the armchair, wrap it around my shoulders, turn to the fireplace, and slump down into the cushioned seat. Tamrin, a blanket draped over him like a cape, stokes the fire while I sulk in the warmth of the hearth. His blanket, almost too small to hide his private parts, forces him to squat awkwardly. His exposed hairy legs indicate he could be part bear, and I snicker at his predicament.

A shadow passes over me, cast by a blanket-wrapped form and the fire, as Jesma walks to the long couch and sits at the end farthest from me. I resist a glance in her direction, which only serves to generate more self-consciousness. Seeing her bare skin before she wrapped herself in a blanket opened the door for thoughts I wished to avoid. A small part of me thinks I saw her smile, but I was too embarrassed to look at her. I tell myself it was my imagination running away with me. If I'm honest, I've been distracted by her since the moment I took the lives of her attackers. Images and thoughts of her haven't stopped tumbling around in my mind since the moment I met her.

Visions of the effervescent makeup covering random spots on her body, smudges of glitter and color sparkling from the sun yesterday, and the fire tonight refuse to release their hold on me. I've never seen anyone like her.

This is the reason I left her in the woods. It honestly didn't have to do with timing at all. She makes me uncomfortably self-aware. Tamrin makes his way to the end of the couch closest to me as Jesmir sits beside his sister. Lost in our individual thoughts, wrestling with too many open questions from the day, four sets of eyes gaze at the flames dancing around the burning logs. My eyes grow heavy.

I pull the blanket around my chin, slink lower in the chair, and focus on getting warm.

Jesma yawns, drawing my sideways glance. I look back to the fire when she stands.

"Goodnight," she says, her voice soft and quiet.

Tam and Jesmir say goodnight. Like an idiot, I keep my eyes directed at the fire. I have the subtly of a wild boar. She hovers at the edge of my vision, waiting, but I don't trust myself to glance in her direction. She pads off quietly, and her brother rises from his spot and follows. I close my eyes and take a slow, quiet breath.

Tamrin backhands my knee, grabbing my attention. The stark contrast between his appearance and Jesma's causes me to smirk. If she is the most beautiful person I have ever seen, Tamrin would be the most burly. No matter how many times I see it, I'm awestruck. His body hair is so thick I almost can't see his pale skin. If not for his cheeks, forehead, and hands, I might have thought we shared my copper-brown skin tone.

No wonder he is comfortable in furs. He is covered in fur even when he isn't wearing his trophies.

I lean back and glance around the room. The Jesting Pot Inn doesn't jest when it comes to hospitality. For thirty gold apiece, which Jesma paid for with a Realm Note, we received their finest room and, for an extra gold, a bottle of red wine.

A large painting with a dragon perched at the top of the mountain, a brilliant sunset behind, adorns the wall opposite me. I admire the work, transfixed by the image of the dragon, creatures rumored to roam Conishant thousands of years ago. The frame, inlaid with gold leaf, looks hand carved. It's one of the most expensive paintings I've ever seen. Behind me, the nighttime sounds of Swill Street echo softly, five stories below through the two windows flanking the room's long wall.

With two large beds, a six-seat table, two large dressers, and nightstands, this sitting area comprises the entire room's furnishings. All well-crafted, all exquisite, all cozy and warm.

"This is the nicest place I've ever slept," I whisper.

Tamrin sips from the bottle of wine and passes it to me.

"Aye, I imagine it is. I've never stayed in a room like this either."

"This floor only has two rooms. It's secure since the other one is on the other side of the main stairs."

"Yeah. At least footsteps outside our door mean only one thing."

I nod, sipping the bottle and passing it back, glancing back at the door to verify I applied both deadbolts. I'm unusually paranoid. I've never played the role of bodyguard before.

"I don't like the look the innkeeper gave when Jesma pulled out the Realm Notes," I whisper.

"You caught that?" Tam takes a sip of wine. "Yeah, of course you did."

As I look back at the siblings, I hear the gentle rhythmic breathing, indicating the first stages of sleep. I stare at Jesma, curled in a ball under the blanket closest to the windows.

"You check the windows?" Tam asks.

"Yeah. Windows are secure."

Jesmir, in the bed furthest from the window, lays sprawled out, one arm and one leg dangling off the bed.

"Clearly, he has no fear at the moment."

Tamrin snickers.

Satisfied, I settle in and wrap the blanket tight around my naked body. I look at my best friend, stretched on the couch, in his naked glory, his blanket barely covering his genitals.

It's kinda disturbing how hairy this man is.

"You are one hairy son-of-a-bitch, ya know?"

He laughs as he takes a big swig of wine and extends his thick tree trunk of a forearm my way. I accept the bottle, pull an equally large swig, and pass it back. He places it on the floor between us.

"You remember when you convinced me to shave it off in Gal-Danang?"

I giggle too loud, and he shushes me.

"I itched for weeks after that. Never again."

"I never thought you'd actually do it. Did I ever tell you it was a bet between my and Brinker? He said there was no way you'd do it."

He laughs. "You're a dick. But yeah, he told me afterwards."

We giggle at the memory and fall into silence as we watch the fire catch a sap pocket and spew a noisy plume of flame.

"I'm glad you followed after us," he says softly after a moment's silence.

"It's lucky I did."

He ponders that. Then looks over at me.

"I can't believe I didn't know you're the Harbinger."

Ugh. That name.

I look at him sideways. I want to deny it, but we know each other too well. My last secret from the man who's risked his life for me too many times is free. I go to speak, but he holds up a hand, stopping me.

"You can keep up the act," he whispers, "but I've known you, what, fifteen years?"

I nod. "Almost, yeah."

"In all those years, I've witnessed you fight some pretty impressive fights, but I was always struck by how you fought, or rather how you didn't."

"How's that, again?"

"You always look like you are holding back. Like you're afraid to go all in. Like you're afraid you'll lose control. I mean, I've always known you were good. I never cared because you never lost a fight. I mean, I suppose if I think about it, I always knew the truth because it didn't surprise me when it dawned on me earlier. It just never occurred to me you were *that* good."

I scowl into my blanket and squeeze my eyes shut.

"Shen," he says, bumping my knee with his elbow. "Seriously. Remember that fight escorting the old merchant from Old Town to Charger's Wharf? What was it, nine of them against you and me?"

I remember that fight and wince, knowing where this conversation is headed.

"You had four down before I unleashed my hammer. It happened so fast that I never saw it. I looked up, ready to engage, and saw four of the raiders dead on the ground. You said it was a lucky day. I've replayed that fight over and over so many times."

"I guess I've suspected since that fight." He pauses. A comfortable silence rests between us. "I saw the bodies in the forest this morning, and I knew it was the work of the Harbinger. There were a lot of footsteps from one guy. The other three? They didn't fight. Four on one and three never got a chance to turn around? Definitely the Harbinger."

He is the absolute best at reading tracks. Too good for my good.

"I figure only the Harbinger can do that. You showed up so fast today. That solidified it for me. I thought to myself, 'If Shen shows up, that will confirm it for me.'" He falls silent again. "I figured if it was you that left the bodies, then it was you who saved these two. Then, I remembered our conversation last night and drew a simple conclusion. If you were their rescuer, you wouldn't let them get hurt.

I even slowed my pace so you could catch up."

I shake my head at him. "It scares me how good you are."

"I wish you had told me. It kinda stings. I thought we trusted one another."

The fire crackles and pops. Sparks fly up the chimney.

"I hate that title."

He looks at me. No change in his demeanor or expression. "Why?"

He doesn't care. He's only upset that I never told him after all this time.

"Do you know where it originated?"

He looks at me and shakes his head, grabbing the bottle and drinking. Red wine slips down his beard toward his ear.

It's hard for me to discuss. No one alive knows the origin. I don't want to tell my friend the truth. It's a horrible story. I committed terrible acts to earn that title. Some of them righteously so, but still horrible. But I also don't want him calling me Harbinger all the time, and he's right. I should have told him. By now, I shouldn't have kept that from him. I look over at the twins to ensure they're asleep and drop my voice to barely a whisper.

"Thirty-nine years ago, the day before my thirteenth birthday, my mother sold me to the Assassin's Guild in Teshket."

He sits up, his eyes wide. His elbows rest on his knees, and the blanket falls to the floor. I shake my head. He looks like he has a third leg, and now I am uncomfortable. My raised eyebrow makes him aware, and he covers himself with the blanket, his pale skin turning a bright shade of pink.

"Seriously?"

He shrugs with a laugh and begins to speak. I raise my hand, arresting his comment before he starts.

"I didn't want to go." I continue the story. "She didn't care. My brother died in the plague of Ditherun Village. That's where I was born."

I pause. I haven't spoken of this since the Guild. Only the Journeyman to whom I was sold and the Guildmaster knew my full name and place of birth. I am entering unknown territory here.

To his credit, Tamrin waits quietly. He hands me the bottle. I sit straight and accept the offer, holding it absently.

"For a year, I tried to escape. The journeymen caught me every time. Which was a surprise to me, my unique traits considered."

He looks at me, confused.

"Unique traits considered?"

"Yeah, you know what I'm talking about."

He shakes his head, "Not sure what you mean."

"You haven't noticed?"

"Noticed what?"

"Seriously?" I ask in surprise.

"What are you talking about?"

I stand and walk around, looking at him expectantly, flapping the blanket like a bat.

"What am I looking for?"

I stop and point to my ear.

"Listen," I say.

I do it again.

He shakes his head.

"I don't hear anything."

I flip an empty palm in his direction in affirmation.

"I don't get it," he says.

"Seriously? You spend much time around people who make no sound when they move?" I spit out.

"Wellllll… nooo… but I figured you were just that good. I mean, I was always impressed by it. But, uhm, it never occurred to me you weren't doing it on purpose."

"How else would I be doing it? This isn't the kind of silence someone practices."

"I'd say magic, but you don't have a patron. I guess I don't know. But still, I thought you simply mastered the art of silent movement."

Sitting on the couch, I flap the corner of the blanket in an attempt to make noise.

His eyes widen in realization.

"I can't believe I never noticed."

"I've never made a sound when I move. It drove my mom insane."

"Never?"

"Never, ever."

He inhales a slow breath in realization.

"See. I figured my natural silence would make escape from the guild easy. It didn't. Members of the guild were masters at observation, surveillance, deception, detection, and murder, obviously."

"You were an assassin?" he asks, incredulous.

Is that a hint of accusation?

I shake my head, then change my mind.

"Depends," I say.

"Depends? Either you were, or you weren't. No middle ground there."

Shit.

I sit back down and drink from the bottle. I sit quietly to gather my courage to speak. When I do, my voice cracks.

"They wanted me to be an assassin. They recognized an opportunity and took it. My mother did, too, I guess." I think about my last moments with my mother. It hurts. "Anyway. They trained me. Punished me for failures, lavished praise and rewards for successes. It was the rewards that began to motivate me. No one ever praised and rewarded me before."

"I spent the next four years learning to fight, mastering every manner of small weapons, poisons, and unarmed combat. I learned how to conceal myself, even in plain sight. I learned how to observe, predict, and identify."

"I don't know if you know how it works, but after your second year, every fight is life or death. Only the best make it. There's a reason the guild charges so much. They only get one new member per graduating class. Classmates fight to the death starting in year three. Only the best one makes it out. One."

My expectant look causes him to consider the words. As it slowly dawns on him, I remember why I love this man as much as I do. There is no condemnation from him, only compassion. I almost tear up as a result. Instead, I fake-cough it away.

He nods in understanding. I look at my hands. How much blood had I shed by my seventeenth birthday? Images of my classmates flood back. There were twelve of us when I started.

I'm the only one left.

"I was the class graduate," I say, stating the obvious. There is no pride in doing so. My hearts beat wildly, nerves making my hands shake slightly. Old, painful memories eat at my insides.

I take another swig and hand the bottle over to him.

"After that, there's The Quickening. What the guild calls 'earning your blood stamp.' I was given my first job. You can't just succeed; you must escape undetected. Then there's the final ceremony. You return with a vial of the blood of your first victim. Part of the ceremony is to drink it in the inner chamber and offer the rest at the altar of Fildeus."

"The Blooding Rite," he says. "All hunters do it."

"Makes sense why the guild does it, then," I say. "I never wanted to be an assassin. I sure as hell didn't want to follow any god. But this was where I found myself, and the praise I received for success was difficult to resist. The contract was given, and I left to fulfill it."

I sit quietly. "My whole life, it always felt like someone was using me, rejecting me, or pushing me down. I wasn't good enough, of high enough class, clean enough, loud enough. My mom worked herself to the bone for the upper classes. They were cruel to her, rude, degrading at times. Sometimes, I think she took that out on me."

"When I arrive at the mark's home I see he's an elderly man, asleep in his bed, in the ghetto of Kerakot, his wife sleeping next to him."

The burning on my chest has reduced to a warm sensation now, but it is there. I rub it subconsciously, shocked at how easily the words flow. What is wrong with me?

"It felt wrong. Killing an impoverished elderly man in his sleep? What could this man have done? He lived in a poor house in the poorest part of Kerakot. It unsettled me more than I already was. I had to know… so I woke him."

Tamrin's intensity makes my soul feel exposed.

"What I found was a man who had done no harm. His crime? He'd offended someone of far greater power and wealth. He'd refused service to someone he didn't like. I knew at that moment what I'd always known; I was no assassin. Training be damned, praise be damned, I wasn't killing someone for no reason, and certainly not for money. There's no honor in that. It's, well… it's evil. It got me thinking of my classmates. I broke."

"So, I fled north, found myself in the Shenshir Mountains, where I encountered a monk from the Drunken Fists Temple sitting in the snow naked, unaffected by the cold. He took me in. Treated me well. That's where I learned to drink."

"I'll say," he interjects, adding a moment of needed brevity. I smile and continue.

"I learned to pray."

He twitches his head and blinks, astonished.

"Yes, for a while, I believed. I honestly thought I could be a follower of Shamna. I learned to fight some more. Learned to drink a lot more. Learned to fight drunk. I spent nearly seven years there. In all that time, not one prayer was ever answered. I tried to convince myself it was a temporary moment of doubt. But I knew it wasn't."

I pause, considering my words. Tam doesn't speak, allowing me the time.

"It's possible I may have even believed it once upon a time. But it was short-lived. No great answers came, no revelations, no glorious change in me or my life."

"When I told the monk about my struggles, he said I was broken. It hurt. I was angry after that. Didn't want to be there anymore, so I left."

"It had been seven years since I left Kerakot. I slipped in quietly and unannounced. I checked in on the old man, hoping he was still alive. I learned he had still been murdered. Only whoever they sent for the job murdered his wife, too."

I reach for the bottle, and he hands it to me.

"It was more than I could bear. All that pent-up rage, building up over so many years." I pause, remembering the moment. "Well, it broke loose. By now, I had matured. My beard was full, my hair was long, my face was fuller and square, and my skills had vastly improved. So had my speed. A few well-earned scars and this crookedly broken nose didn't hurt. I didn't look like the boy who left anymore. It was easier to blend in, so I observed, and I waited, eventually sneaking into the Guild Tower."

His eyes are wide now.

"I see you have heard the story," I say.

"The Massacre of Kerakot," he whispers.

I nod.

"They named the perpetrator 'The Harbinger of Death' because whoever had done it had, in one night, wiped out the entirety of the Assassin's Guild present at the time. I burned all their records, including my name and birthplace."

Tamrin leans back on the sofa, "They've never recovered from that massacre. The way I hear it, there are still scars on the building from the fire." He takes a moment before he continues. "The burning of the records. That's why it's believed 'The Harbinger' is a former assassin."

I offer a slight nod. "The scars are still there, and that's why I don't let my identity get out. There's still a bounty out for me. I've encountered a bounty team several times looking to make a name for themselves." I look at him. "It happened a couple of days ago. It puts people I care about at risk."

I fight back more tears as images of the Tillions' broken bodies flood over me. I take a long pull off the bottle.

"I hate that title." I swig the bottle again. "I hate the stupid names they call me."

Tamrin looks at me with a smile.

"Then I'll call you a different name."

I reply, "My friends call me Shen. I'm rethinking your status on that front."

He leans forward and touches a finger to the side of his nose.

"Ha, yes, Shen, but unfortunately, we will always be friends. I can call you whatever I want."

I shake my head and smile. I can't help it. I love the guy.

He takes the bottle from me, holds it up in salute, finishes it, and sets it on the floor.

Then he lays back down, pulls the blanket over himself, and says, "Goodnight, *Quietius the Second*. Let's get some sleep. We need to figure out what is going on with those two and then figure out what the hell we're supposed to do to help 'em."

With that, he rolls over and, within seconds, is snoring louder than anything I have ever heard.

Thankfully, I am exhausted, too. Otherwise, I'd stab the hairy bastard to get some quiet.

This time, as I drift off, my thoughts are peaceful. I am with an old friend who didn't turn his back on me after revealing my story. I'm warmed by an overwhelming sense of peace. The weight of secrets lifted. No suicidal thoughts drift in to steal the joy of traveling with my best friend. There is no one I would rather have at my side right now.

"Tam?"

"Yes, Harbinger," he says, waking.

"I'm sorry I never told you that."

"Don't sweat it. I understand now why you wouldn't. I'll take it to my grave. Get some sleep, Killer."

I smile in the darkness.

"Asshole," I whisper.

He giggles.

The Growing Darkness

Chapter Ten

Journal Entry:37

I spend a lot of time locked inside myself. Even when

I'm with friends, I possess a propensity to retreat into my own internal dialog. Imprisoned by invisible shackles, locked away from the world, I spiral into the abyss.

The dichotomy of wishing I were extroverted but being hopelessly the opposite drives me to exhaustion. It takes a lot for me to be comfortable around people—a natural byproduct of my solitary existence. Gregarious to a fault at first, the stimulation eventually overwhelms me, and my mind withdraws.

I think it stems from fear of judgment or abandonment or both. This isn't the first time I've considered this. My father left when I was six. My brother, older by a year, took on the burden of keeping Mom happy. Dad gave no hint he was going. He didn't even say goodbye. It's not like Dad was around much before that anyway, but this was different. He said he was off somewhere and then never returned.

My mother was a hard woman. I knew nothing about her as a

person. She rarely spoke of herself or where she came from. My only knowledge of her is she was my mom, she was poor, and she was exhausted. I had no insight into her desires, hopes, and fears. She never spoke of her parents, how she met my dad, and why they constantly fought. After he left, she never mentioned him again. The woman was, and remains, a total mystery to me. She had little patience for her own children, so we tried to stay out of her way.

She did the hard things mothers do, like cooking, but mostly, she did everyone in the town's laundry. It was the only skill she had anyone would find useful. She washed so much laundry. In fact, the hut we lived in was surrounded by clotheslines, always filled to capacity.

Rarely was any of it ours.

Dinkums, Dyes, and Dead Eyes

Dry clothes, a good night's sleep, and a moment of peace do wonders for your mood. After everyone awoke and dressed, our little band of four needed to get some issues resolved. Aimlessly stampeding ahead to avoid our pursuers without knowledge of their motivation seems reckless. Tam, never one to talk on an empty stomach, had food brought up to us. A young boy, barely in double digits, who looks like a miniature version of the innkeeper we met last night, carries a breakfast tray filled with cheese, jams, and loaves of bread. We gather around the table to share a meal.

It's time I asked the siblings some questions.

"Who the hell are you two?" I ask.

I ignore Tamrin's groan. There's no time for subtlety.

I look at him with a dumb expression. "Why beat around the bush? It seems the most logical place to begin."

He rolls his eyes but gestures for me to continue. Jesmir speaks without hesitation.

"We are the eldest children of the fourth Prince of Teshket, His Royal Highness Jhemai of Pal."

Tamrin's spoon slips from his hands onto his plate. Jesma flinches from the unexpected clang it causes. I sit, frozen, mouth agape, food at the end of my spoon, hand suspended, and stare at the man I now know to be a Prince.

"Let me understand. You are the grandchildren of the Queen of Teshket?" Tamrin exclaims.

Both twins nod.

"I'll regret asking this, but why has The Dark Guard of Killinshire, your sworn enemy, embarked on a covert mission to kill a Teshket Prince and Princess lost in Rhinestab? This makes no sense. It's a declaration of war."

My head pounds with invisible war drums. I set my spoon down and rub my temples. A migraine might be coming on. Or it could be a stroke. I never thought for a second that these two were adventurers, thieves, warriors, or assassins. I pegged Jesmir as soft and possibly spoiled the moment I discovered him unconscious on the forest floor. Anyone could see they were out of place; I didn't realize they were nearly two hundred miles out of place.

"We were on our way to Gal-Daro with our father. He was negotiating a deal with the Gal-Korund Tribal Council. He wouldn't tell us why, but he wanted us with him."

"How the hell did you end up in the Rhine Woods?" Tamrin exclaims, his voice rising to an octave I've never heard from the big man.

Jesma almost bursts into tears.

Tamrin looks on in dismay, quickly grabbing his napkin and handing it to her.

"Oh, I am sorry to frighten you…"

She shakes her head. Jesmir comforts his sister with a gentle hand on her shoulder.

"No, it's not that," he says to Tam. "Our father was on a diplomatic mission from Pal to Gal-Daro. He decided to sail directly there rather than cross the straights into Teshket and travel by land."

"But the waters to the northeast are known pirate waters," I say.

He nods, "We… We were attacked by pirates and captured before we arrived at Gal-Daro."

Jesmir loses himself in the memories, no longer seeing me across the table.

"Where is your father?"

He doesn't register that I'm speaking to him.

"You're Highness?" Tamrin asks.

The prince doesn't respond. I begin to fear he's catatonic. Finally, though, he finds his voice.

"He's dead."

Jesma's unable to hold back the tears any longer. Silent trails of tears turn into sobs, and she cries in earnest.

"How?" I ask.

Jesmir continues to speak, his voice hollow.

"Captain Brogen slit his throat," Jesmir replies, devoid of

emotion. "He made us watch."

A flash of a distant memory slaps me in the face. Brogen stands over a bound man and announces to a crowd of Killinfolk a diatribe about cowardice in combat and slits the man's throat. His joy in the act was permanently imprinted on my mind.

I really must kill that man.

"Why?" I ask, forcing myself back to the present.

"He didn't say," Jesmir responds. "I think he enjoyed it."

My hatred for Brogen starts to boil over. I should have killed him long ago. Tamrin notices the tension building in my jaw. He taps my arm, his eyes on Jesmir. I should listen before I lose my temper. Tam's hand bounces in the air, visually soothing me.

"He asked our father for the treaty he was delivering to Gal-Daro. When Father told him it sank with our ship, that evil man didn't hesitate. He declared he had no use for us anymore, killed our father, and threw him over the cliff into the Brine River."

Jesmir took a shuddering breath. The fog seemed to clear as he looked at his sister.

"I panicked, grabbed Jesma's hand, and we ran for it."

He stopped talking and closed his eyes.

"I led us off the cliff."

When he opened his eyes, he stared down at the table.

"We almost drowned. But we managed to make it to shore several miles downriver. I thought staying in the water for a while would be better. The Brine carried us for miles. Eventually, we climbed out and started heading north. On his way to Rhinestab, an old merchant stopped and offered us a ride to Dresdin."

He looked back up at me.

"I thought we could find a way to get a message back to the Queen. But when we arrived, Brogen was already there. Somehow, he knew where we were heading. I became frightened when I saw him laughing and joking with the Mayor of Dresdin. We fled again before they could see us, hoping to get to Valshannon instead."

Jesma reached over and touched his hand. He pulled it away slowly but noticeably. She looked hurt, though she tried to hide it.

Jesmir continued.

"I thought if we could make it to the Royal Emissary stationed here, we could make it home. If we reach our emissary, we can arrange safe passage back to Teshket and inform the Queen what happened."

These poor fools have no idea how outmaneuvered they are. I look at Tamrin, and he shakes his head, admonishing me to tread lightly. I try to hide my displeasure, but it's difficult not to be horribly blunt.

"Who knows about the emissary?" I ask.

"Only royals and Emissaries know the system. It's a covert arrangement between a secret guild and the Royal Family. I'm committing treason just by talking to you about it."

Tamrin speaks, his tone somber, "Brogen knows about the emissary. He knows who they are and where to find them. He sent men to intercept the emissary ahead of our party in case you slipped into Valshannon. I'm afraid your emissary is compromised."

I cross the room toward the window, shift the curtain slightly, and observe the Dead Eye Pub across the street. It's still early. Activity on the street is light compared to last night but filling in quickly with people on their way to open their markets and shops. The pub appears dark, but an occasional patron enters or stumbles out, indicating it is open.

I look back toward the group at the table. Three sets of eyes watch me.

Damn, this insufferable habit. Why does everyone expect me to have the answers? I pull the letter out of my purse and take it to the table, handing it to Jesmir. He reads it and hands it to his sister.

She gasps.

"You read Killinspeak?" I ask.

"All Teshket Royals do. Knowing the language of our enemy is not only good intel. It helps in diplomatic negotiations."

"Then you can see Tam's right. Your meeting is compromised, your Highnesses. We need to think about a new way to get you home."

I'm responsible for fair dinkum royalty now. Just great.

I wish I could just send them on their way.

I wish I could leave well enough alone and wander off into the RhineWoods.

It's not how I'm wired, though.

Responsibility, however, does not mean control. Some-times, the decisions shouldn't be left to me alone. I don't have answers any more than they do. Hell, I'm not sure I even know the right questions. Despite the splendor and size of our room, I'm feeling claustrophobic. The walls close in on me. I'm so much better in the wilds.

The cloudy morning sky and the low light of the room's lanterns cast eerie gray shadows everywhere. From the window, I watch the outside world. It might rain today. Perfect.

I need solitude to gather my thoughts, but I can't leave them unprotected. I don't know if we should take the King's Regal Highway and head directly to Teshket or go the hard way and continue through the RhineWoods. Maybe head to Rogue's Pointe? At least I know what I am getting at Rogue's Pointe. Taking this highway to Teshket? That's too easy. I can't shake the feeling of troubles lurking unseen, monsters hiding in the shadows of the unknown.

If word got out that Killinshire was murdering Teshket Royals, it would be hard to avoid another war. It is Killinshire, though. They start every war, usually out in the open. It's been a long time since war broke out. Longer than the gaps between the previous three wars. So why does Brogen operate in secret this time?

They know Teshket, Rhinestab, and Haabrestand will band together if they try again. Gal-Danang has all but signed a permanent alignment with Teshket. The two realms have enjoyed the most stable alliance of any of the five realms for over five hundred years. Peaceful Gal-Danang won't go to war, however.

But they will supply their full complement of goods to the defense of Teshket. Their weaponry is far more advanced than everyone else's.

Killinshire might not make it through another war. So why?

It's insanity.

I've heard no rumors of war and know of no tensions between the Nation-States besides the usual. Yet, the signs indicate there must be increased tension. It doesn't make sense.

I can't stand when I'm ignorant of the facts. It eats at me.

A storm approaches, metaphorical and literal. I fear tons of collateral damage will result.

Tamrin continues the conversation with the siblings after our meal. I'm glad to see them eat. The coming journey may not be pleasant, and food could become a luxury we don't have time for.

I'm torn between staying here, observing the comings and goings of the pub, or making a break for it now. We should put as much of the RhineWoods between Brogen and us as possible. Then again, what if Brogen's team removed the emissary and replaced them with someone else?

An idea percolates. It might be worth a risky shot to walk down to the pub, take the place of the siblings, and meet their emissary on my own. This last option offers a possibility neither of the others do. A chance to get information.

Everything feels wrong, and information is the only cure for my unease. At least this way, I either end up with the true emissary and can get these two home, or I end up with the spy.

Both outcomes appeal to me.

If the contact is not yet compromised, I can use their resources and simply escort the siblings. An extra layer of protection. Between the big man and me, we can likely manage any threats headed our way for a journey like that.

If, on the other hand, the contact has been compromised, I'm not against some forced interrogation. Say what you will, but torture works. If it didn't, humans would have stopped using the tactic long ago.

I'm well versed in causing non-lethal pain. I hate doing it, but I will. I can drag it out for a long time. I debate the merits of relaying my thoughts to the party. Whatever is decided, I need them to be willing to go along and not question me.

I've been down this road before. I assume everyone's willing to go with whatever I plan. But I'd rather save spur-of-the-moment decisions for when I really need them. Now doesn't seem the time to operate under a lack of communication. An emergency course of action turning into a child's game of "But why?" could cost us our lives.

Better get the "but whys" out of the way now.

Tamrin sidles up and peeks out the other side.

"Thoughts?" he says.

I watch the pub.

"It's surely a trap in there now," I say.

"Yup."

"You can't put a price on good intel, though," I say.

"Nope," he says, glancing my way.

"Don't give me that look," I grumble.

"I'm not. I'd do what you are thinking, too." He looks back out the window. "Maybe not exactly," he says, "but mostly."

"Well, then it's settled. I'll meet the emissary."

"I had a feeling you'd say that."

We both look back to the siblings. Even dirty, they stand out. Their silvery blond hair is pretty rare. They couldn't hide in a dark alley filled with smoke. That's when I remember the expression on the face of the desk clerk downstairs.

"The innkeeper could be an issue," I whisper.

Tamrin nods and says, "And the taxi driver. We need to make them look less like Teshket Royals."

"Hey, take some of the money they're carrying," I say, eyeing him up and down. "As inconspicuously as you can, get them new clothes... by new, I mean..."

He holds up a hand, "I know what you mean." He looks over at Jesma. "Think we can convince her to cut her hair?"

"Would you?"

He snickers, "I'll try anyway."

"How about dye? Her red, him black?"

He nods, his mouth held in a mock frown. "That could work. I'll take care of it."

He steps away, and I grab his arm. He looks at me, questioning.

"I want to say thanks."

His big hand rests on my shoulder.

"I should be thanking you, friend. I should've known better about this job. Don't know what I was thinking. I bought the story. If I get my hands on Brogen, I'll rip him apart with my bare hands. I almost did something I would never have been able to come back from."

"I'll stay out of your way if you go full transformation," I tease, sharing his sentiment.

"Be safe down there, Brother."

He pats my shoulder, and I turn back to the window.

It's all I can do. I don't trust myself to speak.

I spent the better part of an hour waiting for Tamrin to return. At the same time, I watched out the window for anyone suspicious or familiar. He returned with materials to disguise the siblings, and I left without a word. I only hope they move quickly. My mood turned gloomy while waiting due to the sound of the morning bells announcing the city gates were open. Brogen's appearance is inevitable, and I'd like to be gone before he shows.

Valshannon is an almost twenty-four-hour city. The streets never quiet down completely due to night shift workers and their insane nighttime lives. Someone always needs a drink, food, and time with friends.

I marvel at the cleanliness of this city. For all its hustle and bustle, the city's common areas are pristine. Even in the slums, a misnomer since the poor of Valshannon are far from poor compared to those outside the city. To the rest of the world, the poor of Valshannon are wealthy.

All businesses, by ordinance, close when the Twin Moons reach their zenith and reopen well before Ezra shows her face over the city walls. In that short period, the street cleaners move through the streets like a polished army, ensuring the reputation of Valshannon remains steady.

I negotiate the light traffic of cleaners and guards returning home from their shifts or heading to one of the few taverns open early enough to provide their much-deserved revelry.

The Dead Eye is one of the establishments that has early hours to accommodate such patrons. A steady stream of tired workers file in as I approach the entrance. Tamrin, in his infinite wisdom, watches for me from our window in case he might recognize one of Brogen's mercenaries lurking while I make my way across the street.

I cast a wary glance at the giant creeper in the window of our room. Tam's goofy grin flashes while he peers down. Subtle as a crowing rooster, he signals all clear. At least, that's what I think he's doing with his thumbs-up signal.

I don't acknowledge him and enter the Dead Eye. It's unexpected how populated the place is inside. Valshannon's healthy contingent of night owls is more extensive than I realized. Weaving my way through the crowd, I step up to the bar, looking for the best place to scout the room, but I need a drink to do it.

Not just any drink.

Like rolling a five on Shamna Rocks, I have the unfortunate displeasure of ordering a hot Gal-Daro ale.

Yuck.

According to the royals, each emissary has their own developed set of signals. I couldn't imagine having to memorize them as a child.

A yellow feather on my cloak, pinned at my left shoulder, signals a Royal in trouble. Jesmir carries one in a small wooden box. It's rather conspicuous. Frankly, I feel stupid, but I'm always amazed by the differences in cultural customs throughout the realms. I find those differences fascinating, but this one makes me feel exposed.

My fears were validated by several pairs of eyes glancing my way. Blending in isn't an option now, so I face reality and own it.

The barkeep meets me at the bar. One eye is milky white and doesn't move when he glances at me or around the room.

It's a dead eye.

Oh.

I almost laugh. I've got to admire this man's self-deprecating humor. It's funny.

"What're ya havin'?" he asks.

I wrestle with my facial muscles as they attempt to betray my enjoyment of the obvious joke. It takes me a second too long to gather my bearing. The barkeep waits, rolling one good eye, which only exacerbates my efforts.

"Problem?" he asks, pointing at his own eye.

I manage to get myself under control and shake my head.

"Not at all. I'll have a Gal-Daro." I almost snort the words out.

"This is involuntary," he says. "Your yellow feather is a choice. At least I don't look like an idiot."

I laugh. The man smirks.

"Are you aware you answer the age-old question of whether I look someone in the "eyes" or "eye"? Now I know the answer."

"Funny," he deadpans.

I think I'm funny, so I laugh again. The barkeep raises an eyebrow, the one over the dead eye. I choke on my spit because now I'm looking in the wrong eye.

"Gal-Daro, you say?" he asks. I think he's over my jokes.

"Yes, please," I respond.

"Not quite cool enough outside for one of those. Sure, I can't interest you in a local brew?"

"I have the chills," I say.

He shrugs and mumbles, "Wish I could stop selling that garbage. Always such a pain in the ass." He gives me a metal tankard with a dragon-shaped handle. Its contents of bright amber ale from the land of volcanoes and ash reflect the dim light coming in from the windows and door in front. He steps through swinging doors into the back kitchen and comes back with a plate of hot coals.

I scan the room, self-conscious over the stupid yellow feather, and pretend I'm only a patron with a stupid decoration. A few people look at me funny but with only mild curiosity.

Beyond the sea of bodies, I see the stairs to the upper-level balcony. Easy enough. The upper balcony is half full. Hanging out there won't be too conspicuous. The cloudy morning keeps the interior darker than usual here, an added bonus for my purposes. The balcony offers nice shadows to slip into if I need to.

I wait. Fortunately, I have seen this awful elixir served enough to know the etiquette.

Dead Eye takes the tankard and sets it in the coals.

"Be a minute. That'll be a copper," he grumbles and walks off.

I set one of my last eight copper pieces on the counter.

I sure wish I didn't have to drink Gal-Daro ale. I hate Gal-

Daro ale. If by the time the ale is done, the emissary hasn't approached me, then they aren't here, and I have to come back in two hours and do it again. The thought of doing this twice makes me want to vomit.

After a minute, I lift the warm mug and go to the balcony. No sense in letting it get too hot. I hate it anyway, so there's no need to drink it at its 'perfect temperature.'

Looking down from above, the place looks like a sea of heads, bobbing and swaying, all locked in conversation. Alive with activity and noise, The Dead Eye is too lively for early morning. The acoustics here are horrible.

I take in some people watching, witnessing actions from above that are lost when you are down in the mix. I notice a good number of bald spots and realize I have no idea what the back of my head looks like. Everyone else in the world is more familiar with the back of my head than I am.

"Do I have a bald spot?" I mumble to myself.

I count a number of oddly shaped noses, grateful none of them are the familiar bird-beak I'm hoping to avoid. A burst of laughter breaks out at a table below. Off in a dark corner, a barmaid and one of the guards touch each other with a cozy familiarity. On the far end of the balcony from my position, other patrons watch the activity below, their faces contorted in judgment. I almost snicker at the scene. I do that, too, sometimes—pass judgment on others from the background.

Night shift workers are a different breed. I think the change to their circadian rhythm changes their biology, and they become outsiders to the rest of the world. Preconditioned to sleep at night and wake during the day, I think when the opposite becomes the norm, a change happens inside. It's why we don't have night vision like some other creatures around the world. When everyone else gets their day started, night shift crews are winding down, and I think that discordance affects a person. They become somehow rowdier, more prone to excess, and punchier.

I'm feeling punchy watching them.

One drawback to my plan. Everyone here clearly knows each other. The night shift community is much smaller than the rest of society. That makes me more conspicuous than I like.

Case in point, someone pokes me rather rudely in the arm.

"Hey, who are you?" a drunk man says as I take my first sip. *Nasty. It tastes like cough medicine.*

"Passing through," I say.

He pokes my arm again, his face still dirty from the previous night's shift, contorted in a scowl.

"That's uncalled for," I say. I contemplate breaking this man's finger.

"Not what I asked," he says.

I haven't been here long enough for anyone to spot me, so there's no chance this is the emissary. That would be too easy. The passphrase will tell me if I've gauged this guy accurately.

"You throwing rocks today?" I ask.

He gives me a funny look as if I were the obtuse one. "What's that got to do with who you are?"

That is not the response I am looking for. I take two quick sips of my nasty ale, ignoring the guy.

He pokes me again, more aggressively this time.

"I asked you a question," he slurs.

Any other day, I would put a quick jab in his kidney and quietly help him to a chair while educating him on not picking fights with people he doesn't know. Today, I play it cool.

"I'm visiting and thought this seemed like a lively place," I say.

"This is a locals' place. You don't belong here, friend."

I let out a heavy sigh. This guy clearly plans to make a scene.

I lean in and whisper, "I don't want trouble. All I want is a drink after a long journey here."

He leans in closer still. The stench of a day's hard labor and alcohol offends my senses.

"I don't care why yer here. I asked who you are."

I stare directly into his eyes and keep my voice calm and easy.

"I'm the guy you think twice about approaching and making demands of and then, having thought better of it, decide not to." My face is blank. There's no need to express anger. He'll get my point without me adding extra tension.

He blinks. It's a flinch. He stumbles a bit, wobbly on his feet.

He's on liquid courage.

Great.

He attempts to jab my chest, but I grab his finger and pull him close. His body tenses as I whisper in his ear.

"It would be a shame if you ruined my day and made me do something we will both regret."

This guy is ready to pass out. He's drunk and dumb. But he's too drunk to get the message. I hold his finger and press at the pressure point between his thumb and pointer, but I hold up my glass to him in salute. He winces in pain, his eyes dart around. I apply pressure to draw his attention back to me. He swallows nervously, holds up his nearly full mug, and clanks it, rather harshly, against mine. With a tight smile, he downs the contents, his eyes filled with tears.

Is it too much to ask to be left alone? Why are people so intrusive? Why is there always one person who looks to start some trouble?

People can be infuriating.

I pretend to swig mine. It's too gross to let into my mouth.

He mumbles, "Meant nothing by it. Had a little too much."

"I suggest you go home. I'm tired, and I've already satisfied the bloodlust of my blades today. No sense in over-indulging."

His eyes water as I apply more pressure to his hand for emphasis. His self-conscious gulp is the only confirmation I need. He's received the message. I watch him stumble toward the stairs and turn back to the railing. I expect him to take a serious tumble, but he doesn't. I watch him exchange quick goodbyes and walk out the door, glancing back at me nervously. I smirk and take another foul swig. The flavor wipes the smirk right off my face.

It takes every bit of self-control not to vomit. Even more to pretend I'm enjoying it. For better or worse, I have a lot of practice at that.

I take my time with this drink for the sake of the mission. Typically, I would down it and be done. Prolonging the agony is nauseating. The unfortunate side effect of slow consumption of this Gal-Daro sludge is it cools off. As much as I hate it hot, it's worse cold. Lost in the thickened swill within my mug, I almost don't notice a familiar head enter through the front door.

It's about to be an awful day. It hasn't gone well thus far, but the swill is now my least significant problem.

I back away from the railing and blend into the darkened shadows of the second-floor loft. I let out a grateful sigh that the drunk antagonist from earlier stumbled away without incident. Had he stuck around a moment longer, I might not have seen the close-cropped gray-haired head with a pointy goatee and a bird beak of a nose walk in the front door.

I curse silently. Brogen's not alone, and I'm trapped.

Chapter Eleven

Journal Entry:41

We were definition star-crossed lovers. Neither of us knew that at the time. I thought fate had finally let me live a life of hope. Instead, I rolled the dreaded five on Shamna Rocks.

And couldn't pay the levy to remove it.

So, I spent the last thirty-five years cursed, avoiding the past. Avoiding pain.

Emotional pain, anyway.

Truth be told, I've gotten rather good at it, so good I don't even notice I am doing it most of the time. It rarely catches up to me. Today is one of those rare days.

We fool ourselves first and foremost.

New Enemies and Old Flames

Of course, he's here. When I want trouble, I can't find it. But as soon as I want life to be easy, trouble decides to come and find me. The sight of the number two person on my *people I need to rid the world of* list—I still hold the top spot—forces me to exercise extraordinary restraint.

If not for the frightened folks hiding across the street, I'd leap off this loft and come down on Brogen with both blades.

He looks pretty agitated and haggard. The ride on the river must have taxed his patience and resolve. It certainly taxed is coifed appearance. Seeing him wrecked makes me happy. Seeing him at all makes me nervous. I hoped I could avoid him entirely.

Yet, there he stands. If not for his unfortunate timing, I would take a moment to find joy in his recent suffering. Instead, I curse myself for not leaving sooner. What was I thinking? Playing spy over evading this jackwagon was a dumb play.

But running blindly into trouble we can't see didn't seem wise either.

I slink away from the railing and back into the crowd of the upper deck, where shadows offer cover. I haven't had a chance to finish my ale, which honestly doesn't upset me. But I also don't know if the emissary is here. I can't allow myself to get made trying to pretend to be a royal, either.

Damn.

Upon arrival, I made a rookie mistake—I forgot to case the exits. I was too distracted by that damned dead eye.

Stupid, stupid, stupid Shen.

He may not have recognized me in Winding Run, but if he sees me here, Brogen will put together that I'm not who I pretended to be yesterday. It's too much of a coincidence.

I search for a place to observe while concealed. The crowd below grows by the minute, but it's thin enough to worm my way into the relative shadows up here. While I track their movement, Brogen and his two mercenary escorts enter the crowd. I recognize both of his companions from Mistras' Tavern.

Great. Triple shot of someone who recognizes me. There's zero chance of getting out of here unnoticed.

I'm sure I can beat them in a three-on-one fight. But this place is packed with off-duty guards, all armed. Any violent commotion will draw further alarm from outside and ensure my exodus descends into a harrowing escape from Valshannon. Worse, my mission would fail, and I'd find myself forced to abandon the royals and leave Tamrin in a sticky wicket.

Fighting my way out of here is not an option. But, if it comes to violence, I will at least have rid the world of one nasty problem.

I can find solace in that.

Brogen walks to the bar and speaks with Dead Eye. Dead Eye gestures up here, and Brogen spins around to scan the balcony. Whatever Dead Eye said, Brogen is looking for someone. Thankfully, he can't see much beyond a couple feet past the railing.

Dead Eye drops a metal tankard on the bar and heads to the back. Brogen indicates to one of his lackeys, who nods and continues to scan the balcony. That's when I noticed his companion wearing a yellow feather.

Dead Eye must have mentioned my order. I don't imagine he gets two in a day, let alone two in less than ten minutes, wearing yellow feathers. Likely, he commented on the dual coincidences.

Stupid protocol.

They should rethink this one.

I might write a strongly worded letter to the Teshket Royals later.

Their presence confirms my suspicions—there's a spy in the Queen's court. I need to slip out unnoticed by Brogen or his lackeys. If I work my way to the opposite end of the loft, closest to the door, I can pull up my hood and jump down to the first floor after they reach the second.

If I time it right, I can make it out the door and be long down the road before they can get through the crowd. If I'm brazen enough, the crowd will back away and possibly condense at the base of the stairs, a natural barricade to my pursuers. It's not inconspicuous, but it's the only option. Resolved, I make my way around the balcony's shadows toward the front wall of the tavern, away from the staircase, my hood still lowered. I fool myself into believing I look less suspicious than I likely do.

Too focused on the trio and the path to my exit, I don't notice my stalker until a hot pain in my testicles announces a sinister presence. I'm not ashamed to say it has my attention.

Before me, a smaller, cloaked figure presses close, my dangling bits held with aggression born from deep-seated anger. Actually, resentment would be a better word for it.

"You throwing rocks today?" says a quiet female voice.

"I'm looking to lose some money, sure," I reply through gritted teeth, my eyes no longer on Brogen.

My current position forces me to look down, and my throat locks mid-gasp.

It can't be.

Two big brown eyes stare up at me.

"You're no royal," she says.

Screw you, Shamna.

"I don't have time to explain," I reply. "Could you please remove your hand from my genitals?"

"I should kill you where you stand. But for now, I'd be happy with taking your balls, Shen," she says.

"That's not the scheduled reply," I whisper, teeth clenched.

The mental gymnastics my brain executes will someday go into my journal. For the moment, I try to think fast. But a woman whom I grievously abandoned without a word has my balls in a near vice grip, and ruthless murderers approach from behind. I struggle to maintain any mental priority.

But I try.

"Down there is Captain Brogen of the Dark Guard of Killinshire. He intends to hurt your royals. I have them safely stowed away."

Yup, torture works.

I look over and see the trio making their way up the stairs.

I turn back to the small emissary with my nuts in her hand and an encyclopedia's worth of my life's story in her head.

"Either get it over with or get me out of here. I will take you to your royals," I plead.

I am not at my best at the moment. Begging is not beneath me if it will get my man bits out of the awkward embarrassment of their current situation.

She looks beyond me, and her eyes burn with recognition.

She doesn't hesitate, and I breathe a quiet blessing and resist the urge to rub myself.

Priorities, man, priorities.

"This way," she commands and pushes past me. We work through the crowd, our path threatening to intersect with Brogen and the crew. I'm unsure where she leads me, but I need her attention. I grab her arm, and she yanks it free. I'm about to protest when I notice the two swinging doors toward the back of the building.

Oh.

I keep my face turned away from the stairs while we pass through the doors, shadows providing enough cover—the petite, cloaked woman leading the way.

I should have known this was here.

Yeah, I'm beating myself up for the mistake. It's how I learn. Nobody beats me up for my mistakes better than I do.

Well, let's see what this little sprite of an emissary does. I could be wrong.

The swinging doors lead to a service stairway directly down into the kitchen.

Convenient.

Once through the doors, she picks up the pace, and I quickly follow. We hurry down the stairs, past two cooks, who ignore us, and exit out through the back door into the service alley.

I love well-designed cities. Service alleys especially.

She spins around as the back kitchen door closes and slaps me in the face.

Hard.

I hold in the scream that tries to force its way out.

"I'll deal with you in a moment. For now, take off that damn feather and take me to my royals," the fierce woman says.

I comply, quickly removing the feather and stowing it with my left hand while rubbing my cheek with my right.

It stings.

On a good note, the slap made me forget about the slight burn on my chest.

On a sour one, my life suddenly grew significantly more complicated.

I knew it was about to be a bad day.

This clinches it, and now I have a fourth handprint on my body.

The gods hate me.

Can I die now?

A convenient consequence of my solitary existence is I'm never forced to confront my past transgressions unless I want to. It's easy to avoid situations, leaving the past where it belongs, tucked away and forgotten in some other part of the world when that part is hundreds of miles away. Even better when forty years fade those ghosts into the empty abyss of my mind.

That's the lie I tell myself anyway.

Running away from one problem or another my entire life seemed an effective way to deal with those ghosts. Deep down, I recognize I've stunted my emotional growth. Rampant self-defeatism built over a foundation of poor choices has permanency. Burying my head in the sand and tucking the memories away has been less effective than I thought. I should have known something or someone would come and shatter the illusion.

The woman following behind me sent me spiraling out of control emotionally. A vortex of my greatest and worst memories inexplicably re-entered my life uninvited.

Memories of how I loved her more than anything I thought possible return after years in the black abyss of compartmentalization. Regrets over my actions tear at me as I recall how I tossed that love aside, choosing to save my own skin in a moment of utter panic.

The act of a child, immature and afraid, became the poison in my soul.

Even today, thirty-five years later, I believe it was unavoidable.

Inevitable, really. It's what I do.

Kill things.

I'm consumed with guilt as the ghost from my past follows me through the service alleys, pressing our pace to place as much distance between us and Brogen as possible. I take the back route to the Jester's Pot, not looking behind me, afraid to make eye contact with the only woman I ever loved.

I'd like to keep running and escape this ghost as quickly as possible. But I don't break my promises.

My cheek still stings from the slap. It might rank up there as the worst one I've ever received. But that could be due to the emotional connection.

I'm not even mad about it. I deserve it.

The ghost-turned-emissary and I make it to a break in the alley at South-East Main Street. Already, the flood of people through the southeast gate has grown as those merchants living outside the city walls begin to set up carts. Mixed in the crowd are the early risers, intent on shopping before the crowd grows, actively haggling with store owners to get their shops ready. We blend in, two people amongst the hustle and bustle crowd, going about their daily routine unnoticed. I take a quick peek behind us and see no signs that we have been followed or watched.

Those bright brown eyes look up at me, and butterflies flutter in my gut, knowing if I look into them, I'll only see the lost years. I conspicuously avoid her gaze by scanning beyond and over the emissary's head. I'm not ready to confront the past.

Satisfied that we aren't pursued, I turn right, step into Main Street, and make my way across Swill Street to the other side. We pass the row of wooden structures where the Jester's Pot resides and into an alley filled with as much activity as the street we left behind. The welcome crowd offers cover, and we blend in, albeit the density of bodies makes it more complicated to navigate. My hearts pound with anxiety as we turn into the back alley behind the Jester's Pot.

Each step punctuates a new twinge in my chest as I wrestle with the knowledge I'm one step closer to the inevitable and unavoidable confrontation that's lived in my nightmares for three decades.

Why do I have to deal with two problems at once?

Swimming through the sea of laborers, shoppers, and travelers like two sharks, we slide quietly through the throng. Vendors vie for my attention, but I politely wave them off, a disinterested passerby.

The back door of the Jester's Pot, a stark contrast to the elaborately inviting face it wears on the Swill Street side, is no different than any of the rest of the buildings. The hanging sign with a jester stirring an oversized ladle in a miniature pot is the only indicator of the location. It's a silly image, but it is recognizable and conveniently identifies the servants' entrance. We step through, navigating a young kid coming out with an empty vegetable crate.

Once inside, I step out of the way of the servants and turn to her, my intent to make excuses or maybe divert her attention from me, but my voice fails.

She's been crying.

"I thought you were dead, you son-of-a-bitch," she whispers.

Damn.

I wasn't expecting that. Has my ex been crying the entire walk here?

I'm running on instinct at the moment, avoiding over-thinking. She could have screamed at me. I probably wouldn't have heard anything.

"Not for lack of trying," I whisper.

I can't explain what I feel right now. My insides are in knots.

"Where have you been?" she asks.

"Everywhere," I say, my throat tight. I'm unsure how much she knows about what I did, but I fear it's more than I'd like, and I'm about to account for my sins.

"When everyone was killed and your guild burned, I thought you were one of them," she said, her eyes hardening. Streaks of tears lined her face, following the hard lines of age that weren't there the last time I saw her.

Neither was the long, deep scar on her left cheek. That's new, too. I want to reach out and touch the scar. Easily over a decade old, it is well-seasoned by sun and time. There's a story there, and the aching nostalgic part of me wants to know who gave it to her to exact revenge.

"How did you make it out? Why have you never returned," she asks. "Why didn't you come find me?"

My hearts race as a possibility I never considered in the forty years I've been gone occurs to me. This woman from my past is unaware of the sins I've committed against her. She doesn't know that I burned the guild down. She doesn't know the worst details of her own story.

I fall back, the wall holding me upright, the weight of my secret returning.

Memories of rage that consumed me beyond reason, sadness that threw me into despair, feelings that led me to flee north, afraid and alone, return. Fear that waves of assassins, hot on my heels, would kill the one person I loved, driving me away from the only home I ever knew.

The crimes I committed against the guild would never go unpunished. When I returned, in secret, and single-handedly wiped out the guild in one night, setting the place ablaze, I didn't look for her then either.

Of course, she doesn't know. Only Tam, Mistras, and Cali know, and they'd never tell anyone. Worse, they only know half the story. The rest is locked in my double-heart-shaped box, buried deep.

Her big brown eyes still draw me in, and I fall prey to them. She believes I abandoned her for the guild and that I'd been in the fire. The fire that I started.

After I killed everyone in the building.

She has no idea she stands before The Harbinger of Death, the one who scarred the face of Teshket forever.

She would have no knowledge of the ceremonies or the tests we endured. Sworn to secrecy, we took a blood oath payable by a slow and painful death. How could she have known how we were made to fight each other? She's unaware her brother developed an obsession with supremacy, refusing to back down when the recruit pool was reduced to the two of us.

He broke our secret blood oath to not fight each other, no

matter the cost.

She has no idea that he died in my arms, forcing my hand. She didn't know the despair I felt as his last breath was emphasized by the drip of his blood falling from my blade, his life escaping through the hole it made in his chest.

I never told her. I never told anyone.

When I took my revenge on the guild, I fled Teshket as fast as I could. All of Teshket was dead to me. Everywhere I looked, I was reminded of my failures. It became a place I visited only when I had to.

I never wanted to face her and tell her I killed her brother.

Words are failing me at this moment.

"Krin…" I start.

But the words won't come. It requires courage. Courage I don't have.

I simply shake my head and turn away, leading her up the servants' stairs to the rented room at the top of the inn.

The climb up four flights of stairs is the longest walk of my life.

Chapter Twelve

Journal Entry:42

The friends I have scattered over the continent are a source of joy I struggle to let myself revel in. For that reason, it's usually short-lived joy.

I know that's my fault.

I get in my head and feel like I'm overstaying my welcome. The feeling is so overwhelming my joy turns into angst, and leaving is the only respite. When I pop in to see them, I never stay more than a night or two. It works for me because I leave before I feel like a burden. It helps to avoid them witnessing the self-loathing that inevitably creeps in.

I have a lot of self-loathing. I don't think people can relate. It's okay.

I am an island.

Exodus

I stand in the corner of our room and watch the crowd below. In blissful unawareness, citizens and visitors meander about the entrance to the Dead Eye. I do my best to stay out of the line of fire. Tamrin, to his credit, sits quietly on the sofa, doing his best not to eavesdrop on the quiet conversation happening at the table.

Krin and I haven't spoken to each other since the servants' entrance discussion. She speaks in hushed tones with the royals.

Jesma is in much better spirits now that her emissary has found them. There is hope in her eyes that wasn't there this morning. I assume their discussion centers around how they ended up here or some plan of escape out of Valshannon undetected by Brogen's spies.

I was surprised when I came back. Neither of the royals had dyed their hair. Tamrin returned with clothes and dyes for suitable disguises, but they refused. He tried to persuade them, but his words fell flat on the refined royals.

Dirty and scared as they are, they are still royals. I'll never understand the rules for royals in Teshket. They seem arbitrary and strange.

"Royals don't dye their hair," Tam said. His little dance when he mocked the conversation would have made me laugh under normal circumstances.

I'm not in the mood for laughter.

The streets below are busy now. It's not an unreasonable assumption that Brogen is still inside the pub since two ghouls stand out front, trying their best to appear casual. They can't hide their predatory posture, however. Obvious lookouts, the conspicuous duo purposefully shifts their eyes over the crowd, too aware of their surroundings. The menace in their appearance sends subliminal messages to the collective consciousness around them. From above, I observe with disdain how the traffic pattern shifts, a school of fish redirected by the present danger of sharks in the water. These idiots lack the casual observation skills of true spies, unable to assume the demeanor of a traveler or a local.

It's amateur hour down there.

Brogen would have fared better if he'd used Killinshire spies rather than meat-head warriors. But that is a weakness of his I am well aware of. He doesn't value anything but physical presence.

I'm confident these lookouts scan the crowd for two heads of golden blond hair. Hard to say, but since it didn't take much time to get here from there, even with the longer route, I'd bet that Brogen is still inside trying to trigger the emissary.

Which is good news. Brogen may know who the emissary is, but they missed her and don't know it. More importantly, I got to the emissary before his advance team.

I guess I'm allowed to feel good about that. I saved Krin's life. Though she'll never know it.

Too bad Brogen's goons never look up to this window. I'd like to get a better look at their faces. A guild-trained surveillance team would have scanned the buildings at least once.

All brawn, no brains. Typical.

"Alright," I say as I step away from the window, "listen up."

My patience is exhausted. They turn to me, shocked by my aggressive tone.

"I'm here to keep you two alive. While I understand you are used to a certain deference, you'll get none of that from me going forward. I'm in charge."

Krin stands up.

"You? Just like that?"

I avoid looking at her.

"Down in that tavern is one of the most ruthless killers in the world. He has no intention of keeping you alive and will kill anyone helping you in the process. I can't protect you if you don't do what I say when I say."

I walk over to the table where the disguise materials rest, pick up the two jars of hair dye, and toss the red to Jesma. Jesmir catches the bottle of black dye with a scowl.

"Put this stuff in your hair. Now. You stand out like a dragon at a dinner party. Do it, or I walk out that door and won't look back."

Krin walks over and grabs my arm, pulling me to the side to get out of earshot.

"Who the hell do you…" she starts, teeth clenched.

I rip my arm from her grasp.

"I'm the guy that's kept these two alive for the last three days. I'll not have that work wasted. You're as compromised as they are. Brogen knew exactly where to find you and exactly how to trap you. Did you miss that?"

She turns to the royals and then back to me.

"No, obviously I did not miss that," she hisses back.

I look over her shoulder. Tamrin stands, observant. I shift uncomfortably. The royals watch us, concerned.

I lean in and whisper to Krin, "Let's put our history aside for now, okay? Your pursuers likely know exactly how you intend to get these two out of Valshannon. We need to find another way." I pull back and look at her.

"What's it gonna be? My way, or the clearly compromised way?"

Again, she looks back at the royals, who stand afraid, and considers my point.

Forty years, and I can still read her. Even older, I still see the girl I knew. Hardened lines, the scar, even the slight gray in her hair can't hide that it's her. Her face is still more familiar to me than my own. She knows I am right.

She sighs and nods.

I breathe a sigh of relief. That was easier than I thought it would be.

"Do as he says," she tells them.

"But…" Jesmir starts. Krin holds up a hand, silencing him.

"It's a lot to ask of you. But he is right. Brogen showed up, gold feather prominently displayed. They have information that they shouldn't, and that puts us all at risk."

Krin looks back at me, uncertain.

"Do you two trust him?" she asks, her eyes narrowing slightly.

Jesmir speaks softly, "Yes."

Tamrin nods and says, "You could do worse than…"

He catches a look on my face and stops.

"…Shen," he finishes.

I can't help hoping Shamna will shine some luck on me.

Krin stiffens.

"Cursed Luck!" she whispers and looks at me.

"What?" I ask.

"If they know how to contact an emissary here, they know how to contact an emissary anywhere. The entire Teshket Royal escape plan is compromised."

"We have to get moving," I say.

Krin's tone turns forceful as she points to the items on the table. "No time, your Highnesses. Get disguised. Now. We head out in ten minutes."

I'll say this about the twins; when they decide to move, they move. With a single emissary command, they spring into action. Whatever the rules are for Royal behavior, these take the seriously. While Krin helps them tend to their hair and dress, I pull Tamrin aside.

"Listen, we have a problem. Brogen's team is too close. Close enough we risk they'll spot us if we are together."

Tamrin appears to consider a counterpoint. I raise an eyebrow which pulls him up short. He knows I'm not in for a debate.

"Yeah, I thought you might say that," he says.

"We can't run the risk of evacuating these two out as a group."

"Nope. I stand out like a fart in Temple," he says.

I nod in agreement.

"I can blend in and do this solo if you want to go."

He shakes his head and grips my shoulders, his big hands gentle.

"Not a chance. Couldn't live with myself if I didn't stick this out with you."

"Okay, but how do we get out of here?"

He thinks a minute and then snaps his fingers.

"You know Rouge's Pointe, northeast of here, about a day's hike into the Rhine Woods?"

"You're joking, right?" I ask.

He snickers at the expression on my face.

"Yeah, I might know the place," I reply.

"Right. What was I thinking? Anyway, I'll just head out now. You take the emissary and Jesma; I'll take Jesmir. We'll go by the southern gate. The way we came in. No one will think we'd backtrack, so it's the best option. I'll loop around the city and head north on the eastern side of the woods. You cut out and head directly to the east gate. Take whatever route you need to get there, but meet me at Rouge's Pointe, sundown tomorrow."

I nod and hold out my hand, and he clasps it.

"You get there safe," I say. "You're cutting through the eastern RhineWoods, don't stray too far east and stay out of the Garrow's Basin." I look back at Jesmir. "He's not much in a fight, I fear."

"The Raysons. Nasty bunch, that family." Tamrin glances over his shoulder at the prince. "Yeah, I'm sure he's a lover, not a fighter."

"Can you be one without the other?"

Tamrin snickers. "Not in my experience."

I nod. "I've seen it. The kid won't back down, but he'll be a liability, regardless. Listen, you're gonna be awful close to Rayson territory if you plan to be at Rogue's Pointe by sundown tomorrow. Don't dilly-dally. That's inbred country there, and they're borderline undead."

"That whole section is undead," he replies.

Tam's a strong fighter, and his access to magic in battle is impressive. By himself, I wouldn't worry about him going through Rayson territory. But with the prince? Tam will sacrifice himself to protect the young royal, and Jesmir is inexperienced enough to find trouble with little effort.

"Push him through, hard. He's pretty well healed now," I whisper.

"You watch out for those spiderlyches," he retorts, letting loose a shiver. "You're going right through their territory."

I shrug.

"Better them than the Cuska," I say.

He taps his finger to his nose again.

"I hear ya. We should move out if we want to get through the

Basin before nightfall. You should leave now, too, while there's plenty of daylight and those guys are still inside the pub," he says.

He pulls me into a bear hug.

I can't think of the last time I have been hugged.

"I'll protect him with my life," the big man says.

I look over at them.

"The emissary will never go for this."

"It's 'the emissary,' huh?" he whispers.

I glare at him, but he holds up his hands defensively.

"It's none of my business. But it's obvious that there's history there. I'm not the only one that noticed."

I'm surprised by how quickly my glance snapped to Jesma. She was too slow.

She blushes as she glances away.

The internal butterflies take flight again.

Images of last night flash into my memory, and thoughts I shouldn't entertain stir a yearning ache.

Jesmir and Jesma put up a fight over the plan. I should have seen it coming after they fought the disguises. Separating from one another would be a much bigger issue than illegally dyeing their hair. The discussion takes longer than we have, and my patience has worn thin. From my post at the window, I fight aggravation from the bitter debate, my eyes on the street. The sudden appearance of Brogen and his team exiting the Dead Eye pushes me to my limit.

The gods hate me.

Getting out of this inn before Brogen grew impatient was paramount. At least with them in the pub, I knew exactly where they were. Now, looking down on the street, as soon as I turn my back, it's nothing but a bet on Shamna Rocks.

"We have to move. Now!" My tone catches their attention. "Brogen and his team just exited outside the tavern. We need to go out the back way."

I look back out the window. Brogen points at the Jester's Pot

Inn. He appears agitated. The thought of a confrontation makes me momentarily giddy. But it's short-lived. They intend to enter this building.

"I think they are coming here for a room," I say and head to the door. "Or worse."

As I walk out the door, Tamrin and I exchange looks. It's a quick and unexpected farewell. He nods in resignation.

"You sure you want to split the royals up?" he asks.

"It's the best move. Brogen won't expect it. If they find one of us, the other will at least be safe."

He nods, though I can see he doesn't like it.

"Tam?"

"Yes?"

"If you get to Rogue's Pointe before us, don't wait more than a day. It won't be long before word of the bounty for these two reaches that place. There's not one there who won't sell you out for that money."

He nods. "Split up in the alley. You three head east. We'll head south. Stick to the plan," he says.

I turn to Jesma.

"I'm walking out this door. I'm going my way. Follow, don't follow. The choice is yours, but I will no longer accept responsibility for your safety if you don't do as I say."

I nod at Tam.

"I'll see you at Rogue's Pointe, sundown tomorrow. Don't make me wait, and for the love of Mistras' Ale, stay out of Garrow's Basin."

Without another word, I hurry to the servants' stairs. Thankfully, the stairway is not exposed to the lobby. I didn't fail to make note of the exits here like I did this morning in the Dead Eye.

Brogen is definitely coming to this inn. Whether for a room or a hunch, I have no clue. He will ask about "blond couples" when he gets to the front desk. It is safest to assume the worst, so we must make haste for the gates. Tracking us in the city will not be as easy as following footsteps in soft soil was. We have a chance if we get out now.

If ever Shamna wanted to show up, now would be a good time.

The hypocrisy of hoping the gods will help when I don't believe in them crosses my mind. It's strange how prayer is ingrained in me even though I see no value in it.

The servants' entrance is a bustle of activity. A delivery worker with a crate of apples yells obscenities at our presence in his space, but aside from an occasional sideways glances, we encounter no further resistance. Thankfully, our exodus from the building is otherwise uneventful. The back alley is more crowded than before. It's fortunate timing. We will blend in better. Tamrin and I clasp hands briefly before he turns and heads to the southern gate. I grab Krin by the arm and lean in.

"Stay close," I say, my tone cold.

She nods and says, "Just remember, you move faster than everyone else."

There's a hint of a smile there. Maybe Krin remembers me fondly. My hearts skip as we slip into old habits with ease.

I give her my signature smirk and then smile at Jesma. I almost don't recognize her, which gives me hope in the plan. What hair dye and plain clothes will do to a princess is impressive. She could be any young girl working in the city this morning. Her hair, now a subtle dark red, is unremarkable and not uncommon in Valshannon. The ordinary clothes of a traveler don't hide her figure, however. Actually, it enhances it. The pack on her back and the dagger in her well-seasoned belt provide the appearance of a traveler barely living above the poverty level. Her bearing is an issue, however, so I decide a hard pace is required to keep her flustered enough that she loses herself in the effort. The vest and pants, standard for an average female traveler of her age, are the best choice for where we're headed.

Streaks from tears mar her dirt-lined face. I reach up and smudge the dirt around to hide the tears and make her face appear more natural. Tamrin did well in the selection.

"It'll be alright," I say. "You look perfect."

Jesma's sheepish smile is endearing. Our eyes lock, and an involuntary smile forms on my face. Her cheeks blush. Even dirty and disguised, she is pretty. There's no hiding that. I reach behind her and pull her hood over her head. It's best to cast shadows over her beauty and make it stand out less. I can't look away from her eyes as I rest the cowl on her head. I imagine what life would be like if I were different or if she weren't royalty.

Foolish thoughts, Shen. Get your head straight.

"Off we go," I say and indicate down the alley opposite the direction Tamrin and Jesmir went. As I turn to head out, I catch Krin's eyes, and her look makes me feel like I have lingered too long with Jesma.

I don't know what the hell is going on with me right now, but suddenly, I feel like I'm in some sort of romance triangle of my own imagination. It's terrible timing for distractions, so I refocus my attention on Tamrin, taking one last look toward his receding presence. He's so much taller and heavier framed than everyone else that there is no hiding in this crowd for that man. Even in his home realm of Haabrestand, where they are known for their size, Tam stands out. Those damn furs don't help any, either. My only hope is that he gets down the road far enough that Brogen and his team don't happen across him.

I turn and follow my half of the party to the other side of town.

We follow our part of the plan, which is to stick to the alleys to the east gate's main street, staggering the approach away from Swill Street's hexagonal perimeter as we go. The east gate, while still well-traveled, is less busy than the north gate, and while it might be covered by Brogen's spies, they will be easier for me to spot in the less crowded entrance.

We decide to avoid both the northwestern and northeastern gates since their proximity to the northern gate makes them obvious points of egress. If I were Brogen, I'd assume the twins, in their inexperience, would most likely select one of the three northern paths if they were on their own. I'd also assume they would avoid the most obvious path north but still cover it.

It's doubtful that Brogen would consider the east gate as an option due to the dangers the eastern RhineWoods holds. The trek northward to Teshket from there is too dangerous, and even the twins would be aware of those dangers. This fact makes it the perfect option for my purposes. He'd never suspect the twins to go right into the heart of spiderlyche country.

As we reach the intersection of Main Street and the alley, a familiar face turns the corner of the row of buildings. I recognize her immediately and shift slightly to avoid her attention.

It's the woman from the Dead Eye. She hasn't taken the yellow feather off her tunic. I slow my pace and turn my body away from her. Krin notices her, too, and walks casually, blending into the crowd with fluid ease. She leans toward Jesma, feigning a natural conversation between two Valshannon girls. As we pass the lookout, I turn and follow the ladies, taking a quick peek at Brogen's soldier as I do.

I see her step onto a crate to look over the crowd.

My body tingles from an adrenal surge. There is no way she couldn't see that giant bear of a man walk down the alley. I can't take a chance at her catching Tamrin. He may have exited the alley, but I don't know. I'm too exposed to look. I continue across the main road, following the women, and draw close to Krin.

"I need to make sure we aren't tailed. Up ahead is a gap between the buildings on the right. Turn there, go two blocks, then turn left. You'll see Jana's Apothecary when you get to the next main street."

"I know it," she says.

"Go inside and wait. Look around. But keep an eye on the shop window. When you see me, if I look in the window, stay where you are. Come out if I look across the street, and we will continue. I will be with you as quickly as possible."

She turns to look at me but reads my expression and simply nods. Then she grabs Jesma by the elbow and pushes her forward. A loud crash happens behind me, followed by someone cursing. I look and see Brogen's goon pushing her way through the alley in a rush.

It's not hard to determine she spotted the big, fur-covered man. I don't waste time and accelerate my pace.

The familiar burning sensation triggers memories of how much more acute the pain was yesterday during my sprint to reach Tamrin. I don't know why it hurt so much more. I must have pushed my muscles too hard. I wish it didn't ache so much to move this way. Regardless, I wouldn't give up the ability to move fast for anything.

She nearly reaches the Jester's Pot back door when I catch up to her. I caught a final glimpse of Tamrin as he turned the corner a few seconds before, confirming my suspicion that she saw him, too.

She would have no reason to raise an alarm. Tamrin's merely a hired hand that they lost track of, so my assumption is that she moves with curiosity, not suspicion.

I still can't risk her catching up to him.

Valshannon, for all its mazes, is relatively easy to learn with some exposure to its rhythms and layout. As clever as they were in the design, I've explored it enough that I know it well. Particularly the secret places. Sewer access tunnel at every block are my greatest asset in this city. Every alley leads to a main road. Every building has a front and back entrance. It's limitless possibilities are my greatest asset for the moment.

I'm more familiar with this city than most visitors. Far more than visitors from Killinshire. As I follow her past the Jester's Pot, I formulate a plan. Up ahead, the alcove to the sewer tunnels below is on my right. Her singular focus makes this easy. She's sticking to the right side of the alley. It's perfect. The rarely traveled sewer access tunnels, frequented only by sewer workers, suit my purposes nicely. Most people ignore the activity at the sewer gates, the sewer workers considered untouchables.

Thanks to her intent focus on Tamrin I'm able to throw her halfway down the stairs before she's aware enough to cry out. By the time she does, I'm on top of her, hand on her mouth, driving her backward, off balance, into the gate blocking access to the tunnels. Her feet scramble to keep her body upright, but I have the advantage of height, speed, and surprise. Her eyes harden from panic to malice when she recognizes me from Winding Run.

"You," she mumbles into my hand.

"Me. I guess Grankin's trip didn't steal all your memories. What a shame."

The flash of fear in her eyes amuses me. I pull my hand from her mouth, knowing she won't draw attention down here. "You're that drunkard from Winding Run," she whispers. "Get your damn hands off me! Do you have any idea who I am?"

It takes all my willpower not to sigh. If I had a gold coin for every time someone said that while I assaulted them, I'd have a lot of gold coins.

Who am I kidding? I would have given away a lot of gold

coins.

"Your problem is you have no idea who *I* am," I reply.

I can almost feel the indescribable chill run down her spine when it dawns on her. I'm used to it. The reaction is always the same. Palpable fear manifests into tremors and shock—a living entity that becomes its own person in the conversation. It must be an air I give off.

I grab her hair and spin her around, propelling her forward.

"Open the gate," I command.

She resists, but I am not having it. I slam her into the gate and then pull her back. The expulsion of air from her lungs and the clang of her face against the metal bars achieves the desired effect.

Her hands shake as she opens the gate. We step through, and I close it behind me. It's pretty dark in the sewer tunnels, but small glass globes radiate a limited amount of light every twenty-five feet. Those globes are one of the few pieces of magic I am familiar with. Hard to come by and very difficult to make, the engineers' and wizards' guilds work together to create them. The energy required is intense, so most cities that can afford them only install them in places where gas lamps and fire aren't wanted.

Sewer tunnels rank at the top of that list.

The lights are worth seeing, but the stench is awful down here. I push Brogen's soldier down the tunnel far enough to make sure we have some privacy. I glance back at the gate, and I'm satisfied we're well positioned out sight and that I'll have ample warning should anyone approach. With no small amount of force, I slam her against the wall and let go of her. The back of her head impacts the stone wall with a thud that causes her eyes to roll back into her head momentarily. I have no intention of showing here kindness. I'm in a torture state of mind.

She rubs the back of her head as she recovers slightly from the dizziness and fights to catch her breath.

"Why are you after the royals?" I ask.

Her head shoots up, shock on her face.

"How do you know I am after the royals?" she gasps.

I smile.

"Good. Honesty. That's a nice change of pace. I don't usually get that without violence."

She stands up straight, defiant.

"Well, that's all you are getting out of me, Harbinger. Savor it. You caught me off guard."

I shake my head. I knew that was too easy.

"You're him, aren't you?" she says, traces of fear still there.

"I am he."

"So, what now?"

"Well, that is entirely up to you. I don't like killing women. But I will, I do, and I have. Those who deserve it. You're a killer. You understand I do not plan to be lenient."

"Who decides who deserves it?" she asks.

"Stupid question. You know the answer."

She leans against the wall and lets out an involuntary grimace.

It reeks down here. I wouldn't mind a hasty exit back to the surface, preferably sooner rather than later. But I'm not interested in giving Brogen's henchwoman the satisfaction of a shared experience, so I pretend not to notice when she crinkles her face at the feces and sewage passing by.

"What does Brogen want with the royals?"

"You think Brogen wants them?" she laughs.

I whip a knife from my belt and throw it into her shoulder. There's no time for subtlety.

She grunts and bares her teeth but doesn't scream. Looks like it's not her first experience with metal piercing her skin. Aside from the wounds I have caused myself, I have never felt the pierce of another person's attack. I can't imagine what it's like. Seeing it in the face of others is my only experience. That experience comes in two flavors. Hers is the one I like the best.

Seasoned. Like someone who's fought through this level of pain many times before.

Gritting her teeth, she says, "Go ahead. I'm not talking." She reaches to extract the blade.

"Leave it," I say.

Her hand stops, but the venom in her eyes remains. She wants to kill me and I relish the thought.

"You had your chance to kill me back in Winding Run," I say, mocking her. "You have no chance now."

With three quick steps, I move closer to her and grip the knife buried in her shoulder. She sees an opportunity and strikes, attempting to drive her knee into my groin. As with so many before her, she fails to realize I always see this coming. I twist my hips and drive into her, placing pressure on the knife as I push her back into the wall. The force of my counterstrike causes her to lose her footing. My grip on the knife lodged under her collarbone is all that keeps her on her feet. Without mercy, I spin away, taking the knife with me. As her feet gain purchase on the stone ledge, I punch her in the chest between her breasts. It happens so fast her knee catches air.

Her lungs don't.

The distinct sound of bone snapping echoes through the tunnel as her sternum breaks. The gasping sound of her fight for oxygen would be heartbreaking, except I have no sympathy for anyone connected to Brogen. Meanwhile, I continue my motion and land three steps back again. She falls to her knees, sucking wind in as best she can, which makes her take in the nasty air down here in greater doses. She gags on the putrid air of the sewers and vomits.

I wait. I don't have long, but I have a few minutes.

She fights to stand and eventually succeeds. Tears stream down her face.

"I don't have time, so your life is only valuable if you tell me the facts. Who wants the royals, then, if not Brogen? The Emperor?"

She spits on the ground.

"Stupid question. You'll never figure out the answer."

I smile as she uses my repertoire against me.

"Listen, I have no desire to kill you. I don't enjoy hurting you. But I will prolong your suffering as necessary to fulfill my charge."

"The royals hired you?" she asks.

"Last chance. Why were the royals intercepted en route to Gal-Daro?"

"For the glory of Killinshire. To right the wrongs committed against us for so many centuries. You'll never understand, and I'll never talk."

"Then you'll die."

"So be it," she says. Then, she pulls her rapier and lunges at me.

It's not even a fair fight. It's over before Brogen's spy has taken two steps. She collapses to her knees, the damage to her sternum too great. Honestly, I am surprised she lasted that long. My knife severed her axillary artery. It wasn't my intent. The low light and human error caused my aim to miss its intended mark.

It's not my finest moment.

But then again, she was an agent of Killinshire.

Live by the sword, die by the sword, as the song says. Unfortunately, I didn't get the information I was really after.

No, that's not true… she did share one piece of information. Brogen is not acting on his own. The Emperor is behind this.

It's time to get the hell out of Valshannon. It won't be long before some poor sewer worker stumbles onto the body of Brogen's minion.

This isn't my first time in these tunnels. I take the long way, remain underground, and press the pace in relative solitude. My exodus from the sewer tunnels places me well ahead of Jesma and Krin. As they approach the apothecary, they find me sitting with a half-eaten peach, people-watching. My companions walk past me without acknowledgment. I finish my peach and turn to follow. When I step up to them, coughing as I do so that she hears me coming.

"I can't believe, after thirty years, I still recognize your cough," she says.

I smile at that.

"Where the hell have you been?" she asks.

"Not now. Let's get out of Valshannon and away from people. Then we can talk."

"Oh, you can bet your ass we'll talk," she says.

"Do you two know each other?" Jesma asks.

"Long story," she says. "Not the time."

I catch a glimpse of Jesma's face. She looks displeased. Somehow, that displeasure stings. I have no idea why I care.

Late afternoon is in full swing by the time we get to the east gate, and I separate myself from Krin and Jesma, fading into the background. Brogen's team searches for a man and a woman, likely traveling with a third. Two women through one gate and two men through another gate will not rouse a single iota of suspicion.

Especially when neither of them is blond. This is a good plan.

Tamrin splurged on the hair dye. It wasn't some cheap animal blood variety where the colors take weeks to look natural. He spent good money. Thankfully, the traffic is light through this gate. Keeping an eye on Jesma from my position is easy. Krin, on the other hand, is harder to track. She blends in well, even in a small crowd. Most of the street kids became good at that. Memories and emotions of a life long since lost flood back.

I realize that I have no idea who she is anymore. Thirty-five years is a long time. I'm certainly different than that young boy who fled from the consequences of killing her brother.

Or am I? Sometimes, I feel like the same me. Other times, I don't recognize myself. The feeling that seventeen-year-old me and current me are millennia apart is hard to reconcile with the sense that I am still the same me I always was. Memories of memories, I'm sure. But, if I think about it, sometimes it's unsettling. Have I replaced old memories with new misconceptions of myself? If so, the old me is lost forever. But I still feel like I'm that old me, so maybe I never actually changed.

The trip through the east gate, down the steady incline under the wall, and back up to the main road is uneventful. We detect no lookouts. I thank my lucky stars that we made it out of the gates and beyond the city walls…and that Valshannon is as vast as it is.

Now, I can only hope that by this evening, tomorrow morning at the latest, I will find Tamrin and Jesmir safely alongside us.

We travel the Eastern Trade Road for no more than a mile. I maintain a safe distance behind the ladies. A few miles out of the city I watch them slip off into the woods on the right. I maintain a casual pace, make sure no one behind them follows, and then step to a tree on the side of the highway. It's as good a time as any to urinate. I position myself so that I can watch the road ahead and keep an eye out for indications someone follows behind.

A few more travelers pass, followed by a break in the traffic. As I finish my business, a small train of farmers' wagons approaches, their pace casual and slow. I dismiss them as any sort of threat and slide deeper into the darkening shade of the trees unnoticed. Up ahead, the motion between two oaks draws my attention. It's Krin. She's squatting. Clearly, we had the same idea.

I step up, and another old memory flashes by. Habit makes me say, "Nice bum, where ya from?"

"You know goddamn good and well where I'm from," she says as she pulls up her pants, smiling.

The smile disappears faster than a shot of whiskey as Krin remembers she's angry and hurt.

"You don't get to ask me that anymore. Not ever," Krin says, returning to where she left Jesma.

I'm unreasonably surprised at the sting. I forgot myself. I'm the bad guy, either way.

There's a woman, dead in the sewers of Valshannon, that can attest to that.

I see Jesma and walk over. She frowns at me.

"Are you alright?" I ask.

She says, "I'm fine." She's curt.

Not sure what I did.

Krin approaches, and Jesma speaks with her.

"I never thought I'd ever have to use what we were taught." I empathize with Jesma's melancholy. "I never thought it wouldn't work if we needed it, either. It seemed unnecessarily complicated when I was a kid. Now I know different."

"I'll keep you safe," I say.

She purses her lips and doesn't acknowledge me.

Jesma seems to take sudden command of herself. "Let's get going. I want to get to my brother."

Feisty women. I am somehow always attracted to them.

I wonder what people would say about that?

Chapter Thirteen

Journal Entry:45

Krin's and my history is as complicated as any story ever written. Star-crossed lovers. Twisted fates. Pick the trope. That's Krin and me. One an orphaned street mongrel, and the other sold into servitude by a heartless mother. We met in the streets of Teshket when I was fourteen and she was twelve. I remember the day vividly.

It happened on one of the many training missions when I was an apprentice at the guild—a reconnaissance mission, the target a lower Royal of Teshket. I was about to step out of an alleyway from where I observed the Prince when a small girl ran around the corner and bumped into me. We fell into a knot of limbs and curse words.

"Hey," I hissed. "Watch where you are going."

I remember Krin's big brown eyes framed by that dirty face, innocent and apologetic. It was like I had been struck by lightning. My hearts raced. Her teeth, when she smiled, were too white for a street rat, which surprised me. She was pretty, and my stomach did a somersault.

Krin was only a head shorter than me.

"S-s-sorry," she stammered.

"It's okay," I said.

Her stammer was so adorable. It took me a moment to remember what I was doing, her big brown eyes all doe-y. I was entranced. By the time I remembered the Prince, it was too late. He was gone. I had failed.

I turned back to speak to the girl, but she was gone too. It was only later that I realized so was my modest coin purse.

That little thief had not only gotten me in trouble, but she had stolen my only copper piece.

I learned two lessons that day.

The first was that I wasn't as good as I thought.

The second was that love could be the most distracting of emotions.

I spent every free minute of that summer looking for that girl. Each day I scoured the markets of Teshket, in hopeless agony, desperate to see her again. Many times, I thought I had, only to find it wasn't her. It became my existence. I'd finish my chores, complete the day's training, and head out in search of the girl who haunted my dreams.

Then, one day that fall, I finally ran into her when Harley (my only friend in the guild and a year older than me) and I were sent out as a pair. We were alternately tailing someone as part of our assignment. Afterward, we walked the streets together toward the Guild Tower when a small voice yelled, "Harley!"

A girl ran up to him and hugged him around the waist. After he hugged her back, she pulled away, tears in her eyes.

"I thought I'd never see you again," she cried.

He wiped her tears and said, "Shen, this is Krin. My little sister."

I recognized her right away. She didn't recognize me, though. I remember the strange pair of emotions I felt, both excited and disappointed simultaneously. Regardless, after that, Harley and I would take many side missions during our actual missions when we were paired together to arrange places to meet Krin.

The three of us became great friends over the next couple of years. Then puberty took hold of us, and Krin and I became more than friends. We had our own ways and places to meet when I was out on my own. That lasted until the class was down to me and Harley.

I never thought he'd actually fight me. We always knew a day would come when they would make us fight each other. Looking back, I realize why they never pitted us against each other before. What better way to identify a true killer than when the one left standing had to kill his best friend to get to the top?

We had agreed to refuse. We promised to stand together, challenge the rule, and offer ourselves as a team.

He changed his mind. I think he was always mad at me over his sister. The day came, and he didn't even hesitate. His blades, hands, feet, knees, and elbows came with cruelty, intent on harm. I ran around the arena, begging him to stop. Then it hit me. He never intended to be a team.

It was the moment I realized how much faster I was than everyone.

Everything changed for me that day.

He died in my arms, anger in his eyes that I had won—and hatred. I realized he hated me. I trusted him, and he hated me.

Then came that first contract.

Then I set the world on fire.

Sean Gregory

Picaroons, Rogues, and Thieves

The distant rumble of thunder rolls over the northeastern RhineWoods as we make our way through the mess of trees. I can smell the ozone drop to the surface, the first sign a storm brews nearby. By tomorrow morning we will be wet.

The trek through north-eastern RhineWoods takes up most of the day. The air, cooler thanks to the passing of the long days of summer, still carries the weight of humidity, and impending dread. Night falls quicker this time of year, and the road to Rogue's Pointe is still a mile away. Too far away for my comfort.

Calling it a road is generous. The path into the unofficial town is an unkempt, winding, rutted, muddy mess through this wild part of Rhinestab. It's hard to pick up from any main highways through Rhinestab. More importantly, it's dangerous and treacherous. Average citizens avoid it at all costs. In exchange for its treachery, it offers the shortest route through the RhineWoods into Haabrestand. For those in a hurry or on the run, it's the best option. Especially if you are able-bodied, bold, brave, or desperate.

Regardless of the category in which one falls, the risk of robbery, murder, kidnap, or enslavement are high. Government officials are routinely held for ransom here.

That goes double for royals from other countries.

The decision to select Rogue's Pointe as a rendezvous for our divided party was not made lightly, regardless of my status among its denizens. Rogue's Pointe and the road that leads in and out of it are no place for tired travelers, and it's been a long day already. Between our hasty exodus from Valshannon and traipsing through the RhineWoods, exhaustion hangs over all of us. Jesma's gate turns steadily clumsier with each step. Her boots scrape the ground occasionally. She's having trouble picking up her feet.

"Shen," Krin whispers.

I turn my attention toward her.

"We need to rest a moment. Princess Jesma's not used to this."

I glance back to the pampered princess. Her breath ragged and eyes droopy, she wills herself forward, shoulders slumped, in valiant determination. The same determination she demonstrated against her would be rapists. Our pace is already slower than I'd hoped, and this hillier section of the woods won't improve our progress. This hike took its toll on her. The uphill climb behind us was brutal, but thanks to exhaustion, this downhill slog is one misstep from a disastrous slide along rocks and protruding roots. Solo, I'd make it through here in less than half the time.

But we can't dally. All I can do is push these two along. I didn't account for the lesser skills of my travel companions. The air is full of nervous energy. And apparently I'm the only one who knows why.

"It's getting late," I say back. "We need to be on the road before it's full dark. This is spiderlyche country. The safest place at night is the road."

"If that's what you call safe," Krin replies.

"Better than the alternative."

I look ahead. The cusp of twilight beckons the night, and total darkness comes quickly behind. Overhead breaks in the canopy of the giant oaks offers glimpses of the early evening sky. I feel the nocturnal threat of RhineWoods waking from its slumber. It's only a matter of time.

I don't allow a rest. Thankfully, the ground transitions to flat, a good sign.

"We are almost there," I say and turn to Jesma. "Can you make it about another half mile?"

She looks at me, bites her lower lip, and nods. She has tons of heart, so I smile to encourage her.

"Good. Krin, take point," I say and point in the direction to go. I fall behind Jesma in case she stumbles.

I offer slight course corrections to Krin to maintain the most direct route through the woods to the road. Even in the near darkness, I see the small mounds of earth that indicate locations of spiderlyche beds. It's either later than I thought, or my mind is playing tricks on me because I can see the dirt shift on one.

"We haven't much time," I say, "if we want to avoid

spiderlyches. We need to hurry."

Normally, I wouldn't worry so much. Not that death by spiderlyche would be ideal. I'm simply that much faster than they are. Average travelers, like my companions, have to hope, if they fall prey, that the monster actually kills them. Partly dead, well, that means never dead.

It's a wonder the gods haven't inflicted that torture on me. Maybe they don't hate me as much as I think. Perhaps I shouldn't tempt fate.

A faint clicking noise comes from my right. The sound like boughs of treats, but more rapid. I know that sound.

"Ugh, oh," I say. A mound of dirt twenty yards away stirs as a spiderlyche underneath pushes through the layer that protects it from sunlight's dangers. The tips of hairy legs protrude from the surface as they furiously move the earth. The undead spiders wake from their underground slumber.

The clicking increases in volume. The mandibles of the wicked arachnids tapping the earth come from every direction as several emerge from their graves in the deepening darkness.

"We gotta go!" I yell, and I scoop Jesma, unceremoniously, over my shoulder and start to run. Her exhaustion complete, she doesn't even react. Up ahead, about a hundred yards, I see glowing marks illuminate in the darkness.

"Krin? You see those glowing marks ahead?" I shout.

"Yes!" she yells, her voice strained.

"We need to get past them, now!"

"I am aware of that! This isn't my first spiderlyche run!"

"Then move, woman!" I yell.

I'm surprised by how heavy Jesma is for her size, but I'm able to handle the weight. I sprint past Krin as the spiderlyches fearsome noises echo among the trees. It's feeding time. They will be sluggish at first, but that won't last long.

The creepy noises rise from the darkness and escalate into a symphonic refrain. Loud hisses now accompany the clicks. The volume increases until the pressure threatens to deafen us. The spiderlyches are free. The thought of an undead spider's bite tortures my imagination with immediate effect. Brave as I am, even I am unable to withstand the resultant panic.

My body burns with an intense fire as I accelerate, leaving Krin behind to catch up or fend for herself.

Up ahead, about fifteen more yards, I see the safe zone marked by glowing blue glyphs on the trees. The wards, carved into the oaks every fifty feet, protect the road from the spiderlyches. Yet another power I don't understand. No one has been able to tell me who placed the wards, but they have worked for as long as anyone can remember. On more than one occasion, I found myself relying on that magic. Too many times, honestly.

Krin's footsteps are lost in the noise of the rising horde. I'm not sure if she is close behind me. She'll have to fend for herself at the moment. There's no time to slow down if I expect to get Jesma to safety.

As I step beyond the tree line, I feel a slight pressure. It's like passing through a sheet hanging on a clothesline. The barrier takes minimal effort to cross, but I feel its resistance as we exit the line of trees.

I set Jesma down on the other side of the line. The road is quiet and deserted. Jesma stumbles but keeps herself up. I turn to check on Krin just as I hear a thud and a grunt. Krin's taken a fall on the other side of the wards. I can see her, and my hearts sink. She's too far back. She'll never make it.

I don't hesitate. Leaving Jesma in the relative safety of the most dangerous road in Rhinestab, I leap back through the barrier, my body tingling hotter than I have felt in a while.

The spiderlyches' cries reached a crescendo, their awareness of our presence now collective. My ears hurt from the noise. Their demented hisses evolve into ravenous slurps. They are close, the sound as disgusting as it is frightful.

A bad case of tinnitus is less intrusive.

Krin struggles to get up. Panicked, she's unable to think through her problem. Her foot is caught in a root, and she can't get loose. Eight glowing orange eyes shine in the darkness and rapidly approach. The spiderlyche is closer to her than I am. Her panic has drawn its attention, prey in a web.

With an animalistic roar, I distract the undead spider and force it to focus on me. Eight eyes glow in the early night, and the creature turns toward me. My unexpected presence causes it to pause enough to buy precious seconds. More time than I need. The putrid beast turns back to Krin, releases a high-pitched scream, and lunges.

"Oh no, you don't!" I yell.

A deafening crescendo throughout the woods reacts to the creature's scream. Every spiderlyche within miles heard the call.

"That's bad," I mumble as I leap over Krin. My actions fire more pain into my body as my muscles respond to my commands and I accelerate through the air. I don't know if it's adrenaline or fear, or what, but the extra speed and force of the leap send intense pain signals through my hamstring. I grit my teeth in immediate pain, intent on killing this beast before it gets Krin.

The smile that forms on my face belies my discomfort as I fly through the air, knees almost to my chest, arms spread like an eagle. I wink at Krin who lies prone on the ground rolling sideways to watch me, her eyes wide in admiration. The spiderlyche gazes up, turning its attention to the new threat, fangs hungry for living flesh. My hidden blades slide out of my bracers as I come down, fangs of my own. The spiderlyche, with its rotting skin, gray hairs, orange eyes, and massive body, rears up at me in defense. Rotten-smelling poison drips from its fangs as it tries to get into position to bite me when I land.

It's too slow. My blades pierce two of its eyes before it has a chance to get its fangs into position. The momentum of my body weight, aided by the pull of gravity, drives the undead creature to the ground. I'm rewarded with a sickening crunch as its fangs impact a hard mass in the earth and snap off. Its head squishes, and a sickly green ooze spreads from where my knees and fists landed. The nasty creature shudders as it dies.

I am grateful that these things are relatively easy to kill and that their guts aren't dangerous to touch. Their bite and their sheer numbers are their advantage.

Of course, from deep in the darkness, I hear an army of them approach, the screaming of their pod-member drawing them closer. It's a simple matter to turn and break Krin free. Her panic was her problem more than anything. I scoop her up by her waist, set her on her feet, and we make the mad dash to the barrier. This time, I keep her in front of me, pushing her muscles past their limit while yelling at her to move.

She's faster than I remember, which surprises me, but at least we can make good time.

My hamstring screams in protest. My run is more of a skipping, gimpy gallop. I'm definitely slower than I was a moment ago. I'm pretty sure it's a torn muscle. I clench my teeth and bear the pain, bruising my gums in the process. We're about to find ourselves overwhelmed by spiderlyches, and my disdain for such fate is motivation enough to move through the pain. Now isn't the time to lick wounds. Now is the time to get the hell out of here.

"Faster, damn it!" I yell, my voice cracking a bit.

"I'm running as fast as I can!" Krin screams her desperation at its limit.

"Then think fast thoughts!" I scream.

The panic in my voice is a surprise even to me. Krin lets out a guttural cry and pumps her arms and legs as hard as she can. Approaching the barrier, she screams as she leaps through. The clicks over my shoulder loom close. I'm too scared to look behind me, but I can sense the impending attack at my heels. With a last-effort dive, I twist in the air and get an up-close view of the spiderlyches fangs, its glowing eyes beacons of death. If death finally comes for me, my preference is to experience it eye-to-eye. My perception of time slows as I fall backward through the barrier. With a final act of defiance, I flick a knife into the creature's open mouth. Just in time, I might add. Had I not, his fangs would have sunk into my calf.

I scream with the effort as the pressure of the barrier wraps around my body in a protective shield against the spiderlyche's nearly successful bite. An undignified squeal escapes my lips when my body impacts the ground on the other side. The knobby protrusions of exposed roots impact the small of my back with brutal finality. A second undignified sound releases as I gasp to reclaim the wind knocked out of me by the landing. My head slams into the ground, and my vision goes dark, but I manage to retain consciousness while multi-colored dots shoot through my vision.

Spiderlyches slam into the barrier along the tree line, filling the area with screams of pain and anger as flashes of blue light illuminate against an invisible wall created by the wards on the trees, the interactions between the barrier and spiderlyche flesh.

My knife, buried deep in the dripping maw of the one that almost bit me, reflects the blue light. The spiderlyche screams in rage and pain, its flesh burning where it came into contact with the barrier. I watch as it scurries off, presumably to nurse its wounds. More likely to find a new victim.

"Nadur's nutsack, my knife," I whine.

Krin offers me a hand up with a wry smile. It takes me a minute to catch my breath before I can wave her away.

"I need a minute," I say and lay back down.

My back hurts. I'm partly arched backward from my position, and it takes some effort to roll over. Krin steps to me and carefully pulls me up from under my arm.

"You okay?" she asks.

After a deep breath, I say, "No. I'm tired, my back hurts, and I need a new knife. I am decidedly pissed off right now." I lean on her for a minute. "I think I pulled my hamstring," I mumble.

I push her away and dust myself off, leaning to one side, bearing my weight on my left leg. They both stare at me, concerned. Jesma, fueled by adrenaline, is wide awake now. Fear will do that. Krin snickers.

"Remember that time you fell off the wall and landed in the jagger bush?" she asks, laughing.

"Yeah, what of it?" I say, remembering how she and her brother teased me forever after that because of the sound I made.

"You sounded exactly like that time," she says, smiling.

A twinge of nostalgia threatens to overtake me as old feelings return with her smile. It's still dazzling. I put my emotions in check before they can register on my face.

"No, I didn't," I say, feeling defensive.

"Yeah, you did," she says, and pausing for effect, "Jagger Mewler."

"Stop," I warn.

"Well, at least you haven't changed too much," she giggles.

I turn away, angry at the reminder of the trauma of the nickname from my past.

On a bright note, we found the road to Miscreant Town, as I like to call Rogue's Pointe. We accomplished that with only minor injuries, no loss of life, and no spider bites. Not that it was that difficult.

I can only hope Tamrin and Jesmir are in as good a shape as we are.

"Let's get moving," I say.

I don't get far. I turn to head north and my leg gives out under me. I collapse to the ground and land on my knees. Both of the women cry out in dismay and rush to my side. I hold up my hand, stopping them.

The pain is significant, and I need a moment to rise. My lower back hurts, and so does my hamstring. I take a few deep breaths and push myself up, grunting as I do. Placing most of my weight on my left leg, I wobble, barely able to put weight on my right.

"Just great," I say.

This will be a long damn walk to Rogue's Pointe now.

I'm the weak link now, a position in which I'm unaccustomed. I close my eyes and steady myself. It's nauseating, but I hold it together and open my eyes. I test a hobbled step.

"Okay, it's not ideal, but I can walk. Slowly," I say.

Krin blocks my path.

"You plan on slowing us down, now?" she asks. "Or will you let us help?"

"I'll be fine. It might take us longer than I hoped, though," I reply.

"What if we encounter bandits? Or worse, Picaroons?"

"Well, I guess we'll have to improvise."

Jesma comes up to me.

"You have helped me more than I can repay. Please let me help you heal."

My head snaps up. I really hate healers—not this one, of course—and I'm not about to start praying, regardless of my pain.

"I don't believe in healing," I say.

"Yes, you do. You don't believe in gods," she replies.

"How…" I stop. It's the first indication a real personality exists behind the dirty mask she's worn since I met her. She smirks, and it's goddamn adorable.

My stomach lurches. Butterflies again.

"Because at every mention of the Great Eight, you roll your eyes, blaspheme, and smirk at any practice of faith you've encountered since I met you. But you witnessed me heal my brother, and you aren't stupid. You may not believe in gods, but you believe in healing."

"I also saw your scars. The telltale signs of faith healing are all over you. Not all of your scars, but some."

Damn. She's right.

"Fine," I say. "But I am not praying with you."

She smiles. It's charming, soft, and kind.

"You don't need to."

She steps behind me and asks me to drop my pants.

I blush. Krin notices and her face reddens. By the look in her eyes, it's anger. More precisely, it's jealousy.

I look away as I pull my pants down.

From an outsider's perspective, I can't imagine what this looks like. Three people standing in the middle of one of the most dangerous roads in Rhinestab, one red with jealousy, one with his pants around his ankles, and one kneeling down behind the half-naked one, rubbing his backside.

The best insult the gods could put on me right now would be the appearance of a roaming band of Picaroons. Even better if it's someone I know. That would be perfect.

The sticky salve Jesma rubs on my leg burns slightly and smells of mint. The burn isn't unpleasant and ends quickly and gradually turns icy cold. It's a mild shock to my system, but somehow soothing.

She murmurs in a strange tongue. I don't understand any of the words. It's a prayer between her and her god.

I roll my eyes.

Krin huffs, exacerbated by my childish manner.

The pain in my leg subsides to a dull soreness as the warmth of her spell spreads through my hamstring. She pats my butt, which makes me blush and look away from Krin.

"You can pull up your pants now," Jesma says as she stands.

I bend over in an attempt to grasp my waistband but I'm still in pain, even though it has subsided somewhat. I stand there, looking pathetic. Both of women break out in laughter at the helpless look on my face and more blood rushes to my face. Their joy in my state is genuine. Krin shakes her head, forgetting her anger, and bends down to pull up my pants to where I can reach them and finish the task.

"Oh, Shen," she says. "Even after all these years, it's hard to be truly mad at you."

I offer an embarrassed grin as I fasten my belt and test the weight on my leg.

"Better?" Krin asks.

I nod. "Not as bad as it was." I look at Jesma. "Thank you."

She smiles again, having regained her composure. "I only asked. Shamna does the work."

"I won't argue with you," I say.

"Still need to take it easy. It won't be fully healed for a day or two."

That sobers me up pretty fast. Mood killer, actually.

"We don't have a day or two. I'll have to make do."

Standing in the middle of the road, I remember that Jesma walks around with more money than anyone with good sense should have.

"Jesma?" I say.

"Your Highness," Krin corrects.

"Jesma," I say, looking at Krin.

She huffs. Inwardly, I smile. That's what she gets for calling me "Jagger Mewler."

Call it oppositional defiance. Honestly, it's because I couldn't care less if I tried.

"Shen?" Jesma says.

"I need you to give me your purse. Where we are going, you can't have that much money on you. Picaroons will pick your pockets within seconds."

"What money," Krin says. "Royals don't travel with money."

Jesma looks at Krin as she pulls out her purse and hands it to me. Krin snatches it before I take it.

Krin looks inside and then at Jesma.

"Your Highness, you shouldn't carry this," she says.

Jesma blushes.

"It's money I gave her," I say.

Krin looks stunned.

I snatch the purse and stow it inside my tunic pocket.

"Follow me and stay close. We'll likely encounter people on this road. If we do, you let me talk."

Neither responds. I take that as a sign of consent, turn, and head north up the road. Even with a hitch in my step, I can at least put some weight on my leg now.

I hope nothing else goes wrong.

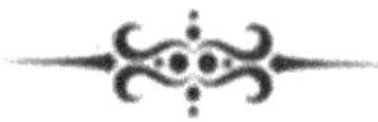

Even at our considerably slower pace, it isn't long before the atmosphere of the RhineWoods shifts. The oppressive aura of undead creatures, though lessened an hour after my uncomfortable undressing, lingers less. The mood changes as natural nocturnal activity takes over and my thoughts drift downward and hang around my loins. Much like the way my pants hung around my ankles earlier. The presence of the Princess, to whom I oddly grow more drawn, tugs at my thoughts with awkward desires. My discomfort grows, exacerbated by the presence of an old flame. With great effort, I force myself to listen to the less frightful nighttime life of the RhineWoods as it awakens around us.

An occasional bakru, with its classic raccoon mask and bunny ears, hops across the road in search of food to scavenge. It's as if we can feel the forest relax as spiderlyche country fades away behind us. But we can't relax.

We are in Rogue Country now.

Typically, by the time I reach this stretch of the road, I've been accosted by bandits or Picaroons who don't recognize me. Less than twelve miles from Rogue's Pointe, this is prime ambush territory. It's unusual for me to make it this far so easily. But it's only a matter of time. I hope this may mean we are lucky and can get to the little gathering of thieves and murderers without much resistance.

I've once again retreated into my thoughts since Jesma performed her prayer. Though healed, my back hurts and my leg hasn't loosened up. I'm not sure what happened, but I keep replaying the moment I felt the muscle tear. I've never experienced such an injury. While I'm used to the internal fire that burns when I push my limits, the feeling is different this time. Between yesterday's sprint and today's encounter with the spiderlyches, a seed of doubt sprouted into growing suspicion that I was too old for such action. The burning sensation has been there for as long as I can remember, but it was never that intense. Although I don't ever recall moving that fast before, either. I've long suspected a correlation, but I'll be damned if I can figure it out.

"Look at what we have here," a hidden caller says from the trees, wrenching me from my thoughts.

I was wondering when this would happen.

"I think we have ourselves a party," says another.

A deep and resonating voice booms, "Let's stick 'em and see if they bleed."

I hold up my hand and signal my mates to stop.

"Now, now. That lacks imagination. Sticking us would end the party before it's even started. Revelry first."

There is a pause.

I recognize the cadence of their speech and realize we are not dealing with bandits. I can't hide my smile. There's a fine line to play when you trade verbal jabs with Picaroons. They love the banter but are offended easily if you don't understand them. They never back down from a fight, even one they can't win, unless they can save face in the effort.

"Revelry comes after the work is done," says a voice.

"Work is revelry when your work is fun," I taunt, my tone sarcastic and laced with menace, "And I *love* what I do."

"Well, maybe a bit of violence is necessary! Quite a delight," the same voice says.

"It's a holiday on the roadway," I say, "why not come out and take the first dance?" I taunt.

Laughter comes from both sides of the road, simultaneously mocking and friendly.

Krin and Jesma look on with frightened curiosity.

Only Picaroons can make mocking laughter feel friendly.

Knowing the enemy before they attack is a great advantage. It means I have an edge. Few non-Picaroons have that edge. I look at Krin and Jesma and whisper, "Don't move from your spots. They'll have bows aimed at you. No matter what, stand still."

I look at Krin. "Keep your damn hands off your weapon."

Krin gives me a resistant glare but nods, moving her hand from her sword. Jesma, frightened, obeys. I spin slowly around, my limp exaggerated slightly. I'm worried about the injuries to my hamstring and back. Concerned that maybe I am aging out of this life. I've never suffered an injury from simple motion, which has me wondering how it happened.

"Well? Who's my first dance partner? It's a beautiful night, and I'm so lonely," I taunt.

"With such beautiful company, I'd imagine your dance card is full," says that voice.

"Maybe I like a different type of partner," I say, projecting.

More laughter breaks out in force, but it's changed. The mocking tone is gone.

Leaves rustle and twigs snap across the road from me in an easy pattern. I watch an older man, his skin tanned and leathery, emerge from the tree line. More hard lines are carved into his face than the last time I saw him. Still, his salt and pepper beard and mustache, far longer than they should be, well-oiled and primped, are immediately familiar. He stands on the side of the road, his hand on the hilt of his short sword.

It's been a few years, but he is known to me, and I to him. I smirk at the Ariki of the most influential Picaroon family. Not the most powerful, but not far from it.

At least, that was his status when I last saw him.

"D'aonar? Is that you?" he says. "Krikhi's scales! It's been too long!"

He turns to the woods slightly and yells, "It's D'aonar!"

"Patrin," I say, releasing my tension as I breathe a sigh of relief.

More rustling in the woods startles Krin and Jesma. From my left, it sounds like a wild beast is crashing through on a rampage. A tall, slender male bursts out, barely an adult, and rushes at me with a gigantic smile. The impact of his body with mine lights my back on fire. His hug is genuine and overly aggressive.

I let out a startled grunt.

Patrin approaches me, his arms open, "That is my youngest son."

My jaw drops as the tall beanpole lets me go.

"Nadur's nutsack!" I exclaim. "Little Ronny?"

He is a foot taller than me. He laughs.

"It's Kashni, now."

Several more Picaroons emerge from the darkness of the tree lines on either side of the road. Familiar and unfamiliar faces begin to surround me. Patrin's family has grown since the last time I saw him. Within the crowd, I feel a hand reach up to my chest, and I slap it away. It's Kashni.

Even if they call me a friend, I still have to watch my pockets with these guys.

"Kashni, is it?" I say.

"Yeah, like grandpa's," he says.

"And just like your grandpa, I will cut off your fingers if you try to take my purse again," I say, laughing.

I almost forgot about Krin and Jesma, so I let Kashni go and limp over to Patrin, arms wide. We stand a moment and smile at each other before embracing.

In honor of Picaroon customs, Patrin and I approach each other with unabashed grins, arms held wide. Our chests touch, and we wrap our arms around one another, left arm above the shoulder, right arm below the armpit. We grip our hands on each other, making sure the other knows where they are at all times. Patrin and I laugh together a moment before we step away, arms wide and hands open for all to see so everyone knows where everyone's hands are and that no items have left the other's possession.

It looks bizarre, but I rather like the custom. It's almost like a dance. The only dance I am willing to do. Picaroons have their ways. Patrin reaches up, grabs my face, and kisses me on the mouth. Another Picaroon custom. This one I don't like.

But, when in the company of Picaroons…

Krin, looking stupefied, and Jesma, oblivious to what is strange activity around her, stand exactly where I left them. I point to them as I walk over to Krin.

"These two are my family," I say. "Krin and Kalin."

It does no good to give Jesma's real name. Patrin and his family will honor them, but other families, especially those I have no ties to, will happily turn her in for any reward if they know her real identity. I may be over-paranoid, but it's too great a risk. Picaroons are Picaroons, after all.

Another reason why I had her dye her hair.

Patrin turns and walks to Krin, arms wide.

"Your family is my family," he says, his smile wide and genuine.

I nod to Krin, and she spreads her arms in like manner. He hugs her and then kisses her forehead. Lip kisses are reserved for those they know and trust. True family.

I could say that I might be a Picaroon, and while I am not, I am the next closest thing.

Patrin steps to Jesma, and she hesitates, but I give her a look that is part pleading and part don't insult him. She reluctantly relents.

Introductions and pleasantries concluded, Patrin gives the all-clear to the rest of the family, who emerge from their hiding places and welcome my "family" similarly.

A Picaroon family welcome is a very long affair. Wars between rivals have been avoided or forgotten because of the appearance of a third mutually known family, converting what could have been a blood bath into a raucous night of drinking and merrymaking and, on more than one occasion, a wedding.

Those who don't like to be accosted by other people are in for a long night when a Picaroon family welcome ensues.

Patrin pulls me aside, "Come here, my friend," he says quietly, his arm around my shoulder. We step aside while the family inundates

Krin and Jesma with questions. Patrin's eldest son, Rohr, a spitting image of his father, slaps a few hands away from Jesma's pack and pockets. The scene brings a smile to my face.

"So, their real names? Or are you in trouble?" Patrin asks.

I tilt my head to the side, questioning.

"Come now, D'aonar. We've known each other for too long. And I am the King of Liars. I am Krikhi's favored. While noble, the ruse of your injury was not fully for show," he says.

"I'll owe you a small favor," I say.

He claps my shoulder and nods.

"A small favor from you, my friend, is a great price indeed." He touches a finger to the side of his nose, "Krin and Kalin it is. The truth stays with me. Now come, let's head to camp. We have much to catch up on. You look like you could use a drink and some bedding." He winks at the last part.

Patrin turns, raises his hands, and calls with a loud and friendly voice, "Family, the day's work is done. Let's take our dear friends and make them welcome."

The band of Picaroon fighters, men and women, cheer loudly and raise their weapons in the air. We are in for a long night.

Another thought occurs to me.

I whistle to Patrin, who turns to me with a smirk.

I wave him over.

"I need a favor," I say.

He smiles.

"I already own a small favor from you. A favor-favor, from D'aonar? How can I resist!" he says, elated.

Asking for a favor-favor means I will owe a favor-favor. Favors, to a Picaroon, are the most important currency. They are only limited by custom, degree, and the lien holder's imagination.

"Name it," he says.

I tell him about Tam and Jesmir. Tamrin has been here with me a few times and is known to Patrin. I give an alias for Jesmir as Octavo.

"Tamrin's taking the south gate?" he asks. "He's coming here? I'd be worried about the Raysons in Garrow's Basin."

I pat him on the shoulder. "I am. Tam's familiar enough to

stay clear of them 'til he hits the road. By now, they are through the tough terrain if all went smoothly. Tamrin knows the Rhine Woods almost as well as me."

"Good. Good," he says.

Entering the realm of spiderlyches would not be a favor-favor. That's a huge favor. I'd be signing up for all manner of unspecified requests, and Patrin knows my skills. I wouldn't put it past him to ask me to kill a king, steal from a dragon, or rob the Emperor's vault.

I rub the tender spot on my chest where Grankin's handprint still stings in the background of my other bodily inputs. Someone has already asked me for that favor, so maybe that's not as big a deal as I think.

Patrin ponders the request for a minute.

"If they came out the south gate to head here, it's a safe bet that they are still out by at least a full day's hike. Don't worry, my friend, I'll send someone to see them safely delivered," he says and turns to the group behind us. "Cristov, Kashni, come!"

The young boy and a man who looks only a few years older than Kashni run up. The older one, his mustache not yet full and his eyes still bright with youth, smiles at me. I don't recognize him.

"This is my daughter's helpmate, Cristov. Cristov, this is the infamous D'aonar."

Cristov smiles, "It is so good to finally meet you."

Picaroons really are fascinated by me. Most of them, anyway.

I smile and nod to him, "Likewise."

"Cristov, take Kashni, grab four horses, and head toward Valshannon. Tell my eldest it's Tamrin and a friend. Make haste. Bring our friends home."

Cristov whistles and calls Kashni, who follows Cristov north on the road. A few minutes later, the pair fly past us, horses in full gallop, their hair trailing behind them like the manes on their stallions.

"Thanks," I say.

He smiles, his eyes filled with mischief, knowing I owe him. The hair on my neck tingles. I'm in no hurry to learn his plans for me.

"Ah, the vigor and recklessness of youth. I miss that energy," Patrin says. "Come, let's get your family settled and rescue them from the hands of these filthy Picaroons."

He laughs, full-hearted, and we head over to Krin and Jesma, who glare at me, overwhelmed by the attention.

"All right, all right!" Patrin exclaims. "Let's get a move on! Tonight, we make our way through to Rogue's Pointe!" He turns to me, "Don't worry, my hobbled friend. We have horses for you. You'll not have to walk on that bum leg the whole way."

And just like that, our journey to Rogue's Pointe turns into a parade of loud Picaroons full of song and mirth along the most dangerous road in RhineWoods.

Krin gives me side-eye entire trip, her brow furrowed. She is not happy about having the Princess in the company of Picaroons.

Jesma studies me with a different intent, her eyes wide with wonder. She seems surprised by the welcome I receive. Her cheeks flush when I catch her staring and she quickly looks away.

I can't help feeling like I'm in a bigger mess than I realize.

Chapter Fourteen

Journal Entry:46

I must seem like a miserable, rotten squonk to you by now. I mean, let's be honest. All I've done is complain. In case you were wondering, I'm nothing if not self-aware.

My life is a total mess. I keep busy to avoid the quiet moments.

That's the problem. It's in the breaks between activities where I find the futility of life creeps in. It saps away my desire to go on.

I can't help thinking that's all any of our lives are anyway. We create little distractions that require enough focus to force other thoughts into the background. Once completed, the background moves forward again.

Sometimes, though, it takes little effort to avoid thinking. Not often, but sometimes, life throws an unexpected obstacle at you, and you have little choice but to push on.

If I wasn't such a fighter, maybe I'd let those moments take me.

Someday, maybe that's precisely what I will do.

Rogue's Pointe

Picaroons are a lot of things—some good, others not so good. The not so good aren't said in the presence of Picaroons unless one wishes for a fight. One fact is universally agreed on, however–they are master horsefolk. Picaroons take tremendous pride in their status in this regard. Picaroon horses are well-trained, but their riders are even more so. Favoring speed over temperament, they lean toward Thoroughbreds for riding. If they like someone else's horse, said *someone* would be better off riding away and finding someplace else to camp.

Picaroons breed, buy, swindle, and steal the best horses in Rhinestab.

Riding this Picaroon-selected horse, I have no issues maintaining my saddle. Bad back and sore leg aside, we make rapid time to Rogue's Pointe with minimal discomfort on my part.

I watch Krin's and Jesma's reactions as we reach Rogue's Pointe. It is not what any first-timer would expect, or maybe it is. I don't know.

Well, for sure, on one hand, it is, I guess.

But from a village versus town versus city versus whatever unit of measure is used to compare, Rogue's Pointe is none of those. At best, Rogue's Pointe is a commune. A loosely held gathering of Picaroons, vagabonds, thieves, assassins, and unscrupulous merchants. It's heard before it's seen. What sounds, at first, like a distant gathering of geese or swans echoing through the trees gains volume and clarity as the distance grows shorter. Simultaneous high and low-pitched sounds blend together in the distance, slowly distinguishing themselves as our journey draws to an end.

It's rowdy, loud, violent, uncouth, and filled with unadulterated revelry. It plays to my baser instincts, but I always have a good time.

My first time here was a welcome surprise and a culture shock. There are no homes in the ordinary sense. There's no town square. No series of permanently fixed buildings flow along a network of roads and streets where an inn or market would generally exist. There are no residents, nor is there a political structure. There's no infrastructure to support modern civilized life, especially not one the technologists of Rhinestab would usually create.

Rogue's Pointe is precisely the opposite of Winding Run. It amazes me how two equally populated places within the same distance of Valshannon could be so radically different. Whether the locale drew in the residents or the residents created the locale is a matter of serious debate among social structure scholars. Whichever the stance, one truth is certain, when on the hunt for the best in black market goods, the strongest, albeit lowest-quality drink, debauchery, or the best thieves-for-hire, there is nowhere better to look than Rogue's Pointe.

Music from fiddles, banjos, and small bongos fills the air, accompanied by raucous singing and laughing. Mingled within the cacophony of sound, the ruckus of minor skirmishes and brawls break out. To those who call this home, it's in the name of good fun.

Rogue's Pointe is always worth a visit and usually can get me out of a funk pretty quickly when Patrin's clan is in town. It's not a place I'd recommend to someone who can't handle themselves in a fight, hold their liquor, or needs silence to sleep.

A giant wooden arch spans the road and offers the only indication we've arrived at Rogue's Pointe. The arch is sturdy and hasn't rotted in as long as I can remember. I've never noticed anyone caring for it, but it's in decent shape for its age and location. A torch hangs on each of the two pillars on either side of the road, that support the well-crafted wooden arch with stylized letters.

Welcome, Friends.
All Others Guard Your Money and Mind Your Manners.

Truer words we never written.

Beyond the arch, on either side of the road, the firelit forms of bodies move, dance, sit casually, and make all manner of merry mingled together. Each clan is surrounded by all manner and style of Picaroon wagons. Jesma gasps when she notices a few fornicators having a time in the open. Whether they think they are hidden or don't care is hard to say, but when she looks at me, blushing, a wave of desire hits me.

Embarrassed by the thought, my face betrays me as blood rushes to my cheeks and I look away.

My ractions catches Krin's attention and I find myself sandwiched between two sets of eyes that make me uncomfortable.

Krin's cheeks are flushed, too, though I'm pretty sure it's from anger. Or jealousy. I turn forward, awkward in my own skin as memories of many teenage nights of passion she and I shared return.

The sooner I get this mission over with, the better.

In the center of the road ahead sits one of the only three permanent structures in Rogue's Pointe, and the only one that can be remotely called a tavern. The modest square building, held up by four massive oak pillars at the corners and a small central building barely large enough to hold a chair, has existed for as long as I've been coming here. The hub, surrounded by a bar that flows around the outer perimeter of the building, is the only reason it can even be called a building. The outer walls of the inner building are lined with shelves housing a wide assortment of mismatched mugs, tankards, chalices, and cups. Nearly every item stolen from somewhere else in the world eventually found its way here, becoming a permanent part of the ever-growing collection until someone with enough guts steals it again.

I wouldn't recommend trying.

While theft in Rogue's Pointe is commonplace and expected, getting caught in the act results in severe punishment. The victim gets to decide what is within established Rogue's Pointe limits. Permanent maiming and death are off the table and reserved for very violent crimes.

Inside Rogue's Pointe, disputes can be, and routinely are, handled "in the ring" whether over disputed possession or perceived insults. Fights break out in Rogue's Pointe often and are immediately halted by just about everyone. Participants of the disputes are taken to the ring. Rogue's Pointe doesn't discourage fights. "Citizens" of Rogue's Point love fights. But they love betting on fights a lot more.

I often wondered why Shamna, the Goddess of Luck, wasn't held in equal regard here as Krikhi, The Goddess of Thieves. But then again, gambling amongst the denizens of Rogue's Pointe is less about luck and more about cunning. Every bet made in this place is just someone offering up their dignity for a chance to get taken for a ride.

Fights are the only fair bet in Rogue's Pointe. All other games are rigged.

Actually, so are most fights.

Bettors bet at their own risk.

Riding into Rogue's Pointe, Patrin and I converse deeply about inane topics. He can turn any topic into a philosophical debate, and his experience far exceeds his age. Mostly, he wants to know where I've been and what I have been up to. It's been almost two years since we've seen each other, and Patrin is, more than anything else, a collector of information. If Rogue's Pointe were the news center of the world, Patrin would be the most subscribed source.

He fishes for information on where I have been, directing his questions around what I've heard and where I've been. It's a give-and-take between us, and we are friendly.

But everything with Picaroons is transactional in one form or another.

Patrin's and my conversation reveals nothing the other didn't already know. It's not unusual for the two of us, so the discussion turns to the news of his family, those who passed and those who've been born, places they've been, and places they plan to go. We cover recent marriages, the growth of his status in the community, and the death of the Tillions, whom Patrin knew well. He offers a gentle hand on my shoulder to ease my shame. In some small way, it helps...for now.

Patrin is well on his way to earning the title of Picaroon King. It's not an actual title, but it is a bragging point among the Picaroon population. It is a status of strength, wealth, and a place of envy. Attaining the pinnacle of the Picaroon world opens more doors for commerce and more lucrative opportunities to match wits against the rest of society. Picaroon Kings act as adjudicators as well, for a fee, of course. Patrin has always had his eye on the title.

It's a title earned solely based on wealth. Hence, toppling the current Picaroon King is a complex task and requires a cunning, intelligent man.

Like Patrin.

We pass several gatherings of wagons, loosely clumped by "family," along the road. Space along the road to place wagons is first-come, first-served. Little campsites, free to whoever gets there first, line the road as we ride past. The wagons with the openly sold items are typically closest to the street. It's as close to a market street as anyone will get here. Shop wagons are identified by the big wooden shutters larger than a standard window.

Among the revelers and partiers mingles a contingent of shoppers looking for trinkets of interest, visitors looking to haggle on jewelry or other supposed valuables, who lack the necessary savvy to protect their wallets—eager to part ways with money for trinkets of significantly less value than they will pay. It's a game, as with all interactions with Picaroons. Visitors who know the sellers never want to lose a sale can come out ahead.

Those who don't better enjoy that costly necklace reputedly stolen from some royal princess but was actually lifted from a costume jewelry shop because they paid gold coins for copper-valued trinkets.

Either way, the sellers are making money. The gullibility of the buyer decides how much.

Walking to the side of the road, Krin notices a couple standing outside one such cart, haggling with the woman inside over a bauble of questionable origins. The negotiation is loud enough to be heard as we pass. This couple is about to get taken for a wild ride.

The world is filled with suckers.

I catch Krin's face as she turns toward the couple.

I still can read her all these years later. Old habits come back as if they never left. Memories of when she abandoned a life of thievery and turned to a life of faith come back to me. Her passion for stealing turned into a passion for helping.

A twinge of sadness rises as I remember how the change in her contributed to my decision to flee when life went sideways at The Guild.

We've been together for less than a day, and I recognize Krin's intent. I excuse myself from Patrin. He follows my sight line with a turn of his head and nods. He's probably assuming I intend to do some wooing. I don't really care what his assumptions are. I need to stop Krin from creating a situation where the Picaroons challenge her to a fight.

I clap his arm lightly and rush to stop Krin before she puts us on the wrong side of a Picaroon's anger. If she stops the sale and offends the Picaroon by selling the bauble, Patrin will have to sacrifice a lot to save her from her own moment in the ring.

Krin is off her horse already. I catch the look on the Picaroon seller's face as Krin approaches. The woman reads Krin's body language and narrows her eyes. I signal with my hand while grabbing Krin and pulling her, rather rudely, back to me.

"Hey!" she yells.

The couple turns to look at me. Krin is about to say what she is doing. I have to stop her from getting the words out. Only one activity has ever stopped Krin's mouth in the past. It's all I can come up with in the heat of the moment. It's not the ideal choice. It's the only choice.

I pull her close, wrap my hand around the back of her head, and kiss her passionately. I do not hold back, knowing I have to sell it. I feel her body go rigid in my arms as she fights me, and her hands try to push me away.

Honestly, I am not proud of this. I didn't even give Krin a chance to give permission. It will eat at me later, but it's not like I have a deep toolbox of options here.

All around me, loud cheers erupt from Patrin's family, and several onlookers gawk at the scene. A few whistles and catcalls are mixed in. While she resists, I keep the kiss going, and suddenly, I feel her body release as she throws herself into the kiss. From the outside, I imagine our behavior, fully necking in the middle of the street, hands roaming each other's backs, looks pretty tawdry.

From the even louder cheers, I imagine it looks ever more passionate. The kiss lasts far longer than I intended, and Krin pulls me back in when I try to pull away. I'm suddenly transported back over thirty years to many moments deep within distant memories. I feel myself crashing against rocks in a wave of lost emotions I haven't felt in a long time. A yearning for her builds inside, and butterflies once again release in a swarm inside me. I'm consumed with desire for her.

When she releases me, her breath is heavy, her chest heaving, and I'm a bundle of nerves. Old feelings flare, and I smile at her, deep feelings rising to my face.

Her smile fades, and too late, I realize it's a trap. I'm too caught up in the moment to notice her hand coming at high velocity toward my face. The tips of her fingers catch my ear as her palm catches the side of my face. The popping sound is deafening. Again. Not a simple slap. The brutality with which she followed through smacks my brain against the inside of my skull. My body twists from the energy, and my right knee buckles. My back notifies me of its displeasure by spasming as I drop my hand to the ground, fighting not to fall face-first into the dirt.

"What the hell!" I cry out.

She storms off while raucous laughter breaks out among the onlookers, many pointing at me, cat-calling whistles echoing in the night.

Patrin walks up to me and grabs me by the arm, laughing as he fights to help me off the ground.

"Well, I'll be damned! I've never seen you on the losing end like that. So much was explained in that kiss. Come, let's drink, and you can nurse your wounded pride back to health. I'd love to hear the back story behind that one."

"At least she had the courtesy to slap the other cheek. The woman hits harder than an angry stepparent," I grumble.

Patrin roars in laughter as he walks away, waving hello to others as they recognize him in passing.

I look up at the woman in the wagon, and she winks at me.

At least my ploy worked on one level.

Jesma and I make eye contact again. This time, my heart sinks a bit.

On another level, I believe I may have opened a can of worms.

I'm stewing over the mixed emotions waging war inside me. Warm feelings of a time, long ago, when I knew true love, are now signed with the sour emotions of guilt. The self-pity I'm about to drown in threatens to overwhelm me. For the briefest moment, I allowed myself to think Krin and I could go back to what we were. I was a fool for falling for it.

My past life with Krin left an indelible impact on my life. Krin's returned passion was so unexpected that I believed it was real. I'm a fool.

Even more unexpectedly, I'm an emotional wreck. The tumultuous rapids of endorphin-triggered excitement that surged through my body now recede as a hopeless riptide pulls me back to reality. My head spins as I slam into the endorphin crash. Sailing around my thoughts, trying to get a piece of my attention, are whispers of a feeling I get when Jesma is near.

What is wrong with me?

Watching Krin on the other side of the bonfire, comfort-able among Patrin's family as the sounds of merriment flow around us, I feel pangs of guilt. Kissing her was a mistake. Killing her brother left me forever broken, and too much time has gone by now. It's the secret I will take to my grave. Running away was the only choice I had. Using the kiss to distract her was a coward's tactic. I was wrong to do that to her. I deserved worse than a slap.

Jesma speaks with Krin in quiet whispers, and my chest aches with confusion from competing emotions toward the two of them.

This is too hard. I can't see this through.

The handprint on my chest starts to burn a little.

Damn it.

"D'aonar!" yells a drunken voice. It's familiar, but I can't place it.

I look up.

A heavy, large, dark-skinned man sporting a pattern of self-inflicted scars on his face stands at the perimeter of Patrin's wagons.

He points at me, "You owe me a fight, you son-of-a-bitch!" he yells.

It's Col-Amot. A warrior from lands well beyond the seas. He's the only person I've ever met who wasn't from the Five Realms. As cruel a rogue as any. Not a Picaroon, but well-informed on Picaroon customs and an able fighter. I've never given him the satisfaction of a fight, though he tries every time we meet. Partly because he's a loud-mouthed braggart. Mostly because he's too eager. I find pleasure in the denial of his tortured attempts to entice me into a fight.

What can I say? I find joy where I can.

Patrin stands up from where he is drinking, interrupting whatever story he tells Jesma and Krin. It requires permission to cross into the inner circle of family wagons. Outer circles are for commerce and intermingling. Inner circles are sacred.

"Col," says Patrin, "he is a guest in my house. You'll have to find another day."

Col doesn't back down. He throws a heavy purse into the inner circle. It lands on the ground with a solid thud.

"I have eighty-one Haabrestand gold in that purse that says I can take him. I'll give five-to-one odds says I can beat this puny bastard. Any rules, any fight."

I let out a heavy sigh.

Patrin picks up the coin purse, opens it, and whistles. I can't see the glint in his eyes, but I know him. Eighty-one gold is tempting. I tense. My back and leg are still sore.

He throws it back to Col, shaking his head.

"Not today, Col. You're too drunk. It wouldn't be a fair fight. The odds wouldn't cover the risk. Besides, he's hurt himself running from spiderlyches."

My heart sinks. Patrin's not denying the fight. He's negotiating the terms.

Damn you, Patrin.

Col smiles, picks up the purse, opens it, and drops more coins.

"One hundred gold, and I'll give you ten-to-one odds."

"Patrin," I warn, "no."

He holds up his hand.

"Two hundred gold, twenty-to-one odds."

Patrin looks at me, then back at Col-Amot, and throws the coin purse back to the man who catches it, his teeth exposed in a grin. He pulls another purse out, counts the gold, and tosses it to Patrin. His teeth sharpened to points, reflecting the firelight.

"Deal!" Col says.

The entire family cheers.

Patrin walks up to me, smirking, "Our favor-favor is settled," he says.

"I hate you," I say but nod. A deal is a deal, and this favor-favor is fair and within the custom.

As I stand, I turn my back so only he hears me, "You better rethink those odds. I'm down a leg, and my back is still sore. I can't guarantee I'll win."

He smiles, "Then I'll hedge my bet by betting against you with everyone else to cover my losses."

He grabs my shoulders, and his big grin flashes in the dying firelight.

Krin stands up in protest.

"We aren't here to fight," she says. "You are hurt already, and we need you."

I walk up to her.

"Krin, it's a debt. If I don't, my standing with this family will be void. My status is all that protects you two from indentured service or sale to another family. Patrin sent his son and son-in-law to get our family. This is him calling in the debt."

"But you are injured," she whispers. "Even now, I can see you aren't fully recovered from your injuries."

I shrug.

She sighs, conceding I have no choice.

I look over at Patrin and nod. His grin grows wider than I have ever seen it. He's always wanted a favor-favor from me.

As we walk, I ask him, "Are you sure *this* is how you want to cash it in? If I lose..."

His look surprises me as he speaks, his voice barely carrying over the gap between us, almost lost in the noise around us.

"I never told you this," he says, "I know who you are. I've always known. You have been there in many ways in the two decades I have known you. I knew the day you stepped in to help us against that shade."

We stop, and he leans into my ear.

"You remember that day?" he asks.

"I remember."

"Well, you never asked for a favor-favor ever, and that was a huge favor you did us. I've never paid you back. I would have sent help to your friends without a favor. So yes, this stupid fight in which you wish not to participate will earn me a lot of gold. Especially the betting. My bet is, hurt or not, you won't lose. So, don't lose my money."

A devilish look appears in his eyes.

"Oh shit," I say.

Whatever he is about to do is good for him, bad for me.

We've reached the second of the three permanent structures of Rogue's Pointe.

The ring.

"Wait!"

Everyone turns to look at Patrin, including Col.

"What now?" Col asks, his tone sharp. "We had a deal."

"And I intend to honor it. But I'd like to sweeten the deal if you allow it."

"How? It's already pretty sugary."

"Yes, I'd like to sweeten it more. Make it forty-to-one odds," Patrin turns and looks at me, "and D'aonar will fight blind."

Col breaks out in laughter.

"I don't need him blind to beat him."

"Well, then you have nothing to lose," Patrin says.

"What are you doing?" I say.

He leans in and whispers, "I may know who you are. Nobody else does. They have been waiting for a fight you could lose. Many of these families want to see me go down. They want the daughters of my family, they want my wagons, they want my wealth, and I want to be the Picaroon King."

"Damn you," I say, "you played me here."

Patrin laughs, "Just a little." He raises his finger to make a point, "But I did not lie."

On that, I laugh. No, I don't suspect the king of liars did anything of the sort. He behaved as a Picaroon would. For that, I respect him. It's my fault if I didn't see it coming.

The ring in Rogue's Pointe is little more than a fence line in the mud on the eastern side of town. Surrounded by large lanterns at the top of each fence pole, it's as pugilistically unfriendly as any space I've fought.

The sky above is a mix of dark clouds and patched starlight. Ezra is hours from rising. Dark shadows flicker in the ring from the oil lanterns. A small, elevated platform with stairs fills one edge of the fence line. The fight announcer, a fat man with multiple gold earrings and a heavy beard, stands at the top. He is the current Picaroon King. All around me, bets are taking place. Some loud and others in hushed tones. The hushed tones are where the major bets take place.

Someone will no doubt lose a lot of money tonight. I hope it's not Patrin.

The rules of the fight are determined mutually among the fighters. If weapons are used, they must be blunt, non-piercing weapons. Once the weapon selection is agreed upon, the challenger chooses his weapon. The challenged may choose the same weapon or any weapon of lesser damage.

"My fellow patrons!" he announces. "There has been a last-minute change in rules! D'aonar will be fighting blind!"

The sound of cheers and excitement that moves through the crowd could likely be heard in Valshannon. It's deafening how much noise a few hundred Picaroons, tramps, and thieves can make. The betting turns into a frenzy. I look at Patrin, and though he is hiding it, his eyes sparkle with delight as his family has spread out among the crowd, taking bets at what I imagine are ridiculous odds.

"Fighters, make your weapon selections!"

Col chooses a wooden staff. I've seen him fight with it. He's one of the best I have ever witnessed. He's also a foot taller than me, at least fifty pounds heavier, and leanly more muscular than I am— by a wide margin. If I hadn't seen him fight before, I'd be apt to think him slow. Thankfully, I have, so I am aware of his deceptive athleticism. He's as nimble as anyone I've come against.

I remove the blades from my banders, which I hand to Krin. I wouldn't trust anyone else with them. They will likely disappear. I tell her to hold them in her hands and not to hide them away. I give her my knife belt, too.

As I do, I notice the missing knife. That really chaps my ass. I don't know when I will be able to replace it. I'm down to three knives, but I put that thought away. Knives aren't part of today's battle.

"Shamna's curse," I mumble.

My boots are against the rules, so I strip them off, too. It would not look good if I were to trigger my boot knives by accident.

Fighting empty-handed with only my forearm bracers and shin guards for protection is not new to me. Sometimes I do it on purpose. Keeps me sharp. If I wasn't injured already, this fight would be easy. Even blind-folded. But I don't know how this will play out.

Col-Amot is not an ordinary fighter. I have watched him. He is outstanding, and I don't like my current odds.

In for a copper, in for a gold is the Picaroon philosophy. It's odd how it's become mine, too.

Krin offers a faint smile as Patrin steps over and ties a blinding rig over my eyes. Specially designed to cover, it holds tight, so it won't slip off but does so without discomfort. It's unique to this ring, and it is impossible to see with it on. It's disorienting, but I've worn it in a fight several times. I don't like it, but I adjust my equilibrium quickly.

My foot catches a divot in the ground, and my leg buckles slightly.

"Easy there," Patrin whispers.

"If I survive this, you and I will have words," I tell him.

I can sense his smile. "I am sure we will. What splendid words they will be."

He turns me around to face the center of the ring.

"Center is about fifteen paces straight ahead," he whispers. "Don't lose my money."

He slaps me on the ass.

"Thanks for that," I say.

He giggles like a twelve-year-old.

If there is a beauty to the moment, I struggle to find it. Maybe in the future, when I think about the day's events, I will see that beauty. For now, Patrin and I are in this together. If I lose, he loses more than money. His family could move to the bottom of the

Picaroon hierarchy. Said hierarchy solely rewards wealth and cunning.

I only hope he hasn't miscalculated. He doesn't care. I can't fight my way and couldn't even if I wasn't slightly hobbled. If I do, I am not sure how it will go with Krin. She doesn't know *who* I am. I need to plan a strategy. If I fight my way, my actions could raise red flags. I risk the discovery of secrets I have spent nearly three decades hiding.

Or am I worrying for no good reason?
I don't know.

That kiss still has me back on my heels, trapped in the fog of love lost. I'm too damned emotional for this fight right now.

"Damn you, Patrin," I whisper in the solitude of my blinding rig.

Have I found love again? Or have I discovered that I only have memories of love where she is concerned, and I'm drawn to another? When did I become a love-sick puppy?

I turn and look back at her. Well, I think, back at her. I've walked to the center of the ring and am unsure what direction I face.

I have no idea how long until the fight starts. I wouldn't care under normal circumstances. But these aren't normal. Patrin seems entirely willing to lay me at the altar of Hakaka. Blinded is fine, but usually, blind fights are mutual and more for entertainment value. This disadvantage Patrin placed on me is overly contrived. I've never heard of only one fighter wearing this stupid contraption.

Did I do something to offend him? Did I miss a clue that reveals hidden animosity?

Jesma.

I spin back, forgetting I won't see anything. Is Patrin trying to eliminate me to take the siblings? Does he know more than he let on?

Oh no.

I shake my head, clearing the thought. Picaroon or not, Patrin would never betray me. He said the debt he owed me couldn't be repaid.

My adrenal glands work overtime. Between this damn blinder, the sudden appearance of Krin, the attraction I feel toward Jesma, and seeing conspiracies that don't exist, my head is a mess.

No matter, the bell should ring soon, and I can focus on what I do best.

From the outside, I probably look lost and confused. In fact, the collective intake of breath the crowd takes tells me that's exactly how I look.

I turn my attention back to…

The collective intake of breath issued by the crowd sends a shiver along my spine.

One hundred pairs of eyes must notice the frantic man lost in his thoughts, wrestling them into submission. But they can't possibly know since my face is covered with this damn harness.

One hundred pairs of lungs gasping means…

The pain catches me completely by surprise. The sound that escapes my lips can only be made by Jagger Mewler.

I never heard a goddamn bell!

I didn't hear Col-Amot approach or the staff moving through the air. But I goddamned well heard the sound of his solid stick of wood slamming into my back with an unnecessarily brutal amount of force.

My feet break free of the mud, the suction of the waterlogged dirt slurping. The solid crack of a staff slams against my shoulder blades and slides up my spine toward the base of my skull as I am sent sprawling through the air. As I experience the unsatisfying exhilaration of flight, I thank the gods I neither believe in nor care about that he didn't target the small of my back or the back of my skull. Had he, this insufferable darkness might have become permanent.

Flashbacks of my extraordinary leap over Krin onto the spiderlyche come to mind. I bet I looked awesome during my graceful and heroic leap to rescue Krin. The memory offers no solace now. My current flight offers no delusions of grace and prowess. My thoughts and dignity shatter into an explosive flash of brilliant stars while my face contorts in pain. The sound of my cry surprises even me.

My brain misfires, incapable of processing the torrent of information thrown at it. My arms flail in the air while I sail, clueless about my proximity to the ground, my trajectory, or the distance my body travels. An image of me landing head-long into the wooden fence of the ring dominates my thoughts, replacing the rather flattering image of former heroic prowess. Thankfully, instinctual self-preservation assumes control of my motor functions. I force myself into a midair tuck, trying to roll across my seriously aching shoulder blades, or at least that's what I try to tell my body to do.

Everybody probably saw this coming. I didn't. I'm apparently much lower in the air than I thought. My roll lands me solidly on my head in the mud. My neck cracks from the impact, and I fear irreparable injury as another unflattering sound escapes my lips. My lower back screams at me as a reminder of how stupid I am for allowing myself to get into this situation.

Today is most certainly not a good day to die. I'll be angry if this is how I go out.

The crowd releases an enthusiastic "Ooh!" when the echo of my back flop in the mud rings out. I can't express enough gratitude to the ground for knocking the wind out of me, mitigating another uncharacteristically high-pitched cry.

Yep, I won't lie, this hurts.

I hear a handful of cheers. Clearly, those who bet against me.

Then there is a handful of curses and several exclamations of "Get up, D'aonar!" calls.

Me? I'm contemplating sleeping here in the mud.

I recall the woman whose life I extinguished only hours ago. Her expression as I knocked the air out of her can't be much different than mine. Little colored dots fly by in the darkness of my mask. My body tingles as nerves respond to the expulsion of oxygen from my system.

My brain fights for oxygen.

Beyond the ringing in my ears, I hear footsteps slopping in the mud.

Get up! I scream at myself. I have no idea how close he is to me.

Get up!

Yeah, it's not happening.

But I can hear him coming. I need to roll away. Most people roll away.

I should roll away.

"Move!" I hear. It's a familiar voice.

Get up, Shen, I tell myself. But I have no idea what is going on at the moment.

"Move! For the love of Ezra! Move!"

It's that voice again. There's desperation in it.

Oh, it's Jesma.

Images of soft, sparkling skin, flush cheeks, and an awkward smile flash to mind. Longing stirs me while I allow myself to fall into the memory of Jesma's naked form in the inn. I can't resist the smile forming on my face. I can't explain why she enthralls me, but she's kind, pretty, and won't leave my thoughts alone.

I remember the moment I first saw her.

She's a fighter. She and her brother are running for hundreds of miles through the unfamiliar and dangerous RhineWoods, pursued by the most dangerous man in Conishant. Here I am, behaving like some lovesick and horny teenager. The last thing she needs is this macho, bloodthirsty psychopath fawning all over her. She put up a ferocious fight against four men who saw her as little more than an object of their desire. I'm one more predator in her world. She's a princess… I'm not even the help. She's so much higher above me I'm fooling myself into thinking there is more there.

She only wants to get home. My role in her life is as her guide. I am a means to ensure her safe return.

My brain is the first to recover.

It's instinct. Many years of ingrained, hard-won instinct. I've never been this far down this early in a fight, but I have been down before. That was against three other assassins. Each one is much more skilled than this slob who sucker-punched me.

I feel a familiar twinge.

I don't like to lose.

I have no idea how long my thoughts left me lying there. However, since Col-Amot hasn't delivered another strike, it can't be as long as it feels.

If I taught fighters, I'd tell them to take notes. My opponent sees an opportunity and approaches, likely swinging his staff with all his might, the violent impact with my head or chest imminent. Rolling away risks him catching me with the tip. Supposing his reach is as long as I think it is, rolling toward him, will catch him off guard. In that case, I stand a chance the angle of the staff will cause it to impact the empty space created by my roll and provide the opportunity to escape unscathed.

Rolling toward him, it is.

It takes far more effort than I anticipated while I fight for breath and have no damn clue where the enemy is. I'm not mistaking this moment; this guy is my enemy.

I struggle, briefly, to extract my body from the divot in the mud. However, the body aches reassure me my movement is still fast, and I manage to roll into Col's path. The soft whistle of an object moving through the air at a high rate of speed makes its sound above me, his grunt giving me direction. I roll toward him with every ounce of energy and speed.

Damn. Col-Amot is as good as he thinks he is.

The slopping sound of his foot lifting from the mud is all the warning I receive before his foot crashes into my stomach while his staff, as predicted, strikes the soft mud behind me.

I curl into a ball. Col's outthinking me, and I will never know what oxygen in the lungs feels like again.

Am I going out humiliated? That's just perfect.

I curse Patrin for this.

I curse Krin for kissing me.

I curse my mother for selling me to a bunch of assassins.

I curse the gods for their utter hatred of me.

I curse myself for not paying attention.

I did this to myself.

I'm tired. Tired of hating myself. Tired of fighting. Tired of possessing only one good skill. Hell, I'm not even good at that right now. I want to cry, but there's no time for that. I want to give up, too, but Brogen lurks in the shadows somewhere. The twins are counting on me. Patrin is counting on me.

Why do I insist on helping? Why is this my burden? Why can't I have a simple life, like Mistras and Cali? Why does this world hate me so damn much?

My frustration boils over and changes into my most useful emotion.

Rage.

I snap. Pain and love no longer matter. Only beating the ever-loving piss out of this guy matters.

I sense his body shift, his heavy breathing accompanied by a slight grunt. He over-planted when adjusting to switch his staff attack to a boot attack, and now he's stuck in the mud. It's not a significant advantage, but it's enough mistakes in execution to give me a brief advantage.

I catch enough breath to say, "Ugh, oh."

It's funny how tides can turn without warning. Sometimes, I get lucky and roll the elusive twenty-three.

Like now.

My snarky two-word comment actually causes him to pause. It's brief, but each stutter to his routine provides a tactical advantage to me. Even injured, tired, mentally exhausted, and emotionally drained, I am still the fastest person in Conishant. Sometimes, less than a second is all I need.

There's one boot I can feel in the mud between my arms and legs… the one he used to kick me.

The other boot I can hear a couple of feet away angled toward my head stuck in the mud.

What I'm particularly interested in is what's between those legs.

I'm actually smiling. I can't help it.

Ask any guy, and they will say there are two types of pain they hate when it comes to their nether regions. The first is a solid blow to the beanbag. Yeah, it hurts. It lights me up instantly. But I can recover pretty quickly.

The other goes by many names. But mostly, we call it "the graze". It doesn't hurt right away. It's a startling moment when we think, "Oh man, that was close." We briefly celebrate how lucky we were that we didn't just take a shot in the nuts.

It's a false moment of security. First comes the twinge. It's a brain stutter as synapses think, "No. Not close. That could be a direct hit." Then go back to "No, I'm okay.", which is immediately followed by "Ugh, oh."

We'll instinctively wait a moment in case the situation changes, which it does. Right when we think we are safe, that tiny twinge flares, like a matchhead that's struck but flashes out, only to flare into a bright, sudden flame as you go to strike it again.

The graze is exactly like that.

It has to hit *exactly* right.

Rolling myself onto my back, I swing my right arm toward his naughty bits, speed offering my only advantage.

The warm, satisfied glow of perfect execution washes over me, and the euphoria of a tidal shift in the fight makes me smile. I wait for the entire crowd to acknowledge how perfect it is. I give myself the moment to wait for it.

I love this moment. I bought myself some needed time.

Even though I'm in the dark, I imagine the scene as it plays out. First comes the expected sigh of relief from Col-Amot as he incorrectly assumes I missed his balls with my backhand swing. The crowd takes a collective breath while he reaches down, checking I didn't remove them. He stands, frozen in place, assessing whether the impulses in his head warning of danger are accurate.

I don't have to wait long before I'm rewarded for my efforts with another collective gasp. Col-Amot's cry of pain and the cheers from those who bet on me bring an elation that is only slightly more satisfying than the disappointed guffaws from those who bet against me. The brief moment of celebration energizes the crowd.

His fight to hold himself up gives away his position, and the location of his feet is easy to discern. I stiffen my fingers and drive them into the soft, fleshy region between his thigh and his hurting beans. A satisfying scream escapes his lips, and the tremors of his body from my relentless assault on his private area reverberate through the mud.

He drops to one knee and attempts to pin me with it, but this time, I anticipate his collapse and reverse my roll, knocking his bo-staff out of the way as I roll under it. The staff falls to the ground, a soft thump in the mud behind me.

His loud groans transition to a growl.

Half the crowd cheers, encouraging my escape.

The cheer when I stand up is deafening.

Col-Amot's condition won't last long, but it buys me much-needed time to escape, stand, and gather my wits. I run, blindly trying to find the fence line, and slam into it with a grunt.

I lean against the fence. Encouraging hands slap my back and shoulders in celebration. I walk along the wood barricade, my brain struggling to recover, using the fence to stay on my feet. As much as I would like to finish this fight, I am blind still except for the stars floating in the darkness of the blinding rig. Adrenaline once again courses through my body.

It's time to think.

My biggest strength in fighting is not my speed. It's recognizing the intellectual component of it and the psychological one.

Everyone knows the physical one.

The intellectual one requires fast thinking. Outthinking my opponent is the tool I rely on the most. The psychological one is harder. Most fights don't last long enough to use it. I need to either build their confidence falsely or tear it down methodically. I use every tool in my arsenal in a fight. My emotions are instinctual. My brain always guides my decisions on a level I can't understand.

The shooting stars finally subside as I regain control of my breath. My leg struggles to hold my weight, but it's solid enough. I take a step forward from the fence and collapse to my knees.

The crowd gasps.

I hear him get up and charge at me.

His steps are still distant, so I have time. His feet splat in the mud, louder as they close on my position. I take a solid breath and think about my height, his height, his angle of attack, speed, likely posture, and every detail I can muster.

It's a guess at the moment. Poor Col-Amot. Unfortunately for him, I have had time to think. He has been waiting for his balls to stop hurting.

I don't think he noticed me recover. He thinks I am down from pain and lack of air.

I almost feel sorry for him. Almost.

My fingers claw in the mud as I feel his presence and hear his foot land less than two feet from me. My legs fire, mostly my left, but my right offers enough support for my intentions. Both of my arms come flying straight up as I cross my bracers slightly above my head. His staff makes an impact with the notch I created. I drive my legs forward, taking advantage of my lower center of gravity and the energy of my upward and forward momentum. His staff, locked in place, tilts more upward as I drive forward. When I feel his hands, I pull my arms apart enough to sidestep into his body and push my hands into his face, raking the two large clumps of mud I am holding across his eyes, rubbing it in as I do.

"Now we are both blind," I whisper.

Now, it's a fair fight.

The staff immediately falls from his grasp as I spin under his armpit and land a solid punch where his axillary artery passes. I feel the staff impact the ground and feel his body arch to the side from the armpit punch.

It's a very satisfying feeling.

Funny truth about arteries. They contract hard on impact. It's a natural protective contraction. The momentary interruption of blood flow feels slightly akin to a limb falling asleep, and I don't hold back. I follow through on the armpit punch in the same ruthless manner he did with his staff attack. It's full force, total momentum, wholly driven by my core and legs.

I imagine my fist severing his arm from his shoulder. That's my intent, anyway.

I chastise myself for overreacting, but I'm furious at how hard he hit me with his staff. I'm reasonably certain his kick to the ribs cracked at least one.

As I finish the punch and my spin puts me at his back, I hop up and put him in a full headlock, locking one arm in the other. His hands go from his eyes to my arms as he tries to pull at my forearms.

"Nighty night," I whisper in his ear as I wrap my legs around his torso and lock my ankles. Then, I take it one step further and elongate my core. The motion lifts him fully erect, knocking him off balance.

I squeeze hard and cut off his angry growl, my arms locked around his head and neck. He throws himself backward, hoping his weight will crush me and cause my grip to release.

This part will hurt, but I couldn't care less. The impact will no doubt suck. But I'm in my happy place. This asshole's going down.

The landing isn't half as bad as I imagined it would be. It hurts, but I'm hurting everywhere right now, so this new pain is mild by comparison. I waste no time cutting off respiration and circulation. Col-Amot's body goes rigid on top of me as his attempts to break free weaken. It doesn't take long. Mud in his eyes, the expulsion of air from his fall, and the pressure from my hold against his throat overwhelm his senses. He flails in panic.

He knows he's done. I imagine he is seeing the same stars I saw earlier.

He taps my arm with both hands, acknowledging defeat and begging for me to let him go.

The crowd loses its mind over my ruthless pursuit of choking my opponent out, cheering me on. I stretch my body tighter, ignoring his taps, which grow more desperate.

A small voice sounds tugs at my conscious mind, and I remember that Jesma is watching me. The mental image of her disdain arrests my rage, and I take control of myself. My hold loosens, and although I want to hold this grip 'til all motion ceases, it isn't the honorable choice. He tapped out.

My arms fall away and land in the mud. The pressure on my chest lessens as he rolls over, choking coughs wracking his massive frame.

He plops beside me, and we lie in the mud, gasping for air.

"You," he gasps, "fight better than anyone I have ever known."

"Thanks," I reply, breathless.

"You should come to my homeland, D'aonar. We could make a lot of money together."

I reach up to release the clasps that hold it closed and pull the mask off. Rolling my head to him, I reach over and pat his arm. He's breathing heavily and barely conscious, his face resting in the mud.

"I have no intention of ever fighting you again," I say, smiling.

He laughs a soft, quiet laugh.

"No. Nor I you, D'aonar. I was wrong."

Rolling over, I push myself to one knee, catch my breath for another minute, and stand up, but everything hurts. I step around Col and offer my hand as he rolls onto his back.

I wait.

He nods slightly, reaches up, and takes the assistance. Col-Amot's a heavy man, so I grunt with the effort.

We shake hands, and I turn and return to where I last left Krin, Jesma, and Patrin.

Patrin's grin, still as wide as his face, creeps me out.

Jesma and Krin are not smiling. Both carry their own mixture of worry and disapproval on their faces.

It's another day in the life of me.

The Growing Darkness

Chapter Fifteen

Journal Entry:51

Picaroons and I have a lot in common. Neither of us makes a permanent home. We travel constantly, finding ways to earn a living either off the land or off the people of the land. They drink and dance (no, I don't dance, but I love to drink) and have a good time when they can (I guess I'm less of a good time these days), but they do not judge people for their choices. There's pragmatism there. They believe everyone has a story, and every story is of value. The inherent belief is freedom over everything else. Of course, they mean it in the most literal sense. It's how they justify their belief that nothing in your hands is off-limits to them.

A famous Picaroon proverb goes, "If you are careless enough to lose it, then I am careful enough to relieve you of it."

But their stance on liberty has a great benefit to the wanderer. Picaroons welcome everyone, as long as you don't come empty-handed (otherwise, how could they con you out of anything). As long as you follow their customs while with them, they will make you feel welcome. Even if it is only to take advantage of you.

That part's not my style.

Their customs are a hard and fast rule, though. Greetings, fare-wells, challenges and betting, marriages, alliances, and most of all, favors.

They don't give you long to learn them.

Offending a Picaroon is the surest way to a fight.

It's not something I've ever worried about, but you can't say I never told you if you should encounter them.

Picaroons are a welcoming group, especially if they find a kin-dred spirit in you. Finding kindred spirits is a big deal to them. If they call you "friend," you have a ready army at your disposal should you need them.

But nothing with Picaroons is free. Everything has a price.

One commonality the Picaroons and I have is fighting.

Picaroons love to fight. It's a pastime of theirs. They fight each other for fun in sparring matches and create silly rules for a fight. Every night there is a match. They bet on fights like it's their sole reason for living. Fortunes and status have been known to change over-night, for better or worse, due to fight-night gambling.

I've never lost a fight.

Picaroons like that about me. I'm a sure bet for them.

They know me by the name 'D'aonar.' It's a Picaroon word roughly translated to 'lonely tooth,' the Picaroon equivalent of telling others I shouldn't be messed with or bothered with unless invited. The name never stops them.

I like Picaroons. They seem to like me.

Especially one in particular.

Nowhere to Hide

For the first time in a long time, I wake up not by Ezra making me angry but by the pleasant smell of coffee. I haven't had coffee in so long. It's the one great luxury of life I crave. I'm rarely privileged with its presence. In fact, I haven't even smelled it in months. The rich aroma wafting into my sleep, softly beckoning me to semi-consciousness, is too enticing to ignore.

I'm not immediately sure where I am. Bright colors and light, cool fabrics surround me. The bed I'm lying in is comfortable, soft, and large. Too comfortable, really. I contemplate not getting up.

But there's coffee.

Rolling onto my back, I recognize the interior of Patrin's wagon. It's not exactly like I remember it. There are some new fabrics and some extra items around, but it's still familiar. I've spent many moments in here sitting with the man in deep discussions. Patrin loves to talk about philosophical and existential topics as much as he does gossip and tall tales.

I stretch my muscles, releasing a groan, too stiff to move effectively. My body hurts in too many places.

As the fog clears, I realize I'm in Patrin's bed. Not wanting to panic or draw any rash conclusions, I try to recall the events leading up to my ending up in this position, but nothing comes to mind. I retrace my activities of the previous night, but a mental block prevents me from remembering much.

I begin to feel some emotional discomfort, but the bed is too comfortable to force myself to jump out. The stiffness and soreness are the more immediate problems rather than debaucherous memories that may or may not have happened. My shoulders hurt pretty good. I am sure they are bruised. If I could rub them, I would, but while I am flexible, I am not that flexible.

There isn't a memory I can recall where anyone hit me as hard as Col-Amot. It was a new experience. One I don't wish to repeat.

I didn't like it.

A quiet cough across the wagon catches my attention. As I force my head up, I see a wide-toothed smile. Patrin sits in a chair, holding two large cups in his hand. Steam billows out of them, a misty siren calling my name. My eyes sting at the crusty sleep I haven't felt in—I can't remember how long. Another rare experience. A solid and peaceful night's sleep. I'd almost feel human now if my body wasn't so sore. Last night may be the most restful sleep I have had in a long time.

No, not last night. It must be midday or maybe early evening.

"Are those for me?" I ask, yawning and rubbing my eyes.

"One of them is," he says.

"Coffee in the evening?" I ask. "I'd think you'd be halfway through a keg by now."

"It's too early to start drinking, even for me," he says.

"Early? Never heard you waiting for sundown."

He giggles a little. "My dear D'aonar. You slept through the day and the night."

I snap upright and notice I'm completely naked again. That familiar twinge of panic builds again. Did I black out? What manner of shenanigans did I allow myself to be a part of last night? The thick fog clouding my memories is unrelenting.

"Wait, did we?" I point back and forth between us.

His laugh comes out so quickly that he almost spills his coffee. Though valiant, his fight to control himself fails miserably, which only makes him laugh harder 'til tears form in his eyes. I shake my head as I realize how silly the question was.

"What is it with you people undressing me while I sleep?" I blurt.

He laughs.

"Oh no, my friend, you did that on your own. But don't worry. Your belongings, including your quite heavy purse of Realm Notes, are in my safe." He points to the iron trunk on a shelf. "And so is your chastity!" He laughs again.

"You know me too well. You went through my bag." It's a statement.

"Of course I did. Reena undressed you and found it. Which, by the way, we should discuss Reena." He gets a twinkle in his eyes.

"She seems to have really liked what she saw."

My mouth falls agape while his eyes sparkle with the mischievous light of a schemer. I sense another game afoot. Before I can comment, the look vanishes as quickly as it appears.

"Anyway, believe me, I was tempted to take your purse off your hands, but, well, maybe I am getting soft," he says as he hands me one of the mugs.

The smell alone revives me.

"Well? Why didn't you?"

His laugh is hearty.

He lowers his voice to a whisper, "I am not the richest Picaroon King in the history of Picaroons, but I am close."

"Oh!" I say softly. "Umm, Picaroon King?"

"Haha! Yes, while you were busy emptying my kegs of ale—and letting my daughter nurse your nice bruise, by the way—I collected the debts owed to me from your fight."

He sips his coffee.

"And now I am the richest of all the Ariki. You couldn't have performed better if I had asked you to. When you struggled to get up after that brute took you down with his first strike, I doubled the odds I would pay out if you lost. The betting and eagerness of those hoping to take me down was exhilarating! It's been a while since I took such risks!"

"You could have lost everything," I say.

He shakes his head. "No. I knew you would not go down like that. Though, I did worry for a second. I thought maybe you weren't overplaying your injuries like I initially thought. But no, that is not how you will lose in this life. This I know." He taps his temple with a flair. "I have faith."

"You'd be the only one in here who does."

He laughs again. "My coffers would disagree with you!"

I drink my coffee. It is a little too warm but tastes so good.

"Well, I think you did your best to break my bank yesterday in retaliation. I'll give you that. I'd forgotten how much you can drink. It put a smile on my face to see you running around like a horny teenager."

"I what?" I blurt, mortified.

His laugh again is joyful and earnest.

"Oh, I have never seen you so lively. Let's say a few of the ladies were smitten with you. If you were so inclined, there are more than a few marriage offers."

I ignore the comment.

"My family?" I ask, changing the subject.

"They are in the wagon at the center. Safe and protected."

He points at my chest.

"What's with the handprint?" he asks.

A dark shadow briefly passes over his face. It happens so fast that I'm not sure I didn't imagine it. I shake it off as my imagination. The attention, however, causes me to rub it. It's not burning at the moment. That's a relief.

"It's a long story for another time. The simple answer is I have a debt I can't escape."

"I can't wait to hear it someday. Marks like those come from powerful magic." I can tell he's leaving out more details, but asking would have a heavy price I'm not interested in paying. He drifts into his thoughts, and I watch, knowing my curiosity would cost some price to satisfy. "You've gotten yourself into a pickle, it seems."

"I can take care of myself," I reply. "Take your worry outside."

His expression grows pensive, concerned.

"What?" I ask.

"It's nothing really. Mere curiosity."

"Information is king, is it not?" I reply.

"Ha, yes, it is!" he says. "Name your price."

I shake my head. Only a fool would name his price first. It's a ploy. We have entered the game, as they call it.

"What is the curiosity?"

"You are curious now. Intrigued by my curiosity?"

Now I laugh. The circular logic can go on forever, and I'm ready to take it to Patrin.

"I'm not curious enough. I have my own matters to attend to. Be gone with you," I say as I wave Patrin away.

He concedes quicker than usual. Whatever it is, his concern is more vital than his desire to win. I catalog that information for later.

"You can't blame me for trying," he says. Then his brow furrows.

I wait for him to ask his question, sipping my coffee. Whatever is bothering him, he is not taking it lightly.

"I have many questions for you, D'aonar. There are too many, and I fear the cost of knowing will outweigh the value of the answers. Not knowing, obviously is anathema to me. But, as you are, at least in spirit, family, I feel I must ask. My conscience will not allow me to let you walk out of here without offering payment of some kind. I only hope you will answer honestly."

Whatever he is about to ask, I now know, is heavy.

"Why do you have a Teshket Royal Signet in with the money you carry? Why do you have a note written in Killinspeak asking you to eliminate someone for twelve thousand Realm Notes? What have you gotten yourself into, D'aonar?"

My jaw falls slightly.

"Have you become willing to kill for money?"

I spit out coffee.

"What do you mean a royal signet ring?"

He looks disappointed, almost angry with me. I set the mug of coffee on the bedside table beside me.

"Do you think me a fool?" he asks, a warning in the tone.

I recognize he feels he knows the truth, and his hospitality requires me to be honest with him. While I don't have to tell him much, what I do tell has to be the truth. My status in his life is important to me, so I answer him truthfully.

"Hell no," I say, honestly. "I thought I recognized the ring, but I couldn't place it. In fact, I had completely forgotten about it until this moment."

My attention is focused on the revelation. Can't believe I didn't remember. Has it been so long since I've been away from Teshket? Years flow, and the memories of another life seem distant and foreign.

I don't know which Royal House, but now I see what has been eating at the back of my mind. There are too many to count. Could it be the twin's father's ring? That seems the likely answer.

Regardless of who it is, he now knows more than I wish he

did. I will have to be very careful how much I withhold versus how much I reveal. Savvy is an adjective used to describe Patrin by nearly everyone who knows him. His ability to read people and situations is only outmatched by his skill at negotiating and wordplay. His mastery over manipulation and observation is legendary.

"If I answer your questions, this will be the largest debt you have ever owed," I say.

"Come now," he scoffs, "I thought we would be beyond games at least a little by now."

"I am not for hire. Ever."

"Tell me your tale, D'aonar. I will help if I can. No debt owed is greater than the one I owe you. It can never be repaid in kind, and that was before the fight."

If I tell him the truth, then the "man with information" will have information that can make him richer than he is now. It's a temptation some Picaroons will betray family for. The risk is too high.

His gaze bores into me, and I squirm in discomfort. Patrin is no fool. He can spot a lie better than anyone I've met. It's an unwelcome gaze, and the silence hangs on long enough to erode hospitality. Picaroons and their damn customs and games. I have to choose my words carefully, so I go formal.

"Father, I do not wish to offend you. What you ask is not mine to give. I am charged with discretion and cannot give you the information you are asking."

He thinks about this.

"The hospitality I show you is more than mere guest. I'll give you a home. That has value."

He is right.

"As you have said, the value is one that, to be fair, has been repaid many times over, notwithstanding last night," I say.

He smiles. He knows I have him there.

"But, as my friend, you have earned trust," I say.

He raises an eyebrow and strokes his long mustache. He nods.

"D'aonar. I wish to make you family. All the rights, protections, and privileges that come with such status. You know I have always wished to call you my son. Reena would be pleased to hitch her horse to your wild wanderings." He looks at his hands as he speaks, "But you have earned that right without marriage," he says and then looks at me. "Without any strings, please accept me as your Ariki and be a part of my family. I will not ask you to stay. I only ask you to check on us more often than you do. Say, at the start of every season, we meet here?"

It's a big deal. What Patrin is offering freely, I cannot say "no" to. In fact, I realize now I don't want to say "no" to it. If I knew writing down my thoughts and raw emotions would profoundly affect my understanding of myself, I might have done it sooner. The feeling I have for this request overwhelms me.

Unable to speak without breaking, I nod.

His smile is the most genuinely honest and pleased smile I have ever seen.

"What I can tell you is I took that purse and its contents off a man I killed who was in the process of attacking my family with me here today. In a vile sense."

He leans back in his chair, contemplating the facts of my story. He believes me. He also knows I'm leaving out details. Details he'd like me to reveal.

"There is a rumor I heard just six days ago while south of Winding Run," he says.

"You were south of Winding Run six days ago?"

He flips his hand in the air.

"Irrelevant," he says. "While performing business, I caught wind of interesting news. A rather significant bounty has been placed on a pair of travelers, a man and a woman. Seems they who are wanted for theft and murder in Killinshire."

"I heard this rumor as well," I say.

"I heard another rumor."

"Go on," I reply.

"I heard another interesting rumor."

"You don't say."

He laughs. "I do say, D'aonar. I do say! A ship departed from the Isle of Pal in Teshket, bound for Gal-Daro. That ship never arrived, apparently lost at sea. Word is the Duke of Pal, Prince Jhemai of Teshket, was on that ship. Further, I heard he may not have been traveling alone."

I hope I am holding a good poker face. Right now, I can feel my ears getting warm. Thankfully, I have long hair. Otherwise, I'm sure Patrin would see them turning red.

He continues, "There is a bounty making rounds within our mutual sphere of influence, young man. Very lucrative, I might add. Someone seeks a pair of siblings. Blond hair, blue eyes, about twenty-four years old, give or take. Rumor is they're the children of Prince Jhemai. One Princess Jesma and Prince Jesmir."

He'd know if I lied here. Rather than reveal my cards, I shrug. "That is similar to what I heard."

He smirks. "Yes, I imagine you would have. What I find strange is you are traveling north, clearly with purpose, carrying a signet ring of the Royal Family of Teshket, with a young man and a young woman, despite their hair color and clothing, are clearly siblings."

I keep my expression flat.

"Would you say blue eyes are very rare?"

"Not as rare as green," I say. Mine are green.

That elicits a wry smile.

"What did you say the names of your family members are?"

"Krin, Kalin, Tamrin, and Cristov."

He purses his lips.

"Right, Krin, Kalin, Tamrin, and Cristov. Not very often do you see two people together with blue eyes. Rarer still, they would be a redhead and a brunette, no?"

He leans back in the chair, his nails drumming the plush arm.

I maintain a steady breath, but my hearts race. Patrin didn't attain his position or live this long without a healthy dose of cunning. I am trapped in the discussion. Without calling me a liar, he's revealed he knows I haven't been entirely forthcoming or truthful, and he knows I know he knows.

The only reason he hasn't called me a liar is because I've been upfront with him about the false names back on the road two days prior.

To continue to lie now would be a great offense.

"D'aonar, it is clear to me you are in trouble. It was clear the moment I saw you. No one braves the spiderlyches so close to their waking, not even you."

"Patrin, I wish I could tell you more. You will have to trust me. It is a big ask."

He waves his hand again flippantly.

"It is not. As I said, I am merely trying to repay a debt and care for my family," he says. "Of which you are now part. You would have to do far more than not tell me everything to lose that. Besides, you made me a lot of money last night. If I were an honest man, I would say I owe you a huge favor!"

I raise a finger, but he stops me.

"Good thing for me. I am not an honest man!" he laughs.

I can't help but smile.

"Can I ask how much you made?" I ask.

"You could, but I won't tell you. Let's say your paltry eleven Realm Notes won't touch what I took in yesterday's betting. The other families will be throwing daughters and sons our way. Some families bet more than they had and now are indebted to me for the unforeseeable future."

He stands and steps to the wagon door.

"You let me know if you want to come back and stay with us? Reena has had an eye on you since she turned of age, and after last night's spectacle, she won't leave me alone." His wink causes me to shudder.

"She's beautiful, incredibly so, and bright, but no, I am not the marrying type."

He nods and points at me.

"No, I would say you are not. But you now have a place to call home. Here with us. Any time you decide, simply show up and stay, son. Welcome to my family." He stands, leans close, and whispers, "Shen-zarl of Ditherun."

I wish I could say I hid my shock. But that was far more information than I thought Patrin meant when he said he knew who I was.

"How?"

"I am the Information King, remember? There's little I don't know," he says. "Now, get dressed. Your friends arrived while you slept. They are waiting for you to get a move on."

With that, he tosses me the key to his safe and walks out the door of his wagon, stopping as he does.

"Shen, I fear you are mixed up in some predicament that could well be the death of you. That signet ring? It's not an insignificant find. Best you aren't caught in possession of such an item. Be careful. Always remember, if you need our help, do not hesitate to ask. Every one of us will gladly put our lives on the line for you."

Patrin steps into the bright, cool morning, leaving me to my thoughts.

Not the least of which is me wondering where the hell he gets his information.

Four cups of coffee, several slices of wild hog bacon, and a hearty handful of Picaroon bread later, the entire party is back together. Tamrin has a new gash across his nose, Jesmir's cheek is bruised, and he has a few new scratches. They look rough around the edges but are safe, and they made it out of Valshannon and through Garrow's Basin alive. It's a victory.

Tam and I hug when we see each other.

I can tell by his manner he's more than well-rested. One of Patrin's sons walks by and touches Tam on the arm with a finger, tracing his triceps as he passes. Tam smirks and watches him walk away.

"Well, I see I wasn't the only one enjoying Rogue's Pointe," I say to him, laughing.

He shrugs.

"When in Rogue's Pointe," he says and brandishes a shit-eating grin.

We sit at the long table, scraps of food all that remains. Enjoying a final cup of coffee together, Tamrin tells me a little about their journey and how they "ran into some trouble" along the way. But when I press for details, he refuses to go into it much, giving no context. I am shocked by his secrecy, but knowing Tam, he will tell me what happened in his own time. Whatever it was, Jesmir seemed a little more reserved, almost traumatized into a mild state of shock.

I made a mental note to ask Tam for more details about it when we are alone.

Most of the morning is spent in discussion of yesterday's fight and my naked dancing. I entertain no delusions that the naked dancing story will outlive the tale of my exploits in the ring. I'll never hear the end of it. I wish I remembered dancing naked.

No, I'm glad I don't.

Tam listened with great interest.

Catching snippets of retold stories, I learn I emptied a barrel of ale single-handedly. I take solace in that legends are usually exaggerated. The revelation that I stripped off my clothes under the encouragement and help from Reena, who took a seat next to me, mid-story, with another plate of food, causes me to blush. My cheeks flush as she leans over to reveal nearly all of her cleavage, watching my eyes as she does. I resist the urge to look, maintaining eye contact to avoid encouragement. But I have to hand it to her; rather than act disappointed, she smirks, accepting the role of the pursuer.

I smile as I look into her beautiful black eyes but do not give in to her temptations. As she walks away, the silk skirt swaying with her hips, I turn and catch Jesma and Krin both watching me. The scrutiny makes me squirm, and I feel the blood rush to my ears again.

Pretending not to notice, I focus back on the plate of food and start shoving another meal into my mouth.

All in all, Rogue's Pointe was a good stop. We didn't get robbed, murdered, or sold into slavery. I gave up little in return besides a bruise stretching across my shoulders and a bit of muscle soreness from exerting myself. The wounds will not slow me down enough to be a liability to the party. The long rest helped my back and hamstring pain, so there's another positive.

Col-Amot has avoided us all morning. It's good. He got played, and I don't know if he's smart enough to figure it out, but I don't want to tempt fate. Hell, half of Rouge's Pointe got played. More than a few Picaroon families lost status in one night's betting. The amount of money that changed hands could probably run a small country. Capital is power, even in the Picaroon world.

One family is especially not happy. The long-reigning

Picaroon King thought he was outsmarting Patrin and placed a lot of bets against me. Apparently, he had been pushing for Col-Amot to egg me on.

I suspect, however, that most of the money that landed in Patrin's chests came from non-Picaroon travelers and merchants thinking they were more intelligent than the most skilled con people in the world. It always amazes me how many people fall for the Picaroon charm. Everyone thinks they are the exception, not the rule.

We gather our possessions and say several farewells to members of Patrin's family. Tam pays particular attention to Patrin's eldest son, Rohr, whose company Tam seems to have especially enjoyed.

I stand with Patrin and watch the events as my party approaches, ready to head out.

Reena strolls up, her hips swaying so the slit in her dress rides high enough that she almost reveals more than the top of her leg. She accomplished her goal and caught my attention. I chastise myself for the indiscretion as her smirk widens, knowing I fell into her trap. Her long dark hair and deep brown eyes sparkle. She's a stunning beauty. In another life, maybe. But there's someone else invading my thoughts now.

Two actually.

"Father," she says, eying me with lust, "I want him."

She sidles up to me, hand on my chest, breasts against my arm, and bites my ear playfully. I pull my head away gently, my eyes pleading with Patrin to make her stop.

"I made the offer. But alas, our D'aonar is not the settle-down type. He has places to go and people to save," he says, only half-joking.

Reena pouts and runs a finger across my lips.

My discomfort appears to bring everyone around me some form of mild amusement. Krin tries to hide her pleasure at my discomfort. She is enjoying this. Maybe she can sense the competing emotions brewing. Patrin pulls his daughter by the arm and shoves her behind himself, protecting me from further embarrassment.

Jesma's glare shoots daggers at Reena. I pretend not to notice but am surprised by my pleasure in her apparent jealousy.

"Alas, dear daughter, he's immune to your charms."

She peeks over his shoulder and says, "He is for now."

Her lascivious smirk, while erotically enticing, makes me feel like a piece of meat at an auction. That continuous river of self-consciousness comes rushing in. I look over at Jesma, wondering if I have been doing the same to her unintentionally while simultaneously trying to indicate Reena's attention is unwanted. But Jesma ignores me.

I feel like it's deliberate, and my stomach twinges with disappointment.

Patrin hands me a small wooden box. It is elaborately built, well-polished, and has a pewter clasp.

"What's this?" I ask.

"Your sigil, son," he says. Reena's eyes sparkle as I watch her lick her lips at me.

"Get out of here before she drags you back to her wagon and seduces you," he laughs.

Tam laughs. "You couldn't do much better than that right there!" he teases.

I scowl at him. We say our "thank-yous" and "goodbyes" and head north along the road out of Rogue's Pointe. As we do, I look up at the sky. The clouds that have threatened to release torrential rains for days are now dark purple, almost black.

A storm approaches.

And right now, I am moving only to avoid standing still. I have no plan or idea how we intend to safely transport these royals home. We gave up a day due to my drinking binge. That takes some of the joy out of me. Until now, I hadn't thought about the consequences.

As we walk, I remember the signet ring, which I haven't had a chance to mention to my mates. I prefer haste out of Rogue's Pointe, putting as much distance as possible between Valshannon and us before nightfall, so I am not inclined to do anything about it now. For the moment, one foot in front of the other is giving me time to think. Then, I can tell the rest of what I've learned.

Thunder rolls in the distance. We each look up at the sky.

It's going to be a long day.

Chapter Sixteen

Journal Entry:53

Please remember, these are my private thoughts. This was never meant to be shared. It was meant to be in my pocket as I walk this life to its final conclusion.

But why write it down if I'm heading toward death? If it's never meant to be shared or seen, then what's all this for?

Is it a series of lamentations?

I changed my mind. I hope I am dead. And I wish it to be a spectacular story. I hope this journal celebrates a glorious tale of virtue, value, friendship, and sacrifice instead of a pointlessly sad ending.

But who am I kidding? I am neither virtuous, valuable, nor friendly.

Unloading these burdensome thoughts is for me. I am putting these down as an attempt to release them. If anyone reads them, then whatever death came about was sudden, unexpected, and likely done on a whim.

If you struggle, like me, with these thoughts, know you are not alone.

> *Actually, I changed my mind again. I hope I'm not dead.*
> *I really do hope all I did was misplace this journal.*
> *I don't want life to get the better of me. I really don't.*

Sean Gregory

Some Pains are Royal

It's as treacherous heading out of Rogue's Pointe as it is coming in. Pick either of the roads, and it will offer opportunities for some trouble. The only benefit of heading north is we are almost out of the Rhine Woods. A benefit easily overshadowed since at the end of the road looms the Valley of Cusk.

Regardless of the end or direction, we are still on the road into Rogue's Pointe and within the Rhine Woods. The ever-present danger hasn't changed.

What does change is the terrain. The ground is starting to make a steady climb uphill. The northern parts of Rhinestab are lined by the Toerge Mountain Chain, which runs the full border between Teshket and Rhinestab. It's a critical barrier keeping Killinshire out of Teshket forever. Rhinestab is the first line of defense for Teshket. The Toerge Mountains are the last. Killinshire has never been able to cross the mountains. They aren't equipped for the cold or the climb.

A treaty going back longer than the oldest person alive established the border between Rhinestab and Teshket as the peaks of the Toerge chain. The natural border between the two also creates a significant difference in climates. It's strange how some arbitrary geographical barrier can change the behavior of an environment.

Getting through undetected won't be easy, and losing a day at Rogue's Pointe wasn't ideal. Unless we choose one of the two established trade routes through the mountains, the Rhine Woods will be the beginning of our struggles. We will reach a decision point soon as we'll be through the Rhine Woods well before sundown. Sufficient for today is that hurdle. However, we still have some tough miles ahead before the mountains become a concern.

After some consultation between Tamrin, Krin, and me, we decide to get back into the woods and off the trail sooner rather than later. There is a natural break in the tree line marking a standard trailhead that makes its way to one of only two passes through the Toerges. We plan to stay on this road for a mile beyond the trailhead and enter the woods, where it is a little more treacherous but less likely to be tracked.

Hopefully, we aren't molested by bandits on the way.

Hope is the faith of fools.

I wish the altercation wasn't inevitable. But Tamrin and I expected it after Patrin delivered the news of how much wealth has shifted within the Picaroon hierarchy. Hell, it's possible as anything, anybody would have seen this coming. There was no way there wouldn't be ramifications from the fight the other day. More than one Ariki lost status after so much wealth exchanged hands. One of them was bound to seek retribution.

As we reach the trailhead and leave the road before it heads back to the King's Regal Highway, we encounter three wagons blocking our path. Eleven men and women, strategically stationed in a semi-circle, weapons ready, face us as we approach.

"D'aonar," says the Ariki Morgan. I recognize the fat fight announcer. We've never really gotten along, and he harbors resentment over my unwillingness to grant him the same access to me Patrin enjoys. It's always been a source of contention between us.

Unfortunately for him and us at the moment, he was, until yesterday, the reigning Picaroon King. I assume he's here to exact his revenge on us. He smiles as we stop about twenty feet away.

Tamrin doesn't hesitate. He pulls his giant hammer from his back. I hear Jesmir's bowstring stretch.

I guess we all expected not to escape Rogue's Point without some altercation.

"Morgan," I say, matching his tone and inflection.

He steps forward. I step forward.

Thankfully, my limp is gone. My back only slightly hurts, but Jesma's salve did the trick on my hamstring and shoulders this morning. She wasn't gentle when she applied the pain suppressor before we left, but at least she used it.

"You cost us everything," he says, the statement an accusation. "That little ruse you and Patrin pulled had quite the effect on more than a few families."

"There was no ruse on my part."

He looks skeptical.

"Well, it's the way of fortune. For me, it's the nature of Picaroon life. I will be back to the top soon enough. It isn't the first time I have fallen and clawed my way back."

He looks at his family behind him. "But they aren't as hopeful as I am. They want recompense."

"I have no quarrel with you or your family, Ariki Morgan," I say, giving deference to his position. I am hoping to talk my way out of this.

"Ah, yes. You know our ways and provide the deference of a Picaroon." His eyes narrow. "But you are no Picaroon."

"Oh, but I am now," I smile.

"Bullshit."

"Ariki Morgan, what you say is not true as of this morning. I am a son of Ariki Patrin. This title has been granted to me without the requirement of marriage. As such, I am provided the protection and the rights of such membership."

He scoffs.

"He made no such offer, and you are afforded no such claim."

I look to Tamrin and Krin. They both nod to me. Turning back to Morgan, I pull out a small chain from around my neck, dangling the tiny, barely the size of a thumbnail, hand-cast platinum sigil in the form of Patrin's family symbol.

I don't need to say anything. Morgan knows my possession of such an item can only come as a gift.

"This can't be. Patrin has D'aonar as a son?" The Ariki is stunned by the news. Behind him, his family begins to fidget. If only my reputation didn't precede me, even disguised as D'aonor.

"He does," Tam says.

Morgan's scowl deepens, if that's even possible. He points his rapier at me.

"Then clearly, you two were in cahoots. Patrin would never extend such a favor otherwise. That man loves no one but his harlot daughter and money. The rest is an asset to be bought or sold."

I shake my head. That didn't go as I hoped. I raise my hands. The sounds of bowstrings stretching, one on either side of the line of wagons, draw my attention.

"Ariki Morgan..."

"You can stop with the formalities, D'aonar. You aren't fooling anyone here."

I continue. "I do not wish to see you and your family harmed. Please allow us to pass. I am not looking for a fight."

He laughs as a man half-crazed with anger and jealousy. His losses must have been staggering; he's gone insane, the laughter manic. Uncertain, his family cast furtive glances at one another, shocked by their Ariki's behavior.

The elders of the family fidget, their stances lacking resolve. I recognize only duty keeps them in place. Morgan is their father and Ariki. But he is barely holding on as the leader of his family. The loss of his status broke his mind. This must be his last-ditch effort to hold on to control.

"Well, you have an unfortunate habit of attracting fights to you, now, don't you?"

I look back at my allies, signaling them to keep their weapons down.

"This will not return your status. But I have eleven thousand Realm Notes. I offer them as payment for your loss. You can have them freely to rebuild your status. Let us pass without a fight."

"Father," says one of the sons with a bow. "It's a fair offer. Please, let's take it."

He doesn't even look at his son. Instead, he yells, "What he has with him is worth far more than eleven Realm Notes!" His voice screeches as he screams.

He points his rapier at Jesma and then at Jesmir.

My heart sinks. Morgan is after the bounty. That is how he intends to regain status.

"Royal blood runs deep in those two. You can try to hide your hair with pretty and expensive dyes, your Highnesses, but your hands are soft, and your eyes are blue. The bounty for you is the greatest wealth any Picaroon has ever known. It will put me right back on top."

He points his weapon at me.

"Your family isn't here, Angel, to the Picaroons," he says.

"There's a new title I haven't heard," I mumble.

I'm unable to talk my way out of this predicament. He means to take the twins and turn them in for the ransom. No amount of money will stop him from trying. Looking around at the men and women of the blockade, it is apparent Morgan's family is unsure of this course of action. I have one chance.

"Ariki Morgan," I say. "You dishonor me, Ariki Patrin, and your family with this action. I beg you, don't do this. I will kill you if you force me."

I look to his family.

"If you fight alongside him, we will have no choice but to end your family line here. I won't only kill you; I'll burn your wagons to the ground. Everything… and everyone… inside."

Looks of horror bloom across the faces of Morgan's family. They exchange glances, unsure if I mean what I say, but knowing my reputation, they have little doubt about my authenticity.

I look to Morgan.

"I will spare your family and fight you. Alone. If I win, your family will let us pass. If I lose, you can take my family as payment for your loss. Mind you, you are wrong about who these two are. It will net you nothing but good fighters and strong genes."

"Lies," he hisses. "My family stands with me. You will die here today, regardless."

He twists his torso in preparation to lunge with his thin blade. I take zero joy in the moment this time. I honestly wished to avoid this.

As always, it's this feeling of everyone moving slower than me.

He thrusts his hips forward. Before his feet have stepped, my hands drop to my knife belt, and I flip two knives toward his sons, impacting their notched arrowheads. Both arrows slip out of position and fly in a tumbling arch. Before the arrows land back on the earthen roadway, my hidden blades slide from my wrists.

Morgan hasn't even landed his step, and I am spinning away from the tip of his flexible rapier. I slap it down with one blade as I finish the spin move. The other slides into the base of his skull.

He never feels my blade. His body, lifeless, falls forward from the momentum, sword dropping from his grip.

I come to rest facing the rest of his family. When I stop moving, my blades are ready for more attacks. I watch as dawning realization overcomes them. Their father is dead, and they haven't even had a chance to move.

I don't know what came over me. Keeping my speed down when there are witnesses has always been instinctual. A habit honed over the years to protect myself. This time, however, restraint never entered my mind. Only one person in the world moves as fast as I did. They take their eyes off the dead father and look at me. Swords, staffs, and bows drop to the floor.

"D'aonar is The Harbinger!" one exclaims.

The words ring in my ears. The world becomes a blur as I realize Krin heard the words, too. I spin around to look at her. Her eyes are filled with tears.

I have nowhere left to run.

The rain came almost as soon as the words that I am The Harbinger of Death landed on the eardrums of my party. Never doubt the cruel irony of fate. Any delusions I harbored that the past would ever be reconciled between me and Krin dissolved the moment she heard them. My thoughts accelerate through stages of grief. It was a fool's dream to think it could be any other way. Run as I might, I can't outrun who I am or what I've done.

I rolled Shamna's cursed five.

Death is the only way out of the nightmare now.

The rain has turned the roads into a muddy mess. Leaving Morgan's family without a word, we push past the blockade. They don't raise a finger after the death of their Ariki. News of Ariki Morgan would reach Rogue's Pointe before Ezra reached her zenith behind the dark clouds.

Worse, everyone in Rogue's Pointe will know who I am now.

Patrin will be happy over the news. His status as Picaroon King will never be challenged once it is revealed The Harbinger of Death is one of the sons of Ariki Patrin.

My life, as I knew it, is over. Krin hasn't said a word to me since that moment. Slogging through the RhineWoods, hours later, she stays well to the right of me, avoiding eye contact and proximity. I only know she is still there because of her quiet conversation with Jesma and Jesmir, who walk alongside her. I keep looking over, but it's as if I no longer exist.

By this time tomorrow, the identity of The Harbinger as D'aonar, son of Ariki Patrin, will reach Valshannon. By the end of the week, the news will arrive in every town and village within one hundred miles.

Then Patrin's joy at the word going out will be short-lived. Within days, bounty hunters from all over will flood Rogue's Pointe. I've been Patrin's son for less than a day, and without even trying, I have become his burden.

I never wanted this.

Krin has every reason to distrust me; the twins see me as the monster I am now. Jesma only sees the killer when she looks at me. I will be stuck behind this mask forever. Until recently, I had never let myself think I would ever be free of it. But then I had these moments between me and Jesma or me and Krin. Or me and Patrin. Somehow, in a brief span of a few days, I lost myself in little moments of peace. Peace I hadn't felt since the early days with Krin.

I find myself lost in a spiral again. These thoughts circle, pushing me ever more distant from the rest of the party. I stumble, not paying attention to my steps. I wish I could be invisible.

A gentle hand touches my shoulder.

Tam.

I've been mildly aware he's been watching me. I see the worry on his face. It's unfair to him to travel with me like this. But it's all I can do to not run away. How long will it be before someone links D'aonar to Shen-Zarl? Patrin already has that connection. Will he keep the secret?

My thoughts drift to him. How does he know me as Shen-Zarl? He doesn't even know my name is Shen. Until this morning, Tam was the *only* person in the world who knew all three personae— Shen, D'aonar, and The Harbinger—were me. Or so I thought.

The big man stares at me, gentle and kind, and I see the love there. His big beard is soaked from the rain, pulled almost straight by his periapt of Fildeus tied there. I know how he feels romantically, but his love is more complex than simple romance. He's my brother, as genuinely as can be without blood ties. I'll never understand how he's able to cope with the emotions inside himself, but he does. He never burdens me with it. I'm not sure he even knows I am aware.

That makes me feel guilty.

I'm so sick of these highs and lows. It would make sense if I were a teenager, but I'm a grown man. I'm tired of the ride.

I smile weakly at him, trying to reassure him I'm fine. He knows me better than that.

"Shen, you can't carry this burden alone."

I'm grateful for the rain. At least Tam can't see my eyes water. But he can see my shoulders slumped from the pressure. He pulls me into a gentle hug, not a bear hug. It's a brother's hug, strong, stable, pure.

I weep silently. I'm not able to stop as the tears come. I don't remember the last time I actually wept.

Yes, I do. Thirty-five years ago.

"Now, you'll ruin my furs with your damn tears," he growls after a moment.

I laugh and wipe them away. There's no time for tears. Tam has once again pulled me out of my head. If I'm the anti-hero, he's the hero-hero. I push him away.

"Get off me, you creep," I jest.

He pushes my shoulder. "You're the one sweet on me."

"It's that hairy beast of a body and your chocolate skin. I can't resist it," I tease.

He laughs. "If only."

I point at him. "Don't get any ideas."

He points his chin over my head. I turn to look at Jesma, Jesmir, and Krin. Thankfully, they never noticed, and they are still pushing ahead. Krin turns to look for us, realizing she doesn't see where we are. Tam waves at her.

"We're fine," he says.

"Tam needed a hug!" I yell back. "He gets scared of thunderstorms in the woods. Lightning," I say, twirling my finger at the sky.

He pushes my shoulder again. "I don't get scared. You do." He turns and starts walking again. I follow him, grateful he never makes a big deal out of vulnerable moments.

We continue through the woods for several miles. My thoughts return to the needs of the moment. It's unclear whether we are free from Brogen. If he hasn't already, he will eventually figure out he missed us in Valshannon and come looking. I don't know if he'll try to intercept us at ValleyView, Coraside Bay, or if he thinks we are crazy enough to risk the Cuska and try to cut through to Hericot. Regardless of his choice, Rogue's Pointe will find itself on the list of options.

There are only a few ways we can go through the Toerge Mountains, which are well-known and most well-traveled. It's not an unreasonable assertion that Brogen will have planned ahead, either. He could have any number of spies at each location, making our choice moot and arbitrary.

My only real hope is we get the twins on the other side of the Toerges before running into him. I'm not worried about fighting him any more than I am anyone else. I've got that covered.

I'm not sure how many he'll show up with, and there's only so much I can do, even as skilled as I am. I'm confident the twins will be safe once we cross the Toerges. Brogen would never be stupid enough to cross into Teshket.

Then again, he murdered a royal. He somehow got his hands on a signet. The revelation from Patrin about the royal signet weighs on me. I have pieces of a puzzle but no clear picture of how they go together. The answer may be obvious, but I don't like the obvious. Rarely are answers so simple.

Rogue's Pointe is now several hours south of us. Time is hard to track in this rain, so I'm unclear how much time elapsed.

Tamrin has been uncharacteristically quiet since my little breakdown. An awkward silence hangs between us, and he seems a little haggard. My thoughts center on him. He hasn't mentioned it since breakfast, but I can't help but feel the flight from Valshannon to Rouge's Pointe carried some trauma with it. Our altercation with Ariki Morgan also weighs on him. Whatever it is, when he's ready to open up, he will.

But the silence is getting to me, and I'm exhausted with my own thoughts.

I sidle up to Tamrin, looking ahead to ensure Krin and company are out of earshot.

"I need to show you something," I tell him.

He gives me that sideways glance of his. It's his "I'm listening" look.

"Ever seen this emblem?" I ask as I drop the signet ring in his hand.

He inspects the ring and offers a mixed nod and shrug.

"That's a royal emblem from one of the Royals of Teshket. I'd think if anyone knew, you would."

"Yeah, but who?"

He looks at it again and shrugs.

"I thought you learned this years ago?"

"You know I haven't been in Teshket since the Season of Inipin."

"Wow, it's been that long? I hadn't realized. Time does fly," he ponders. "Well, see the dragon?" he asks, finger pointing to a dragon in a two-footed stance.

"Yeah, that's the Royal Family emblem of Teshket."

"Yes, but look at the position it's in."

It starts to come back to me as he talks. I chastise myself for not remembering.

"In this case, the dragon is on the right, facing out. Whoever this belongs to is in the northeastern territory."

"Right," I say

He nods.

I study the ring again. "Then not Pal," I say.

His brow furrows.

"No, not Pal. It would be facing up if it were the island territories. Why do you say that?"

I indicate with my head toward the trio ahead of us.

"They are from Pal," I say.

He lifts his head in understanding.

"So not theirs."

"More importantly, not their father's," I say.

He nods in agreement.

"Is there a way to tell whose ring it is, specifically?" I ask.

He stops walking.

"I am sure there is. I mean, we know the territory. These other features," Tam points to a sword in the dragon's paw and a star overhead, "mean anything?" He raises an eyebrow, "You're from Teshket. You should know this better than me."

"I didn't pay attention during that part of 'murder for hire' school," I joke.

We walk in silence for a while.

"There may be other royals at risk," I say. "We should ask ours if they are aware of others going missing."

Tam doesn't reply right away. "I don't like this, Shen. Killinshire can't be trusted, obviously. But The Dark Guard chasing Teshket Royals through Rhinestab? That's an aggressive move. Then there's the Teshket Royal signet ring in the hands of bandits with more money than makes sense? What if the twelve Realm Notes were a coincidence and not the payoff from the note?"

I nod. We are both thinking it, so I say it aloud.

I respond, "If the bandits murdered another traveling royal of Teshket as a contract and wanted to be paid, they'd need proof of the death. A royal signet would provide such proof the job was done."

"Even though royals don't carry cash, their escorts do. Likely a sizable amount. A stack of money would be a lucky take if said bandits succeeded in the primary goal. A random robbery in the most dangerous territory in the realms would explain it."

"You know, though, the money is Haabrestand notes. Not Teshket," I say.

Tam waves that off, "Many people travel with Haabrestand currency. It's the strongest in Conishant." There's pride in the statement from the man from the eastern realm.

"The bandits assaulted the twins. Robbing foreign royals is risky. Under normal circumstances, Teshket royals travel with skilled guards. It would take a seriously skilled bandit to accomplish a successful robbery. One as good as those I dis-patched when rescuing these two. It would explain his skills and answer so many questions."

"This could be a coincidence, though. Assuming it is, the next question is, what is Killinshire up to here regarding these two?"

Tam nods. "But if it isn't a coincidence, we must ask other

questions.”

“Right. Is this a much bigger play on Brogen’s part? Or on the Emperor’s, right?”

“Hard to believe Brogen would embark on a play this big without the Emperor’s approval,” he says. “Let’s think about this. Teshket is a significant ally of Rhinestab who has the second-largest military in the Five Realms, rivaled only by Killinshire. If Brogen takes out royals throughout Teshket, there must be a pattern. It can’t be random. There has to be a reason The Duke of Pal was targeted.

And poor Rhinestab, stuck between the two realms, is always at risk. All three Great Wars were started by Killinshire. Her lust for control of the continent and utter hatred of her northern border neighbor goes back centuries. If it suited their purposes, they’d have no problem creating tensions between the allied nations.”

“I don’t like this,” I reply.

I look up at the twins.

“You don’t think there’s some truth they aren’t telling us, do you?” I ask.

“I don’t know. But let’s catch up,” Tam replies.

We pick up our pace, not wanting to lose sight of our party.

I’ll have to talk to Krin.

Unfortunately, I have no idea how to approach her anymore.

Usually, wandering the RhineWoods provides a sense of tranquility. Regardless of the dangers contained within, I manage to exist with few troubles. Now, however, after three days and nights, I’m honestly tired of looking at oaks and maples. Since leaving Rogue’s Point, we haven’t been dry for a second. The RhineWoods begin to wear even me down after a while, regardless of how much I prefer their presence. The forest is vast, covering more than half of Rhinestab. Sometimes, these trees never end. Getting through them takes forever. Two forevers when going off-road.

Being hidden for three days of travel from Rogue’s Pointe, Ezra has had little opportunity to reheat the air. The three days of constant rainfall have broken our spirits. The ground, soaked, muddy, and slick, causes an occasional slip or fall. What protection the trees offered at first ended when the sheer volume of water worked through the leaves in heavier drops than naturally fall from the clouds above.

And the palpable tension amongst us isn't helping.

Tamrin, usually so positive, curses at every root he trips over and every slick rock his foot slides from. His water-logged and matted furs make him appear as a drowned wolf rather than a man. I offered to take some off his hands, but he refused, not wanting to burden me.

Up close, he looks and smells like a wet dog.

We are making him stay downwind from us, which only makes him feel worse, but the smell is foul. His apologies are heartfelt, but no one cares, no matter how sorry for him we are.

Midway through the fourth day of hard, slow travel in the saturated forest bed, the trees finally begin to thin out. The rain hasn't slowed, but the widening gaps between trees allow some wind to come through, at least providing fresher air. The difference is noticeable. Unfortunately, the temperature drops, which causes a chill we can't escape.

The RhineWoods, never one to give an inch, begin to increase the grade right when we receive a reprieve from the stagnant air. The foothills of the Toerges, fewer than fifty or so miles north of us, already coax the land into a gradual slope upward, turning the previously flat trek into an effort-inducing climb, making walking even more treacherous. Losing footing results in a backward slide, further adding to universal misery.

More than once, one of us has slipped and fallen twenty or more feet back. Even I haven't been immune to the treacherous footing.

The ferns and other foliage lining the forest floor thin out as the soft earth and tree roots are replaced with rocky earth... and tree roots. The maples and oaks give way to a smattering of evergreens. Temperate plants will give way to the cold, hearty varieties within a mile. Rivulets of water come down the slope as we climb. More slipping hazards, slowing us down further.

By the time the Ezra has made her way to the horizon, we arrive at the end of the oaks, maples, and ferns... and to a decision point.

We haven't hit the actual mountain range yet.

Before us sits a more sinister, dark, and dank obstacle, its mere presence pressing against our psyche.

Even I don't find solace in this part of Rhinestab. Standing on the ridgeline of a steep ravine, the lower valley before the last stretch into the Toerge Mountains opens up like a wound in the earth. Before us, stretching for miles in either direction, a cliff with a fifty-foot sheer drop down into the darkest patch of marshy trees anywhere stares back at us. The easiest way into the valley is a half mile west of where we currently stand. That's all the time we have to come to a decision.

If we choose to go that way, there are no spiderlyches to worry about. Oh no. That would be overkill. There is no need for the valley to throw more at us. We stand at the cusp of the Valley of Cusk.

Tamrin steps up beside me as I look down. "Do we really have to go this way?" he asks.

Jesmir stands on the other side of me. "What is it?" Jesmir asks.

I look at him. They're the first words he's spoken in three days. His eyes are barely paying attention to what he sees.

"The Valley of Cusk," I reply. He stares down, his expression unreadable. No reaction to the news.

I look at Tamrin and whisper, "You will have to tell me what happened to you two at some point."

Tamrin nods but remains mute. Who am I to judge? One of them will talk when the time comes. Whatever happened, Jesmir is dealing with some torment inside. As long as he does what he needs to stay alive, I guess that's all that matters now. I look at him. His eyes are locked on the valley below.

Jesmir doesn't blink.

"So, we are going into Cuska territory?" His voice seems hollow.

"That hasn't been decided yet," I say. "Jesmir?"

He doesn't answer.

"Your Highness," I say, commanding.

"Yeah?" he says absently.

"We need to speak with your sister and Krin. I have some new information to provide. Then we can decide what to do next."

He simply nods. It's starting to worry me. Not because I am concerned about him. I hardly know him. I'm concerned the Prince is a liability in the journey ahead. I wouldn't care except that his and Jesma's safety is my only concern. My job will be unpredictably more difficult if he doesn't snap out of it. I can't deal with it right now, though. I have my own churning thoughts, too many to deal with his issues.

Something gnaws at my gut, and I can't wrap my head around it.

Forget about the other personal stuff. The twins, or more accurately, their situation, has me unsettled. Leaving the two men staring at the valley, I head to where Krin and Jesma are sitting and to my fate. Whatever is wrong with Jesmir, I can't solve it. At least not now.

I sit down next to Krin. She stiffens. I feel the pangs of regret again.

"Your brother is…off somehow," I say to Jesma, not glancing at Krin.

"We were just talking about that," Krin replies. Her voice is flat and cold.

I take some jerky from my pouch and break a piece off for each of us, handing one to Jesma and Krin. They both take it. Jesma says thanks. Krin doesn't respond.

The uncomfortable silence lags on as I try to get the courage to speak again. Krin beats me to it.

"What are we doing?" Krin asks.

"Well," I say, looking at Jesma, "That is a decision we need to make together."

"I thought it was your way or the highway?" Krin jabs.

I ignore the comment.

"I need your brother to come over here so I can talk to all of you," I tell Jesma. I look over my shoulder at the men standing at the ravine. "But he seems to be trapped in his own head."

"You think he's the only one?" Krin snaps.

I flinch at her tone. Ignoring Krin, I look to Jesma.

"He won't talk to me," Jesma replies. "He's never shut me out."

I look at her with her head bowed, fiddling with the jerky I gave her.

It's occurring to me that this band of travelers would be less dysfunctional if I left.

"Clearly, he is working out an issue," I say. "Eat your jerky. If we go the route I think we must, you'll need the energy."

She nods and takes a small nibble. She nibbles rather than eats, but at least she is listening. She looks up.

"He's coming," Jesma says, looking over my shoulder.

Jesmir sits next to his sister while Tamrin takes a knee. His look tells me he didn't get anywhere in the moments since I left them staring down at the valley. I shrug my shoulders and pull out the signet ring, handing it to Krin.

"What's this?" she asks.

"My hope is you can tell me," I reply.

Krin looks down at the ring and immediately pops her head to look at me.

"Where did you get this?" she demands.

"Whose is it?" I reply, my voice flat.

She hands it to Jesma, who accepts the ring and looks at it, then back to Krin and me.

"That's the crest of the Duchess of Tal, our Aunt Fila," she says. Then she looks at me, "Why do you have this?" she asks. Her tone carries desperate concern rather than accusation, like Krin's.

"Those bandits who attacked you the day we met. It was in with the money."

Her eyes grow wide. "I never looked inside the purse."

Krin stands up and points a finger at me.

Her voice rises to a yell. "You've had this the whole time and didn't tell me?"

I hold up my hands.

"Whoa. Back off!" I snap, "I had no idea what it was until a couple of days ago."

Krin leans over me, her hand on her hilt.

"You're telling me you had a Teshket Signet ring in your possession this whole time, and you didn't know? How is that possible? The Guild teaches that! You've been keeping secrets from us this whole time, *Harbinger*." Krin's last word is delivered with a venom I have never experienced from her.

I look at her, fighting back bitter tears and anger.

"I have kept no secrets from you that were relevant here. In fact," I say as I stand, towering over my ex, "I as much as gave both of you a chance to look inside that purse. I never kept any secrets you were entitled to, *Emissary*."

My icy tone is involuntary, but it feels good. I refuse to relent.

We stare at each other, both seething.

"You had it in your own goddamn hands," I continue, my finger pointing at her nose. "I didn't hide it. In fact, I am doing this out of my own sense of honor. I will happily leave you to your efforts if you don't need me!"

"You have no honor, *assassin*," she says.

Jesma launches from her seated position. "Emissary!" she yells.

My temper flares as I stand there towering over Krin. Krin turns to look at Jesma.

"That's unfair. Shen has put himself at risk for us. He doesn't deserve your anger. He deserves your thanks." Jesma looks at me, the first sign of compassion since the confrontation with Morgan. "All of our thanks," she says softly.

"You have no idea what he is, your Highness," Krin spits.

"You know nothing of who and what I am, Krin," I say and walk away.

"I know you're a killer," she says after me. "Everyone knows."

Behind me, I hear Krin speak to Jesma, but I don't care.

"I just peeked in, saw the Realm Notes, and never looked beyond it, your Highnesses. I should have known," she says more softly.

"Well, what does this mean?" Tamrin asks.

Krin lets out a slow, heavy breath.

"I don't know. But there's only one reason a non-royal would possess that ring," she says. "I fear the Duchess is in danger too."

I ignore the conversation as I walk to the ravine and stare down. The valley below appears more inviting to me. Once again, the familiar fatigue overwhelms my mood with a wave of despair and regret. Self-recrimination for a life poorly lived threatens to drag me into the vile, Cuska-filled marshlands a hundred feet below. I lift my gaze toward the sky. Dark clouds float by, pushed by unseen forces. A metaphor for my fifty-three useless years in this world.

I don't know how long I stood there, but it was long enough for the light behind the clouds to move beyond the mountain range's peaks. Darkness grows around me, literally and metaphorically, and I can't see the light of hope anywhere.

Footsteps crunch the rocky ground behind me. Too light to be Tamrin, I don't acknowledge them. A gentle hand touches my elbow. I don't want to look back at Jesma.

"This is all wrong. There's rottenness within the system." The voice isn't Jesma's. "Emissaries are usually notified when royal travel is taking place, so we are ready in emergencies like this."

It's not Jesma. Turning around, I look down at Krin. She smiles weakly.

"I had no idea what it was. If I had, I would have said so."

She nods.

"We have unfinished business, you and me. But now isn't the time. I wasn't fair back there, though. I'm sorry. You've looked after my Royal charges, and I should be grateful."

"At least we can agree on that," I reply

I take a moment and then say, "If the Duke of Pal and his children were kidnapped by pirates at sea and the Duchess of Tal taken somewhere in Rhinestab, there has to be a spy in Teshket. The Duke's trip was taken secretly since you weren't notified. The protocol for their safe return is compromised. What's most bizarre to me is the Captain of the Dark Guard of Killinshire leaves his post to personally come after them… and you. He is traveling, barely incognito. It's a risky move on his part."

She stops and looks at the ring in her hands.

"And now this?"

"Do you think they killed Aunt Fila, too?" Jesma asks as she approaches, standing next to Krin.

"I don't know," Krin says. "I hope not."

"We need to get you both home," Tamrin says.

"No," Krin says, "We need to get them to the Queen. She

needs to be informed these two are safe." She pauses, "And of the death of her son."

I have a thought.

"How is the disappearance of a Royal handled?" I ask Krin.

"Dispatches are sent to every emissary outside of Teshket. Two in Gal-Daro, three in Haabrestand, and three more in Rhinestab. Six in Killinshire."

"You have six emissaries in Killinshire?" I ask.

"Yes. It's harder to move around there, so we have more. It's a different network. We know who each other is, but we do not know contact protocols for the royals with other emissaries. Each emissary is different, living in different areas with different customs. Our signals are tailored to where we are stationed and developed personally by the emissary in station. We only know the rendezvous points. But we have all met and can identify one another on sight."

"Is it possible the ring is a counterfeit?" Tamrin asks.

Krin and Jesma both shake their heads.

"Not without some significant help on the inside," Krin replies. "The signet is ordered by the Throne. Each phase of work is parceled out, and each component is created by a different smith. Works are secured and held by the Throne. Then, the Throne Jeweler assembles the ring and engraves his emblem inside. It's a pretty thorough and effective system."

"Once the ring is assigned, the personal engraver of the throne carves the recipient's name."

She takes the ring from Jesma and points to an engraving under the setting. It's small but legible.

"That doesn't say 'Fila'," I say.

"No," she says. "It is a name known only by other royals and emissaries. Each royal has a public name, and a secret name issued by the Throne. I can't tell you what it means. I can only tell you it is accurately the secret name of the Duchess of Tal, Fila Danwire. It's authentic."

"You would have better luck counterfeiting a Realm Note than a Royal Signet," Jesma says.

Her confidence is reassuring but leaves us with more questions and fewer answers.

"Did you receive notification these two and their father were missing?" I ask.

"No. But…" Krin says, looking at Jesma, "how long ago did you leave for Gal-Daro?"

"I don't know. We left Pal on the eighteenth. I have no idea what day it is right now."

"How long before you were attacked by Pirates?" Krin asks.

"It was the middle of the first night. Not even a full day."

"Where did they take you?"

"A tiny village on the coast in Killinshire. We weren't there long before we escaped. Only a couple of hours."

Krin looks at me, "Nine days they've been gone. Today is the twenty-seventh. Assuming they were expected at Gal-Daro by the twentieth. When the ship didn't arrive by then, the Embassy in Gal-Daro would have communicated the delay immediately. That's four days by courier back to Teshket and the Queen from there and four days to me. I should have received a courier, worst case, by the twenty-fifth. I have a colleague who is two days closer. I would have received notice two days ago, assuming the courier and I don't miss each other."

"At best, I would have known you might show up two days before you arrived. At worst, I would be finding out today."

She pinches the bridge of her nose.

"I didn't receive any word."

"A day is within any travel issues," I say.

"Yeah, the timeline is too close to make any assumptions. The courier could have arrived as we were fleeing. Shades, they could have been at my safe house waiting for my return yesterday morning. They wouldn't know we wouldn't ever make it there."

I pace, restless, and indecisive.

I don't know how long Grankin delayed Brogen, but his presence in the Dead Eye came much quicker than I expected. His choice to enter the Jester's Pot Inn may or may not have been for the same reason we chose it, strategic proximity. But then his lackey showed up in the alley.

Why? What triggered that action?

My thoughts continuously return to the fact the emissary

protocol is compromised. Details that shouldn't be known are known. A signet ring that shouldn't have been in the possession of bandits was, until a few minutes ago, in my possession.

Brogen's intel is thorough. But he also seems to have extraordinary luck. Avoiding him is the only goal I am sure of. My choices are to trust my instincts and assume the worst or believe there are coincidental truths in this world.

Neither option helps resolve the current dilemma. How do we cross the border into Teshket? Hericot or ValleyView? ValleyView is by far more accessible. A third option would be to add as many as ten days to the journey and head west to the ocean beyond the end of the Toerge mountain chain. There, the border town of Coraside Bay leads straight to Kerakot. We could follow the base of the mountains to the Cora Sea and into Gal-Danang, an entire nation of high deserts. We'd need supplies at the minimum, and horses would be nice.

But time is not a luxury we have. The longer we are out here unprotected, the greater opportunity our path and Brogen's intersect. I can't shake the feeling he is right behind us or one step ahead of us. We've wasted days already between Valshannon, Rogue's Pointe, and the damn slow travel in this storm. Either way, I don't believe for a second there isn't a rotten apple somewhere in the Royal Circle. If what Krin says is true, someone very close to the royal family is in on this. Which means even Krin is at risk.

Stirred-up emotions or not, I'm unwilling to walk her into a trap where the enemy can't easily be identified. If Brogen knows who he is looking for, then ValleyView seems the worst choice for avoiding Brogen or whoever the spy is. If I am wrong, the obvious choice is to head to the safest and shortest route through the mountains. As long as we beat Brogen and his spies there, which we have no way of knowing if we will, then we can head right to the Royal Command in either town or return the siblings to their homeland.

If I am right, however, we could be walking into a trap.

In that case, a direct path down into the Valley of Cusk, the shortest route to Hericot, is the most logical choice. Nobody, not even Captain Brogen of the Dark Guard, would suspect the royal siblings would make their way into the valley. Which means they would not waste resources staking out Hericot.

Hericot is the easiest and fastest way to the other side of the Toerge chain. The mining town was built less than fifty years ago to develop a second way through the mountains to speed up travel. The tunnel was completed less than a year ago. Too bad they haven't finished the bridge over the Valley of Cusk yet. The damn Cuska keeps killing the workers, so it may never be completed.

I look at the women before me and say, "Let's take a vote."

They nod, and we walk back to where Jesmir is sitting.

As Krin walks away, I realize she can't possibly know what the guild did and didn't teach me.

Chapter Seventeen

Journal Entry:60

I never wanted the life I live. Whether the man I am today was formed through my own choices or not, the trajectory of my life was not of my choosing. Sure, micro-decisions made on the fly turned the wheels of inevitable destiny, as micro-pulses of time blaze a backward path from today to the day I was born. But the options available to me at each crossroad were limited, pre-shaped as they were by decisions made without my consent.

The connective chain of decisions culminating in this inflection point in my journey does not rest solely at the feet of my choices. I was pushed down this road. Oftentimes, I wonder who I'd be if my mother hadn't sold me to the guild. Or if she sold me instead to a different guild, or a monastery, or a simple shopkeeper. Or if she had simply been a better mom and hadn't sold me at all.

She had her own issues, though. It couldn't have been easy raising two rambunctious boys with no money and no husband. Still, I hold a deep-seated resentment toward her. Of the ways my life could have gone, ten-year-old me never once thought, "I'll be an assassin."

This life was thrust on me without my permission. If I'd been given a choice, I might have chosen the life of a Picaroon. There was, when I was younger, this roving band of Picaroons that always came through town. They'd entertain us, sell us cheap bobbles for too much money, and offer games of chance (illegally, though I didn't know it at the time).

The girls were beautiful, their hair dark, eyes black as the night sky. Full lips and wide hips. I was enthralled by their liveliness and joy and proud voices and music and all-out revelry. Always full of bright colors on their cheeks and eyes and lips, their clothing flowing soft fabrics.

They looked so rich to me. Their lives looked fun. A stark contrast to the reality of the world I inhabited. When they'd leave, I'd cry at night, secretly wishing they'd take me with them. I dreamed about it a lot.

But, with adulthood and life, childhood delusions fade, and reality sets in.

Sean Gregory

Rainy Days and Somedays

The Valley of Cusk is the most universally avoided region of Rhinestab. Spiderlyches suck—undead eyes, rotting flesh, and awful clicking aside. However, they are relatively easy to kill. Even undead, they still squish. Garrow's Basin is treacherous because the Raysons hold a strange power over anyone entering their territory. Netherstacks, for all their mystery, can kill in an instant.

All of Rhinestab is a dangerous place. But the creatures of the Valley of Cusk are another story. Nobody knows where they come from. Nobody knows how they are trapped in the valley. Nobody has ever killed a Cuska that I'm aware of. If the quicksand or the Netherstacks don't get you in, the Cuska will.

The valley has its own vast ecosystem of wetlands. Mountain snowpacks melt in the spring, flooding the valley every year. Rainwater through the warmer months keeps the moisture level high year-round. In the heat of summer, a stench of rot and death emanates up from the valley floor, pressed upward by the netherstacks scattered throughout. It's a never-ending engine of dank, dark death. But the season change approaches, cooling the air in the valley, and a foggy mist hovers at the top of the trees, blanketing out some of the stench from climbing up to the ridge lines.

Walking the ridge line overlooking the valley is treacherous, but at least it's in the open. None of us wanted to be in the trees any longer. Having the gray sky overhead, in spite of the gloom of the valley below, felt less oppressive than the wet forest canopy. At least out here, the raindrops are smaller.

Stuck between the edge of the maple and oak forest of the RhineWoods and the frozen Toerge Mountains, this nearly one-hundred-mile-long, eight-mile-wide valley is boggy marshlands self-contained by sheer cliffs. Tall pines, beech, and cedars clog up the view, keeping the dangers below hidden from our vantage point. These wetlands carry some of the worst tales I've ever heard.

The only firsthand experiences I've heard of the valley come from the mining town of Hericot. Workers there bear witness to Cuska taking workers in the early days of the bridge's construction. Work on the bridge was halted as a result, and no one is sure it will ever restart. Off in the distance, the skeletal remains of spires meant to support the bridge loom like the remnants of some ancient civilization. The Crown offered unheard-of riches to anyone willing to brave the valley in support of their effort. The few crazy enough to take up the offer didn't last long. Short of slavery, the bridge effort died a quick and foreseeable death.

It's deceptive, though. If I didn't know better, I'd look down at the breathing trees of the valley below and wonder at the serenity. I imagine the Cuska down there doing whatever it is they do, the history of their origins lost during the burning of the Great Library in Dresdin during the first Great War. Cuska are now legends and lore.

Much of the world's history was lost in that fire. Most of what we know today about history is now passed down verbally over generations and recorded in new books, the oldest of which dates between the first two Great Wars, less than two millennia old. But who can trust them now?

Even the writings on the gods are suspect, known to be, at most, barely eight hundred years old. It's a serious bone of contention I have with the whole concept of faith.

The only fact known for sure is that Cuska never leaves the valley, and only two types of people enter the valley: the ignorant and the suicidal.

"I've heard rumors Cuska are cannibals," Tamrin says. "I don't know if it's true, and it's a disgusting thought, really. But I guess, if I were to think about it, we are just another type of cattle. Still, I'd rather not be eaten."

"I've never been down there," I say.

"Yeah, I'm happy to be avoiding it too."

We are walking single file. Jesmir leads the party with Jesma behind him, followed by Krin, me, and then Tamrin anchoring us.

Krin turns to speak as we walk.

"Highway is how much farther?" she asks.

We choose to return to the King's Regal Highway. I can fight men. I can fight undead spiders. I have no idea if I can fight Cuska. As much as I fear spies are a real concern, we universally agreed the risk of encountering surveillance was worth any effort to avoid the valley.

"About an hour or so out," I say.

She nods and turns away.

My thoughts travel to her.

We have unfinished business, you and me, she said earlier.

She's not wrong. I wish I could tell her it wasn't my fault. I wish I could make her see. But she wasn't there. She didn't witness my attempts to stop Harley, to plead with him to back down. She didn't see the determination in his eyes. He only ever cared to be the best. To win.

She didn't know what I figured out too late.

He never was really my friend.

Up ahead is the trail into the valley. If we were to go through Hericot, this path would most likely get us down into the valley without climbing.

Krin stops and stares down the trail. I pull up beside her.

"It's a treacherous chance," I say.

She stands frozen, staring down. Tamrin stops next to us.

"Let's keep going, you two. That way is insanity."

Krin turns to Tamrin.

"Tamrin, can you give us a minute? We need to speak," she says.

I nod to him. "We'll catch up. Don't wait. From here to the highway is safe as long as we don't go down there," I point.

Tamrin looks at me and winks a knowing smile. But he really doesn't know. His assumptions are far from the reality. But it's better if he believes what he believes. I shake my head, feigning disapproval. He giggles lightly and hurries after the twins.

"Don't be long, you two," he calls back.

I look at Krin. Even with the raindrops rolling down her face, I could see tears welling in her eyes. Her sorrow is evident, and my chest aches in response. I wish I could tell her the truth. I wish I had the courage to hold her and tell her how much I hated leaving her, how every day I lived with regret.

That she was the only person to ever show me love, unconditionally. That I was so sorry I threw it away. Looking down at those big brown eyes, I start to melt away, and without realizing it, I pull her into a tight embrace.

I can feel her sobs shaking her body. I don't speak as she rests her head against my chest. We stand in our communal grief for a good while. I feel her take a deep breath.

"Was it horrible?" she asks.

I am unsure how to answer.

"What?"

"Killing Harley."

The question surprises me. I'm shocked by Krin's knowledge. A heavy sob escapes my lips, and I fight to choke it down. I hold her close, each mutually consoling the other over unresolved hurts. It's my first indication we might reconcile. I squeeze her closer and cry into the side of her head. Emotions long held deep inside begin to flow from me, and the release of the truth feels good, though it is hurtful to acknowledge.

"He said we'd never fight. He said we'd stand together and resist the rules. He lied. I tried to run, but he wouldn't stop."

For the first time in a long time, I feel pent-up energy begin to break free.

It feels like… I'm looking for the words but can't find them. It's like a sharp object piercing my rib cage, letting out years of emotion.

Wait, that's not right.

Oh no.

A sharp object is actually piercing my rib cage.

My arms loosen their grip on Krin as she steps away. She is holding her dagger in her hand. Bright red blood drips from it as rainwater runs down the blade, thinning the blood into diluted puddles of light red as they drip to the ground.

"You killed Harley. He never died in the fire. He died by your hand. It's the only way you survived to run. I saw the records. I was an apprentice when you destroyed everything and now, our account is settled."

She slides her sleeve up and shows me a tattoo. It's the sign of Fildeus, Goddess of the Hunt. I had the same tattoo in the same place. My most prominent scar is from the day I burned it off. The mark of the Assassin's Guild. It's the apprentice mark. The tattoo gets finished after your first kill. She's missing the rest of the final mark.

I'm having a hard time breathing. My lung tries to expand, but a sucking sound comes from my wound. She reaches up and snatches the necklace with Patrin's sigil from my neck.

She's an apprentice.

Who's her mentor? Have we been set up?

I can't think. The pain is excruciating. I stare into her face. The tears are real. Aren't they? But so is the menace. Her eyes are cold, stained with the blood of classmates as she climbed her way to the top of her class.

How could I have missed it? How could I have been so stupid?

I stumble back from her, horrified at myself for not seeing her true intent. Dismayed by the loss of what I thought would turn into a chance to reconcile my past, I weep. Maybe this is making things right?

The ground is slick from the rain. Or is it my blood?

"Krin…" I plead. This isn't how I want to die. Ashamed and alone.

It doesn't matter. Krin plants her foot in my chest, and she heaves me over the ravine. I lose my footing and fall back. It's a desperate, reflexive motion. My hand grips her ankle, my bracer snagging her leggings. The look of surprise on her face as she follows me over the edge is kinda funny, except it isn't. Her hands windmill through the air as she falls toward me. Her body rotates 'til she is head first.

It's a long fall. It feels like time has slowed.

Who knows? I only know I am going down, and death finally found me.

The dark clouds looming overhead turned a gentler shade of gray, surrounding Krin as her arms and legs flail. Ezra is now well past the horizon, and the calm of twilight, once again, has arrived. I note the beauty of those clouds as best I can. Even in her shock, Krin's face as she watches me fall is beautiful. Too bad I'll never learn how she received her scar. She's angry, too. She wasn't expecting to come down here with me. I didn't mean to bring her down here. I was trying not to fall. Then I see fear in her eyes, and I can't tell if it's because of the fall itself or because she's about to land headlong into the Valley of Cusk with me.

It's hard to reason out if I am glad death has finally come or upset because I thought maybe I could stop running. At last, impact with the ground finally arrives. I guess either way, my running is over.

I bounce off some object but barely register the pain, flipping into a tumble. I think I hear a scream.

Did someone call my name? It's a female voice. Did Krin call out? Does she want to take it back? Can she?

No, wait, it can't be her. She's falling with me.

Or maybe it is her calling out to me as we fall. It must be her.

The tumble down the trail into the Valley of Cusk is a long fall. More bruises would bother me if I wasn't dying. It's of little consequence. In fact, I relish the pain from the bumps and scrapes. I'm savoring each one as it happens. These are my last moments. Funny how death puts those types of experiences into perspective.

Krin lands next to me, a solid thud. I turn my head to look at her. She isn't moving. Her body is twisted and broken. Her eyes are closed.

I think she's dead.

I weep.

It's too little too late, though.

I feel the cold, wet ground against my face as I stare at her. She looks so peaceful. Soon, I will, too.

I'm so tired.

The handprint on my chest blazes, but I don't care. Grankin can't touch me now. Rain lands on my cheek, and I smile. I can finally sleep. I hear footsteps coming. I hope against hope it's Quietius and not Cuska.

Then again, even if it is. The Cuska can't hurt me now. I close my eyes and take a long, slow breath.

I forgive you, Krin. Don't torture yourself over this. It's what I deserve.

Resigned, I finally sleep.

I hear

"I'm trying. It's all too wet," a male voice says.

"There's so much blood," a female voice says.

"We have no choice," the male voice says, "we have to move him."

Pain shoots through every part of me. I'm so cold. Breathing is an effort.

"He has so many scars," the female voice says. "There's a lot of fight in him. Let's get him home."

My body is jostled about. It's unpleasant, though it seems the hands accompanying the voices are gentle, or at least trying to be. I can feel both hearts slowing down. The familiar bump-bump-bump, whose timing I am so familiar with, is slowing down. There's no energy left in me.

I can feel pressure on my back now like a cot and the sensation of gentle swaying. I think I am moving. Floating. An occasional bump jostles me awake.

The pain in the side of my rib cage is excruciating, but I have no energy to rail against it.

Bump.

Bump.

Bump.

Slower now. The beats get further and further apart. I hear a voice calling in the distance.

"Sleep, child. Sleep," it says.

It's all I want. I don't fight it.

I hear the crackle of fire.

Bump.

I feel a single heartbeat. Faint but present.

Bump.
A distant dripping, like water in a bowl, echoes in the distance.
I feel pressure on my side. It hurts so bad I want to scream.
Something is different.
Only two bumps? I think, finally, one of my hearts has stopped. I welcome the change. Soon, maybe, this will be over.

I have chills. My teeth are chattering, and my joints and muscles ache. I'm so cold.
"The infection is spreading," I hear a voice say. Male or female, I can't tell.
"We've done all we can," another voice says. Again, I can't tell. It could be the same voice.
Bump.
"It's up to him now."
I hurt. Why is death taking so long?
Bump.

What is that? It sounds like scraping. It's a familiar sound, like a utensil on a pot.
Bump.
A creaking sound. What is it?
"There are strangers in the valley," a voice says.
A clang and a thump.
"Two times in as many days?" says another. Or is it another?
Bump.
"They seem to be searching," says one.
"Where are they?" asks another one.
"Where we found this one."
"Let the others deal with them. We have what we need to get through."
"Not if he doesn't survive the infection, we don't."

My one heart is so slow. I don't have much time left now. Quietius will be here soon.

I've been this close before.

Please, no healers. I'm so tired.

It's daylight. Sitting on the edge of the Bird Song Waterrise at the mouth of the cave atop the Sanctum Mountain plateau, my feet dangling over the edge, I watch in awe as the water rises from below. The Great Rankin River's flow sends the water rushing up the mountain face with tremendous power. From up here, the view is even more unbelievable than I imagined. A thick, cool mist surrounds me as the waterrise splashes down onto this plateau and runs past me and into the cave behind me.

I'm not sure how I got here. But it is peaceful. Incredibly peaceful. I had always intended to make the climb up here but never had a moment to indulge myself. This is my new favorite place. I resolve to make an annual pilgrimage here from now on.

I touch the location of the knife wound. There's no pain there. The wound is gone.

I listen for my heartbeats.

Hmmm, silence.

Okay, then. I am dead.

"Finally!" I scream out above the roar of the water.

It's a happy moment. I laugh joyfully. I can sit here forever. No part of me hurts. No one is counting on me for anything. At last, my suffering is over. If this view is where I get to spend eternity, I couldn't be more pleased.

"Is it what you hoped?" a voice says to my right.

"It's better," I say, smiling.

"Hmm. You had low expectations of the afterlife?" the voice says. I turn to look at the speaker. It's Grankin. I blink.

"You aren't Quietius," I say, surprised.

He laughs. "No, I am certainly not that charlatan. Thank you for noticing."

I must look confused because he raises an eyebrow and says, "For a relatively smart man, you are pretty slow."

"I don't understand."

"Well, let's start with this. Look at your hands. Notice anything strange?"

I do as he asks. There's nothing out of the ordinary about them. They are my hands. Except the scars and callouses are gone. I mean, sure, maybe I thought those would go away, like the pains and other damage. They are my hands. I make fists with them, and they do as I ask. No issues there. I slap them on the wet rocks beside me and splash the water. Yep, I can feel that. Rugged rocks and wet wa…

Wait.

I look at my hands again. They aren't wet. I look at Grankin.

"Damn it, am I under the damn river again?"

Grankin shakes his head, clearly disappointed by my question. He expects me to understand one of his riddles. But I don't.

"Look out there," he indicates with his hand to the river below. "Does it look like you are under the river again?"

He's right. It doesn't appear I'm under the river. I look up to be sure. It's a typical sunny sky. No shimmering layer above me and no fish swimming overhead.

I'm not underwater.

"Okay, so why am I not getting wet here?"

Grankin sighs. Clearly, I am not as bright as he hoped I was.

"Because you aren't really here."

"But I am."

He shakes his head.

"No. You are where you were. Dying on a bed from an infection in a wound you suffered from one you once trusted."

"Wait. I'm still alive?"

"For now."

"I'm in a fever dream?"

He shrugs. "Perhaps."

I've had enough. These gods, or whatever they are, play their little games, and I am tired of being a pawn in it. I look at him, anger boiling over.

"I've had enough of you all! Stop with the games and the half-answers. Whoever the hell you are, because let's face it, you are *not* gods, I don't care anymore. I am tired, no, exhausted. I am finally about to die, and you can't let that moment go in peace? What is wrong with you people?"

I stand up and give him both middle fingers.

"You can torture me all you like. I am dying and won't do your little task for you. Find some other poor fool to get your tome. I've had enough. I have been betrayed by the only woman I ever loved after decades of running from a past I never asked for."

I go to turn away but then think better of it.

"Screw you, Grankin."

He stands up and laughs. Of course, he laughs. He seems to only ever torture and laugh.

"Bah!" I wave at him as I turn away and head toward the cave. "Be gone and let me enjoy this dream in peace. I want to go see what's in here."

"Oh, Shen," he says and smiles. "This isn't a dream either."

I turn back.

"What do you mean?"

He points at my chest. I feel his handprint there. It doesn't hurt, only tingles.

"That is my periapt on your chest. I can communicate with you, and you with me, any time we want. That's what we're doing right now! We are meeting at a place of common interest, on a spiritual level."

"I'm sorry?" I question.

"One of your most endearing traits, dear man, is your complete disdain for the gods and your unwillingness to follow a single one of them. It's admirable and a testament to your intellect, I might add."

Did he say "them"? Why not "us"? I hold up my hand.

"Not them. You either. You mean 'us,'" I reply.

He shakes his head.

"No, I don't. I am not a god. Never claimed to be. Notice I have no temples? No clerics? No followers? Those who've met me and returned are the only ones calling me a god, and I have never answered a single prayer."

He's right. I have never encountered a follower of the God of Time. The thought had never occurred to me before. I've never seen a temple erected in service. In fact, of the gods, I have the least knowledge about the one standing before me now.

Well, the not-gods, but still.

"What are you, then?"

"Now that is the question you should be asking," he exclaims. "You should be asking that of all of us."

He paces. It's a familiar moment, reminiscent of when he held me under the river. Back and forth along the edge of the waterrise, he walks. He seems to be contemplating. He is having an oral debate with himself.

"Maybe? No, not ready. Too soon. But if not now, when? Not before he's ready. He wouldn't understand. No, he needs to draw the conclusion on his own. But how—if he dies in that valley? Who then? Good point, good point. But not that way. Can't just come out with it. No, that won't do. Perhaps purpose? He seems to be seeking purpose. A reason to go on. Yes, that's it. A reason to go on."

He stops and looks at me.

"You are in terrible danger. Dying will keep you from immediate trouble for sure. Unfortunately, it won't do your friends much good. Or the world, come to think of it." He says the last part absently. "They came looking for you, your friends. You have access to far more strength in you than you realize. You are stronger, smarter, and… faster than you know."

He walks over and puts his hand on my chest, right over the mark he left. I feel it warm but not painful. It's actually pleasant.

"I swear not to toy with you any longer. But I cannot give you the information you seek. You must find it on your own. It's the only way you will understand."

He removes his hand.

"And the only way you will decide to do what must be done."

He turns and walks to the edge of the waterrise and then turns back to me.

"Your friends are in danger. They cannot survive without you. If you choose to die, they will die as a result. Tamrin, Jesma, and Jesmir will not survive the day. You must fight. It's who you are. It's what you do. It's your purpose in this life."

He takes a step back closer to the edge.

"You are not unique in the world, Shen. Others believe as you do and fight as you do. Each one of them is special, like you. Find them. Learn together. And kill the ones who enslave us all."

I realize he is about to leave me as he takes one last step backward.

"Wait!" I exclaim, my hand reaching out to stop him.

"Oh, and Shen, not all that is real is as it seems. You'd do well to remember that. Beware of the power of three."

"Who?" I ask.

But it's too late. Grankin is gone, and I am alone at the top of the waterrise with only more questions. I wish Tamrin was here to at least talk it out.

Tamrin.

He said Tamrin was in danger, and Jesma and Jesmir.

He didn't mention Krin. Why not?

I have to go save Tamrin. But how? I don't know how I got here. Only one way off this plateau. Down. But the river is un-swimmable. At least in the real world, it is. I'd just end up right back up here. But I can't stand here waiting for events to unravel for me. If he can jump, then so can I. I walk to the edge and try to jump, but I find the leap impossible.

Is it fear? No, but for some reason, I am stopped.

I look around for any indication of a path out of here.

The cave.

I've always wanted to know what's in the cave and the river flows that way. Maybe there's another way out?

I walk to the dark cavern. The river roars inside as I approach, much louder than I ever imagined. Dripping water echoes louder than the river's flow, yet somehow distant. The rhythm is accompanied by a beat like a drum in the distance. It's a familiar pattern.

Bump-Bump-Bump.

I follow the sounds into the cave.

I feel a cold cloth press to my head.

Bump.

"Take a look," a voice says.

"What?" says another.

Bump.

"He seems to be coming out of the fever dreams."

"Maybe he'll make it?"

Bump.

I hear it. I feel it.

Bump.

Bump.

Bump.

Both hearts? Well, I guess I'm not dying. Whatever is coming, I'd like to be ready for it. Whoever is caring for me seems kind enough. They could have let me die.

Bump-bump-bump.

I open my eyes.

"Easy now, child," says a feminine voice. "You are injured and have an infection. We are treating it, but you need rest."

I hear scraping and smell pungent food cooking. The crackling fire flashes blurry shadows on the wall. A dark figure leans into my blurred vision. I can't make out what it is. Scraggly hair and pointed ears on a long face whose features I can't discern stare down at me as cold hands take the compress from my head.

I drift off to sleep and hear water drops again, and the cold compress is placed back on my head.

"That's good," says a masculine voice. "The fever is breaking."

"We will survive the winter," the feminine voice says.

I have no idea what they are talking about. I'll ask them later. For now, I need sleep.

"He's a fighter. Good energy."

"We'll need it. This is the year of the long winter."

Darkness comes as I drift off again.

Chapter Eighteen

Journal Entry:61

My fast temper is my fatal flaw. I offer this warning as you go through these pages. It likely won't shine the best light on me.

Yet another reason why I don't believe people really like having me around. I am angry. All the time. Maybe that's what fuels my natural talents. I wish I understood them.

I wish it didn't hurt all the time.

I never wanted this. I never asked for this. I never tell anyone the stories. I don't celebrate my exploits. The people I save tell the stories. But memories are what they are, and the details get exaggerated or blurred.

Memories of memories become fictional legends of our previous experiences.

I leave no survivors in a fight. If we are fighting, you made it happen, and we are fighting until one of us dies (well, unless we are in the ring at Rogue's Pointe. Someday, we may talk about that).

These pages are the first time I've recounted the stories in my own words. Only my closest friends have a hint at what I am capable of. But even they don't know fully. I'm not sure I even know. It would be nice to understand it, but it's always been there.

Writing this down, I'm no longer sure, is helping.

Sean Gregory

Resolve, Rescue, and Retribution

It's a strange feeling coming back from the brink of death. I should be used to it by now, but I am not. The laborious climb from the door-to-the-other-side is always the same in one manner or another. The acceptance of the end doesn't come as easy as my thoughts make it seem, but once accepted, the end becoming the beginning again is a shock. There's a small, irrevocable change in the aftermath. I don't really know what that change looks like. I only know I'm different. Sometimes better, sometimes worse.

I've really got to stop doing this to myself.

The big difference this time versus other times is this time, I wanted to return. One would be correct to expect that since this has happened more than once I should maybe change how I live my life. A logical person would turn away from this life and find a peacefully quiet existence doing anything else. Instead, Grankin's words echo, his handprint a warm, gentle accompaniment.

"Your friends are in danger. They cannot survive without you. If you choose to die, they will die as a result. Tamrin, Jesma, and Jesmir will not survive the day. You must fight. It's who you are. It's what you do. It's your purpose in this life."

That is what he said. It's all I need. Clawing my way back to consciousness was an ordeal. I am covered in sweat. Everything around me feels soaked. Heavy blankets cover my body. My vision is blurred as I open my eyes, but I can make out the rafters overhead within the haziness of my sight. At least, I think they are rafters. It's hard to say. My mind could be filling in the blanks to make sense of my surroundings. The distinct flicker of firelight bounces softly around the room. It's definitely a room.

I can hear the wood crackling and smell cedar and pine burning. That acrid smell of strange herbs is there, too. It's an unfamiliar smell. Strange shuffling sounds occur to my right, out of view. I turn to look, and two figures sit by the fire, their backs to me. Off in a corner sits a chair where a third person looks to be sleeping.

Or dead. It's hard to tell.

Their dark, blurred forms, all three slightly elongated versions of humans, appear to be sitting by a fire. I think they are speaking, but I can't make it out. I am sure the third one looks dead.

I try to sit up, but a crackling noise beneath me draws the attention of the strange occupants.

Both of the strangers turn and look at me. One stands and approaches. My eyes, struggling to focus, imagine a black figure, limbs abnormally elongated, walking toward me. As it draws near and comes into focus, I recognize the light, coupled with my blurry vision, is playing tricks on me. It's a woman, not much older than me, maybe even my age. Her eyes are gentle, and her face soft and kind. Her hair is long and unkempt but not dirty. The lines on her face are gentle, and the early signs of age have only recently become evident. She smiles softly, stroking my hair away from my face.

"There now," she says. I recognize her voice. She puts a hand on my forehead. "Rest. Your fever broke faster than we thought. You must be blessed by the gods."

"Where…"

"Shh, there will be time for that soon enough. You fought hard to beat the infection from your wounds, but it's still there. It is lucky we found you when we did. Rest. When you are well enough to eat, there will be plenty of time for questions."

Honestly, I am famished. I can't remember when I ate last. Was it this morning? Yesterday? How long have I been out?

A warm feeling begins to wash over me again, starting from my chest. But I'm so tired.

I try to clear the brain fog while I lay there looking up at the ceiling. I was right. It is rafters. I'm in a small hut. Various items are scattered around. From the looks of it, I'm lying on the floor in a bed of twigs and blankets. There is no furniture in the hut aside from the one chair. Everything else is in small piles or stacks on the floor.

The couple, I assume they are a couple, sits by the fire. The male is stirring some food in a pot, steam slowly rising from within. The steam rising tells me the pot is the source of the smell. It's making me a little woozy.

I realize I am thirsty.

"Is there water?" I ask.

The woman turns and looks at me, then back to her companion, who nods. Picking up a bowl from the floor, she holds it close to the pot, and the other scoops a ladle of liquid from the pot into the bowl.

She comes over, sets it on the ground next to me, and helps me sit up. The move makes me dizzy. Likely residual effects of the fever. She reaches down and hands me the bowl. I take it and nod my thanks. She pats my head. As she does, I catch sight of a necklace dangling between her breasts. It looks like the type of item devotees of the gods wear, but I don't recognize it. It's not of any of the gods—three circles with descending lines, intersecting a horizontal line, with two vertical lines beneath.

"What does your necklace mean?" I ask.

She looks down at it and holds it to the light.

"It's the symbol of our faith," she says. "It's the Tripartite. Each one is a head. It stands for me, my husband, and our faith. A trinity."

"Trinity?"

"Yes," she says, her voice soothing. "Three heads in one body. United through life so each may be stronger than the sum of the parts."

I nod. The Tripartite is not a god I am familiar with. I've never heard of the god Tripartite.

"Drink your soup. Then get some rest," the strange woman says, returning to her husband.

I watch as she walks away. Her movements seem odd. Slow and lumbering, a mismatch to her frame. I look down at my soup. It smells horrible but looks the same as any broth I ever had. My mouth is dry and sticky, so I put the soup to my lips.

"Beware the three-headed man."

Isn't that what Grankin said?

I stop. The husband glances at me. His presence and features make me shudder, but I can't grasp why. He appears neither sinister nor caring. He's devoid of any emotion, and it's unsettling. He gestures in the same slow, lumbering way his wife walks. It's uncanny how similar they behave. Around his arm, a sloppily wrapped cloth appears to cover a wound. He winces in pain as he moves it, clearly hurt.

"Drink," he says.

His voice makes my skin crawl like it is coming from somewhere other than his mouth. It sends chills up my spine. I look down at the bowl. The liquid resembles a bone broth. Glancing back at him, he watches me intently. My body visibly reacts with a shudder. As thirsty as I am, my desire to drink the liquid is gone. This whole place feels surreal, like I'm stuck in a dream. Sweat beads on my forehead begin to slide down my temples and brow. Chills cause me to shiver, the fever driving my thermal response discordant signals.

My perception must be skewed. I haven't had a fever in so long. I don't remember what it's like. But I'm sure the term fever dreams didn't come from nowhere. Maybe I'm being silly.

I look back down at the bowl and back to the man watching me.

No. This man definitely gives me the creeps. Even in this state, I trust my instincts. It's how I survive. I set the bowl on my lap. The dryness in my mouth screams for me to drink, but the voice in my head warns of a sinister nature.

"Tell me about Tripartite?" I ask, my voice hoarse. "Is that your god?"

The husband stands, walks over to me, limping, and points at the bowl. I notice a similar sloppy bandage on his leg. A dark spot of blood seeps through. He's injured.

"What happened to your leg?" I ask, lips parched.

"Drink, sick one. You are not well."

I look at him closer. Like his wife, his features are soft, rounded even. His lumbering gate and motions make my head hurt. The entire situation feels off. He lets out a heavy sigh.

"Here, I'll help you," he says, reaching for the bowl in my hand.

I shake my head. "I need to catch my breath first," I say.

He takes the bowl and lifts it to my lips. The hair on my neck stands up. The handprint on my chest gets warm. I narrow my eyes at him, distrusting. When I do, my vision blurs slightly, and he looks different. Somehow, his limbs and fingers look longer. His skin appears dark black and burnt in color.

I snap my eyes open and slap the bowl away.

The woman stands and spins to look at me. The husband stands over me, his posture still bent in the same helping manner.

"Why did you go and do that?" the woman asks. "You need all of this to be better."

Her tone is icy.

"Tripartite?" I ask. Tripartite sounds like triple parts. Three parts. Three heads.

"What are you playing at?" I ask the woman.

The husband stands unmoving, hovering there. His frame still bent over me.

"We're trying to help you get better," she says.

"Why?"

"Because you are in the Valley of Cusk," she says. "It's a dangerous place. You are injured and have no hope of surviving."

"I am much tougher than I look," I say.

Her eyes narrow as she contemplates my words. I glance at her husband.

"Please give me space," I say.

He doesn't move.

"I think," the woman says, "you should drink your soup. I will make you another."

This is surreal. It's like nothing I say matters.

Three-headed man. Valley of Cusk.

The thoughts repeat, over and over, grasping for their meaning. Could the pendant be of a three-headed man?

"I think maybe I should go," I say and try to stand. The husband puts his hand on my chest and presses down.

"No, my boy, you need rest. You still have the infection. That just won't do. We need to cleanse you," the woman says.

The husband looks at his wife, his hand still on my chest. It's a heavy hand. Far heavier than it appears. My head is still spinning, so I am having difficulty commanding any resistance against the pressure. I look at my own hands and realize, for the first time, I have none of my weapons on me.

I have no idea how long I have been here, but I don't like

strangers touching me, even if they are trying to help. This feels so wrong as if I'm held against my will. I look back up at the husband. He still defers to his wife, who lumbers over with another bowl of whatever is in that pot.

Now, I definitely don't want to drink it.

I summon every ounce of strength I can muster and drive my right arm up into his elbow and my left down into his wrist, catching whatever is under the bandage. I am amazed at how easily it snaps. For all the mass and strength in his hand, the elbow bends almost perpendicularly in the wrong direction.

The woman screams in rage… and pain.

"What in the hell?" I whisper.

The high-pitched scream hurts my eardrums, reverberating off the walls of the hut. The husband's hand immediately lets me go. My vision gets blurry again. But this time, two images compete for prominence. One is of a woman and her husband in a hut, and the other is out of a nightmare—dark, looming, sinister. I scream in response, and suddenly, the woman and husband fade away, replaced by a long-limbed, three-headed creature holding its broken arm, screaming in pain. The walls of the hut shimmer and change from a modest family home into a dark and dirty structure of logs and mud.

One of the monster's heads dangles to the side, lifeless.

Now I know why everyone fears the Cuska.

The fireplace has been replaced by a pit in the center of the room. I am on the floor, naked, again. The three-headed monstrosity roils back in pain, screaming obscenities at me.

I have never woken up naked so many times in my life, and I'm tired of it.

My side hurts. A strange paste covered in moss hides my wound, pulling at my skin. It hurts but somehow isn't bleeding. Chills wrack through my body. I'm still running a fever, which means whatever infection I have is still present.

Two of the three heads snap their gaze toward me, speaking

simultaneously. The voices are the same as those of the husband and wife, but somehow, they come out in harmony.

"You will pay for that!" the creature screams. It extends its good arm, the broken one dangling to the side, blood running freely. I have no weapons. I have no bracers. I have no strength.

But I can move.

Painfully rolling to my side and pushing myself up with my right hand, I try to crawl away. The creature, limping along, gets to me before I can get fully upright and grabs hold of my hair, throwing me to the other side of the wooden cabin. The move is sloppy, and I land on my feet, somehow managing to stay standing as my body impacts the wall. Pain explodes everywhere. Stars fly across my vision as I suck air into my lungs.

The creature on the other side of the fire moves toward me, its left leg buckling slightly. I pay attention, recognizing it's incapable of hiding specific details in its illusions. I'm slower than expected, which isn't surprising but no less concerning. My only hope is that with a useless left arm and a nearly useless left leg, I have a chance. Stalling for time, I circle the fire, keeping it between me and the Cuska.

"I know what you are now," I say quietly.

Fear causes my skin to tingle. It has to be fear. There's a similarity to what I experienced in Grankin's presence, only far more sinister. An oppressive presence crashes against my mind, and part of me attributes it to another illusion by the Cuska. The feeling angers me. I catalog the sensation and fight the unfamiliar thoughts. As I resist, an unseen force presses back, invading my internal monologue.

"Be afraid," the thoughts tell me. *"Cower in fear."*

The subliminal assault threatens to overwhelm my instincts. I've never experienced this type of psionic attack. My mind swirls in a cloud of jumbled thoughts, some my own and others that may or may not be.

No. This isn't real.

"You can't win." a voice that sounds like mine says.

But the thoughts aren't mine. I know my own thoughts.

This fear is not my own.

One benefit of a solitary life is the amount of time I spend in my own mind. This monster picked the wrong victim. With a wicked grin, I prevail against the invasion into my inner sanctum and prevail. The pressure against my mind subsides.

"Not so easy, am I?" I snarl.

The creature remains quiet. We circle the fire, and I split my focus between the psychic onslaught and assessing the monster. I catalog this new experience for future reference. A skill I've acquired over thousands of fights.

In this case, if I survive, I want to be able to pass the information along.

Standing nearly seven feet tall, its long, gangly limbs and torso look emaciated. Its hands almost touch the ground as it walks, bent over, leaning to its right, taking weight off the injured limb. The two living heads track me as I circle the fire, long, sharp teeth bared in malice, bright green eyes intense. With the fire between us, the flames dance and light up the features of its skin. Wrinkled with age and clearly deprived of food, I have no idea how it is still alive. It looks as if it should have died centuries ago.

"Damn, you are ugly," I say, almost to myself.

"I will consume you slowly," it threatens. "You'll keep me fed through winter. We'll cut the infection out of you."

As we circle the fire, I notice a door to my left.

Now, if I could locate my clothes.

It's not easy keeping an eye on a monster in a dark room with only a slowly dying firepit to light the space. Especially when trying to simultaneously identify my surroundings. It's fortunate I'm well-trained at exactly that. But I'm getting dizzy from the flicker of the flames, the circling path we are walking, and the fever. I'm fighting vertigo.

And my side hurts so bad.

If Tamrin, Jesma, and Jesmir are truly walking through this valley looking for me, I need to get to them before they encounter other Cuska. In the corner of my eye, I notice a pile of items. It is a large pile. It's too far from the fire to get enough light, but my gut tells me it's my stuff. Maybe the stuff of many people. It's hard for me to imagine this vile creature cleaning up after itself.

The Cuska lunges around the fire, its useless arm dragging the ground as it crouches for the lunge. The odd skip in its gate slows it down, providing me ample time to keep the fire centered between us. The move takes me too far around, and I lose sight of the pile.

I'm cognizant enough to know the Cuska is only slow because it's injured. It would likely have gotten me already. This could go on forever. I can feel my body getting exhausted. I'm in no state for this fight. I need a plan.

But at least the odds are even. Somewhat.

"Why resist?" it asks, the chorus of male and female voices making my body hair stand on end.

"Why does he resist?" asks the female head.

"He thinks he can get away," the male one says.

"Why don't you let the other one talk?" I jest, pointing at the lifeless head.

"It will. Once you have become part of us," the female one says.

"Such a lovely addition you will make to our Tripartite," the male one says.

"Oh yes," the female one replies.

"Three heads are better than two," they both say.

Oh.

That's what it meant by "become part of us." Now I feel fear of my own. The thought of an eternity conjoined with these freaks makes my stomach heave. Death by Cuska is far worse than I ever imagined. There's no chance I am letting this abomination make me part of its Tripartite. I'd rather let Grankin torture me under the river for eternity. At least he is somewhat likable.

"How about this?" I suggest. "You let me go, and I promise to only rip one of your heads off?"

No, that's not right. I'm a horrible negotiator when I'm delirious. They both laugh as if I told a joke.

"Oh yes, he will make us laugh," she says.

"Enough of this," the male says, "I am hungry. It's been too long since we fed."

"Not gonna happen," I say.

If I believed in gods, I would pray to them immediately to get me out of this. The irony isn't lost on me. Desperation to live is not a feeling I've experienced before. It's a strange feeling.

Is that why I am afraid?

I don't know how I feel about that. But now isn't the time to dissect those thoughts.

Now is the time for me to dig deep. My mind is swimming in a fog, and the usual pattern of my short attention span makes it harder for me to concentrate. The monster feigns left, then shoots to the right. I stumble in response, my body losing the battle to endure the shivers. It's unfortunate timing.

Up to now, they've toyed with me. Well, at least it feels like it has. My stumble seems to have changed its plan. The Cuska, noticing the moment of weakness, lunges. I don't move fast enough to keep the fire between us. I can't. It's on my side of the room before I can push myself away. The elongated fingers on its hands reach for me, dark flesh peeling off the tips. This time, I don't know if I am resisting a fever shiver or a shudder of disgust. But I am loathe to let it touch me.

My only option is to roll forward through its legs. I'm not sure it's a good idea, but brain fog messes with my decision paradigm. The gap of its lumbering stride gives me the room I need.

One advantage of my average size, I guess.

The dive is one of panic. It would be neat if it was part of a larger strategy, but I have none. I'm all tactical right now: survive.

I curse myself for not thinking fast enough and taking out its hurt leg.

Clearly, I am off my game.

Behind me, the sound of claws scraping the ground tells me I narrowly made the dive unscathed. The mossy paste on my side pulls, opening the wound to the fresh air. My head explodes in pain, and I scream in response. It's not a flattering sound. Nor is it one I am used to hearing come from my lips.

It's much different than the Jagger Mewler sound of my youth.

All my years of supremacy in combat built up one hell of an ego, yet in less than a week, my ego is shattered. My confidence is broken. I'm missing opportunities. I'm tired of fighting against powers I don't understand, as if I'm on some mythic adventure. The events of the last couple of weeks left little hope I'll ever find peace. I want to return to Mistras' and ask if he'll let me stay. I've had enough.

So far this week, I've managed to get myself hurt saving Krin from spiderlyches, battered by the distraction of two women and a sadistic pugilist, stabbed by Krin—a rather ungrateful act on her part—and kicked over a cliff. Now, I'm about to be the winter meal for a Cuska. All of these events seem directly related to my inability to say "no." It's enough to make me think maybe I'm seriously fucked in the head.

Fighting the desire to protect my injury and pushing this stack-up of self-loathing and pity aside, I spin myself around on the balls of my feet as I recover from the roll. Muscle memory is my most trusted ally. At least that isn't failing me right now.

The hideous creature isn't even halfway turned around when I stand.

I must be delirious. The Cuska didn't seem that slow a minute ago. Though the familiar burning engulfs my body, the sensation feels no different than at other times. Yet I somehow was faster. The fever must be altering my perception.

It's impossible that I moved as fast as it seemed. This must be another illusion. If it is, it's a strange one.

No, it must be slower than it looks. That's it. The Cuska is slower than I gave it credit for. I use the confidence boost to press my advantage. The space is more expansive than I first thought. Another lucky break. The ring of light from the fire isn't bright enough to il-luminate the walls, leaving a thick band of darkness along the perim-eter. Darkness combined with my innate silence is all I need to slip into the shadows at the room's edges.

As the heckle-twins turn their hideous, and thankfully slow, body toward me, both heads look in different directions. It's actually comical. One head swivels to the left, the other to the right.

And one hangs there, dead. Until it doesn't.

I swallow back and audible gasp, nearly giving away my po-sition, as the head begins to sink into the shoulder, slowly disappear-ing, its mouth gaping, emitting a sickening noise like a melon squeezed under a wagon wheel.

"Made a space for you," both voices say, the pitch of their voices harmonizing in the most upsetting manner. A disturbing image of my head mounted in place of the dead one causes a shudder. I'm sure that's what they intend. At least I won't be stuck in the middle. What a horrible way to spend the rest of my days. Talk about an unfair end to an already subpar existence.

So little is known of the Cuska. The mystery of their lifecycle is a topic of discussion whenever Cuska comes up in a story. None of it seemed real until now. Now, this feels very real.

The unattended fire offers less light than when we first started our little dance. Logs, burned through, no longer provide structural support to the stack and collapse, sending sparks into the air. The room gets brighter momentarily, but the light dies down as suddenly as it flares. I slide my body along the wall, keeping my eyes on the dark form, using the dark shadows to my advantage.

"It likes to play games," she says.

"We have lots of time to play games with it," he says.

"Yes, thousands of years to get to know each other," she replies.

The 'thousands of years' comment makes me want to vomit.

I have so many questions, but I am afraid to speak. Instead, I work my way clockwise around the room, staying out of the furthest reaches of the light.

"Where did he go?" she says.

"Shh," he says, "he's staying to the wall. Use your ears."

I fight back a sigh of relief and a giggle.

Silence is golden and I am the master of silence.

The monstrosity can use its ears for all the good it will do it.

A twinge of adrenaline surges as the creature tries to find me through sound. Skirting the perimeter of the room, I see a dark mound in the shadows to my left. It's the pile of stuff I saw earlier. It's tempting to take a moment to feel around for my gear, but the Cuska is too close still. Still, in a moment of clarity, my disappointment hatches into a plan.

I reach down for anything with mass and grab the first item I touch. It's a log. The pile I saw earlier is a stack of wood for the fire. A twinge of disappointment hits me. Ordinarily, I would throw the log across the room as a distraction. But this sucker isn't stupid. No way that will work on these two and it's a pretty obvious ploy, anyway. One I plan to execute in a less obvious manner.

I don't have a lot of time. I'm battered and tired, and the slowly dimming light indicates it's only a matter of time before the two sets of eyes scanning the darkness adjust enough to see me despite the shadows. In fact, up to now, it has stayed in the light. This monster isn't dumb, though. Within two steps, it switches to circling to the edge of the room. If not for its sheer size, keeping it visible, it would be impossible to see. The thought sends a shiver down my spine. At least its black skin doesn't offer it too much advantage over my dark copper version. Thankfully, the shadows are very dark, and I am somewhat covered in mud from my dive through the legs, dulling any reflection from sweat or body oils.

Time to move. I hurry around the room again, but this time, less than a quarter of the way around, I drop the log behind me and watch which way the creature attacks. It surges, dangerously close to the fire, straight at the log.

The ruse sort of works.

Sort of.

"I have you!" both heads say as the Cuska lunges over the fire to land directly behind me. It anticipated my movement and decided an intercepting path was the best action. I can't believe how fast it moved.

It's been toying with me.

But these two aren't as smart as they think they are.

Although they moved to intercept my forward progress, they landed, so we are back-to-back.

I don't know where my extra burst of speed comes from, but desperation makes people take crazy risks. The monster grasps empty air as I spin and lunge onto its back.

A real Shamna twenty-three.

Too late, it realizes the mistake. Wrapping my legs around its torso, I grab both of its living heads.

"How?" the female head shrieks.

"No!" the make head cries.

"Surprise!" I yell, maniacal.

"Get it off us!" she screams.

A sense of rapture overtakes me as I slam their heads together, expelling a scream as their heads collide. I may have gone insane. I'm laughing gleefully at the carnage I'm creating. Exerting tremendous force into the first hit, I feel the satisfactory thud followed by two angry, startled screams. The Cuska tosses itself backward, attempting to crush me between itself and the wall. The combination of my weight and its panic causes it to place too much weight on its injured leg. The buckling of its knee drives it forward instead, my weight creating the leverage needed to keep it there.

With another maniacal laugh, I clash their heads in rapid succession like cymbals, dull thuds echoing. My arms ache from the speed at which I move. Each successive impact drives my hands closer and closer together. I'm in a frenzy, and it takes me a few hits to realize there's a sick, wet, cracking sound as one of the skulls gives way to the other.

The female skull goes limp, a warm, sticky fluid oozing down the left side of her head, down the Cuska's back, and onto my chest. I smash them together a final time as bloodthirst grips me.

The male head lets out a grunt, telling me he is still alive, but he is putting up no resistance. The Cuska drops its other knee to the ground, and I slide off its back. As soon as my feet hit the floor behind it, I pivot my right foot, taking a half-step back to gain leverage and drive my right fist into the back of the male skull. This time, the fire in my body burns like a white-hot fire. I can tell this isn't related to the fever. The intensity burns hotter than anything I've felt before. The pain is intense, but I ignore it, giving in to the feeling.

I expend every ounce of strength I have left. The energy I put into the punch is unnecessarily brutal as I torque my hips, driving with my back leg and throwing my fist forward. My ribs cry out in protest, my punctured lung screams in pain, my bruised back, still tender from the fight with Col-Amot, spasms, and my head pounds from the fevered headache, yet I still throw all of my energy and power into the act. A horrible pain in my triceps causes me to scream, but I don't relent.

The primal, rage-filled scream carries my frustration, fear, hatred, and anger. It transfers the negative energy contained within a tightly clenched fist into the back of the creature's skull. Bones break with a satisfying crack, but the blood lust overshadows the pain. My hand, covered in a sticky mess of blood, shattered bone, and brain matter, continues through until it sticks out from the face of the male head. I blink as I realize I drove my hand through the skull and broke several bones in the process.

"Well, that's a new one," I say aloud, tilting my head in curiosity.

My knuckles hurt terribly. I'm sure I split them open.

The Cuska's body falls forward, lifeless, catching me off guard and yanking me forward on top of it, my arm still sticking through its head.

Time is meaningless. Hours could be days; days could be minutes. I don't know how long ago I felt the cold steel of Krin's dagger. I don't know how long I laid there on top of the dead three-headed body, hand buried inside its middle skull. It seems like forever. Devoid of thought, the moments after the Cuska released its final breath passed, their duration meaningless to me. I don't know if I was catatonic or tired, but I needed the moment, and my brain, thankfully, gave me that.

As the adrenaline charge wears off, a feeling of shame overwhelms me. I'm disgusted with myself. Whatever drove the rage, the gleeful exhibition of violence, was far different than any fight of my past. As much as I feared losing to this monster, the rapture I felt in the violence was far beyond any acceptable pleasure I find delivering justice.

Emotionally spent and nauseated by the smell of the creature's ancient blood all over me, I vomit on the ground beside the monster's head.

In normal circumstances, I would probably take time to study the dead body, especially since nobody has been able to gather information on them for centuries. My existing knowledge about Cuska couldn't fill a single page of my journal. Nobody has ever survived a one-on-one encounter with one and shared that knowledge with the world. A shudder runs through my body as I imagine what my life would have been had this thing bested me. It's either the fever or an overactive imagination. My imagination runs rampant, and visions of what my future could have been flitter in my mind. The thought sickens me. If I believed in a god, I would likely thank them for saving me from that fate.

Blinking myself to the present, the fire dimming further, my body shivers as a chill works through me. Feverish, naked, covered in mud and blood, my body hurts more than it ever has. I'm so utterly spent I struggle to rise. A part of me wants to stay here, oblivion, feeling so close. It's an internal silent plea to which I shouldn't succumb. But it's hard to find a reason against the thought.

I'm so tired. So very tired.

A warm sensation begins in the center of my chest and spreads slightly until my shoulders feel the benefit. I touch my chest absentmindedly, and a momentary calm washes over me. A gentle urge to move comes from somewhere, a reassuring pat on the shoulder. I suddenly don't feel alone and don't know where it's coming from. The feeling is distant, unlike the presence of friends, yet equally intimate. It's pretty disconcerting, and I would chalk it up to a fever dream, but I'm fully aware of it. It's like someone is reminding me of something.

Then it hits me.

It's the nudge I needed. The handprint on my chest responds as Grankin reminds me of his presence. Taking a deep breath, I pull one knee up, and then, using my hands as an assist, I push myself upright, extracting my hand from the mushy remains of the head.

"Gross," I mumble. I'm covered in the gore of war. This wasn't my usual fight. This was a different type entirely. A sense of shame hits me, but I push it aside. They meant to harm anyone crossing their path. I refuse to succumb to guilt or remorse.

It's a long stagger to the stack of firewood. There's not enough light to see my surroundings, and a little more warmth would be a welcome feeling.

As dry as the Gal-Danang sands, my mouth cries out in protest. The combination of fever, exertion, fighting this monster, and the warm room turned my tongue to sand. I stumble along, slowly picking up pieces of wood. Waves of pain cause me to double over. My chest wound aches from the effort. Thoughts of water float in and out of my head. I try not to breathe through my mouth, but keeping my mouth closed causes it to stick shut. I need water but can't locate my gear. The thought I might never find water again threatens to transition into a panic. I sense a distant attempt to soothe me, like someone reaches out to me from a faraway place. I glance around, startled, but nobody is there. A wave of warmth spreads within my chest.

The mark Grankin placed on me glows.

Grankin? Is he trying to communicate with me?

I thought that was a dream. The sensation somehow has a calming effect.

Does he actually care?

Seems unlikely, but regardless, it helps me pull my thoughts back from despair and allows me to reason through my situation. The irony of the idea that a god I don't believe in is helping is not lost on me.

If I could find my gear, I'd find my canteen. The last memory of gear I have is of us filling our canteens at a small run-off spring right before I took a blade in the gut. My gear can't be far. Without light, it would be a fruitless endeavor. I drag my feet, concentrating on not falling over, while I approach the firewood stack. My memory is foggy, and I end up on the wrong side of the room. I use the wall to support myself 'til I find it, each step an eternity of misery.

Everything feels like forever right now.

It requires extraordinary effort, but I eventually find the stack and begin taking logs to the fire, one at a time. Small but satisfying flames flicker along the surface, blue and white flashes of precious heat trying to find a path to feed themselves, sparking to life only to die out, reigniting again elsewhere. As I push the first log around to stoke the flames, heat singing the hairs on my arms, new wood ignites, the fire roaring back to life. It's enough to start loading more pieces of lumber. After a few moments and more logs, the fire rolls to life again, and it eventually starts blazing.

Within a few minutes, I realize I may have been overzealous as the fire becomes too hot to put more wood on. The intense heat forces me to push my naked body away as I begin to feel like I'm cooking.

The chill subsides, and I can finally see around the room.

Firelight illuminates a log-framed six-sided room with a dirt floor. Definitely not the cozy space within the image the "couple" treating my wounds led me to believe. My thoughts wander to the memory.

What was it? A hallucination? Or did the Cuska create an illusion? Is that what they do? What were they trying to get me to drink? Did they actually plan to eat me?

It has always been assumed that Cuska were cannibals. But the choice of words seemed somehow oddly specific.

If they aren't cannibals, then what? Why were they trying to heal me?

Another shudder runs through my body as I realize how lucky I am to be alive.

For now.

Looking up, the ceiling is almost twelve feet high with a hole in the center. Smoke and ashes float through, rising on heat vapors into the night sky or canopy of trees. I can't really tell.

The fire provides enough light so I can study the Cuska better. I shiver at the hideousness, and another shudder shakes through my body. Grotesque doesn't describe it. Its skin appears ancient, the elasticity gone. Wrinkles, so deep they fold onto one another, cover every inch of its blackened skin. Random patches exhibit fewer signs of aging than others, with fewer age spots.

Beneath its wrinkled skin, wiry, lean muscles barely hide the bones and joints. It appears to be human, yet obviously not human. Long nails, thick with age, are yellow and cracked, not quite claws, but almost as effective as weapons. The fingers, arms, legs, and toes stretch awkwardly, elongated unnaturally. However, the oddest feature is not the length of the limbs, three heads, or wrinkled skin. It's the distinct transitions in skin color. One of the arms carries significantly more melanin than the rest of the body. In fact, the one head that seemed already dead was of the same tone as the arm.

The more I study it, the more I realize the Cuska is not one creature, but three different creatures joined together like some macabre experiment. The mixture of dark and light skin, male and female features, limb sizes, and three heads is unsettling. It's like pieces of humans were bound together by some horrible spell and stretched or like the monster took pieces from humans to replace…

Ohhh, absorb!

Another shudder runs through me. Somehow, Cuska absorb their victims.

But then, why would they nurse me? Why not just eat me? No, not eat. Absorb.

My side hurts. Sweat drips down my face. I wipe it off. My body feels cold, so why am I sweating?

Fever. That's right.

Infection!

They couldn't absorb me. Absorbing infected flesh must be dangerous. They had to heal me first.

I can't look at it anymore. Its existence is an abomination I can't deal with right now. If demons were real, Cuska is what I imagine demons would look like.

They did say *thousands of years*. I wonder how old this monster really was.

Looking around the room, I don't see anything other than the Cuska, the fire, the stack of wood, the pot by the fire, the bowl they tried to feed me with, and the door I saw earlier. My gear is nowhere to be seen. I'm not motivated to look for it other than I need water. If not for that, I'd probably lie down and pass out.

By sheer will, I push away thoughts of sleep, rest, and giving up. Struggling to maneuver, my right arm utterly useless, I eventually stand and reach the door. Grunts of effort escape my lips involuntarily as I try to walk. I push the door, and it opens easily. I am not prepared for what I see.

Based on my experience so far, the room borders on the unbelievable. I look back at the Cuska, confused, and then back to the room beyond the door again. Quaint and cozy, it's an actual room with actual furniture. The quality and condition of the furniture, proportioned for the Cuska, surprises me. The furniture appears well cared for, possibly antiques. A small reading table, a single chair, a few bookshelves, and a hammock fill the room. The chair faces a rather large fireplace, still burning with glowing embers. A lamp on the chairside table offers enough to reveal more surprising details. A book that rests on a small reading table handcrafted with insets, beside the chair. The skin of an animal I do not recognize covers the floor, its head facing the fire. Three horns, a couple of inches long, protrude from the head.

I have to blink to make sure I am not hallucinating or falling for another deception again. The contrast between the room and the creature intent on killing me is difficult to connect. A vicious and ruthless monster harboring refined tastes contradicts my preconceived assumptions.

I enter the room and notice a pile by the fire. My gear, tossed carelessly aside, beckons me, and I make a clumsy dash to grab my canteen. Thankfully, it's full.

"Oh, thank you," I say out loud.

I struggle with the pain of moving and contorting my body to dress. The sticky blood covers most of my body, making it difficult to slide already bloody clothes on. It takes me a while to get dressed, but I eventually succeed, except for putting on my bracers. With torn triceps, a broken hand, and a knife wound rudimentary motions are difficult..

Moving takes so much out of me, especially since the adrenal surge has worn off. I've broken out into ae sweat from the effort. A quick search of the room helps me locate a burlap bag filled with the same paste and moss the Cuska used on my wound. I'm grateful for the find and stuff it into my small pack already overstuffed with my bracers.

No matter their reasons, the bastards were trying to cure me, so I am mildly happy about that. I imagine if they knew who I was, they would have left me on the trail to die next to Krin.

The monster would still be alive if it had. Further snooping reveals the books on the shelves cover a range of subjects. Books on poetry, science, and history fills the shelves. Some seem to be so old I couldn't begin to date them. The book on the table has an elaborate title. "How We Fell: Mankind to Man Cruel." I absently pick it up.

There's a bookmark sticking out the top. I marvel over the idea the Cuska was actually reading it.

I open the book. I'm too delirious to absorb any factual information, but curiosity gets me, so I read the words on the page. It's a chapter titled "Why We Feed".

A life of millennia costs a great price. We must continue to feed off the energy of others to maintain our rightful place as the rulers of this world. While the gods, if they can be called gods, rail against our methods, it is crucial for us to remember these weaker mortals are ours to subjugate. If inclined, they could grab the power, but they are too weak-minded for such advanced considerations. But the gods did discover the key. Power can be taken slowly over time or entirely in the immediate...

I don't know what this is, but it sounds like nonsense. I'm sure my delirium hampers my cognitive capabilities, so I stop reading. Besides, I don't have the energy for high-level thoughts, so I put it in my pack, a mild curiosity that might prove useful later.

I walk to the door on the opposite side of the room from where I entered, and as I do, a small chest catches my eye to the right. It appears well-aged and uncared for. It could easily be the oldest item in the room. A broken latch hangs from the front, offering no security to the contents inside. I open the lid and find a jumbled mess of tangled chains with various stones and items. It looks like a mix of necklaces and jewelry.

It's an odd assortment of worthless treasures, if one would call it that. I pull one of the items from the tangled mess. A braided leather necklace with a stone gem. A quick flip of the stone reveals it to be another periapt of Shamna.

Upon further investigation, I find a trove of various religious talismans from every known god. I'm curious why the Cuska would keep so many of these. Could they be from their victims? Trophies maybe?

An idea forms, and I fight to hold onto it. I return to the other room and retrieve the amulet from the carcass. If Cuska take trophies, then I will, too. Whatever Cuska are, I don't think we have a clue.

They are far more complex than simple cannibalistic monsters. There's a humanity to them I never knew existed. Maybe it's more an intellect than a humanity.

I'm now the only person to ever survive an encounter, let alone kill one. That would also make me the only one who could report these findings. If that's what you'd call them. I can at least provide new and valuable information to the world.

Then again, I haven't actually escaped the valley. I've bought myself some time. One fact I think I learned, though? For the Cuska, winter is barren, as it is for the rest of us. It's their hunting season. This time, however, the Cuska aren't the only hunters.

There's a fevered, battered, tired, and rage-filled anti-assassin hunting, too.

For the world of good, that will do.

Clearly, I am delirious.

Chapter Nineteen

Journal Entry:64

There's this girl. I'm afraid to tell her how I feel.

Maybe it's infatuation.

It's too early for more than that.

I can't tell her, though. I'm a killer, and she's a princess. We aren't compatible.

Actually, I'm unworthy. Mongrel, monster, miscreant. There's no chance she'd pick me.

Besides, everything I love gets hurt or ruined. If it were possible, what kind of life would it be?

I don't even want to talk about this here. It's insane that I'm even thinking about it.

Tracking Trackers and Bakru Trails

It's a struggle to stay upright. Standing outside, I look at the home of the Cuska and realize it is an actual two-room cottage nestled within this marshy land of the valley. It's an odd thought, Cuska as some kind of human experiment.

My head feels like I'm in a fog and trying to reason out what recent events causes me more stress than I can handle. My thoughts are wild and spinning. Mostly, I'm miserable, and I need to get moving.

My body is unable to support itself for long. The search for a suitable branch to aid my walk is a fog of thoughts, jumbled and disjointed. I stumble around, barely able to hold on to the thread linking action to my primary task. After what feels like eons, I find one, bent and gnarly but strong and not too thick, barely confident it will hold me. Thankfully, I stumble onto what looks to be a gurney leaning against the side of the cottage. Likely the same one used to bring me here. With a few slow cuts with my knife, I try to concentrate on essential motor functions, and the pole comes free from the gurney. It's not like the Cuska needs it anymore.

I lean against it with slowly increasing pressure, testing to ensure it will hold me. The stick is good enough, and I toss the branch aside. A vision of myself as an old man, bent slightly, grasping his cane for all his worth comes to mind. If I was in the mood, I would laugh about it. Maybe later. Right now, it's too soon.

Water helped my state of mind, eliminating the parched soreness in my mouth. I allow myself time to let the water do the job of ending my dehydration. Gradually, my brain regains some ability to focus, clearing some of the brain fog and dizziness.

I'm still disoriented but feel better about reasoning out my situation. A plan begins formulating. Admittedly not a great plan. It's the only logical action I can think of; tracking my steps to where the Cuska found me. If the memory of my fevered dreams is accurate, my friends may have come looking for me. I vaguely recall some conversation about "others".

I consider taking a moment to meditate and center myself. My old teacher at the Temple of Drunken Fists would force me to meditate right now. I don't have time for such frivolity.

I'm overwhelmed with worry. Cuska are not easy to kill. I got lucky the first one was injured and hungry. Backtracking through their territory is not ideal, but getting to everyone before they get into too much trouble consumes my thoughts.

The Cuska did me a couple of favors. They have distinctive footprints. I noticed them in the dirt of the cottage, and they are easy to locate here. If that was all I had to go on, I'd be in trouble, though. This is its home. As a result, the footprints are everywhere, going everywhere.

But Mister and Misses Cuska drug me here on the gurney, leaving distinctive marks I located with little effort. Memories of two voices and me floating come to mind… vastly different than the reality of how I landed here. I suppress another shudder at the thought of the Cuska. The illusion seemed too real.

The clear trail of a wide, flat item drug through mud and brush is visible from the cottage door. I can see where it passes through the cedars and pines. Flattened foliage marks a muddy, crushed trail toward where I stand. They look to be a little over a day old. It's a safe bet this is the way the Cuska brought me.

The trail is over a day old. The thought fills me with dread.

A fern, recently crushed, is turning brown at the breakages. Only the edges of the broken pieces show signs of dying. I think it's a safe bet a day has passed but less than two, confirming my suspicions of the tracks overall. Indications the rain stopped several hours ago are everywhere. What was waterlogged earth has drained somewhat into wet, low spots filled with muddy water, unable to drain into the saturated earth. I can tell the rain continued at least a little while after the passing of the Cuska with a gurney full of me.

Still, the trail is muddy and difficult to navigate when leaning on a stick, but not as bad as it would be if the rain had recently stopped or, worse, was still coming down. Even for the approach of fall, it's muggy down here in the valley. Between my fever and the moist air,

I start sweating as soon as I start walking. Thankfully, the rain doesn't seem to have been hard enough to wash out tracks. I vaguely recall it slowing down prior to Krin's attack.

A wave of regret crashes over me at how our time together ended. It pains me Krin is dead. I never meant to kill her.

There's no way to know how deep into the valley I am or how far the Cuska brought me. All I can do is follow the trail, which a blind man could do, but I currently find taxing.

After what feels like several hours later, but probably isn't, I arrive at an odd intersection of tracks trampling all over the trail I've been following. Less than a day old, the patterns in the trail look to have occurred after the rain stopped, as there is no sign of running water disturbing them. Within the flattened mud of my trail are signs of boot prints coming from my right, in the same direction as the gurney trail leads. Coming from the left, more prints, horribly similar to the prints the Cuska left around its cottage, enter the area.

At this intersection of tracks, there appear to be signs of a struggle.

Bile rises in my throat as panic grips me. My imagination takes hold, and I'm sure I'm too late.

Boot prints of three distinct patterns indicate three people came this way, following my captor's trail. I have no doubt it's Tam, Jesma, and Jesmir. I recognize Tam's boot prints right away.

Leaning against my walking stick to catch a breath and fight the rising bile, another shiver moves through my body. My side explodes in pain as I dry heave, nauseous over the fate of my friends. My sweaty body has converted to feeling cold, so now I have chills.

Fevers suck.

Taking a moment to rest, I continue to inspect the area, trying to decipher what happened. My worst fear has come true. My friends have been taken by Cuska. Multiple Cuska. They came down here looking for me.

There are only three sets of boots. There's a conspicuous lack of the fourth set confirms what I already know. Krin is dead.

I reimagine her falling, gray sky surrounding her like a fog, a scowl on her face. I'm revolted by the pain I caused her. Now she's dead. Why I'm still alive is a mystery. It felt so spur of the moment. I didn't mean to drag her down here with me. I was trying not to fall into this cursed valley.

Maybe she was hoping I'd suffer down here.

I can't blame her.

An image of Tam's face appears in my mind, which re-turns my thoughts to the present. I look around, trying to decipher what happened, and a deep depression in the mud, impact from a relatively large body confirms my worst fear. Telltale striations in the mud, thin marks of matted fur, is all the confirmation I need. It's Tam.

The Cuska tracks head from and to the left, indicating they came and went the same way. Further evidence the worst has happened. Mixed within the Cuska tracks is a set of smaller female boot prints. The boot prints belong to Jesma.

The Cuska prints vary in size and pattern. Still, I can see the similarities enough to know at least three are walking together. I don't want to think about what fighting three would take.

Two of the Cuska seem to be walking heavily loaded on their exit. Their prints sink farther into the muck leaving than they do coming.

Another wave of nausea rises. Leaning against my walking stick, its solid nature offers comfort and enough support to stay upright. At the same time, I steady myself, vomit spews from my mouth. Tears well in my eyes.

This is a different level of despair than I've ever felt.

The heaving causes my side to hurt, and I fight to resist the urge to press my side where the Cuska medicine is holding my wound closed. Whatever is in that strange paste has some sort of analgesic effect from the medicine because the pain is manageable. Still, it hurts, and as another surge of pain pulses through me, I take a moment to breathe through it.

I have no idea what to do next. I only know the trail goes away from where I came. Clueless, tired, hopeless, and angry, I trudge on, following four pairs of footprints. Three of which will likely see to it my death comes soon.

It's painful to move this fast, but desperation drives me. The *plop-plop-plop* of my staff, accompanied by the more forceful impact of my boots in the mud, indicates my inability to control the energy behind the movements. I feel, rather than hear, the impact I make as I push myself, stumbling onward. Prominent tracks, easy to follow due to their sheer multitude, make it feel like I'm chasing a marching army. That thought scares me.

My pace isn't setting any records, but I'm still gaining on the party of captors and captives. The line of egress is tromped foliage and displaced mud.

The faint aroma of burning cedar finds its way to me, light on the air. The pleasant scent does little to cover the stale, musty air down here under the fall fog above the treetops. Someone has a fire going. I yearn to be near that fire, resting.

Off to my right, I hear a whistling sound, like steam escaping a pressure pot. It's a familiar sound. The last time I heard the sound was over a week ago when I first rescued Jesma and Jesmir from those bandits. A twinge of panic flows through me as I look around for the telltale signs of a netherstack. I see it, inside a cluster of trees to my right, the black flow of darkness shooting upward as it whistles through the tiny hole at the top of the narrow four-foot pillar like steam from a tea kettle.

I give it a wide birth, staying well away from the dead ground where the fog rests, keeping the tracks within view but to my right, between me and the netherstack, not wanting the poisonous plume anywhere near me.

I wish I knew what caused them. I've noticed them more frequently over the years. The gloom of the darkness falls around it, roiling outward like a fog, only to settle onto the ground. Everything within this settled swath of land is dead.

The tracks lead me to a rocky portion of the trail. Muddy imprints in the ground transition to muddy prints on rocks, fading as they go. It's only a matter of time before I lose the trail on these rocks.

My side hurts so bad I want to cry, but tears will only make following the trail harder.

Uneven and smooth, the rocky walk is worn from time, water,

and traffic. My staff offers little support on the terrain as it slips to one side or the other on, unable to find a stable surface. Every placement of the staff takes concentration, slowing my pace. I'm aware of the shift in terrain into an uphill climb. A curse escapes my lips more than once as I lose footing, slipping to the ground, violently. I focus on following the light trail of slowly vanishing muddy prints, fighting to maintain balance. The path grows steeper, each step taking more effort than the last. My side starts to throb in protest, demanding I forfeit the effort.

I will myself to continue but find myself standing, brow furrowed, uttering all manner of curses.

The trail has gone cold. After following it up a rocky incline, I arrive at the last muddy step, clueless about which direction to head. A wave of dizziness wobbles me, and I lean on the staff for support. Three clean, easily traversable paths spread out and down the rocky face before me. A number of mildly difficult paths, adding variety, offer no indication which direction is correct.

I'll never find them.

This is all my fault.

Tears of frustration blur my vision. I've already broken down once. This emotional thunderstorm needs to stop. I'm better than this. But for all my rumblings, rantings, and despairs, I've never felt so exhausted or defeated. I have to continue on. But it's all I can do to stand. Spinning around, I look for any sign of passing Cuska or a person. Tears blur my vision, and standing still, my body starts to shake from chills again. The temperature is dropping, and I am soaked with sweat. My side hurts so much more than earlier. I have to take a moment, so I sit on a rock with a heavy sigh.

Now is not the time to fall apart, but it's no use. The tears come. This moment, I realize, is as low as I have been since the day Harley and I fought.

Tiny rivers run down my cheeks, streaming into my beard. My closest friend is possibly dead. All because of me. The twins could be lost. All because of me. Had I never fled from Krin all those years ago and instead faced my actions, maybe she would have understood. Perhaps I'd be a farmer or trapper like Tam.

Why didn't they keep to the plan? Why would they risk

coming down here for me? Tam should have known better. Foolish man-child. I'll have to put an end to his feelings. He's got to stop blindly putting himself at risk for me. I'm not worth the sacrifice.

Damn you, Tamrin Saltar.

The twins should have forged ahead. Foolish decision on their part, too.

Shivers tremor through my body uncontrollably. Fatigue is tearing me down. All I want to do is lie here and sleep. The mark on my chest gets warm again.

Great. Go to Hell, Grankin.

This damn mark flares every time I succumb to despondency. It's like Grankin's tied into my thoughts. It's exasperating. His impatience is wearing on me, too. I didn't ask for his task.

"Get your owned damned book!" I yell.

My voice echoes back to me. Probably the most brilliant move I've made to date: announcing to a valley full of cannibalistic monsters I'm here. I drink more water, leaving a quarter of the canteen full. I haven't encountered a drinkable water source since I left the cottage. I'm going to die here. I have no idea why I'm electing to save the water.

Congratulations, world. You finally found a way to take out the Harbinger. Took you long enough. I tried so many times. Many tried. Many times.

Ironically, the idea of dying makes me viscerally angry. I'm not made about the where. I'm not even mad about the how. It's fitting, actually. I'm angry about the actual act of dying.

Has my death wish been an illusion, I tell myself? A pathway to wallow in self-pity?

Crying isn't a method of release I subscribe to, but I'd be lying if I didn't admit it helped. I can count on one hand the number of times I have allowed myself such behavior, most of them happening in the last two days. But this time, it seems, that sort of release is giving me a chance to blow off some building tension.

My own internal netherstack, releasing the pressure of dark thoughts of death instead of a dark, deadly fog.

Feverish or not, I need to think. Surveying my surroundings, it's evident I climbed higher than my fevered state was able to comprehend. The outcropping of rocks on which I sit elevates me above the local tree line. Sporadic hints of fall colors pepper the landscape as cedar trees begin to turn, little pockets of yellowing among a sea of evergreens. It's early yet so it's only a handful of color changes, but fall's signs of arrival are present. Above me, the steamy layer of clouds is almost within reach.

Scanning the forest for anything, I finally notice a small plume of smoke rising through the treetops to the west, disappearing into the low ceiling as it does. Towering a few miles away, the peaks of the Toerge Mountains trace a faint, jagged line across the horizon, barely visible through the fog.

The smell of firewood burning is stronger now, and I'd lay odds that it's the best place to find my friends. Relief overwhelms me, and I fight back a new set of tears as I realize there is only one smoke trail. With no facts to guide me, I set out, determined to reach the plume by sundown.

Choosing the most direct path down the rocks, an easy imaginary line leads from where the muddy trail of tracks faded toward a trailhead in the trees below. It takes the better part of an hour for me to get back down to the valley floor safely, but it lands me right at the trailhead I saw from above. My left palm stings from an abrasion I earned on a particularly nasty spill on the way down, but otherwise, I am no worse for the trip. Thankfully, it's not the hand I use with the walking stick. Otherwise, I might have cried again.

As I ease myself to the forest floor, I search for any sign I am on the right path. A heavy sigh of relief escapes my lips as familiar footprints show up in the mud. Small boot prints surrounded by the prints of Cuska.

I found them.

Tears form again.

"Let's not make this a habit," I whisper aloud as I brush them away.

The newfound hope helps me push through the fog, accelerating my pace.

It doesn't take long for the thick trees and roots to make following any trail difficult. Lighting down here is poor on a sunny day; it's so much worse today. Eventually, I lose sight of signs of passing.

My ability to process information is fading fast. Stum-bling my way through the dense trees, I decide to walk a straight path from where I am. The path is lost, and I'm too tired to turn back.

Fighting against despair, I realize I don't even know when I lost the trail. In an effort to keep moving, I choose a tree straight ahead and focus on it, trying to stay directionally aligned with the trail as I remember it from above. Selecting a new tree as my focus upon reaching the original.

For all I know, I am going in circles, but I do the best I can. The only sign I'm doing well in the effort is the smell of wood burning, getting stronger as I go. With the cloud cover, it's hard to tell, but the shadows have grown darker down here on the valley floor. The day is coming to an end, and daylight is barely present in the gloom, muck, and dense trees.

Distant voices make their way to me through the trees. Not far off, but to my right more than I anticipated. It's laughter. One laugh in particular is very familiar. If I hadn't heard it, I would have passed by their location and never found them. Clearly, my efforts to walk straight to the source of the smoke hadn't worked. I am off by several hundred yards.

Laughter draws me in again. I worry it's a trap, remembering the laughter that first drew me to Jesma.

This time, however, the laughter is joyful, friendly, and jovial. A booming laugh echoes through the woods over all others. It's defi-nitely Tamrin's. I'd recognize it anywhere. Grateful doesn't begin to describe how I feel upon hearing that laugh.

My pace slows as I head in the direction of my friend's voice, the terrain climbing slightly. Cresting the small hill, the distinct re-flection of firelight casts bands of color on the trees ahead, their lead-ing edges lines of yellow and orange. The darkening shadows stop their forward advance, while the flickering glow of the firelight acts as a signal, drawing me closer. I can hear the popping of firewood and the distinct sound of conversation.

As I draw closer, the voices distinguish themselves from one another and I can make out my friends and a couple of voices I don't know. I stay at the edge of the shadows, outside the revealing light cast by the fire. Inside a clearing, I can make out another small cottage, this one covered in moss, windowpanes reflecting the fire back to me.

I'm afraid to move forward, cautious of my perception. But there is no way the Cuska would know I'm here. Besides, this one feels vastly different from the other cottage. There's a peaceful friendliness to the laughter and banter coming from around the small fire.

There, in front of the cottage, sits Tamrin, Jesma, Jesmir, and three men I do not recognize. They are deep in conversation, laughing, and drinking what looks like pints of ale. My party seems calm, at ease, even merry. The three men are dressed very similarly to Tamrin. One is nearly as big. Did they happen on a trapper's camp? In the Valley of Cusk? I take a minute to close my eyes and clear my head. It's not the scene I expected.

I thought I was on a mad rescue mission and headed toward certain doom. This is an unexpected surprise, but I'm loathe to celebrate or reveal myself. My encounter with the Cuska left me skittish. I search for prints, working my way around the perimeter. If there are Cuska about, I should have no issues finding the tracks. After a few minutes of searching, I locate a giant boot print. It's Tamrin's. Surrounding his are several boot prints, including Jesma's and Jesmir's.

No Cuska prints. Just the prints of my friends and those of what I assume to be the three trackers communally conversing with my party. I'm unsure of the circumstances but seeing them safe gives me a sense of relief. For once, I feel lucky and step into the firelight.

As I step into the firelight, Tamrin looks up and sees me.

"Hey! There's the man himself!" he exclaims.

He is genuinely happy. So are Jesma and Jesmir. The three men smile at me and wave me over.

"Come on and sit with us," the middle one says.

"What happened to you? You look haggard," Tamrin says, concerned.

He stands, walks over to me, and claps me on my back. I wince in pain, but Tamrin doesn't seem to notice. I search for any sign of trouble, eying the three strangers. They seem normal. Jovial. Real.

"What in Nadur's nutsack is going on here?" I ask, my voice cracking. "I thought you guys were taken by Cuska."

Tamrin gives me a startled look, almost confused.

"Come have some ale with us," the smaller man on the right says. He is older and has a long, graying beard and wispy hair. He looks fit for his age, but his eyes are hard and filled with experience.

Tamrin's expression returns to a smile. "Taken by Cuska? No, no. We came looking for you after you headed down here." Tamrin looks down at me, "Which, by the way, you shouldn't have left unannounced, you know? What was that about?"

"Leave unannounced," I say in exasperation. "I did no such thing."

Jesma and Jesmir both look at me like I am speaking riddles. Jesma goes to get up and then stops herself.

"You and Krin left without a word. What would you call it then?" Jesmir says.

I crinkle my brow at him. It's the most normal and engaged I have ever seen him. Shaking my head, I try to make sense of the scene. This fever either has me hallucinating now, or I was hallucinating earlier.

"Have you seen her?" I ask in desperation.

Tamrin looks at me strangely again. I can't tell if he thinks I'm insane or if he is confused.

"Right before you two went down to the valley," Jesma says.

"No, Krin stabbed me. We fell down the rim of the valley." I close my eyes, trying to remember. "I watched her die," I say, my voice cracking.

"Krin stabbed you?" Jesmir questions, his tone skeptical.

"Yes, Krin!" I cry out and rip my tunic open to show the wound. "Last I saw her, she was lying next to me, dead. Then I passed out. When I woke up, I was a captive of a Cuska."

Tamrin glares at me, his face contorted in confusion. Jesma behaves like I speak Killinspeak. The three men stand, their expressions nervous.

"You escaped a Cuska?" one of them says, his eyes wide.

"I... I... I killed it," I say. "Look at me! I'm covered in blood!"

"Impossible," says another one of the men. "No one has ever been able to do that. You must be a god."

Tam looks at them and shakes his head, "No, he's something else. But Shen, come on. Everyone knows Cuska are a fairy tale. They aren't real, and there is no way you were able to make it from the Valley of Cusk to here in a day and a half."

I shoot him a glance. He looks down at me, clearly perplexed. "What? Where are we?"

"The Ferile Forest outside of Kerakot."

A wave of nausea washes over me. I fight the dizziness this conversation, and my fever are causing.

Shaking my head, I say, "No, Tam. I heard the Cuska speaking. It said other Cuska found three travelers. That was you. I..." I stop speaking, trying to remember. It feels so long ago, and I can't tell if it was real.

My body hurts so much, and I can't think.

"Shen, what's wrong?" Tam asks his hand on my shoulder.

This feels wrong. Tam's hand doesn't have the same weight. It's tender without his characteristic strength. There's no strength in his touch, only tentativeness. It's like he doesn't believe me, and he's placating.

It's frustrating.

"No!" I yell. "I followed the tracks. They... they... led me here!"

The three men approach me, and I step back, confused and scared. I look at Tam.

"Hey, pal," one of the men says. "There's a volume we don't use around here lest we attract the wrong creatures."

I shake my head some more, stepping further back. I have to run. Get out of here. This is too much.

"You aren't really here, are you?" I whisper.

Tam looks perplexed or agitated. He takes a step forward.

"Don't come near me," I warn.

"What are you saying?" Jesmir asks.

"We are in the Valley of Cusk," I say.

Tam's expression makes me want to scream. He is looking at me like I have three heads.

It's as if my last three days were a dream as if the natural world and the one I am in now coexisted, and I was trapped inside my own head, living a reality that wasn't real. It's possible I might actually be going crazy. I can't seem to reconcile the discordant nature of my surroundings with my memories. My friends should be captive to Cuska. But my friends are clearly fine.

Or they aren't really here. I pull a throwing knife from my belt.

Tam's eyes get wide, fear evident. I tilt my head at him. Why would Tam fear me? He knows I wouldn't hurt him. I watch as he takes several steps back, standing next to Jesma, who looks at him with an eyebrow raised.

The three men rush up, standing between me and my friends, who may not be my friends. I glare at them, and they raise their hands—trappers trying to calm a rabid animal.

"Whoa there, buddy," one says. "You can't come in here and threaten our friends."

"They're my friends," I say, pointing my blade at him. "Not yours."

He looks at me with concern and compassion.

"Fildeus, help this man," he says.

Fildeus? I am so confused. I grip my head with my hands, my blade hand a fist.

Have the last couple of day's experiences been an illusion? Did I get too close to the netherstack? Were my friends simply rescued by three strangers? I get no sense of the danger I felt the last several hours. In fact, aside from Tam's terrified look, all seems normal.

"Hey, come sit," the younger of the three says. "These are our new friends, and these are my brothers. This one is Rihan," he says, pointing to the one on his left. "I'm Rivan, and this is Rolan. You don't look well. Come let us help you."

"Tamrin, I'm so confused. I swear we were just walking the ridge of the valley."

I wince as a wave of pain grips my side. I press my hand, and yellowish puss oozes out.

Tam's expression is a mixture of concern and fear. His mouth moves, but no words form. He appears to struggle between worry and fear. I can't discern which. He shakes his head like a man clearing cobwebs from his brain.

He closes his eyes and grips his periapt, dangling from his

beard. I notice his knuckles turn white, the grip intense, the muscles in his forearms bulging. Suddenly and without warning I see him take a deep breath and release it as he screams a single word: "Pravé!"

A loud pop releases from behind Tam and echoes in the woods.

I stumble back from the force of his voice, nearly falling on my butt, my staff slipping from my hands. My vision blurs briefly before it clears as I manage to maintain footing.

"No, don't fear," three voices say in unison as I take another step back. I recognize the melody.

As my vision clears, the world as I see it vanishes. Tam vanishes in a shimmer only to reappear, tied to a post behind a tall, dark, three-headed creature. I scream, startled. The enormous creature before me is the biggest monster I've ever seen and my throat catches. Nearly twice as tall as me, multi-armed, multi-legged… and three-headed, the Cuska towers over me. Its heads are dwarfed by its massive body, the proportional difference preposterously misaligned. The faces of the three men who mere seconds ago tried to reassure me it all would be fine, stare down at me with malicious intent from atop the single set of shoulders.

I've decided that I do not like fear.

My attention snaps to Tam, confused once again. But I recognize he's sprang into action. Through the monster's legs, I watch as he frantically yanks Jesma and Jesmir up from where they sit, his spell of true sight shattering the illusion. Jesmir's expression of shock turns shift into fierce determination. Jesma, stricken with terror, freezes, her eyes glued to the Cuska standing before me. She breaks her gaze, and we lock eyes its forest of legs. I watch, partly mesmerized, as she takes a deep breath.

"Run, Shen!" she screams.

I don't know what to do, but I snap out of whatever held me frozen and reach for my staff. The monster lurches toward me, causing me to abort the attempt. In the background, I see Tam, Jesmir, and Jesma running away. Looking up at the hideous six-armed, six-legged monster, skin black and dangling, its emaciated frame moves toward me. The never-ending threat of tears continues as I accept I am in no condition to fight. I prepare to sacrifice myself to save my friends.

I stare up, jaw agape, at the Cuska. It's bigger than the other one.

This time, there are no shadows to hide in.

This one isn't injured.

I don't stand a chance.

Tamrin turns in the background, his body preparing to take action.

His voice booms. "Run, Shen! Run!"

I don't hesitate.

I run.

My lungs burn as my breaths come shallow and fast. I'm running, but I have no energy. My legs are pumping, but the ground is not the blur I am used to. I'm in so much pain I can't tell if the familiar burn inside comes from my speed or the fever. Branches slap against my face, leaving behind scratches I run, frantic. My feet stick in the mud with each pounding step, requiring energy I ban barely muster to keep them moving.

Loud crashes reverberate behind me in rapid succession, each one closer than the last. Feet strike the ground like powerful horses, six legs pounding, drowning out the beating of my hearts. Fighting an injured Cuska no longer feels like much of an accomplishment. Fighting an uninjured one, especially one as big as this monster, only ends one way.

My death approaches.

"You won't get away!" the melodic sound of three voices in harmony screams.

I break through the brush ahead of me, running blind, with no map or trail to mark my way. The wet and slick ground causes my feet to slide, costing me precious seconds. Dodging trees, my ankles give as I step indiscriminately on roots and soggy ground. My ankle buckles beneath me, and I feel it sprain, but I keep going, using my hands to push me around trees, digging hard.

Both of my hearts feel as if they are about to burst. The bump-

bump-bump rises in tempo at an alarming rate. It doesn't take much. The impact terror has on my psyche is incredible. I'd take it in if I wasn't so damn frightened.

It's humbling.

The monster is on me, breathing down my neck. I can feel it. I can hear the breath of three mouths, the pounding of three pairs of legs, the swatting of three pairs of arms knocking trees out of the way.

Any moment it's hands will grab me. The inevitability of my doom is an established truth. The earth vibrates under the impact of feet stomping the ground, the hunter in pursuit of the prey. For the first time in my life, I am prey, no longer at the top of the food chain. More bile rises, impeding my breathing. Tears blur my vision, and I bounce of tree trunks, stumble over roots, a lose myself in the growing darkness.

Violent fingertips lightly brush through my hair. Or was it a branch I pushed out of the way? I have no way of knowing. I dare not look back. Warm, sticky fluid runs down my side. The wound bleeds freely once again. The copper smell of blood mixed with a sickly smell reaches my nostrils. I'm in trouble. The infection still has its hold on me, my fever climbing as fast as I climb the upward sloping ground.

I run around a thin sapling almost the size of my arm. I hear it snap asunder less than a second later. I'm the weak one in the herd, I realize. Injured, slower, easy prey for the monster whose hands barely miss me again as I swing around a tree, the beast screaming in rage as its hands impact the tree with such force it reverberates on my eardrums. My hearts beat harder than they ever have. My joints hurt from the pressure, and my knees scream in protest as I run harder.

Nighttime shadows once again play on my vision. I'm lost. I have nowhere to go. But the monster pursues. I trip over a root, losing my footing, my sprained ankle taking me to the ground. Images of Krin and the spiderlyche come flooding back. Before I impact the ground, I force myself into a roll, instinct doing what it does, and spring to my feet at the end, screaming in pain as my ankle tweaks a second time.

"Yes, keep screaming, little one," the voices taunt, their sing-song melody enhancing my fear. It's as if I've taken a psychedelic medicine. The world feels unreal. Voices laugh and call all around me.

"It's been a long time since we've enjoyed a hunt," one of the voices says.

"Shut it, Rolan. We don't have time for this," the oldest says. "We need to feed."

I start to weep in fear.

I don't want to be eaten.

My muscles tighten with built up lactic acid, and the fire inside burns hotter than I've never known. I don't know how long the Cuska and I have been in this race, but I can feel my pursuer on my heels, matching my distance klick by klick. I push myself harder and harder, but my muscles no longer cooperate. My hearts feel like they are about to burst. I've never felt them ache like this. My chest heaves with the pressure from my lungs as they beg me to stop. Both hearts stutter up as my blood thickens. My body is soaked with sweat and desperately cries for water.

The trees around me are little more than dark shadows in a dark swamp. Creatures of the night come to life everywhere but remain quiet as I pass, paying a silent vigil to the prey unwilling to admit his time is almost up, grateful it's not their turn.

"Don't let it get away!" a voice screams. It's the third head, the middle brother if they are brothers.

The slope of the ground changes. I'm running downhill, the sudden shift causing my legs to fumble for a foothold but it's no use. The ground is too wet, my ankle refuses to support me, my mind refuses to push me on, my speed fails me. There is no footing to be gained if I wanted it. Even if there was, my feet couldn't keep up anymore. My joints hurt. My head hurts. My muscles have no more to give.

I don't care anymore.

The fall is unflattering, lacking in grace, style, and skill. Me, a fully bloodied, tired, defeated, useless man-child, taking the final tumble to his death. Several impacts with smaller trees make me cry out in pain. My life seems to be an endless repetition of moments like this. I roll down the slope of the ground, mud and nasty swampy water covering me, filling my mouth, nostrils, and eyes. I cough it out as I fall, but my spirit isn't in it, so the mud stays there.

Then, suddenly, the ground beneath me vanishes and I'm in open air.

Once again, I'm in freefall.

But it's short-lived. I come to a thudded stop less than a second later, my body tumbling a few more feet into what feels like brush and grass. I fight to catch my breath, but why? It's no use. I can't run anymore.

I give up.

I can't catch my breath.

I can't stand up.

I don't care.

A loud thud sounds a few feet away from me.

"I told you not to lose him!" the younger voice says.

"He can't have gone far," the middle one says.

"Shh! I'm trying to listen for him!" the oldest one says.

Footsteps approach. I feel a foot squeeze mud up around my face as the brush cloaking me rustles. I open my eyes and can make out the outline of an elongated toe inches from my face. My eyes are wide with fear. The toe moves away slightly and then back again. I fight an audible gasp, but in doing so, I take in a slight breath.

"What was that?" the older voice says as a rustle in the distance approaches us.

"Ha! Found you!" they say in unison.

Here comes the pain.

The foot lifts up, and I can feel its shadow over me. It lands right behind me, a foot or so away. Another foot lands at the top of my head, nearly touching me. I close my eyes, waiting to get stomped. More mud presses against me, followed by the sounds of more feet, and crashes through the brush, headed toward the sound.

"You can't hide from us," the voices say as the footsteps move away.

I lay there, listening as the sounds of hands and feet searching work their way through the woods, getting fainter and fainter as time moves. I take a quiet, slow breath. Fearful they can hear me, even though I know it's unlikely.

I listen for what feels like hours as the Cuska works its way around the area. A couple of times, it comes back close to me, and I'm sure it's found me. But it passes by as if I'm not there.

"Shh," I hear a voice say in the distance, but I can't tell from where. I assume it's the middle one. Hard to tell. More footsteps approach, and I realize the Cuska is coming back.

"He has to be here somewhere," the younger one says.

"No. The human got away," says the middle one.

"We can't leave until we find him," the younger says.

"We need to go home," the older one says, "I don't have the energy to continue. The assembly is less than four days away. We must conserve our energy."

"You just don't want to be replaced," the middle one says.

"Would you?" the older says.

"We all get replaced," the younger says.

The middle one seems to grumble in agreement. Still, I hear the footsteps lumber away again, this time going in the other direction.

The waiting is excruciating, but I wait anyway. Quietius should be here soon to take me home. My tears dry up because I have no more to give. I'm no longer paying attention. The ground, cold and wet, begins to cool my fever some, offering a welcome grave. It hits me I will never be found, and my journal will rot away here, never to be read.

The thought makes me sad.

I have so many regrets. I should have told Krin the truth, and now she's dead. Jesma, Jesmir, and Tam are lost somewhere in these woods. Brogen gets to live while I die.

The gods are cruel. I hate them.

I laugh inside as at least some part of me is still there. Fat lot of good that will do me as I feel motion around me. Animals of the valley, likely scavengers waiting for me to die.

"This is where I die," I whisper, risking the sound. Why should I care anyway?

"It will be if you don't shut up," whispers a familiar female voice.

I feel a gentle hand on my back. Small, light, friendly.

"He's here," Jesma says, her voice soft, quiet.

I close my eyes and weep.

The Growing Darkness

Chapter Twenty

Journal Entry:65

I've been told it's odd how much time I spend wandering the world alone. My friends say people, regardless of race, have one universal trait: the need to be socially connected. I get it. I do. Indeed, the entirety of mankind, whether Human, Fae, or otherwise, cannot survive as a race without community. Every race has built societies for this reason. Bands became tribes, tribes became chiefdoms, chiefdoms became nation-states, and nation-states became realms.

Settlements become villages, villages grow into towns, and towns explode into cities.

Gathering around a fire becomes gathering around a table. Pubs exist for one reason. Gathering of people around a common environment. Socialized good times.

If I am honest with you, I am no different. Yes, I travel alone, and yes, I live in solitude.

Yes, I have very few people I trust and call friends.

But I have them.

Somehow, they always show up.
Like now.

Sean Gregory

Return of Light, Returning to Plight

I've lost track of the days. I've been in and out of consciousness so often that time has lost all meaning. Every minute could've been an eternity, and I wouldn't know. I'm not sure I'd care. Blissful images of the object of my desire kept me company. Or it could have been fevered dreams. I don't think I'll ever really know.

All I can remember is the peacefulness of those images—my soul at ease.

Mental images blend together, different versions of her looking down at me, washing my face, stroking my cheeks with gentle caresses. Images of us running through a field full of wildflowers together, hand-in-hand, tickle at my memory. Remembrances of soft touches of her hand to the back of my head as she lifts it and adjusts my pillow, her hair falling about my face, the scent oddly organic and soothing, invoke feelings of contentment.

Without warning, I stand alone at the top of the waterrise where I last saw Grankin, overlooking the river below.

Then *she's* back, holding a tankard of broth to my lips.

The sky changes, and soft breezes send waves of motion through the field. She's laughing at something I said but can't remember as we pick fresh berries in a land I don't recognize. Then she lays with me, head on my chest, looking up at the night stars until finally, the darkness fades, and flickering firelight bounces off strange rock walls.

I'm not disturbed by the images I see. But in all of them, I see someone I'd die for, maybe even live for. Whether in the background or front and center, Jesma is a comfortable companion. There's a serenity in her presence I can't explain, but she feels like home.

A soft rumble, low, quiet, resonates around my lower abdomen. A sensation of emerging from deep water overwhelms my senses at first, as consciousness returns.

I open my eyes to flickering light once again. A dead weight presses on my legs, keeping me from moving them. Looking down, a mound of red-brown hair with light streaks of silver peeking through spreads across my body like pools of platinum amber ale. Jesma, her head across my lap, asleep, holding silent vigil, is the muse I have seen in every image of recent memory. A slight line of drool falls from her mouth onto the sleeve of her blouse as soft purring snores escape her lips. She is sleeping soundly, one arm folded under her head, her hand dangerously close to my private parts. Her hair covers a large portion of her face and flows in every direction, unkempt and dirty from days of travel and trauma. Once again, I realize how beautiful she is.

A flutter of butterflies tickle my stomach. It's a familiar feeling now when I look at her. I'm drawn to her. The woman who lives in my dreams haunts me when I'm awake. If somehow I could prove worthy of her, I would. I'd give so much to have lived a different life. I wanted to find myself with the status that gave me a chance with her.

But I can't, so I brush those aside.

Unrequited passions aside, I can't put words to how much better I feel. It only slightly has to do with the sleeping beauty. Stiff but rested, my body doesn't hurt. The headache is gone. I'm dry, although my skin is sticky from the residual salts and dried sweat mixed with my body oils. Dizziness abated, so I reached over and stroked the hair of the girl who haunted dream's. It's soft, cool to the touch, and comforting. She stirs but doesn't wake.

I pull my hand away, suddenly aware my behavior is inappropriate. It wasn't too long ago four men tried to commit terrible acts against her. As I try to sit up, the motion disturbs her further. She lifts her head and immediately wipes the drool from her cheek. As she opens her eyes, she realizes I am staring at her.

The natural blush of her cheeks as she quickly sits up and looks away is the most adorable thing I have ever seen. Her sheepish, self-conscious smile as she turns to hide her embarrassment makes me giggle. She shoots me a playfully shy look.

"Sorry," I say. "You just looked so cute."

"I drooled," she groaned softly.

"You snore," I whisper, smiling.

We linger a moment in the silence, eyes locked on each other.

It's not my intent to embarrass Jesma, so I look away and try to gauge where I am and what happened, pretending the comment wasn't said. Besides, looking closely at her only makes the distance between our worlds more real.

I think she looks disappointed when I look away, but I'm too self-conscious to turn back.

The room looks familiar. A shudder goes through my body as I recall fighting the Cuska. Suddenly, I realize why this place looks familiar. It's the home of the Cuska I killed. I don't know how I got here, but I recognize the chair and table and the pile of stuff by the fireplace.

"Where are we?" I ask, unsettled.

Jesma smiles. "I am glad you are awake. The fever held on a long time," she says. "You gave us a scare… a couple of times."

Her expression is a mix of relief and wonder.

"Did I fight a Cuska?" I ask.

She shakes her head slowly. "I don't know. But there's a dead one in the other room."

"I remember two. Did I fight that one too?"

"No, thankfully, you ran. You both ran so fast. When you disappeared into the forest, I feared the worst. I thought we lost you," Jesma says. "Tam is so good at what he does. He followed you while keeping us away from that monster."

She pauses, but I can tell she has more to say, so I wait.

"I don't know how you do it." She closes her eyes as if she had a vision. "Shen, what you did… I don't know how it's possible, but you got away. You moved so fast it was like you were invisible. When the Cuska followed you, we were able to escape." She pauses, about to say more, and stops. Then she simply says, "Thank you."

I look up at her, confused.

"I don't understand," I say.

She gives me a wry smile and gently touches my cheek.

"Neither do I. But you saved us. You saved me. Again. If you hadn't come looking for us, Tam says he never would have realized we were trapped in an illusion. He never would have called to Fildeus."

Her touch sends shock waves through me. I can't help it; I

press my face into her hand. Desire burns in me from her touch as I allow myself to entertain feelings for her, finding them simultaneously scary and comforting. She doesn't feel what I do, but thinking about her brings me peace.

The deep blue of her eyes draws me in. I lose myself momentarily.

She leans in and kisses me on the lips. Her kiss is soft, moist, and tender. She lingers there a second, no more. But long enough, I convince myself there's more than a simple thank you.

Can I be wrong? Does she feel what I'm feeling?

I feel blood rushing to my face. My ears burn with the increased blood flow, and for a brief second, I want to pull this woman who invades my thoughts close, but I stop myself and allow the urge to fade. I am sure she's simply extending kindness to her patient.

She pulls away, eyes watering, a smile on her face. Her forehead touches mine.

"And this time, I was able to save you. With Shamna's help, of course."

At this moment, I realize I feel better than I have for a while. For the first time in days, I'm pain-free. Not in my side, not my back, not my head. Every ache, pain, and injury is healed. Vague memories of injuries sustained linger, but I can't place where they were. Any residual ache or pain of them is gone.

I am me again.

For all that's worth.

Jesma strokes my hair and squints her eyes like she has a question.

"What?"

She shakes her head. "I never realized you had so much gray in your hair. It seems somehow grayer than when I last saw you."

"Umm, thanks?"

"I like it," she says. "Makes you look austere." She stands and offers me her hand, expectantly, an invitation to come with her.

I want to address the kiss, but my nerves get me. Attempting to speak, I stop myself several times, and she raises an eyebrow.

"Let's get you moving around." She winks and says, "I won't hurt you."

I chuckle. Jesma's returning another favor. I accept her offer to help me stand. The room spins, the effort making me dizzy. She helps me steady myself. Pondering the evolution of our relationship in the few days I've known her, I find myself dwelling on impossibilities. I won't fool myself with senseless hope. She's a royal, and I am little better than a street mongrel vigilante.

"Easy," she encourages. "You've been out for three full days."

My gaze snaps to her.

"Three days? We've been in the Valley of Cusk for three days?"

She nods. "More, actually. You've been down here for five. We felt this was as safe a place as any to get you healed. Jes and Tam have been hunting close to the cottage. They should be back any moment."

Five days!

I release her hand and walk over to the door. My mouth is parched.

"I need water."

"Just outside. Don't drink the ale or eat the food. It's drugged. I think that's how the Cuska keeps us docile. They cast illusions, get us to drink their potions, and then… I don't want to think about 'and then'. I think the drink causes us to sleep, giving them time to do whatever they do."

"How do you know this?" I ask.

"I found a book in your pack. There's a lot about these Cuska. I've also been going through the books here in this room."

I look back at her. "I think they eat us."

Her face pales slightly. "It's worse than that," she says. "They use us to stay alive by enveloping us, I think. It's hard to put together because I've only found pieces of information. It's all quite confusing."

I nod and open the door. Light from the day comes in. It is brighter than it has been the last several days. My eyes squint involuntarily against the light. I turn my head down and try to focus on my footing and the ground. The air is crisp and cool. Fall is moving through its phases.

"You've been asleep for days. It will take a moment for your eyes to readjust," Jesma says.

I feel her wrap an arm around my side and the other gently presses on my arm between us. Her touch sends a tingle up my spine. Butterflies again.

"Here," she says quietly, "I'll help you walk to the fire."

I accept her help, grateful I don't have to stumble my way. Even more grateful, it allows me to look into her beautiful blue eyes.

I suspect I might be smitten. I don't know how, and I don't care. I'll let it live here, inside me, for now.

She leads me to a log, and I sit, the low flames of the dying fire warming my feet and giving me a new focus. My eyes begin to adjust as I feel her step away and hear her shuffling behind me. A moment later, she sits next to me and hands me a mug of water.

"These Cuska are smart," she says. "They catch rainwater in barrels and then filter it through sand inside and send it into another barrel. It's rather ingenious. I don't imagine there is much drinkable water down in this valley. But this is safe to drink."

I accept the mug and take a large swig of it. The coolness is refreshing, and it takes effort to stop myself from downing it like a thirsty dog.

"Any idea how far in we are?" I ask.

She closes her eyes. "I don't know. The monster caught us off guard when we came looking for you. He beat Jesmir and Tamrin and then offered to allow me to walk."

She drops her head.

"I thought we were dead, but I couldn't let the creature take Jes and Tam. I thought if I went along, maybe I could find a way out." She shakes her head. "No, I thought maybe I could buy us time for you to come find us." Her head hangs low as if she's ashamed of that. I long to reach over and raise her chin, tell her it's okay, tell her I am happy I was able to find her.

Before I do, she shakes her head. "And then you did show up. Fevered, battered, confused, covered in so much blood, and fearless." Then she looks up at me. "Instead, you ran. We yelled for you to run, and you did. I was so grateful you did. When it went after you, I was scared. Angry at it. I was afraid you wouldn't survive."

I close my eyes and focus on the memory of the Cuska. Three

heads again, three sets of legs and arms, the memory, while vivid, feels like a dream. I remember it clearly. The visions of night terrors. I turn and look at her, and the fear of monsters is replaced by a different fear.

I've never experienced so much fear.

"I was scared, terrified," I say.

She shakes her head. "You are a warrior. You don't know fear."

"Warriors know fear. Until this place, I didn't really know it." I look at her. "I know it now." I want to change the subject. "How did it get you?"

"It went for Tam first. Before we even knew it was there. Jesmir, though he fought hard, isn't as skilled as you two are. It had him before he could draw his sword."

I can see the pain in her face over the memories of the encounter with the Cuska.

"He's not like you. He tries, though. He swallows his fear, even if he is unskilled."

I look at my hands as I realize what that means now. I didn't swallow my fear. I ran, afraid in a way I never knew I could be. We sit silently, each lost in our thoughts. I find myself thinking about my encounter with both Cuska.

She adjusts her position, turning toward me. Her knee touches mine.

"I'm glad you ran." She sits silently for a moment. "I wasn't sure it wasn't part of the illusion. I didn't even realize it was an illusion. Thank Fildeus for Tam's true seeing. He broke the illusion." She turns her head to the fire, lost in the memory.

I ignore the declaration of faith.

"It never touched you. I think you moved so fast that you snapped tendons. Your arm had no outside injuries, but it was hanging oddly, swollen. So was your knee. Your ankle was so swollen I thought it was broken. The infection was the worst part. But you are alive and healed, and for that, I am happy," she says.

I feel a faint heat on my chest.

The handprint.

Oh, go to Hell, Grankin. I'm busy.

That's as much of any prayer I can offer. I'm no disciple.

Evening settled by the time Tamrin and Jesmir returned. Tam carries two small bakru and a medium-sized pheasant. Jesmir avoids looking at me as he enters the glen. It's uncomfortable and awkward when Jesmir does look at me. I don't know why he is so distant.

Tamrin, on the other hand, walks over and, with a big smile as always, lifts me into a bear hug.

"Fildeus be praised!" he exclaims. "You gave me quite the scare, Shen. I thought I lost you forever. How about we stick together from now on?"

He sets me down, and I smile at him.

"I sure am glad to see you," I say. "Are you okay? I hear the Cuska got you before you had a chance to teach it a lesson."

Tamrin reaches the back of his head and rubs it. His chagrin is evident, but he keeps his spirits.

"Well, yeah, it got a hold of me pretty good. I was focused on the trail you left, or well, more like the one whoever took you left. It surprised us. As big as it is."

He puts a hand on my shoulder and looks at me earnestly.

"I figured you were dead. But I couldn't rest until we found you. One way or another."

I place my hand over his.

"Thank you. But you should have gotten these two to safety."

He laughs.

"You try telling these two not to do something they want to do. Neither one of them was having it. Jesmir noticed you and Krin were missing and immediately rushed back to find you."

His demeanor darkens.

"We found a puddle of blood at the edge of the ravine. I spotted more down the trail into the valley. What happened?"

I give him a look, conveying my lack of desire to discuss Krin.

"Krin stabbed me," I say.

"What?" Jesma says.

"Krin stabbed you?" Jesmir says. He has come over and is standing next to the big man. His face is one of concern. "How is that possible? Why would she do that?"

"She surprised me. Then she pushed me over the edge. I was holding onto her when I fell and ended up pulling her down with me," I say. "You guys didn't find her?"

Jesmir looks at Jesma, then back to me, "Where did she go?"

I look down at my feet. It's too painful to discuss.

Or is it?

I know, deep down, the best choice is to let it all out, the entire history of my time with Krin. I wish I had more courage. I've never been good at intimacy. How can I tell these two, who were counting on Krin to do her job, that my mere presence in their lives caused their situation to grow more tenuous? How do I tell them they are the unfortunate collateral damage of decisions I made years ago? How do I say the current predicament is entirely my fault?

I should tell them.

But I can't.

But I have no other option. I'm done with secrets. My identity is no longer a secret.

Without looking up, I whisper, "I killed her brother."

Actual crickets sound in the woods.

Why does it always feel like I finally see the light, but the darkness only grows?

The Growing Darkness

Chapter Twenty-One

Journal Entry:67

I'm not sure what to believe anymore. This mark on my chest constantly reminds me I'm no longer alone when I'm alone. These people don't seem to tire of my presence either. Could I have been wrong this whole time?

Are these records of my thoughts giving me the strength to open my soul to the world?

The truth is, I need this. I need to know that someone will read this someday. I think putting this down is helping already. If I am lucky, maybe I'll find a purpose for myself that doesn't involve death.

Maybe there is a life to be had in the presence of others.
Maybe there's a chance at a normal life.
If I can get them home safely, maybe I can settle down.
I'm shocked to realize how much hope the thought gives me.

The Light at the End of the Tunnel

Unburdening myself of this lifelong secret is a tremendous relief. Tam sat quietly, having learned most of the story that night in Valshannon. I don't fully know why I tell the twins but seeing as how they risked their lives for me by coming into the most feared place in Rhinestab, there's a debt to them I can't repay. They deserve to know the reason we are down here.

Besides, their emissary sent me into this stale, moldy hellscape. They deserve to know why they were betrayed.

The truth about my relationship with Krin and her brother poured out of me. I confessed to killing Harley and burning down the Guild Tower in Kerakot. I spared no details. Once the words came, they poured out. It was a flood of words, and with each new reveal, pieces of the emotional armor fell away. It was cathartic, visceral, and a huge relief.

I even told the story of the Tillions, which Tam took with some sadness. He'd met them occasionally, and their hospitality was well known in our circle.

A lot of questions were asked, but none gave me any indication they held me to blame me for Krin's actions. In fact, they were pretty quick to see her as a traitor, which made a lot of sense when looking at it from their perspective.

Tam expressed concerns about not seeing her body when they came looking for me, and that was a topic of discussion. The Cuska tracks around the spot where we landed were hard to read, according to Tam, because the rain washed away most of the evidence.

"If not for the gurney tracks," he said, "we never would have known which direction to go."

I omitted no secret intentionally, the revelations at the completion of my tale leaving me emotionally raw. Jesmir, stone-faced, kept quiet throughout the entirety of my story. When I exhausted my words, no one spoke. Each of us sat quietly within our own thoughts.

Jesma was the first to finally speak.

Turning to me, she takes my hand, holding it between hers, one friend comforting another. "We," she looks at her brother and back, "the collective royal family have taken advantage of all of you. The Assassin's Guild exists solely as a political tool for us to influence the world to our own desires. What you are is not your fault." She lowers her head, "It's ours."

"Too much is asked from the people we're supposed to serve," she says. Then she looks up at me, her eyes moist but her face determined. "You are a good man, Harbinger. Wear that title with pride. You're not the horrible person you see yourself as. I bear witness to your sacrifice. Whatever your reasons, you continuously throw yourself into harm's way to help others. I've been grateful you exist since the day you first appeared through the brush many days ago."

"To me, you're a hero. Not a killer."

Her voice, at once soothing and alluring, calms my spirit. I'm drawn to her Siren's call. Her compassion and kindness quicken my hearts, each beat emphasizing the emotional ache within. Tam, smiling, taps the side of his nose again and points at me with a slight flick of his finger.

He agrees.

Jesmir, however, stands, his shoulders slumped, clearly wrestling with his emotions. Not wanting to waste the vulnerability of the moment, I'd rather he be honest with me about how he views what I said. It won't do for there to be hidden animosity if he views things differently. This liberating feeling won't last if he hides resentment.

"What is it?" I ask. "I think, at this point, honesty is best."

He looks at his sister and then back to me. We stare at each other, both expectant, but I have difficulty reading him. I sense his discomfort. It's not what I expected. His gaze falls to the ground, and I realize he's withdrawing inside. I recognize the look.

"No matter how I try, I cannot seem to be the warrior my father wished." He glances up at me. "Like you." He shakes his head slowly, the display deliberate. "Thrice, I've failed to protect my sister."

I finally understand him. I take for granted what I'm capable of. I even flaunt it at times. What torments him is another version of the self-loathing I carry. He feels inadequate and hates himself for it.

Two sides of the same coin. Where I've hidden in solitude and violence, Jesmir has hidden in extravagance and privilege.

"If not for Tamrin, I would have died again in Garrow's Basin." He glances at Tamrin. "Or worse."

I stand and walk over to him, placing a hand on either shoulder. He looks up at me, and for the first time, I see a vulnerable young man, still a child in many ways. We stare at one another, and I 'm ashamed for not remembering the life he knew ended the day his father was murdered in front of him. They've been so busy running there's been little time for him to process the dangers he's encountered. Dangers he never thought he'd see. Been through horrors his former self never imagined and he's been helpless to do anything about it.

"Do you think yourself less because you cannot fight?" I ask.

He looks up at me, tears in his eyes. "Yes."

I'm a fool. Jesmir's hands shake as he speaks. All this time, I thought it was about me as a person. Here, I believed he judged me, looked down on me, and even despised me. I thought he was soft, relegating him to the minor character in a story where his existence was unimportant outside my duty to return him home safely.

I cared little about his trauma or the internal battle waging inside. In some ways, it is a lot like my own. I've been caught up in myself, in my own ego, in being the hero. I failed to realize I could have been helping him more significantly.

He feels like a failure, useless and unworthy.

He feels like me.

"What kind of ruler can I be to my people if I can't even protect my own?"

I look back and forth between the two of them. Jesma goes to speak and then stops herself.

"I understand," I say. "And I can help you there."

They both look at me expectantly. I don't have a lot of valuable skills to pass on, but in this one instance, I'm the best person for the job. And for once, it doesn't require me to kill any-one.. I can see Tamrin smirk, listening while he rotates the meat.

I look at Jesma. "You two are fighters in every sense of the word." Turning to Jesmir, I say, "You made it from deep inside Killinshire to the Great Rankin River. Few wouldn't struggle with that journey. Most would have been dead. But you managed to get so far while avoiding the most ruthless killer in all of Conishant."

Jesmir looks at me with surprise.

"Your Highness," I say, "your ability to physically fight has no bearing on your ability to lead. Compassion, intellect, empathy, cunning. Those are the skills you will need to lead. If you want to learn to fight physically, that's easy. I can teach you."

Looking to Jesma, I continue. "Both of you."

"I have been trained to fight," he says. "I'm just no good at it."

I shake my head. "No, you haven't been taught to use what you have. It's more than weapons and fists." I tap my head. "I outthink my opponents. I've practiced for many years to get to where I am. I don't fight my enemies on their terms. I fight them on mine and it's all up here." I tap his temple. "You are one resourcefully cunning man."

Jesmir's genuine smile is the first indication he has a personality I can relate to.

"Really?"

"Yes. You evaded trackers and stayed ahead of Brogen. Trusted your instincts. Dumb luck brought those mercenaries to you. You weren't outsmarted or outfought. You were out planned. Fighting is easy."

"I'd like to learn."

Jesma puts a gentle hand on my arm. "I'd like that too."

"Good," I say, "it's settled. You start now."

I stand and look at both of them. "Your first lesson. Stop the stinkin' thinkin'. Now let's get some food. Tam, please tell me it's ready. I'm starving."

"Ready." He looks back at the barrel of ale sitting under the shelves of tankards. "Too bad the only ale we have is poison-ed."

"Let's eat, rest, and hit the road in the morning. I want to get out of this valley. I will climb above the tree line to see which way the sun is setting."

He points ahead of him.

"West is that way," he says.

"Well, now I have nothing to do," I say, clapping my hands on my thighs.

"You can eat," he says.

This feeling is freeing. My body no longer hurts. Jesma's powers are extraordinarily effective, and I'm moving like me again. Watching her as we walk, I'm enthralled by her presence. What was a physical infatuation has become a somewhat emotional need to be connected to her, near her.

We've become a united group with my secrets out in the open, the shared trauma of the last few weeks, and the simple act of sharing meals.

I'm content with this feeling of belonging. Our familiarity brings with it a level of comfort with one another.

As we walk, I contemplate other questions. Questions about Krin still linger. But no answers come. I fear she was also taken by Cuska, a fate I would not wish on her, but I cannot fix that. Looking for her would put the twins at risk. As much as it pains me, if she survived, the outcome of her actions is entirely on her.

I try not to think of her head sitting on one of those creatures, but the image conjures itself, and I shudder, trying to break free of the thought.

She abandoned her post, and as shocking as the image is, she did it to herself. It's easy to understand why she did what she did to me, but abandoning her mission as emissary makes no sense. Krin is lost. She made that choice. I can't carry that guilt with me anymore.

Focusing on our way out of this valley and into Hericot, we push north. The fastest way home from here is through the Toerge Mountain tunnel into the mining town. We've been in this valley long enough. Too long. While the stench around us is oppressive, we've grown accustomed to it. It's a disgusting thought.

I glance at Tamrin. Our friendship is more profound now than it ever was. Those little parts of myself I held back from him are now out in the open. At one point on our trek north, we exchanged glances. I knew he wanted permission to have *the* talk, and he knew I wanted to discuss it, too. In that brief look, he realized I already knew how he felt.

"How long have you known?" he asks, embarrassed.

"About your feelings for me? Couple of years. It was when we were hunting down those horse thieves near Rankin Lake."

He nods, remembering the moment to which I am referring.

"Wow, that long?"

I smile.

"I'm sorry, Shen. I know it's uncomfortable."

I stop and grab his arms. "It's not. I feel bad that I don't feel the same. I hold back some of myself in an effort not to lead you on or hurt you. You are my brother. Your feelings are never wrong." I let him go, and we start walking again.

"Besides, I know I'm awesome. I'd be shocked if you weren't in love with me."

He snickers. "I hate you."

"No, you don't," I say.

It's all out in the open now. For the first time, the thoughts in my head are quiet.

Ezra occasionally appears through the dense trees as we make our way north. The cloud cover that added an extra layer of gloom is lifting. The metaphoric difference amuses me.

So far, the valley has left us alone today. No dangers have approached. Tam's run across a few tracks similar enough to the Cuska we previously encountered, but they look days old. Whatever came through is likely long gone. The few netherstacks we pass are far enough away to only slightly darken our mood, which fades as the netherstacks slip into the distance behind us.

Still, we are on high alert.

I pat a spare coin purse discovered on the Cuska's shelves to ensure I didn't lose it. The Cuska necklace, my trophy, tucked inside. The necklace and book, when combined with my journal entries, contain more information than collectively resides in the libraries of the Five Realms.

The world needs this information. Maybe we can learn some

facts and eradicate these monsters. Jesma knows some scholars who will find a use for these items. I've decided to donate them to the Scholars' Guild in Teshket.

A rock lands at my feet. I turn to my right, and Jesmir points at his eyes and the ground. I look around and let out a light bird call. Tam and Jesma, up ahead of us, turn and look at me.

Comfort.

We are a band of adventurers now.

I signal toward Jesmir, and they follow me to where he squats, moving debris carefully on the ground. Tam leans over him.

"That's fresh," Tam says. "Can't be more than a couple of hours old."

I scan the area to ensure we aren't under observation.

Jesmir stands and points to his right. "Looks like they turn. They are going in our direction."

He looks at me with fear in his eyes.

I nod. Jesmir's fear is justified.

"We'll be fine," I say, though I'm not entirely sure it's true. "This time, there are four of us. I am not fevered, tired, or injured." I look at each of them and smile. "Thanks to you three."

Jesma smiles at me. Butterflies flip my stomach again.

Tam says, "Good work, Jes. I'll take point." He points at Jesmir. "You keep us going north. I'll need you to tell me if the trail strays off our path. Otherwise, I'll get hyper-focused, and we could go way out of our way. We don't want to follow these tracks if they take us in the wrong direction."

"Understood."

Tamrin grips the periapt in his hand and whispers, "Prave vetas."

Jesma inclines her head toward Tam, her eyes locked with mine.

"I bet he could do that without the periapt," I say.

"So much evidence, yet you still won't believe," she replies. "And what of the handprint on your chest?"

"I'm not saying magic doesn't exist. I'm not even sure I believe your gods don't exist. I simply don't believe they are gods. Either way, they are selfish and cruel, and I have no desire to pledge fealty to one."

She shrugs and offers me a half smile. I shrug back and change the subject.

"Jesma and I will take the rear," I say, smiling at her. "You're with me."

She is frightened still but nods. Memories of Cuska replaying in her head. But she seems relieved I'm keeping her close.

I'm not entirely sure if my motivation is purely protective.

The path we take weaves through the valley as the floor starts its climb out and up toward the base of the Toerges. Unfortunately, we are walking a line that does, in fact, follow the tracks, making us all a little uneasy. Collectively, tension rises in the group, and furtive glances come more often. If this continues, it's only a matter of time before we risk another encounter. Regardless of the outcome of the first two encounters, I don't relish the idea of a third.

I keep replaying the battles with the Cuska.

I whisper to Jesma, "Cuska? Cuskas? Cuski? What is the plural of these things?"

Jesma looks at me curiously, and I wave it off.

"My brain went on its own path mid-thought."

"Mine does that all the time," she says. "I think it's Cuska, though."

"I was thinking about my fights with those Cuska, and when I tried to pluralize, I got stuck on it."

She laughs. "Cuski or Cuskas sound funny."

I laugh a little too loud. Tam spins around and shushes me, his eyes stern. I wave an apology and drop my voice to a whisper.

"I keep playing the scene over and over again in my mind. It's unfathomable to me we've survived two encounters."

"Honestly? It's what frightens me the most. I don't know how we are still alive. Either they aren't as fearsome as we made them out to be, or something we missed gave us an advantage. What if, despite everything, I fail next time?"

"I don't think that's possible," she says. "Can I ask you a question?"

I look at her. "I don't think I could say no to you."

She blushes, and I feel my ears burn again.

She clears her throat quietly and then asks, "How did you get so good at what you do?"

"Fighting? Well, that was easy. I've always been stealthy and fast. I don't ever remember a time I wasn't. Your Highness… Jesma."

"Jez," she corrects. "My friends call me Jez."

"But we aren't…"

"Yes, we are," she blurts angrily, then covers her mouth in shock. "I'm sorry. I didn't mean it to be so…"

I smile and step closer to her. "No, I am. You are right. We are friends… Jez."

Her smile makes me blush again. She stops, so I stop.

"How did you get so good?"

I look at my feet, and her hand touches my chin. Light fingers lift my face up 'til our eyes meet. Those deep blue lakes mesmerize me. Her eyelashes, long and dark, flutter as she looks at me. She leans in and kisses my lips, soft but gentle.

I don't pull away. I don't push either. I let it happen, returning a slight kiss back.

"You don't have to be afraid of me," she says.

We both blush… I think hers is in response to mine. It's hard to say.

"I'm not afraid…"

"Yes, you are."

I tilt my head. "You have a habit of interrupting," I say.

Her smile makes my body tingle. "Only when I know what you will say is wrong."

I laugh a little too loud and shush myself. We both giggle like children.

I turn, and we start walking again. I pick up the pace to ensure we don't fall too far back. As we do, we talk.

"I'm an assassin, Jez."

"I know."

"Then I don't know what you mean. That's how I became what I am."

She stops and looks me dead in the face.

"No, your powers. You have no god, no periapt. You make no prayers. Yet you move like a man possessing limitless power."

I furrow my brow, contemplating her comments.

"I really never thought of it that way. I do it."

Casting a sideways glance, I add, "It hurts. All the time."

"What does?"

"My body. All the time." I let out a soft sigh. "Most of the time? Like now? It's this dull throb all over. Inside, outside, like this rhythmic pulse of discomfort. Sometimes, it aches. I've grown used to it. When I'm pushing myself to be fast, though? The feeling intensifies. Lately, it's been so much worse."

"That sounds like the feeling I get when I pray for Shamna's blessings. When she answers my prayers, it's this intense discomfort. Sometimes, I don't want to do it, but it's how I prove my devotion, and she answers the prayers."

I stop and look at her. "Tam said a similar comment a long time ago. What do you think it means?"

She shrugs. "That's why I'm asking you how you do it? Are you saying you don't know? I've never seen you pray."

I shake my head. "No clue. I don't pray. I do. I've always been silent, and I've always been fast. It's why the Guild was willing to pay so much for me."

I smirk at her. "I can't believe I'm telling you this."

We continue in silence for a while.

"I can," she says, smirking back. "You're falling for me."

My mouth falls open, and her smirk turns lascivious. She suddenly jogs away. I am dumbfounded at the thought. Why would she make such a flippant statement?

"I most certainly am not," I whisper after her harshly.

She looks over her shoulder, her expression telling me she thinks otherwise. I don't have the courage to tell her how much I want to know more about her. She's a kid playing games. What I'm feeling can't be returned by her. Street thugs and princesses don't go together, not in Teshket society.

"Shen!" I hear a hoarse whisper call.

Jez stops, and I come to a stop close to her, our bodies almost touching. I can feel the heat coming off her as I look into her eyes.

"Shen!" I hear a different whisper call.

Am I falling for her, though?

"Shen!" both whispers call.

I turn, frustrated. "What!"

Tam and Jesmir stare at me, wide-eyed, waving us over. I look back at Jesma, who stands looking at me expectantly. I abandon my plan to kiss her, tilting my head in their direction instead. She lets out a disappointed sigh and turns back to Tam and Jesmir.

"We have a problem," Tam whispers.

When I think of monsters, especially those I don't understand, it's rarely in any context other than "they want to kill me. I have to kill them to survive." Cuska definitely fall into that category. In that regard, I imagine them to be solitary creatures. It's not without some basis in the evidence I have. Accounts of encounters from supposed eyewitnesses tell of the horrors and are rare. The facts vary based on the age of the story and who is telling it, and all of the accounts are secondhand or worse. In all of those accounts, there have never been stories of hordes of them or packs. It's always one. The stories, though, are that. Nobody has proof or empirical evidence—until now.

We've experienced Cuska firsthand. The four of us can attest to their intent to do harm for no reason other than we exist and they want to. Our evidence suggests they work alone. We have yet to encounter multiples. Tracks from the one that took my friends may have indicated more than one, but it still turned out to be just one.

From my perspective, the monsters are solitary malignant tumors in the circle of life. I'll admit perspective is everything. I'm aware I see the world from a skewed perspective and am unable to see it from any other. But, considering the two I encountered behaved precisely as in every story I ever heard, it's hard to convince me my perspective is wrong. From where I stand, Cuska are solitary monsters. Devoid of social structure. There would need to be evidence to back up that argument before I could restructure that paradigm.

Like a sense of community.

Like four sets of tracks coming from four different directions, meeting at a point, then heading together down a common path.

Exactly like what we are following right now. For the last several thousand yards, we have followed a clear set of tracks of multiple Cuska moving together. We discovered more tracks converging on the trail.

"That's a lot of footprints in the mud," Jesmir says.

"Yeah, I am counting six distinct sets now," Tam says.

Jez and I walk about twenty feet to either side of the tracker and his new apprentice, scanning for more prints. I wish I could say it was for efficiency and thoroughness, but I split us up because I didn't want to talk to her about what she said. I catch sight of her scanning her route, intently focused on the ground ahead of her, and my thoughts shift from the task at hand to what she said.

"You're falling for me."

She said it so self-assured. It's ridiculous to think that is possible.

Sure, she's beautiful. I can admit there is infatuation there. The events of the past weeks have bred familiarity and comfort, which I've never experienced. Not even with Krin.

I'm human, and I like girls. But that doesn't mean I am falling for her. I know so little about her and I'm not foolish enough to even consider that a Princess of Teshket would be interested in anything more than a fling with someone other than another royal. They are pretty strict on that front. I'm of such low status in Teshket society I wouldn't even be considered for a role as one of her servants. Mom was an untouchable. That makes me one.

The idea that she thinks I would allow myself to fall for her is preposterous.

Regardless of the heartfelt talks, I'm still the same guy I always was. These thoughts about monsters are really a euphemism for me, the worst monster of all. I don't fool myself into thinking I'll ever be allowed the opportunity for love, peace, and family. I am The Harbinger. The whole world fears my presence or loathes it.

Love is not in the stars for me.

"Psst!"

I look over to Tamrin.

"Do you plan to join us or just stand there, stuck in your head?" he whispers harshly. He's frustrated. I realized they had been trying to get my attention for a while.

Oops.

I nod and head over.

"Sorry," I whisper.

"You plan on remaining lost in the nether regions of that thick skull of yours? Or do you plan on sticking with the rest of the class?" Tam admonishes.

I look at Jesma, who gives me a slight smile. I wonder if her thoughts match my own. Tam snaps his fingers in both of our faces.

"Nadur's nut sack, I get it, but enough. You two are lost in your mutual admiration society, but can you please focus?"

"Sorry," I say again. "What's going on?"

"Well, if you were doing your job, you'd see we have more tracks. I am counting eight Cuska now."

"Oh. This can't be good," I say.

"Well, I'm glad you got us all up to speed there, Skippy," Tamrin mocks.

I give him a look meant to convey he should tread lightly. He raises his hands in surrender.

"Okay, I'll stop."

I look ahead at the mess of muddy footprints converging and heading in one unified direction. Hundreds of prints trampling over the top of each other make it hard to tell the total number of creatures. We've left the realm of scary and jumped right into apocalyptically terrifying. One of these is dangerous enough. Two would be one hell of a fight. Eight or more, we'd be foolish to not find a different path. Up to now, we've been following these prints partly because they are headed the way we are. But also, because we got caught up in the dramatic curiosity. Foolishly so.

The chance to gain knowledge ran away with us. Even Jesmir is lost in tracking, pushing his fear aside, and thriving in the group's collective mind. The decision is easy, continuing to follow the tracks is too risky.

"Let's find a different path," I suggest. "If these beasts are merging to this path, whatever the reason, others are likely merging elsewhere as well."

I look up through the trees. The sky is still blue enough, from what I can see. We have between three and four more hours of solid daylight, and getting out of these woods is more important than following this trail any longer.

"We don't want to be stuck here at night. Especially this close to a Cuska gathering," I say.

Jesmir nods in agreement. "I'd like to get out of here before dark."

I put a hand on his shoulder. "Agreed." Remnants of terror-filled memories linger in the not-so-dark corners of my mind.

"Any thoughts on which direction?" Jesma asks.

We look around the woods. Forward continues the slope up the valley, presumably taking us out. Behind us, the grade slopes back to the valley floor.

"Which way have the majority of the tracks come from?" I ask.

Tamrin points behind me. "Most of them originate from that direction," he says.

"It's safe to assume we likely are behind them, so if we go that way…" I start.

"It's also likely that is the wrong direction since that is where they are coming from," Tam says.

He's right.

"Okay, we are agreed. We head that way," I point over Tam's shoulder. "Let's go walk perpendicular to our path for a mile or so. Then turn back up the slope and get the hell out of here."

Tamrin and Jesma nod in turn. Jesmir hesitates.

"Jes," Jesma says, "agreed?"

He looks at me. "I can't believe I am saying this. But isn't it odd they are gathering? Why would they gather?" He looks at Jesma. "We could learn new information here. Take the knowledge home."

My jaw falls open.

"Jes, I want to go home," she says. "We have to find out what Brogen is up to. The Queen needs to know we are safe."

Jesmir thinks a minute and then nods. "You're right. I'm not thinking. I got caught up in the adventure."

Tam snorts a small laugh.

"It kinda gets inside you, doesn't it?" he says.

Jesmir shrugs in acknowledgment.

"Well then," I start but don't finish.

Above us, up the valley slope, a low thumping begins. Three rapid beats, repeated in a pattern, the sound of a bass drum. In unison we turn our gazes uphill, our chatter silenced. The beats repeat a total of three times. Then, as if in unison, we hear the creepiest sound come down to the valley floor. Voices of monsters, raised in song.

It's hypnotic. A new Siren's call. We stare at each other, eyes darting back and forth. Jesma's smile sends a chill up my spine.

"Let's go check it out," Jesma says.

I look at Tamrin, "What the hell is happening here?"

He shakes his head. "I want to know too."

The beating of the drums is not a cacophonous barrage of sound. If not for the sinister nature of the valley, it's almost soothing and reverent. Calming. The low rumble, controlled and deliberate, moves like a slow roll of distant thunder. The voices filling the valley are somber, soft, and filled with emotion. It's eerily human. Harmonious. I do not recognize the language of the words. Still, if not for the chills of previous experience, it's a beautiful sound.

We make our way toward the chorus, concluding we are much closer to the end of the Cuska trail than anticipated. Barely more than a quarter-mile trek up the valley slope, we find a ring of Cuska circling a large drum. Hiding in the shadows of brushes and cedars, we stare in awe.

The song, a wail of lament, sounds ancient and formal. The sublime harmony, marking time with our slow approach, evokes emotions of loss and sadness.

Ezra's late afternoon light provides an easy view of nineteen Cuska, eighteen of which stand circled around the large drum in the center of the clearing. One stands at the drum, three arms held high, a large stick in its hand, three heads tilted back to the sky.

It looks very much like they are in a form of prayer.

The four of us stay deep in the shadows of the evergreens

around us, doing our best not to allow any of Ezra's light to reveal our presence. Shocked and fascinated, we watch the scene in awe, exchanging furtive glances. These creatures are gathered in communal worship. They act as one, the ritualized behaviors telling a story of their own. Cuska have a culture. It is as beautiful as it is terrifying. We lose ourselves in the observation the spectacle.

Looking at the various Cuska, I see they are physically vastly different, yet somehow the same. Some are like the first Cuska I encountered, long and spindly, two legs, two arms, and three heads. Others, like the one in the center, have three arms. Some have one arm and several legs.

Three specific traits are shared universally, though. Three heads. Each and every one has three heads. Mismatched skin. The body parts seem to be a mismatch of parts from various races. One even has a Korund hide covering its back. It's hard to see, but I am pretty sure it has a Korund head as well.

It's almost as if someone cut up several people and patched them together in a mix-and-match pattern. The thought of how different my presence here could have been if I hadn't defeated the first Cuska makes my skin crawl.

As the song ends, the one in the center lowers its hands and looks around the clearing, all three heads taking individual stock of their brethren.

"My dear family," the three heads say in unison, that same melodic harmony giving me the creeps. It's as if the three minds are connected. My experience of the previous two Cuska would suggest each head has a distinct personality. This Cuska demonstrates there is a hive mind as well. I look at Tam and he is fascinated.

"As is readily apparent, one of our number is missing." The heads look at each Cuska in the circle in turn. "Fashkor is not here today. This does not bode well. Fashkor has led this vigil for thousands of years. Their absence reminds us that we must find a way out of here. Fashkor would never miss this assembly. We fear that can only mean they have passed into the next world. Morgan has come with news as well."

The three heads turn to look at another Cuska. I gulp the massive monster with six legs, six arms, and three heads, immediately familiar to me, begin to speak. The same creature that chased me three days ago steps in front of the leader.

"The hunger we feel cannot be satiated and only grows worse. Even I, the largest and strongest of us, cannot hold out much longer." They hang their heads. "I had four perfect meals within grasp two days ago. But they escaped."

An audible gasp echoes through the trees.

"I searched for the last two days and did not find them. They broke my illusion spell. One of them, injured, moves faster than anything I've ever seen. Even injured, that one managed to escape. I can only assume they are here with the help of the Hated Eight."

"They know our time is waning!" a trio cries, wailing. "Why can't they leave us in peace?"

The leader steps forward, holding three hands up. "As we feared, our entrapment in this forest has finally caught up with us. Few humans travel into this valley anymore. For those that do, we fight amongst ourselves for the sustenance and now, these humans seem able to escape us. Our supply of new members to our bodies has dwindled to the point where only two of us have hosts younger than five years old.

And, as predicted hundreds of years ago, the slow erosion of the lifespans of man has impacted us as well, requiring us to feed more often. The Great Eight have succeeded in their plans and have grown more powerful as we fade into history. Our once great numbers, at one time hundreds, are now down to this small group. I fear the marvelous creation of Cuskatana could vanish from this world."

A murmur works its way through the gathering.

"Please, brethren, calm down. After our vigil, we will take Inndia and Morgan to see Fashkor. Together, we will go to our missing brethren's home and seek answers. We know Fashkor was on the verge of a breakthrough. We will search his books for answers. We would suggest we reconvene in four nights. We will report to you our findings. We must find a way to break the barrier that traps us here. We must work together and push the gates of our prison asunder."

The three heads pause.

One of the others calls out, "To what use? Fashkor has tried since the beginning! We squander time in useless efforts. In one hundred years, none of us will be left. The Great Eight have won. Cuskatana has failed us."

A murmur through the crowd echoes among the trees.

"Enough! Do not blaspheme our Goddess again, Chimgar. We must maintain faith. For if we don't, we shall perish."

The collection of Cuska nods to each other as more murmurs work their way through the crowd.

"Let us pray," the leader says.

"Let us pray!" the rest say. It's much louder than I would expect. Fifty-four voices make a hell of a racket.

"Oh Cuskatana, creator of eternal life, we beseech you again to help your creations and free us from this prison. Twenty thousand years have passed since you left us here. Twenty thousand years have passed since Nadur and his ilk have imprisoned us in this valley. We have gathered in solemn prayer for twenty thousand years on this day, the day of your passing. Forever your faithful, we have lost access to magics that once were ours to command. Return our power and help us seek revenge on those who imprisoned us. Guide us, Great One, for yours is the path, the power, and the glory. Forever do we serve Cuskatana."

"Forever do we serve Cuskatana," the crowd repeats in unison.

The reach out and grab hands. It's a prayer circle. These monsters have feelings and very real pieces of humanity, and the thought frightens me more. The thought of them banded together chills me to the bone. Wild thoughts run through my head as I imagine the worst if they were to break free of whatever barrier they are talking about. That must be the reason they never leave the valley.

But my mind is stuck on the scariest part of this whole scenario. Cuska gathers. They are organized and they want out.

I sneak close to Tamrin and whisper, "This is not good."

He shakes his head in agreement.

"If they disband, they are sure to find us here." I look at Jesma and Jesmir. "We have to get out of here."

Tamrin grabs my arm, fear frozen in his expression. "It sounds as if they are stuck in this valley. That's why we never see them anywhere else." He looks back to the clearing.

"If they get loose…" he whispers so low I almost can't hear him.

I put a hand on his shoulder and a finger to my lips. I look at Jesma and Jesmir and make the same indication to each of them. I wait for each to confirm they understand with a nod.

Jesma shifts her weight to move away, and a twig snaps under her foot. I close my eyes in horror. When I open them, she stands frozen. Her body shakes in terror.

I return my attention to the cluster of Cuska gathered. Two heads on the nearest Cuska look back in Jesma's direction. I can't tell if it sees her, but both sets of eyes squint, peering through the trees. The hair on my neck stands on end while it searches the shadows. The decision is easy.

With a shudder I glance at Tamrin, who watches me and shakes his head vigorously. He reads my intentions on my face. There's no other option. We have mere seconds to act. This monster is coming. Tamrin knows I'll never allow these evil creatures to draw close enough to threaten my friends. My friends would never survive. Not against nineteen.

He knows I'm about to act recklessly.

I can't let these Cuska break free of this valley if it's their prison. If they got loose, the world would never be able to fight this many. Towns would be slaughtered. People I care about could die.

What I am about to do is utterly insane.

Chapter Twenty-Two

Journal Entry: 71

I only did what most people would do. Or did I? Of course I did. I am not special. I am not really unique. Sure, I walk quietly. Sure, I am a better fighter than anyone I ever met. Sure, I have two hearts. But in the grand scheme of this world, I am an unremarkable person. I am not particularly handsome or witty. I have a better-than-average intellect, but I am not wizard-smart.

I did no more than anyone else would do for those they care about. It wasn't heroic. It was dumb. But it was necessary.

What other choice did I have?

There are much worse reasons to die.

Fear the Enemy You Don't Know

In my hand rests the trophy I stole from the Cuska I killed. I exchange silent instructions with Tamrin. He knows to be ready to run when I give the signal. He will do as I ask. The safety of the twins is his priority now. For them to get away, I have to redirect this Cuska.

I'm the decoy.

I point to the twins and then at Tam. It's a command. They are to follow him. Neither acknowledges it, but I have to trust they got the message. I give Jesma an apologetic smile. Tears stream down her face in an unspoken apology. I smile because she's right, I *am* falling for her.

Actually, I fell. This stranger, who feels like a friend, stole my heart. I can't let this Cuska bring to us the attention of their entire group. I blow her a kiss and place a hand on Tamrin's shoulder.

"This is the end of the line for me, dear friend."

He closes his eyes, and a tear winds a trail down his cheek into his beard. I put my forehead to his.

"I've always loved you," he whispers.

"I know," I say. I reach into my pocket, give Tam my ledger. It's hard to let go, but it's better in his hands than in the collection of these monsters.

"Keep this," I say. "Get the twins home safe."

With reluctant resignation, he acquiesces. Without another word I bolt around the perimeter, tossing a rock twenty yards ahead.

I don't look back.

My body tingles more intensely, and I consider Jez's words about magic and power. Too bad I'll never get any clarity on that.

The two heads turn where the rock lands, and their motion draws the attention of other Cuska. I arrive at the point of impact and throw another a few feet ahead of me. It's good to feel whole again. The familiar adrenaline-boosted exhilaration, as I approach death with a different mentality, turns into a state of rapture. For the first time, a true sense of peace flows, and I think back to the moments of my life that led to this one.

More eyes glower my direction. Not all of them, but enough for my purposes. I take a deep breath and close my eyes, count to three, and, opening my eyes, walk through the trees into the clearing, my trophy high over my head. It's the greatest bluff of my life. I'm smiling like an eight-year-old me about to execute a mischievous act with the bell Mom made me carry.

"Yoohoo!" I say. My voice lilts an octave or two.

Fifty-five more heads turn toward me. The visual threatens to shatter my resolve. It takes all of my strength not to bolt. Likely, they'd follow me, so it's not a horrible plan. I even start to turn away but stop myself. I need them to stay here, in this clearing. But, for a moment, I think I could get away and lure them a mile or two, but that's a risky plan; they will separate and find my friends.

This is the only way.

Besides, I ran once. Running is not my style and now I'm a little angry.

"What is this?" the threesome in the middle demands. "You dare interrupt us in prayer? You foolish man. We will happily accept your sac..."

The three heads choke on the words as their eyes focus on my trophy.

"May I address the audience?" I ask.

"What do you have there?" the leader of the group demands.

I glance at the necklace hanging over my head. It dawns on me that I possess the religious symbol of the Cuska. They have an object of worship.

Cuskatana.

I have to admit I have never heard of this Cuskatana, but now that I have, I intend to use the name to my full advantage. My brain fires again. I also have another name.

"It appears to be the Periapt of Cuskatana," I say. "I took it from Fashkor after I put my fist through the back of their skulls."

I love that I'm a quick learner.

Most days.

Their eyes narrow at me. "That's impossible. How have you

come to be in possession of such a talisman?"

"Would you believe I am a worshiper of Cuskatana as well?"

The other eighteen Cuska break their circle, turning toward me, a few stepping closer. I suppress a swallow. I'm definitely going to die here. But as long as they are looking my way, my friends have a chance to get away. I'll give them the fight of their lives.

This is nuts.

"How would that be possible? You hardly look old enough to remember her," another Tripartite says, in the same melodic sound of three voices. It's really creepy.

"Good point," I say, lowering my arm and looking at the emblem on the stone surface. "That can only mean I am telling you the truth. No? You missing any friends?" I look around the audience. "I mean, I would certainly assume Fashkor wouldn't be sloppy with their only connection to Cuskatana. Noooo," I draw out that word, "I'd say they gave this up without much of a fight." I narrow my eyes. "Because they are dead."

Wow, I sure can read a room.

These creatures are hell-bent on survival. It is good to know they are afraid of death. That tidbit of information is my only armor at the moment. Well, that and curiosity. Their curiosity.

They fear the enemy they don't know.

They know their time is short in this world. I'm hoping to convince them it's shorter than they realize now. I never have feared the end. Even now, I don't fear it. I'd prefer it didn't happen as I would like to entertain the possibility of a future with the woman I now know I love. But again, it's a fool's dream. It can't happen.

My life has been building momentum to this moment. I don't get to ride into the blissful ease of old age with a great circle of people I love. That was never in the cards for me. If this is it, at least my death can be gloriously and epically selfless.

Songs will be sung.

Today, I will die not by my own hand as I've often thought about. Today, I will be happy in the knowledge it meant more than a whiny old man lamenting the loss of his youth and hope. My death will serve a purpose. It will be for the love of those who selflessly cared for me, with all my faults and flaws, not because I want to die, but because I want them to live.

Now, my death will have meaning.

Tell my story, Jez.

It's time to drive home to these vile monsters they are *not* the apex predator in the Valley of Cusk anymore. I look at the one to the right of the Cuska closest to me, singularly focusing my attention on it. All three heads focus on me and acknowledge the threat I represent as I put the talisman around my neck. I point to them. They aren't the tallest or the most muscular. A natural choice by predator-prey standards. Make the kill as easy as possible.

"This is my trophy," I say as I narrow my eyes. "I'm looking for more. Yours will do nicely."

"What!" says the lead Tripartite in the center.

The one I am focused on smiles at me, menace laced in their crooked lips. They accept my challenge, their three sets of pointed teeth bared. Their muscles flex, and the hunger in their eyes glows.

Good. Then this will really throw you.

It's nice not to be hurt. It feels good to be me again. The return of my speed, agility, and faculties makes me high on adrenaline. Sometimes, I wish I could see myself from others' perspective.

Am I a blur? Do I vanish and reappear? What must I look like in this perfect lunge?

But I can't.

But I can see the look of shock as I stare them in the eyes, and they struggle to keep up with my motion, stuck watching as my trajectory catches them off guard. As I stare at its center head, the trio of eyes struggle to follow me, shock registering as they realize they are *my* decoy. My blades come out as I land on the shoulders of the one closest to me instead, the second largest of the group and the most muscular.

I shout with glee. Taking out the weakest wouldn't send the message. But this will.

I drive both hands into the sides of the outer heads of the muscular beast on my left, swinging my arms in as if I intend to box their ears. Only metal blades don't box.

I'm smiling right now, my teeth bared in a sinister grin as the two outer heads smack the middle one with such force my blades skewer them together.

I ride its lifeless body to the ground, the momentum driving the Cuska backward. Retracting the blades as I remove them, I snag up the necklace off the center head, smoothly transferring it over mine when the dead Cuska impacts the ground.

I don't stop, continuing to step into the circle of Cuska, walking confidently, hoping they fall for the act, straight to the leader. My bladder reacts in protest, wanting to relieve itself all over me in response to the genuine fear I'm hiding.

"They call me Cuska-Slayer," I say as I point to the leader. "Fildeus, Nadur, and Shamna bless my cause. Quietius sends his regards. You will never leave this valley."

I have no idea where that came from, but it sounded good. I assume the Hated Eight referenced in their discussion is the same as the Great Eight currently ruling Conishant.

I must have struck a nerve because the creature lunges. I dodge around the Cuska easily, landing atop the big bass drum. Sitting, ankles crossed, I wait for it to turn around, my grin never wavering. I could play of a drumbeat in the time it takes for the monstrous beast to turn and face me. The heads look around, trying to figure out where I went. I kick the side of the drum.

"Looking for me?" I jest.

Every set of eyes in the clearing turns in my direction. The leader stands straight and turns to face me. The sea of eyes staring wide in complete wonder boosts my confidence. The one called Morgan, the massive behemoth that chased me through the valley, takes a step forward.

I wiggle my finger at them. "No, no, no," I say. "You don't want to do that. As you can see, I am not injured anymore. It's a special gift to be a favorite of the gods." I bare my teeth, "This time, I won't run."

They stop.

"Who are you?" the leader asks.

I'll be damned. I actually have their attention and their fear.

Holy shit, this might work!

I wrestle my emotions into check, knowing it wouldn't do for me to let them see my surprise.

"I'm The Harbinger of Death," I say, hands resting on the side of the drum. "Maybe you've heard of me?"

They glare at me, their anger growing. I need to move this along.

"Or, if you prefer, Quietius the Second."

"I know Quietius. You are not he," says the leader.

"Hence 'The Second,'" I say. "He and I do a lot of work together. I sacrifice blood to Fildeus and souls to Quietius, restore the balance for Nadur, and keep chance alive for Shamna. Shed blood for Hakaka. Bathe in the glory of Ezra and bring glory to the metals of Krikhi. You might say I am their emissary. Hand-picked and uniquely blessed by more than one."

"Oh," I say, pulling open my shirt, "and touched by the hand of Grankin."

I make eye contact with every one of the Cuska. Mixed in with the malice directed at me is a sense of awe. Somehow, I captivated this audience. It's like I am a circus leader drawing the attention of adoring fans. Not that any of them are fans. Or adoring. Though they should be. I can't imagine they meet many people with my pithy monologue skills. But at least they are captively captivated.

Fear. Definitely my sharpest tool.

Then again, I could just be an entertaining fool. If I can't dazzle these Cuska with brilliance, I'll baffle them with banter.

"So," I say, lifting up my trophies with the tip of my blade, which is now number two, "Blessed as I am by not one, but eight," I continue, as I hold up two fingers and pretend to be confused, holding two more up with my other hand. "Yeah, eight, gods, it seems you have a real conundrum. A bit of a pickle, I like to say."

I drum my fingers on the side of the drum. Morgan takes another step forward. I extend my blade as I point at them.

"You can continue walking toward me, which I promise will not go well. I mean, it seems you are worried about your numbers dwindling, and by my count, you're down two in less than a week. Care to make it three?"

Morgan stops, scowling. I cross my legs, a predator fearless of the overwhelming numbers. One of the monsters in the back starts to move, clearly not willing to back down.

I snap my attention to them, a little extra speed to drive the point. It stops and looks at the leader, then takes a step back.

"I'm glad we understand each other," I say. "As I was saying. I can continue to whittle your community to nothing, or… you can take a truce, and we all go our separate ways."

I look directly at the leader. "I offered Fashkor the same option when I encountered them yesterday. They refused to accept my truce. As you can see, their necklace is now my trophy."

I make eye contact with every set of eyes. None look away. I'll say this. They are intimidating. A second wave of adrenaline surges, and my skin tingles in response, and my pleasure receptors spike. I must admit to a particular love of the adrenal response. It's a high like none other. But this time, I'm acutely aware its source is fear. I'm not used to my own fear. While they aren't moving, they aren't necessarily afraid either.

I distract myself from the tremors in my hands through nervous motion, hiding my fear behind the action. It'd be nice if the entire congregation of Cuska would back down already. Apparently, while I have their attention, I haven't yet achieved their subjugation. Hopping up, I stand on the drum and bounce. It makes a decent trampoline, the bass tone echoing through the clearing. I fill the verbal silence with words.

"I don't want to actually destroy you. I simply wanted some help from your dead friend. They thought to kill me instead." I stop bouncing, shaking my head, mock sorrow, "Such a waste of life." I let out a heavy sigh and then smile, bouncing again. "Anyway, I wasn't sent to kill you. I was sent to check on you. But it seems I got turned around, and now I'm lost and need to find the way home. You seem hellbent on eating me along the way. While I am happy to engage with you, I have urgent business north of here, and all I wanted to do was get a head count like Shamna asked.

"Now, I have a wedding to attend, and I'm afraid I'll be late. If you agree to point me in the right direction, I will abandon my self-appointed mission to destroy all of you and leave you to your valley. Unharmed."

I stop bouncing and point at the leader. My grin shows all my teeth.

"Test me on this, and you will be the first one I kill. I only need one of you alive to get what I want."

"You can't kill us all," they say.

I shrug.

"Maybe. But each one I kill reduces the likelihood you'll ever have enough power to get out of here."

I see a few of them stand up straight at that, their heads turning and looking at one another. I think I may have struck a chord there. Murmurs work their way around the group.

"Quiet!" the leader yells. "You don't get to come in here, kill two of our kind, and intimidate us. I will gladly lose a few to add you to my collection. Clearly, you have a power I'd like to own."

The resultant silence is tangible. The collective hesitation shifts into malicious intent faster than I could ever have anticipated. The circle of Cuska tightens as they step toward me. I crouch, leg muscles gathering potential energy, ready to lunge. The three heads smile, a predator that simply sees me as prey. My peripheral vision picks up motion through the entire crowd.

Okay, I struck a chord. Unfortunately, it wasn't the right one.

It seems I have overestimated the effect I have. A bead of sweat rolls down my temple. My armpits start to sweat and drops roll down my ribcage. A third adrenalin surge pumps my hearts ever faster. This time, it's terror. Death is preferable to allowing these creatures to capture me. I intend to trigger their thirst for unmitigated violence. Rage is what I need from them now, as this has suddenly taken a turn for the worse.

The knife is in the air before I even realize it, embedding itself into the eye socket of the middle head of the leader. The Cuska reaches up and screams in pain and anger, hands flying to the knife. A second knife pins the hand in place.

I need more knives.

The Cuska drops to its knees, screaming. Morgan begins to move at me.

"Tarake Ang Preta!" a voice growls from the back of the clearing. Everyone stops.

I immediately recognize the prayer and the voice. Tamrin steps into the clearing, his muscles bulging out of his furs, with teeth elongated into fangs, nails extended and hardened like claws, and eyes glowing red.

I can't help but get excited when Tamrin casts his hunter spell. He's an intimidating beast when he transforms. In his left hand, he holds his war hammer, lazily resting on the ground. His Talisman of Fildeus is prominently displayed and hangs from his chin. He holds his right hand high, another Periapt of Cuskatana dangling from his fingers.

How the hell? Damn you, Tam.

He's flanked on each side by Jesma in one of the meditation stances I taught her only this morning, her periapt held forward, and Jesmir with his short bow notched and ready. My hearts leap. I'm surprised by how relieved I am. I've never been so overjoyed at some-one for ignoring my wishes. I scan the crowd. Their menacing advance to deal with the threat I present stalls and their collective posture turns into resignation.

"By the way," I say, gaining confidence, "I forgot to mention, I'm not alone."

Hopefully, this ruse works. I play it like it was part of the plan.

Tension builds as nobody moves. Morgan's muscles flex, and their breathing grows deep and measured. I recognize the signs of an imminent attack, and the hair on the back of my neck stands up. Bumps rise on my arms. My shoulders tense and flex in response.

"Need I remind you, Morgan," Tam's voice booms. "My power overwhelmed yours. We ran rather than fight because that is our missive. We didn't come to kill you. But you make one move, and you will leave us no choice."

Morgan turns to face Tam, who doesn't flinch or react. The big man rises to his full height and demonstrates his strength and love for me by snarling at the scariest monster I've ever encountered. To my utter surprise, the beast flinches. Morgan's muscles relax, and their shoulders slump.

Ezra's light! It worked!

"All right!" the leader screams in pain.

They pull the knives out of their hand and eye socket. The middle head drops, lifeless. Both knives fall to the ground. Tears streak the face of one of the heads.

"We will do as you ask," the two remaining heads say.

A collective sigh of relief works its way through the gathering. I do my best not to let mine be one of them.

"It is clear the Hateful Eight sent you to send a message. They slew Cuskatana all those years ago, and clearly, they seek to continue our torture. Their cruelty knows no limits. It seems they still wield power over Cuskatana, and her return is yet to come."

They point to my left and behind me.

"Take yourselves a mile in that direction. You will find the trail to the mountain pass northward."

I look in the direction they point. We weren't even close to finding our way out of this valley.

I point in the opposite direction and narrow my eyes in warning.

"Leave this clearing, all of you, and return to the valley. I will leave you to your lives as long as you never try again to break the barrier. If we are called back here, you will all die. It's a take it or leave it opportunity."

Inside, my soul is shaking. Self-control requires more effort to maintain as I fight to hide my genuine relief. But besting this leader has given me confidence this will work. I'm of no illusion that if they change their minds and decide to rush me or my friends, everyone dies. But the shock of Tamrin holding a periapt as well has taken their fight from them.

How did he get his hands on one? Is there another dead Cuska?

The leader stands, both heads glowering at me.

"We will leave. But know this. You think your gods support you, honor you." The eyes of both heads narrow. "They use you. Cattle for their power. Pawns in their games. What they take from you far outweighs what you get from them. Power costs. But it costs less when the ones you wield it over give up theirs so readily." It turns and starts to head out, speaking over its shoulder as it does. "Now, get off my drum and get out of our temple. The stench of your gods makes me sick."

The seventeen remaining Cuska follow it out, leaving their dead comrade behind. I watch as they pass. The ones behind me give wide birth, various heads looking my way with malice and no small amount of fear.

When the last one passes beyond sight, I let out a heavy breath. Tamrin, Jesma, and Jesmir run up to me. Tamrin shakes his head. I can see he seethes with anger.

"I can't believe that worked," I whisper.

"Next time you try to kill yourself, do me a favor," he says harshly, "leave me out of it." He slams my journal into my chest with so much force I stumble back. The book falls to the ground. Tam shoulders past me and heads in the direction indicated by the Cuska leader without another word.

Jesmir smiles and says, "That was crazy!" He slaps my shoulder.

I look at Jesma. She avoids eye contact.

"Let's go," she says, her voice low. As she walks past me, our shoulders touch slightly.

I can't help feeling like I am in the shit house.

Jesmir pats my shoulder again. "You scared her. She'll be okay." He follows after.

I pick up my journal and slide it into my pocket. Then I pick up my knives from the grass, blood dripping from the blades. Rubbing them in a clean tuft, I imagine a life with Jesma and feel like it slipped away. An empty feeling grips me.

It feels like more than Cuska died here today.

I straighten my back, take a deep breath, and turn to follow my party.

Chapter Twenty-Three

Journal Entry: 74

I've been thinking about Mom a lot lately.

The only tangible memory I have of my mom is her attitude toward me. I don't think she liked me much. Mom had a thing she would say if I got in her way or made a mistake. It's incredible how often my mind repeats it. Her tone and cadence are as clear as if it were happening now.

"Why can't you be an asset and not a liability?"
It had a way of making me feel small.
Sometimes, if I think about it too much, I can almost feel myself shrinking, everything around me growing larger, overshadowing me.

It's become a mantra, driving me to actions I sometimes don't want to take. Mom found a way to turn me into an asset for herself, though. At twelve, she sold me into slavery. I don't know if I have the energy to think about it right now.

So, if I am dead, I hope I didn't burden anyone in the process. I hope it was in an effort to help. I try always to not be a burden. I guess, at least, Mom got that right.

It's funny. Even now, as I write this thought, I hope I just lost this damn binding of stupid thoughts. I really don't want to be dead.

Thinking about Mom makes me think of home and the tiny village in Teshket where I almost grew up. I barely remember what having a home felt like. Any memories of home have faded into the fog of a distant past, distorted into an amalgamation of feelings rather than memories. Even those feelings may no longer be accurate, tainted by what came after.

I find memories to be oddly fluid. I mean, sometimes I question their validity.

I once heard it said we don't actually remember anything and that what we do is more like we remember remembering. As the theory goes, each time we remember a memory, we actually conjure the last memory of that memory. It's a strange thought, remembering a remembrance. When I was an apprentice, they taught me that bits and pieces fall off when we do this, and bits of other memories or fictional details get slipped in to fill the gaps. It's a way we protect ourselves from cognitive dissonance. Why taking in details at the moment matters so much.

It explains why we can remember doing something with someone, and they swear it didn't happen, but we know it did.

And if all that is true, then whose memory is more correct? The one who remembers it most often or the one who remembers it least often? I wonder how many arguments could have been avoided if we did away with memory altogether.

Or how much of this pain I carry would go away if memories didn't exist.

If the theory is true, it makes memories little more than fictional stories we tell ourselves of our past. It's a sad and frightening thought, really. It's like we can't ever really know our own past. Which begs the question.

Can we ever really know ourselves?

The Path to Understanding

It takes us less than an hour to get to the trail indicated by the Cuska. Ezra has settled to the west, the furthest stretch of the Toerge Mountains casting deep shadows. The trail up the valley meanders another few miles, which we follow. The winding path eventually straightens and begins to pass between a series of tall stone pillars, easily ten feet square and thirty feet tall. The shadow of the unfinished bridge looms overhead and covers the entirety of the path. The westernmost mountain shadows overrun those of the bridge's skeletal remains as Ezra's rapidly fading light slips further beyond the reach of the valley. Evening tints of orange, amber, and purple color the sky, illuminating the edges of clouds wistfully floating overhead.

Jesmir walks beside me.

"Can I ask you a question?" he asks.

"You just did."

"Oh. Well… it's… umm."

"Spit it out, your Highness," I say, not really wanting conversation.

"Well, okay, I've been thinking. It seems, maybe, you, umm, have a thing for my sister," he says.

I let out a heavy sigh. I'm not sure I am ready to discuss this with anyone. Especially since Jesma's ignored me for hours.

"No. I don't," I lie. "I care about you both enough to protect you. I consider you friends; therefore, I want to get you both home safely." I cast a sideways glance at him. "I have no romantic intentions toward her. You can relax.."

He shakes his head.

"You misunderstand me," he says.

"Do I? You're royals. I'm the mongrel son of a peasant mother. Seems obvious you would never approve of anything more than friendship between us. Ours is still a class society, last I checked. We still haven't followed the way of Rhinestab or Haabrestand."

His hand shoots to my arm and grasps it tightly. It's the most forceful I have seen him.

"I am a Royal Prince of the House of Jhemai, Duke of Pal. That doesn't mean I am not human."

I pull my arm from his grip.

"Your tone suggests otherwise, your *Highness*," I emphasize the last word more forcefully than I intended.

"You don't like royals, do you?"

I don't know why I am taking out my frustrations on him. He started a bit brooding, but he's been open and never acted like he believed he was better than me. In fact, he has behaved the exact opposite.

I'm behaving like a jerk to him, and I'm not even mad at *him*. I'm angry because of the situation. I almost ask how I can be worthy of Jesma, but my pride won't let me. So, I swallow the question, deflecting my inner thoughts, and offer half an apology.

"Until you, I've never met one. I don't know enough about you to dislike you as a group."

We walk quietly for a while.

"I find perfectly good reasons to dislike people on an individual basis. I don't dislike a group simply for existing. Neither of you has given me a reason to dislike you," I say a few moments later.

"You don't like Cuska as a group."

I snort out a laugh. "Well, you got me there. Does anybody?"

"Can I make an observation?"

"Can I stop you?"

He chuckles this time.

"You spend a lot of time hating yourself."

We walk in silence for a while. Jesmir's not wrong. I'm not sure how he knows it. I definitely don't like hearing him say it.

"What makes you say that?"

"I've never seen anyone put themselves through such punishment needlessly," he says. "Back at Rogue's Pointe, you allowed yourself to be manipulated into a fight. Seeing you in action today? No way that match in the ring should have gone the way it did."

He surprises me with a knowing look. "You took a beating on purpose."

"I didn't take a beating on purpose," I say. "I actually got distracted. It happens a lot more than I would like to admit."

Jesmir nods. "You get stuck up here a lot," he says, tapping his temple.

I nod.

"Back to my sister. You like her. I can see it. Before you deny it again, thereby lying to me or to yourself, I want you to know I'm good with it. She and I do not subscribe to the same ideals the Queen does. In fact, neither did our father. He married a common girl."

He stops, which causes me to stop.

"My mother was anything but common. She was amazing. Jesma looks like her. Mom had a certain air—that little extra in personality. It drew people to her. The Queen, my grandmother, wasn't happy about it at first. But father wouldn't take no for an answer. He wanted to marry her. So, he did." I squirm under the scrutiny of his gaze. "You should tell her how you feel."

We both look up ahead. Tamrin and Jesma are deep in conversation as well. His hands move with his words, indicating he tells her a story. I smile because she indeed receives the complete Tam treatment. He's a master storyteller and a master embellisher. I'd never call him out on it. It would hurt his feelings.

I'd rather be a participant in their conversation than this one. But here I am, waxing the emotional with the Prince of Pal instead of hearing Tamrin tell wild tales of battles with giant lizards or whatever story he can spin.

I look at Jesma's form as she is walking. Her hips sway gently, unassuming yet tantalizing. Her hair, red from the dye and tied in a ponytail, sways side to side. I am mesmerized.

"Come on," Jesmir says, "let's not let them get too far ahead."

I can't help but focus on her, and my thoughts turn into butterflies once again.

We return to silence as the sky turns from the multi-colored sunset to the darkening purples of twilight. In moments like this, it's hard not to think what I would have been if life had been different. If I hadn't been forced to take the life of my best friend that day. If he didn't happen to be Krin's brother.

If I had come clean with her and dealt with the consequences thirty-five years ago.

If my mom hadn't been who she was and hadn't sold me to a group of murderers.

If my dad hadn't left me.

If my brother hadn't died from the plague.

If I was anybody else but me.

I am unsure how long we walked because it startled me once Jesmir started speaking again.

"She'll be fine," he says.

"Huh?"

"Jez. She'll get over her anger at you."

"Anger at me?"

"Yeah," he says, "for what you did back there."

"What I did back there! You mean saving your lives?"

He shakes his head again. "Wow, Tamrin was right. You are dense."

"Hey! Watch it."

He flips his hand at me as if the question is insignificant. He carries himself more like a prince than the beleaguered traveler I've seen thus far.

"Why do you think she isn't back here, walking with you, trying to get you to notice her?"

"Because now she knows who I really am."

"No, that's not it at all."

I shrug. "You tell me, then, because that's when your sister stopped looking at me."

"I am trying to, you ox." He points up there. "She won't admit it, but she's been smitten with you since you saved our lives before Valshannon. She talked about you the entire time she dragged my busted-up ass from that glen to the river."

"She was upset you didn't escort us. But she understood we weren't your problem."

He's quiet.

"But then you showed up when Grankin grabbed us. I saw the look on her face when you appeared. Even though we had no idea what happened. Even though we were afraid for our lives. Even though she was terrified. When you showed up, she relaxed. She believed in her heart that everything would be alright from that moment."

"When you went missing, she was the one who ran down to the valley to find you. Tamrin wouldn't leave you behind, but she made the decision for everyone when he said your tracks could only mean you went below. She didn't hesitate. We had to chase after her."

He sighed. "Jez is the most compassionate person I know. She cares deeply for everyone. But this was different. She was desperate to find you. Relentless. I only saw her that passionate once before. When the bastard Brogen killed father."

"She wouldn't leave your side when we finally had you back. For three days, she lay there next to you. Praying, crying, then praying some more. She wouldn't let either of us near you. So let me ask you again. Why do you think she's mad at you?"

My voice is barely above a whisper. "Because I'm stupid?"

He laughs, "That's one way to put it. You rushed out to confront those Cuska without regard for your own life. You were willing to sacrifice yourself for us. In her mind, for her, and you didn't even give her a choice in the matter. Then you told her to stand back and watch. Which she didn't, by the way. She again gave us no choice in the matter and stepped out to help you."

He places a friendly hand on my arm.

"She is angry because she knows what life with you means. You are not the settle-down type. You're a restless soul. She will always carry the burden of worry that you may not return if she chooses you. Giving her heart to you means she has to find peace with the reality of living without you. It means she has to choose between sending you away forever or suffering your loss later. We've lost our mother and our father. She and I were all we had left. Until you came along."

I look into his eyes and realize he believes what he is saying. Little twinges of shock make my ears tingle. It slowly spreads through my body.

Tamrin whistles from up ahead. We both look up at him.

"You two want to come up here and look at this, or will you continue whispering amongst yourself like schoolkids?"

We both run up to the plateau where he is standing.

Before us, the southern mountain face looms overhead. Giant iron doors, mounted inside the entrance to what appears to be a tunnel entrance, block our path. The curved doors, well over fifteen feet tall and eight feet across, seal the tunnel shut. Engraved in the stone, following the arch of the man-made tunnel, are the words "Hericot Vertice—Knock Thrice to Enter."

Tamrin takes his hammer out and bangs on the doors with it. The booming reverberation behind seems to last forever as the sound echoes down the tunnel beyond. He looks back at us and raises an eyebrow.

"Well, that was louder than I intended."

Jesmir clasps his mouth with his hand, and Jesma backhands him.

"Grow up," she laughs.

Tamrin's grin grows wide, and I admonish him with a look.

"C'mon, man. It's been a shitty week."

I shake my head and Tamrin hits the door again with the hammer, this time harder. His wicked smirk grows more pronounced as soon as the heavy hammer impacts the door. The echo resounds through the tunnel beyond and throughout the valley.

We can't contain ourselves and break out in manic laughter. Above us, a smaller metal door opens from what looks like an overlook in the stone mountainside. A helmeted head peeks down. The wearer is old, much older than me, and his beard is thin and wispy. His face is covered in dirt and seems unbathed in days.

"What the hell was that?" he yells. Seeing us, he frowns. "What did you hit my door with? A dragon?" He disappears back inside, and we hear echoed voices yell back and forth from the window. Two minutes later, a smattering of voices comes from behind the door, echoing in the chamber beyond. A small hatch opens in the center of one of the doors, and another face peeks out.

"What do you want?" It's the same man from above.

"To come in," Tam says.

He eyes Tam up and down. "How did you get here?"

Tam looks at me and then back to the man. "We walked?" he says sarcastically.

He lets out an exasperated sigh. "No, you big hairy ape. By

what path did you get here?" He speaks as if to a child.

Tam points to the trail behind us.

The man's eyes open wide, and he starts to stutter, "Pr-pr-pr-preposterous! No one comes that way. You are an illusion. Cuska!"

I roll my eyes and snag his beard before he has a chance to get the hatch closed.

"Help! It's got me! Cuska!"

Echoes of his cry repeat behind the door as others sound the alarm. I pull his beard, his face squeezing out the small opening.

"If I were Cuska, would I waste my time holding you like this?" A hand touches my shoulder, and I look. Jesma gives me a look of annoyance, shaking her head.

She steps forward and shows her ring.

"Princess Jesma and Prince Jesmir, by order of the Queen, demand entry to Hericot."

The man focuses on the ring and begins to stutter again, "Y-Y-Yes, your Highnesses. Right away." He turns and yells back, "Open up, you goddamn fools! Royals at the gates!"

Another round of yells comes from inside.

"Royals at the gates!"

I hear a faint call, "Well, which is it? Royals or Cuska?"

"Royal pain in the ass," I mumble.

Tam laughs.

Hericot looks precisely like what it is. A rundown, forgotten mining town. Dirty, unkempt, filled with quickly erected stone and wood structures define a handful of crisscrossing dirt roads, haphazardly planned. If it could be called planned.

The walk through the torch-lit tunnel took about ten minutes. Upon exiting, the sky above already reveals its stars, purple having deepened into the black void beyond. Hericot, even in twilight, is bright. A blanket of snow, less than an inch deep, covers the ground. Fall temperatures behind us have dropped to the mildly cold beginning of winter here.

North of the mountains, winter has come, and it catches me off guard.

Tamrin looks at the three of us as we shiver slightly. He removes his two furs and hands Jesma and Jesmir each one. They accept them gratefully. He looks at me apologetically, which I dismiss with a wave. Two guards escort us through the tunnel. They both behave nervously around the royal twins, unsure of custom. Royals don't visit Hericot much.

"I don't imagine you get many royals visiting here," I say.

"No, sir," one replies, his voice cracking. He looks to be barely an adult. In fact, I am not even sure he actually is one.

"Take us to the Baron, please," Jesma says to the guard.

"Yes, your Highness," the young man replies. "He's this way." The guard points ahead as we walk the road from the large tunnel. Various townsfolk sit around small fires, talking amongst themselves, casting curious glances our way. Jesma and Jesmir proceed, the dignified poise missing in their flight through the woods suddenly present among the citizens of Teshket. Tam and I slip in behind them, giving them the position of authority customary in Teshket society. I mostly try to blend into the background.

Little comments of, "Who are they?" and "I think those are royals" and an occasional "they can't be royals" are directed at the twins as we walk along the trampled snow path. Several onlookers express confusion as the siblings seem to forget they disguised themselves. Neither of the siblings looks like themselves or are dressed as royals. Their hair, no longer the customary silvery blond that has long been the hallmark of the Royal Family, hides behind dyes of black and red. However, the color starts to fade out. Their worn, dirty, and tattered clothes identify them as ordinary folk. Not as the prince and princess they are.

But their stature, their poise, and their graceful gait are every bit royal. I feel awkward, moving behind them, unrefined as I am. I carry myself as a predator, a realization that makes me self-conscious. Maybe I recognize my appearance because I walk in the royals' presence. I never thought about it until now.

Have I been fooling myself into thinking I blend in all these years?

I feel exposed. Unable to blend into the anonymity I am accustomed to, I think some comments were directed at Tamrin and me. The chatter disquiets my mind as I imagine all sorts of spies and enemies. I begin to scan every face, every doorway, every alleyway, every shadow for possible threats. My skin tingles with anticipation.

Another group stacks tools in a shed, closing for the day. They stop what they are doing and watch the curious band of travelers.

"They must be bodyguards."

"They don't look like bodyguards."

"What else would they be? The little one looks violent."

Tam appears equally uncomfortable as I am as we pass, turning onto another street.

"Baron Bun-Marlon is in the building on the left, your Highness," the guard says, pointing to a stone structure with a small coat of arms on the door. A light flickers inside to indicate someone is present.

The guard blushes as we step to the front of the building, and he prepares to knock. From inside, sounds of what can only be described as aggressive effort and ecstasy emanate through the closed windows and doors. The guard hesitates a moment, but his look pleads with the royals. Jesmir steps up and bangs on the door loudly.

"Go away!" comes a breathless voice from inside. Grunts can be heard. From the side, I can see Jesma's cheeks flush.

The guard looks dismayed. Jesmir flashes a childish smirk and bangs on the door twice as aggressively. Sounds of a tussle and moving furniture followed by a few choice swear words come from inside. Loud boot steps make their way to the door, the perpetrator clearly agitated by the disruption of his acts of passion.

The bolt on the door clicks, and the door flies open.

"I said go away!" yells a portly man with a hairy stomach, thinly trimmed mustache, and a pointy goatee. His shirtless body jiggles as he fights to hold his trousers around his waist with one hand, clearly unable to let go without the embarrassment of the situation escalating.

The bureaucrat gives the guard an angry look. The guard coughs conspicuously, glancing sideways at Jesmir and Jesma.

"Who the hell are you?" he yells, his voice gravelly, as he

looks them up and down and then leans to the side to glare at me and Tamrin. "I haven't got time for this." He flips his hand down the road. "There's an inn three doors down. Take yourselves there and get a room. I'm busy, and we are closed for the night."

He swings the door closed, but Jesmir stops it by sticking his boot in the doorway. The man's eyes narrow.

"Take your damn foot out of my way before I have you thrown into the valley for the Cuska to have at you."

The guard shakes his head vigorously, his face contorted in embarrassment.

"I am Prince Jesmir of Pal. This is Princess Jesma of Pal," Jesmir says.

The Baron opens the door.

"The hell you are. If you are Royals of the Crown, then I am the Queen. Now move your damn foot before I have this guard run a sword through your gut and leave you in the street."

Jesma puts a fist in his face, her signet ring inches from his nose. I flinch at the aggression behind it. His eyes grow wide.

"Now, may we come in, Baron Bun-Marlon?" she asks.

He begins to stutter as he opens the door to let them in.

"Ye-ye-yes, most certainly, your Highness. Pl-pl-please do come in."

I want to laugh at the people of this town. I've never heard so much stuttering in one day.

Before Jesma can step through the doorway, a barely dressed woman runs past us while she clutches a wad of clothes in her arms, her face flush with embarrassment. She keeps her head down, eyes intent on the ground and with a slight curtsey, mutters in a mousy voice, "Your Highnesses," and flees down the road.

As we step into the room Jesmir raises his voice and with a raised eyebrow says to the Baron, "Do put your clothes on, Baron, you are in the presence of royals."

The Baron glances down at his shirtless top half and his haphazard pants and says, "Umm... yes, excuse me just... one minute." He makes haste to the bed, grabs a white tunic off the floor and throws it on while simultaneously tying is pants. Then he throws the sheets and bedspread that were lazily tossed on the floor over the bed. He turns to face us with flushed cheeks.

Tamrin breaks out in laughter, and I have to hide my face to keep from smiling.

Tam's laugh is reduced to giggles by a glare from Jesma. She glances my way, and I choke on my own smile.

Inside, the Baron's home is sparsely furnished. As Hericot became a forgotten town due to the suspension of the bridge construction, its ability to attract commerce declined. Now, it is little more than a haven for nomadic miners who look to find a big score in the hundreds of ore mines that surround the area. Even the Baron's lodge shows signs of wear and tear.

Two threadbare lounge chairs, a worn couch, a small dining set, and a desk, positioned slightly akilter and, in desperate need of restoration and new stain are the only accouterments adorning the cramped space. Two lanterns, one on the table and one on a mantle by a lit fire, offer the only light sources.

A small hall leads to two rooms in the rear, from one of which the sounds of the Baron changing clothes echo to the front of the home. Jesma and Jesmir sit in the lounge chairs, each with an unimpressive glass of red wine. Neither drink them.

Deep mumbles in the Baron's bass tone emanate down the hall, but the words are hard to make out. He sounds like he grumbles about the situation or at himself for not recognizing the twins. Ten minutes later, he emerges from his room, properly dressed in the garb of a Baron of Teshket. His robe is threadbare in spots, further testament to the forgotten nature of the town.

Jesma and Jesmir carry a forlorn look on their faces.

"Your Highnesses, please accept my sincerest apologies for my behavior again." He is one step away from prostrating himself and kissing their feet. They both hold their glasses out to me.

"Emissary, do you mind?" Jesma says.

This role is easy for me to play. It's my role. Servant class to the royal class. This is where my relationship with a princess should fall. It's more than I deserve. Taking the cue, I secretly thank her for offering me a disguised identity and do as she asks.

"Not at all, your Highness," I say as I take both glasses and carry them to the desk, depositing them next to a stack of papers. Returning to the other side of the room to stand over the twins, I eye the Baron. We lock eyes, and he swallows hard.

"Forgive me as well, your graces. I did not realize you were Emissaries of the Queen."

Tamrin and I play along and nod in affirmation of his apologies.

"There is no need to apologize, Baron," Jesma says. "We obviously do not look like ourselves. Do you have your signet book?"

He nods. "Locked away as required, your Highness."

Jesma reaches into her purse, pulls out a small key, and hands it to the Baron. He takes it and retrieves a key from his own purse. I watch as he walks to the hallway and enters the other door. The sound of keys entering and triggering locks emanate softly from the room. A minute later, the Baron comes out with a book. It is the color of the Royal Family, a deep purple with gold inlays on it.

He sits on the couch across from the twins and opens the book. Jesma hands him her signet ring. Bun-Marlon compares the ring to a wax image in his book. His eyes grow wide. He hurriedly hands the ring back to Jesma, closes the book, and carries it back to the room beyond. More sounds of clicking and a latch catching emanate from the room, followed quickly by the Baron. He hands Jesma her key and bows as he does.

"May I sit?" he asks.

Jesma nods and leans forward after he gets settled, placing a hand on his knee.

"Baron, we are not angry you didn't recognize us. Please relax. It's not your fault."

He visibly relaxes as his eyes water slightly.

"May I ask why you are here? Why wasn't I notified? Why aren't you in appropriate attire?" He looks nervous, asking the questions. "Why have you broken the law and dyed your hair?"

Jesma and Jesmir look at each other and then back at us. Jesma is floored by the questions.

"Baron Bun-Marlon, were you not warned we might be coming? Did you not receive the missive stating we were missing?"

He looks at both the royals, his mouth hanging open.

"Your Highness?" he questions. "I have no idea what you mean. No such missive arrived. What do you mean you are missing?"

Jesma and Jesmir exchange alarmed glances. Jesma looks back at me.

"Emissary, the missive didn't go out. That means the Queen has not been informed. How is that possible? We have been gone for weeks." She looks at her brother. "Jes, I'm frightened."

First impressions of the Baron were far from flattering. However, as the night wore on, I got a true sense of the man and quickly began to like him. Rough around the edges, he is of a kindred spirit. Lacking in pretense but savvy and knowledgeable, he appears every bit the product of a remote life in a forgotten part of the realm, slipping quickly into helping us try to solve the mystery, casting a shadow over the twins since the moment they were taken from their ship.

The conversation with the Baron continues well into the night, past the zenith of the stars. Most of that time was spent discussing the possibilities of why he wouldn't have received the missive and the related issue of the orphaned signet of Duchess Danwire. None of the answers leave us with a peaceful, easy feeling. Questions we had long stopped asking ourselves due to competing priorities begin to pop back to the forefront of our minds.

As our transition from survival to problem-solving evolved through the night, those buried questions moved to the center stage of our living world. But answers were few. Gloom settled in the tiny home of the Baron. The lanterns have long since been extinguished, darkness sits heavy, and the fireplace is the only light source.

Over and over again, we hash out the facts. Every time, we land on the same unanswerable questions.

How was the emissary protocol compromised? Why was the Duchess of Tal's ring in the possession of bandits? Why did Brogen kidnap the royals at sea? How did he know where they'd be? Why was the Mayor of Dresdin friendly with the Captain of the Dark Guard of Killinshire? Are there spies in Hericot we should be worried about?

I assume the answer to that last one to be a no-brainer.

Two questions nag at me more than any others. To the point my side aches from the memory of a knife blade.

Why did Krin betray her charge, and where is Brogen now?

I'd never get answers to Krin. She's dead, and her secrets are dead with her. Brogen was a different matter. I'm shocked he didn't catch up to us. Then again, even he isn't stupid enough to enter the Valley of Cusk. Not knowing where he is, however, is a problem. Yet another one I can't solve.

Jesma is asleep on the couch. Jesmir and Tamrin sleep in the loungers. The Baron and I sit on his front stoop, him billowing smoke from between his lips, pipe resting there. It is cold out, the night having coursed along, Ezra on the other side of her path around the world. The night sky is clearer than I have seen in a long time. The stars brightly reflecting off the snow-covered ground provide near daylight visibility for several hundred yards.

Wrapped in one of Tam's furs, I marvel at the warmth is provides, although it stinks from the sweat and wet travels. But it's better than freezing.

"You aren't like any emissary I ever met," the baron says.

I don't say anything.

The smell of his pipe is pleasant, almost enough to cover the musty fur smell. As he puffs on it, wispy smoke trails upward in mesmerizing clouds from the mouthpiece. He reaches under his fur shawl into a pocket of the wool coat he wears and pulls out a second pipe.

"I always keep a spare," he says, offering it to me. I accept it gratefully.

"Thank you," I say as he hands me a box of matches and a bag of tobacco. I fill the pipe and strike the match. The sweet, spicy aroma surrounds me, pushing the last hint of the musty fur smell away from my mind. The nicotine hits me immediately, calms my nerves, relaxes my muscles, and makes me slightly lightheaded.

"So?" he asks.

I give him a sideways glance.

"It's alright. You don't have to say anything. But if you are an emissary, then…"

"You're the Queen?" I finish for him.

He smiles and nods.

"They trust you. That's good enough for me," the baron says.

"Then that's good enough," I reply.

He pulls a large puff from his curved pipe and blows a smoke ring.

"One thing bugs me about all of this. The missing missive. Only three ways that doesn't happen." He scrunches his face.

"Go on," I encourage.

He shifts and turns his body to face me slightly. I reciprocate in kind.

"First, the Emissary of Gal-Daro would have to fail to get a notification to the Queen. When the traveling royals didn't show, a dispatch would have gone out within minutes. Strict timelines where the royals are concerned. Every town they planned to visit would have been notified weeks before a Royal comes for a visit."

"Either the emissary didn't send it, which means they are dead or complicit. Or the emissary's messenger was intercepted en route."

"Second way, and this one is the scariest. It's so awful I am afraid to say it."

"I'll say if for you," I say, "The Queen never sent the missive once she was informed."

He squeezes his eyes shut and pinches the bridge of his nose. "I can't believe that for one second. She's the Queen. She'd never betray her own son and grandchildren."

He opens his eyes and looks up at the stars.

"The only other explanation is the missive itself was intercepted en route."

"It's either the first or the last. It could never be the second."

I shrug my shoulders and turn back to face the road.

"The Queen has assassins," I say. "She uses them. She's not without her sins."

He gives me a sideways glance. My impugnment of the Queen offended him.

"I don't mean anything by it," I say. But we both know I do.

"I don't fear much in this world," Bun-Marlon states.
"Me either," I say.
He hums a moment.
"Know what I do fear?" he asks.
I shake my head.
"The enemy, I don't know."
I tip my pipe to him in salute.
"I fear the friend I don't know is an enemy," I reply.

442

Chapter Twenty-Four

Journal Entry: 77

It's hard to judge whether people actually like me or simply tolerate me. The ones I don't kill, I mean. It's no secret how those people feel.

Sometimes, my behavior seems like a defense mechanism designed to push people away before they have a chance to really know me. That way, they won't dislike me for the reasons they should. But then I think it's all imagined, and I try to get out of that dark place and engage with people.

Tam is easy. He plays along sometimes and sometimes he tells me to get out of this place I'm in. He's the only one with the sack to do it. Everyone else just indulges me.

It would be nice to have a few other people with whom I felt comfortable. That seems a worthy dream.

I think I need to try to be more open to the possibility they are out there. It's not easy, though.

Homestretch

"Shen."

I feel a light touch on my shoulder. Small, gentle hands. The call is barely a whisper.

"Shen, it's time to wake up," Jesma says.

I open my eyes to a dim morning light. Jez's face is close to mine. We lock eyes, and she smiles. Her hand caresses my cheek, and she leans in and kisses my forehead.

"I'm sorry I ignored you yesterday," she says.

My heart leaps more than I thought it could.

"No," I whisper, "I understand why you were mad. I've never seen it from your perspective. Thank your brother."

"I already did," she says. "Jesmir made me see it from his perspective." Her lips touch my ear as she whispers, "You're a good man, Harbinger. I'll never hold that against you."

As she pulls away, I can't help the wave of emotion that causes my eyes to brim with tears. If only I believed fulfilling my desires was possible.

"Now, let's get on the road before Ezra comes up. It's a three-day ride to Kerakot by carriage. The Baron is giving us his."

I nod, throwing the blanket I don't remember covering myself to the couch across the room. Stretching, I stand and observe my surroundings one last time. The Baron sits at his desk reading a paper.

He looks up as I approach. I stick out my hand, which he takes and shakes firmly.

"You have a friend in this town, Emissary," he says. "If you ever need anything, come see me. If it's in my ability, it's yours."

"You as well," I say. I clasp the side of the baron's arm, and he nods once.

"Safe travels," he says. "Stick to the plan. Breakridge is a day-and-a-half ride north. You should have enough food and water to get you there. Avoid the other towns on the way. If what we fear has happened, there are likely eyes everywhere. I'm worried about spies here.

Best you are gone before the town wakes.”

“You are a good and loyal man, Baron Bun-Marlon,” I say.

“Kervan. My name is Kervan.”

I reach into my tunic and pull out the purse with the remaining Realm Notes, hefting it. Then I hand it to him.

“There’s ten thousand in Realm Notes inside this bag. Use it however you want for your town. I have no need of it.”

His eyes grow wide in astonishment.

“I don’t know what to say,” he whispers.

“There’s no more to say. You may never get your carriage back. Let’s call it a fair price?”

He laughs and takes the purse.

I smile and lean in to whisper.

“Shen. My name is Shen.”

He gives a satisfied grin.

“Well, Emissary, I shall remember that for when we meet under better circumstances.”

“Goodbye, Kervan.”

Without any more fanfare, I walk out the door.

The sky is turning pinkish orange to the east. Ezra will peak over the horizon within the hour. Already, a number of Hericot citizens move within their homes, lanterns turning on in the still early dawn. Jesma and Jesmir sit inside the carriage, the curtains on the side facing the Baron’s home sit open. She waves me over. Once again, I feel a strange compulsion to comply with her wishes.

“Yes,” I say.

“Come closer,” she says.

I do, and her hand shoots around the back of my head as she pulls me closer still. Our lips meet and linger for longer than I thought possible. As I pull away, I catch a glimpse of Jesmir brushing dust off his pants, a self-satisfied smirk on his face. I slap his boot.

“Wipe that smirk off your face, your Highness.”

“Wipe that shit-eating grin off yours,” he says, “that’s my sister, mongrel.”

I stifle a laugh as I step away.

“Hey,” Jez says. I stop and look. “Don’t be stupid up there. You remember we’re in this together.”

"Keep the curtains closed, but only partially. We want you to look like you don't care if you are seen but still be able to hide in the shadows if needed. I'll let you know when it's safe to come out, and you can take turns up front with us."

They both nod. I slap the sill of the carriage door, head over the front step, and hop up next to Tamrin.

"Get a good morning kiss?" he snickers.

"Shut up," I say.

He laughs as he flips the reins, clicking his tongue. The two horses move together, and after a subtle jerk forward, the carriage moves down the road and out of town. Tamrin and I keep vigilant, scouting for anyone watching who shouldn't be.

The exit from town is uneventful.

A nice change of pace for once.

We take short rests along the way to give the horses a chance to wander and our butts a chance to un-numb themselves. Tamrin and I swap places with regularity so we can each nap in the carriage and offer the twins an opportunity for open air without risk to their safety. At one point, Jesma and I sat side by side in the carriage. We didn't speak much at first.

"You aren't going to say it, are you?" she asks at one point.

"What?"

"How you feel about me."

It's not the usual playful banter she employs. She's serious.

I can't look at her. I stare straight ahead, frozen, not wanting to go into how why it can't work.

"Shen?"

"Yeah," I say, still looking forward.

"Would you look at me?"

I turn my head and look at her face, the contours of her cheeks high and regal. The almond shape of her eyes, set wide apart and bright, is hypnotic. The silvery strands of her hair show through more as each day passes. I trace her lips with my eyes, their soft lines willing me closer, dimples on either side of the corners like tiny holes in her face.

I shake my head and look away.

"Why won't you say it?"

"Because I'm not worthy of you, Jesma."

She sucks in a breath. "That's not fair."

"It's okay. I've accepted it," I reply.

I see her head shaking vigorously. "No, Shen. That's not fair to me."

"Huh?" I say, startled by her tone. "How is that?"

She turns away from me. "You don't get to decide for me who is worthy and who isn't. I decide."

I don't know what's happening. "I'm not the one who decides. It has to be you."

"No." She turns on the bench and points at me, her finger close to my cheek. "You are deciding for both of us. You've decided you're such a bad person you don't deserve happiness. Then you project that onto me so you can sit there in your self-pity and go, 'Woe is me.'" She jabs her finger into my cheek.

"Ouch."

"Deal with it," she says. "Big baby."

I don't know what to say to her, so I sit there silently for a while.

Ezra rises, sets, then rises again before we reach the first town on our route.

Jesma and I haven't said much since our chat, and it's been eating at me. I don't know how she gets under my skin, but she does. Her words stir my emotions, and I suspect it's because she's right.

Tam and I keep watch on the horizon. I don't see any signs of a small village ahead, nor do we expect to today. It's still too far away to discern, but it's there. In about six hours, we will reach it at our current pace.

I pull the carriage to a stop, and Tam taps me on the shoulder.

"Go for a walk," he says quietly. "I'll unhook the horses and give them a chance to rest."

Behind me, I hear the carriage door slam. As I peek around, I see Jesma wrapped in one of Tam's furs, hugging it close to her and walking off. I've hurt her, but I can't understand how. I look back at Tam and nod. Hopping down, I look into the carriage. Jesmir is stirring from a nap.

"You okay in there?" I ask.

He nods, yawning. I tap the door sill and turn to watch Jesma. She stops a couple hundred yards away, and I bow my head and follow her.

When I reach within thirty feet of her, I pick up a rock and toss it at her feet, not wanting to startle her. She looks down at it without a word and looks back to the southern horizon, not acknowledging it. I step up and cough quietly, standing behind her.

"I'm sorry," I say.

She shakes her head.

"I don't understand."

She turns and looks at me. She's been crying. I reach up to brush the tears, but she pulls away. She turns her head to the side, looking away from me.

"I don't know why I have these feelings for you. I try to fight them, but I can't. I wish I didn't feel this way." She looks back at me. "You are so busy deciding who you are worthy of and who you aren't you fail to see that your choices hurt those who care about you more than you seem to realize." She looks back at the carriage.

"Tam loves you with his entire heart. Nobody in this world is more important to him than you are. Did you know that?"

"Aye. I know that."

"Do you worry if you are worthy of him?"

"No. Tam's my friend. Has been for as long as I can remember."

"Right. Do you love your friend?"

"Of course I do."

She nods, biting her lip.

"Why am I not allowed the same?"

I go to speak, but my throat locks. I don't have an answer.

"Is it because I'm a princess?"

I shake my head.

"Is it because you're a monster?"

I meet her eyes and choke up. "Yes."

She steps forward, tears in her eyes.

"Let's say you are a monster," she says. Then she places a hand on my chest gently and pats it. "You're my monster. I've fallen for you, Harbinger. It's my right to do so. If you won't throw Tam's love away, then I should get the same."

She steps around me and starts to walk away. I catch her arm, and she turns back to me.

"Jez, if you are in my life, you're at risk. My life is a continuous series of people getting hurt. Especially those close to me. That's why I keep you at arm's length."

The image of the Tillions comes back, flooding me with regret and sorrow.

Her eyes soften as she looks at me.

"It's my life, too. I get to decide the risk of it. Not you." She pauses and smiles at me. "And I choose the risk of a life with you over the safety of one without you."

She steps to me and touches my face.

"I decide who is worthy of me, and I've decided only you are worthy. Not some nameless prince I couldn't care less about."

She lifts herself to her tip-toes and kisses my lips softly, then steps back.

"Your move, Shen."

I grasp her arms, pull her close, lift her off her feet, and kiss her, tears falling down my cheeks. She kisses me back, and my stomach flips into somersaults. The world doesn't exist for a few minutes, and it's just us.

Part of me wants to hold on to this woman and make a permanent life right here in this frozen tundra. But she and her brother need to return home. When I set her down, she smiles at me and punches me playfully in the arm.

"Now, that wasn't so hard, was it?" she quips and returns to the carriage.

I look to the southern horizon and consider how far the Toerge

Mountains are now and how far the hidden glen where I first met the girl who stole my heart is beyond that. It's been a long journey. I never could have seen how it would end.

Certainly not with my heart in the hands of a princess.

Riding up top again with Tamrin, Ezra is about a third of the way along her winter glide across the lower portion of the southern sky. The light covering of snow that blanketed the ground on our exit from the Hericot Vertice slowly melted away in the rays of Ezra's warmth, too light a coating to survive the direct rays this early in winter, revealing brown tufts of winterized grass, long asleep after the lullaby of fall. Up ahead, the town that is our stop for the day appears on the horizon.

Breakridge.

So-called for the broken edge of rocky cliffs on the eastern side of the town. Breakridge is actually about two days out of our way to Kerakot from Hericot. We could have taken the main roads straight from Hericot and been to the capital city before nightfall tonight. But that would be the obvious choice for anyone trying to find the twins.

Jesma spent her morning praying to Shamna that our journey would continue to be eventless. I can only hope her faith is well-founded. I prefer not to roll on luck.

The four of us have been quiet the last couple of hours, each of us nursing our own fears. Each worrying about what Kervan had termed "The Enemy You Don't Know." Our comfort as a foursome has grown by incredible strides over the last few days and hours, which eliminates the discomfort that comes with silence.

Digging at my thoughts, nagging at me as we travel the last bit of desolate expanse of high desert between Hericot and Breakridge, are open questions. Every new horizon, I keep expecting Brogen to show up, ready to kill us all.

As the ride progresses, a deepening sense of gloom builds inside me. I can feel myself getting stuck inside my thoughts again. I reach out to Tam, continuously communicating with nods and glances. I clap Jesmir on the back offer pointers on controlling the horses. I exchange soft flirting touches with Jez. Each action is a deliberate rejection of my former self as I try to build new habits with these three people I have grown to trust with the secrets I have held tight for two-thirds of my life.

Occasionally, my mind gives itself a break and allows my thoughts to think about her. Her voice, her scent, the curves of her body. Images of her naked body back in Valshannon float, rent-free, into my mind, little sparkles of her body make up flashing in the flickering fire. The embarrassment of the moment is long gone, and the vision of her is a joyful image of yearning and promises yet to come.

Breakridge approaches ever closer, snapping me out of my daydreams of soft skin, warm touches, and effervescent beauty.

I tap the side of the carriage with my boot. The sound of curtains closing reassures me the twins are paying attention. Tamrin shifts in his seat next to me. His unease oozes onto my side of the carriage bench.

"Eyes open," I say.

"Yup," he replies, his war hammer in easy reach.

Breakridge is so small we can see it entirely from one hundred yards away. Six small huts— a wooden structure sporting the hallmarks of a dry goods store, tavern, or both, and a smithy shed, black smoke rises from the large stone chimney—make up the entirety of the village. Sheep, goats, and a native three-toed draft animal called a gazard meander in the nearly vanished snow, grazing on frozen grasses.

The gazard, its thick black fur, rounded head, squished nose, and awful underbite, bleats at us as we approach.

I see no horses and only two covered wagons. Their archaic design has been out of use for nearly twenty years.

A woman emerges from one of the huts and stares at us, a baby goat in her arms. She sets it down and wipes her hand on her apron, and I can hear her admonish the goat.

"Na yesh shtay out of my hesh," she yells, shaking a finger at it. Her speech is strange, and the dialect and pronunciation are hard to distinguish, whether from style or impediment.

We pull up to the edge of the first buildings, lining a path anyone would find hard to call a street.

"Hello, ma'am," I say.

She eyes me suspiciously, squinting as she does. She spits a brown stream of tobacco-filled saliva without any head movement. The fluid flies from her mouth, landing on the ground and blending into the dirty, melted snow.

"Who da hellsh er yesh?" she asks. No friendliness in her voice.

"We are heading north to Vourend," I say. "Relocating from Hericot. Work dried up and heard there was work up that way."

"Wellsh, yesh an kep on goen," she says, waving her hand north.

I adjust my hips, feigning anxious energy.

"I was hoping to buy some supplies. Water, feed for the horses, jerky, if you have it? Maybe rest a bit?" I say.

She eyes me coldly.

"Wesh got none te shpare," she says.

"I have silver if you're willing to part with some supplies. Haabrestand silver," Tamrin says.

"Haabarshtend, yesh shay," she says. "Wellsh, maybs can helpsh yesh."

I hop off the carriage, and she takes a startled step back.

"I din't shay yesh'n come dahn," she says harshly.

I hold my hands up. "Didn't mean anything by it. Just need to stretch my legs. Been a long few days. You wouldn't happen to have a fire we could warm up near, would ya?"

She squints again and points to the back of the carriage.

"Whosh ya go hidin in der?" she asks.

I look back at the carriage, unsure if she is asking what or who. I squint back at her and crinkle my nose like I am unsure what she is asking.

"Yesh get rocksh in yesh hed?" she asks.

I shake my head. "Me? No."

"Wellsh?" she asks expectantly.

I swing a light arm back at the carriage casually. "Well that there is my best mate, Teagan. Inside the carriage is his wife Kerigan and my baby brother Torrence. I'm Barkly."

She spits again. This time the brown saliva sticks to her lip and falls to her chin. She wipes her chin with the back of her hand and nods.

"Alrighsh," she says, "Come dahn te de shtore. Cashee'll git yesh shettled."

She turns and starts walking between the huts to the stone building that could be a tavern or store. The goat she admonished runs up to her, and she shoes it away with a booted foot.

"Gesh on, git."

I nod to Tamrin, who hops down and opens the carriage door. Jesma and Jesmir hop out and stretch their legs. Jesma puts her arm around Tamrin's waist. A twinge of jealousy runs through me at the fake affection before I remember she pretends to be his wife. I look back at the woman leading us, who watches us rather closely.

Small-town people are suspicious folks. It doesn't get much smaller than this village. I remind myself to keep cool.

We follow the woman to the unknown building. As I pass a couple of huts, I see motion to my right and look nonchalantly. A child in the window sees me looking and disappears hurriedly. I smile as I look away.

The woman knocks on the door to the store. "Oy, Cashee, lesh esh in. Yesh, get cushtomersh!"

The door opens, and the woman steps inside. I follow her in. Before my boot lands on the stoop, the door slams shut, and I hear a deadbolt slide.

"Trap!" I yell as I spin around. My blades extend as I bolt, lightning fast, to Jesma's side. Tamrin, Jesma, and Jesmir make a dash for the carriage, and thatches fall from the roofs of the huts, revealing hidden bowmen. I flick my three knives, my hands fly in a rapid triple strike. Two of the bowmen take knives, one in the neck and the other in the chest. Their crossbows release wild as they fall from the roof.

The third knife hits the last one's crossbow, bounces off the roof, and falls to the ground uselessly. I see the crossbow bolt flying through the air, off its intended target, Tam, and head straight for Jez. I push myself toward her to deflect it, but I'm too slow. The bolt catches Jesma in the thigh, dropping her to the ground.

She screams in pain.

Damn it, I wish I had my fourth knife!

I scoop Jesma up as she screams in pain. The bolt passed clean through and is sticks out the other side. As I run to the carriage, Jesmir picks up a rock and throws it with all his might. He hits the crossbow as the bowman attempts to reload it. The weapon falls from the man's hands and slides down the slope of the roof to the ground.

Jesmir rushes forward and picks it up. With oddly fluid proficiency, he pulls the bowstring back. He draws a bolt from the harness on the stock, loads it, and fires it into the throat of the bowman up top, who falls off the back of the hut with a thud. Reloading, Jesmir scans the area, looking for more enemies.

Three more ambushers come from around the back of our carriage, swords in hand. I recognize one of them as the man who accompanied Brogen in the Dead Eye Pub back in Valshannon. The other two I don't recognize but they have the same look as the first guy. They are Brogen's men.

I hear Tamrin say a prayer I've heard many times before.

"Tarake Ang Preta!"

Jesma gasps as she watches Tamrin's transformation. Oddly, Jesmir doesn't react. I've seen it so often it no longer phases me. Tam's muscles begin to grow twice their size. Simultaneously, his hair grows longer, his nails extend and harden, and his incisors grow in length to become fangs. A familiar redness fills him as blood lust takes over.

He lets out a low, rumbling growl, preparing to charge into battle.

"Enough!" yells a commanding voice from behind.

I turn around slowly, Jesma held tight in my arms. The voice is familiar to me now. I want to silence that voice permanently. There, in the middle of the small village, stands Brogen, Captain of the Dark Guard of Killinshire. His cropped gray hair and pointed gray goatee infuriate me. His bird-beak nose begs to be broken. He smiles, his super white teeth perfectly straight, and his thin lips even thinner with the smile.

"God, you're ugly," I snarl.

"You!" he exclaims, his eyes bulging at first, then narrowing. The smile fades. Four more goons come from around the huts on either side of him. Tamrin growls. One of them is the young guard who escorted us to Baron Bun-Marlon.

"I will kill you with my bare hands," Tamrin growls, pointing at the spy. The kid's malice-filled grin eggs Tamrin on.

Brogen holds his hands out. "Nobody move!" he commands his men. They obey his command without hesitation, swords and spears at the ready. I scan each one. Footsteps sound behind me.

"I've got your back," Tam says in a much lower timber.

I look down at Jesma. She winces in pain but says, "Put me down."

Once again, I can't resist her commands. I'm wet clay in her hands, moldable like I never was before. I nod and gently set her down, helping her steady herself. Jesmir steps beside her to offer support, his ready crossbow aimed at Brogen.

"Easy, Jes," I say. "Save that bolt. I've got the big guy. Anyone gets near me, take 'em out." I turn and smile at him, "Please don't shoot me in the back."

"You worry about Brogen. I'll worry about your back." I shake my head with a smirk, remembering his earlier shot with the crossbow. I'm anything but worried.

"The wandering vagabond from Winding Run?" Brogen shakes a finger at me. "Our last encounter didn't sit right with me. I couldn't put a finger on it, and it's been bugging the piss out of me," he says, waving his hand around the back of his skull, "poking at me back here since that day. I thought you looked familiar then, but you seem to have aged some since I saw you last. I bet you'd like to know why. It's finally come to me how I know your face."

I'm confused by what he's saying. It doesn't make any sense. The only explanation is he's trying to get me off my game, so I shake it off, focusing on the various people, weapons, obstacles, and paths to fight.

He looks around at his men. "You are outnumbered here," he says, "and seriously outmatched." He spins around, counting his men with a deliberate pointing of his finger. "You took out the hirelings. They were expendable anyway."

He tilts his head as if he is looking around me on either side. "And you are out of knives."

"I don't need 'em," I snarl. Both my blades are out. I retract and extend them for effect.

He nods. "No, I don't believe you think you do… Harbinger."

I come to a stop.

He laughs. It's not a fake laugh. It's a genuine pleasure at my shock.

"Oh, I know you much better than you know yourself. What was it? Eighteen years ago? When you killed the Yarl? We locked eyes then. I was madder than a hornet." He rests his hands on his waist, shaking his head, a smirk forming. "Oh, how I wanted to get to you then." He starts to circle. I keep him at a distance, circling in formation.

"Tell me," he inclines his head, "was it personal? It seemed personal."

"It was nunya," I say.

"I'm sorry? Nunya?"

"Nunya damn business why I killed him,"

Brogen's laugh is genuine. "Man, I wish I liked you. We'd make a great team. You are entertaining."

I don't respond.

"I've heard rumors that you are nearly superhuman fast. The stories are legendary." He looks to his goons, "Unbelievable, really. Everyone thinks they are exaggerated." He points at one, "Strethos, you say it all the time. What is it?"

"Ghost stories to scare children into submission," the one called Strethos replies.

"You don't get it, do you, Shen-Zarl of Ditherun Village?"

My head spins.

How does he know that?

My skin tingles as I feel myself breathing too heavily.

"I know all your secrets, young man," he says. "I've been around a long time. Much longer than you. Much longer than anyone in this village today."

I have been stunned a handful of times in the world. But none like this. I can't imagine how he knows who I am.

"Oh, I see the wheels turning up there," he says, circling his finger around his temple. "Let me look at you." He looks me up and down. "Wow, it's uncanny. The apple does not fall far from the tree. It's like he's here with me again, your father."

I stumble, my foot slipping on a rock as his words race through my mind.

"You don't know my father," I whisper.

"Oh, but I do. Or did. You want to know why your father left?" he asks. "I'll tell you."

It's the fastest movement I have ever seen. It's as if the man vanished and reappeared.

He grabs my shirt, lifts me off the ground and with incredible force, he slams me into the wall of the store. My head impacts the wooden planks behind me. Stars shoot into my vision, tiny multicolored dots flying every which way. My sight blurs and grows dark. My blades involuntarily retract. The air escapes my lungs. I can't breathe.

"Because he was just like you," Brogen says. His mouth is so close to my face his breath fills my nostrils, the warm air choking me while I try to catch my breath. He lets go, and I fall to the ground. I land on my knees and barely get my hands out ahead of me before I face plant in the muddy grass.

"Shen!" I hear Jesma whimper.

He turns his back to me and walks back out to the street. He spreads his arms wide as he continues his speech.

"Your father was fast, too, Shen. As fast as you. Maybe faster." He turns to me. "He walked away from his family. Too afraid to be what he could be."

Brogen squats to look at me, locking eyes. "Oh, what a King he would have made! If only he had the vision!" He stands. "We were schoolmates. Best friends. We found each other on the training field. One day, we were paired to fight. We learned we had the same skill. Lots of speed! We trained together for years. Honing our skills, learning to access the power granted by Hakaka! We stored it within us like little nuggets of energy. There when we needed it we released a vast reservoir of power."

"We planned to rule Killinshire. Take over the world from there." His expression grows dark, "but he grew a conscience. Tried to make me 'see the error of our ways.' Well, I wasn't buying it!" he screams, his thumb pointed at his chest.

Silence.

Breathe, goddamn you!

"You know I thought about coming to find you? After I killed him. After he left you and your brother. Shame what happened to your brother. Too bad your mother was a loon."

"Shut up," I whisper.

"What's that?" Brogen says.

I push myself up and stand, focusing on my breathing. I tilt my head back and close my eyes. A deep breath. Then another. I look at him.

"I said, stop talking. Let's dance."

He laughs. I lunge. His body twists with a slight motion, his speed much greater than mine. The move is wildly effective. His hand catches my wrist and with a roll of his hips, he throws me across the road. Inertia does the rest, as momentum is conserved, and I fly through the air against my will. I allow myself to flow with the energy and tuck my shoulder into the dive and roll through. I complete the roll with a hip-twist, and pop up with a grin, ready for his attack. Brogen stands, unimpressed, his lip curled into a smirk.

"Like I said, boy, I am like you." He pulls out a talisman. It is the only god the Killinshire folk worship. Hakaka.

"I'll strangle you with that necklace," I snarl. I push myself harder than I ever have and lunge again. This time, I control the lunge, twisting before the bastard can grab my wrist.

His massive fist blasts the side of my head, sending me to the ground, sliding in the wet, cold mud. More stars explode from the impact. I try to get up.

"Shen!" I hear Jesma scream in panic.

How is he so fast?

Pushing myself to my knees, I catch my breath again and shake the cobwebs from my rattled brain.

"Come on, son, let's get this over with," he says, boredom in his tone.

I'll die tasting the bitter medicine I have dealt to hundreds of enemies over the years. This was not how I thought I would die.

I stand and let out a heavy sigh.

If I'm about to die, I'll die fighting for all that I'm worth.

I extend my blades again and stand facing him. He sneers at me, licking his thin, ugly lips like some draconian lizard. I walk this time, deliberately and slowly. My mind races, churning through scenarios. I recall past fights with people who had a chance, but nothing in my repertoire ever prepared me for someone better than me. Everyone I ever fought was never good enough. This time, I may be the one that isn't good enough.

An idea begins to form, and I latch onto it. Maybe I can play some mind games of my own.

I do the very thing I hate. I run through a complex, rich, and specific routine: a drunken fist kata from my time at the temple. My arms move and sway, my feet slide and dance, my breath controlled and deliberate. My weight shifts from one foot to the next as my body curves and undulates, drunken stumbles meant to look random, thoroughly planned, and flawlessly executed.

I tell him exactly what I will do with each step, each motion, and then I beckon.

He rolls his eyes, "My god, son, I thought you'd be an actual challenge."

He pulls his sword. It rings with a familiar sound. Gal-Danang steel.

He turns his body sideways slightly and rests the tip of the sword on the ground, the grip firm but relaxed. His shoulders slump.

"I really thought you'd be a challenge. You have no idea how hard it is to find anyone worthy to fight. Your father was nowhere near as good as he thought he was. That was the last worthy opponent I ever fought." He smiles at me, "he'd be proud of you, though. You're better than he was. But still. You are not the challenge I hoped for."

He steps to me, his sword drawing a line in the ground as he does. The blade moves fast, and I give him the first logical steps of the specific pattern he is expecting, confirming his suspicions. He takes a few tentative strikes at me, and I dodge and weave in the most likely and anticipated moves. His blade slices a cut along my cheek. It stings but is a necessary ploy.

He steps in, and I abandon the routine altogether. I don't even stay in the same style. As he strikes his killing blow, I dash from the blade's path. I press my hand toward his face, blade retracted

Expecting the presence of a blade, he swings his sword to block, and it passes through empty air but catches him off guard. I activate my blade, and it extends as I reverse my move, catching him off guard again. But his speed is unreal. I don't know how it's possible, but he sped up at the last second. The tip of my blades barely catches the birdman's nose, opening a small cut across the bridge.

He steps back and touches his nose.

How is he doing this?

I hold a minute. Unsure of what to do.

"Well, now," he says. "That was a surprise. Too bad it will only work once. Gotta land the surprises on the first attempt, boy."

"I am not your boy," I snarl.

"No, you aren't. If you were, you'd be better. I'd have made sure of it. Not left you to fend for yourself like your father did. In fact, why don't you come and join me? Be my right hand? We'll kill the twins and your useless friend, then head down to Valshannon for some brews?"

I push down the rage at his words. For the first time, my rage works against me and will only make me sloppy against this man. I charge at him again, controlled but speedy. Muscles tear throughout my body. I can't pinpoint the source of pain, but I don't care. The sensation of flames engulfs my body as I access speed I've never tapped before. There isn't time to process the continuous increases in speed over the past few weeks or the increased internal pain. I only push harder.

Our blades collide as he blocks and parries. His blade comes fast. We exchange a series of blows as I try to push him to the door of one of the huts. He stumbles as he steps up to the porch of the store, and I take advantage. Pushing hard, I come for his head, trying to impale him to the door.

It's too late, and I realize the stumble was a feint. Brogen dodges my blade as it impacts the door. Before I can retract it, his sword comes down on my blade with such force it shatters. Gal-Danang steel against Gal-Danang steel. His sword is heavier and moves at blinding speed. My small blades are no match. Especially when stuck in a door, unable to flex or bounce out of the way. My arm absorbs the shock of the impact, and I cry out in pain.

The sudden release causes me to stumble. I spin and dodge backward toward the carriage. My legs are burning. I smell the metallic scent of blood on me. Somewhere on my arms and legs, I hurt. Cold steel has sliced me in several places. I can catalog them all over my body. The adrenal rush pushes the pain into the background, but I can feel every wound.

The loss of blood accelerates. The warm liquid distracts my thoughts. The scent of copper drowns out all other scents in the air. While I dodged and clashed about, his blades sliced my body in hundreds of little cuts. I stumble backward to give myself room. I'm as frightened as I've ever been. I'm not able to beat this man. My friends will die because I failed them. My position as the apex predator was a lie. I need to buy some time.

The burning sensation in my chest starts up again.

"Not now!" I scream.

"Oh, now, for sure," Brogen says as he approaches. He thinks I speak to him.

I back away toward the hut closest to the carriage. There's no escape. Brogen leers at me, his sword whistles through the air. I block with my last blade. His force drives my arm to the ground and continues as if he intends to cleave the earth. My last blade snaps in two. With a last-ditch effort, I lunge away from the next blade strike. He misses as my legs drive my body backward. I lose my balance and fall to my back.

Oh, thank you, Grankin.

A glint catches my eye. Loose steel against the brown grass beside the little hut.

It's right where it landed.

With an incredible display of discipline, I contain my joy. I dig my feet into the ground with desperation and drive myself backward, the panic only partially real. With one last aggressive kick, I push myself overtop of the blade with an unsure hope my plan goes unnoticed. My hand closes around cold steel. The familiar feel of my forgotten throwing knife resonates in the scars on my wrists from the multitude of attempts to take my own life. It's a sweet, familiar friend. My last hope.

Lucky break, it hit the crossbow and not flesh.

Shamna twenty-three!

Brogen is faster than me, stronger than me, and more experienced than me.

But the man who murdered my father underestimated me. I'm a fast learner.

Brogen plants his boot down onto my chest, leans into it and compresses my lungs. My eyes bulge as I fight for air, my body already winded. His sword nips at my throat, held fast by steady hands, and he turns and looks at my friends.

"Your Harbinger has finally heralded his own death."

It's the best day of my life. I realize there is a good life to be had if I'm willing to fight for it.

And fight for it, I will. I may not fear death, but now, death has no hold on me. I'm no longer willing to hand my life over, not even to myself. It belongs to the woman I love. For her, I will fight to live.

My hand moves so fast that nobody notices. The last of my knives, having slid from the roof after it's failed impact with the bowman's crossbow, thankfully ignored since it fell, and, Grankin be praised, clasped in my hand, right where it landed.

My last ploy, a feigned fall. Brogen never thought I would be stupid enough to use his own tactic on him so quickly. Maybe he never thought I was smart enough. No matter. I maintain my posture of fear while he's gloats, his eyes on Jesma. Her face, contorted in rage and anger, shakes as she lunges toward him, the crossbow bolt still in her thigh. Brogen turns his pointy face toward me.

The world moves slower than I've ever seen.

Jesma raises her dagger to strike. Inside, pride wells up as I see the woman I love ready to throw herself at my attacker.

I suppress the smile that threatens to spread across my face and strike.

My blade slices tendons at the back of Brogen's knee. The same knee that supports the foot planted on my chest. The sharp edge severs the tendons and his knee buckles. The tip of his sword slides up as he loses his balance and catches the edge of my chin. I grimace at the pain but continue my attack. My hand drops to his leg, and I stab the knife deep into the muscle of his calf, just above the boot cuff. His expression turns into shock as he attempt to shift his weight back to his rear leg, but it buckles, too.

The first rule the monks taught me was always keep your balance in your stance. It's an amateur mistake. Or an arrogant blowhard one. The sword falls back toward my neck and misses, burying itself in the ground dangerously close to my jugular.

I hear the twang of a crossbow and wait for the impact to pierce me somewhere.

Instead, a loud thud lands next to me. Brogen's eyes are wide open. A crossbow bolt protrudes, feathered side up, straight through his neck.

Brogen tries to speak, but the bolt cuts his vocal cords.

I shoot a glance at Jesmir. He smiles.

Jesma falls to her knees, dagger in hand.

"I never miss with a crossbow," Jesmir says.

"Well, why didn't you say so?" I yell and cast a smile to Jesma. She just shrugs.

Tamrin releases a ferocious growl and charges at the three men at the back of the carriage. Saliva drips from his fangs, and claw-like hands rip through leather and skin. Jesmir loads another bolt as the four men at the other end of the village charge at us. I push myself up, ripping Brogen's sword from his dying grip.

The fight with the remaining seven soldiers is over before it begins. Tamrin makes short work of the first two on his side of the village. Jesmir's work with the crossbow takes down two others on my side before they can get to us.

Brogen's sword feels good in my hands. It sings as I move it through the air, slicing the last two assailants on my side in mid-stride.

A primal scream pierces the air, and everyone turns to look at Jesma. Brogen's final henchman stands on wobbly legs. As he turns away from her he lifts his hands from his crotch. He stares at his blood-covered hands.

My eyes fall to the hilt of the dagger, the entire blade buried deep in the flesh of his manhood. Jesma spits at him.

"Oh, fucking Krikhi's cradle!" I cry.

Tamrin cringes at the sight.

"He tried to touch me," Jesma growls.

She's beautiful in her rage—her face a warrior's mask and I smile at her in spite of my pain and her blood-covered face. The sense of pride is only partially shadowed with the echo of guilt that I've led her to violence. But it's hard to deny the results. Our enemies lay dead throughout the village, and the four of us remain together, alive and panting. Tamrin sports a slice on his cheek. Jesma kneels with a bolt in her leg and waves me over to her. I stumble my way to her and fall to my knees in exhaustion, multiple lacerations on my body, all individually nonfatal. Jesmir stands with a shit-eating grin on his face.

"See, Jes," I say. "You are a good fighter. We just needed to find your weapon."

The ride from Breakridge to Kerakot is as uneventful as it gets. Two days of travel, lots of prayers from Jez, which I no longer roll my eyes at, and plenty of wine taken from the store in Breakridge. We paid them for it. It's a small village. Brogen and his men would have hurt everyone there. Punishing them would have been cruel and unfair. But we did buy everything they had. The journey is much different from Breakridge than it was to the village. Laughter, a night with a fire, this time under the stars, some tasteless jokes, and camaraderie. It was perfect.

Not all of Jesma's prayers are answered. For some reason, Ezra wouldn't answer her prayers for herself.

Gods and their games.

But she is in high spirits and has been bragging about the scars she'll have, even though her leg hurts like mad. Thankfully, I happen to still have the Cuska paste from the first cottage. That eased her pain and at least stopped the bleeding. She has mild hallucinations from it, and her brother uses her momentary loss of lucidity for his own entertainment.

I choose not to intervene but decide instead to enjoy the sight of them as I imagine they usually are together. Lighthearted and full of mirth.

A few rough bumps along the road caused Jez discomfort, but she bore it well.

Jesmir regaled Tamrin with his ability to throw rocks and his crossbow action and even embellished it slightly. Tamrin approved of the edits and even added a couple of his own.

I'm writing down my thoughts here. I hope it won't be judged too harshly if this is ever public knowledge. Even at fifty-three, I guess I can learn. I'm not saying I won't have my bad days. Reviewing my life in retrospect, I know that profound fatigue is still there. It may come back. Then again, maybe it won't. Who's to say?

But right now, at this moment, as I put pen to paper, riding inside the carriage, Jez's injured leg elevated on my lap, I am happy in a way I haven't known since I was a teen. It's joyous to be with people I love and who love me. Peace can be found outside my mind. Not inside.

I know that should there ever be readers of this journal, they'll wonder, so I've put it down here.

Even injured, Jez couldn't stand to wait any longer. Neither could I, really.

Her skin is prettier without the effervescence. It's smooth, soft, and warm.

The details won't go in here. Those memories are mine to keep. I hope to build many more of them.

We've built two already.

She's kicking my journal with her foot.

The curtains of the carriage are closed because we are both still naked in here, tucked under Tam's furs. Looks like I won't be getting dressed just yet.

The Growing Darkness

Chapter Twenty-Five

Journal Entry: 78

I wish I knew if Brogen had been lying about my father. That obsessive part of me won't let that go. Someday, I'll have to chase down the truth.

But it will have to wait. Today, I have to celebrate the victories.

Call it part of my burgeoning new outlook on life.

Hell, I may even believe in gods now.

Grandmothers and Grand Tales

Our arrival in Kerakot is quiet. We chose to enter the city unannounced and head straight to the Queen. It's a long ride from the gates to the castle. The revelry of the road from Breakridge is over. Jez and Tamrin ride out front while Jes and I sit in the carriage. We still have those lingering questions. But we know together, we can get to the bottom of what happened.

Our first step is informing the Queen. Jez decided she should be the one to tell her about the death of her aunt and their father. If she does know, then at least she will have the peace of mind of knowing the perpetrator is gone, and her grandchildren are still alive.

The castle guards stop us as we approach. Jez hops down and walks to the Guardmaster. After a few quick words, he recognizes her and nods to the other guards to open the castle gates. Kerakot Castle is small. The circular stone drive leads to a wide three-story stone and marble structure that looks more like a very large mansion than it does a castle. There are no towers and no balconies. A long, broad flight of stairs leads to the main entrance, where two doormen stand.

Jez opts to climb them without support, the poise of a Royal Princess held high. The doormen, dismayed by our collective appearance, opens the doors and curiously glances at the royal siblings. We appear as soldiers after a long war, except for our smiles and laughter. Jesma and I bask in the afterglow of two days of rigorous coitus, and from the look on the doormen's faces, it could be pronounced.

The entirety of the staff, engaged in last-minute flourishes of activity to receive a prince and princess, comes to a stop. Shameful gasps escape a few lips, but neither of us acknowledges them. The Queen's handmaiden, on her way down the staircase from the living quarters, turns and runs upstairs upon seeing us, presumably to get the Queen. Everywhere I look, tapestries, paintings, ornate furniture, vases filled with flowers, and rugs from around the world decorate the grand entry. The opulence of this one room is more wealth than I will see in a lifetime.

A few guards and servants eye me suspiciously, but I shake that off as typical paranoia of royal guards. Probably afraid Tamrin and I will try to take off with the silver.

The Queen comes down ten minutes later, still in her bed robes. Her face immediately darkens at the sight of the children of her son, shifting to relief and joy as she suddenly realizes it's them with dyed hair. She rushes to hug her grandchildren. Tears flow as Jez and Jes run to her. She looks perplexed.

I'd never seen the Queen, so I didn't know what to expect, but not this. Based on the twins' age, I expected a frail, slow woman well into her twilight years. Instead, it was a surprise to see a barely aging woman, still light in her steps, bearing only light wrinkles, glide down the grand staircase, barely looking ten years older than me.

"What is the meaning of your appearance?" she asks her grandchildren, her tone stern.

They look at each other and then back to her.

"Grandmother, we only did this to survive," Jez says.

She looks at them, confused by the comments. "Survive? Survive what?"

The twins, stunned by her question, don't respond immediately. Then Jez begins her tale of their trip, starting with Pal. The Queen stops them when they get to the pirate attack and waves them into a parlor beside the stairs. As Tam and I follow, she stops.

"And where do you think you two are going?" she says, narrowing her eyes. "Who are you anyway?"

Jez gives her grandmother a nervous glance, then walks over to me and puts her arm in mine. "These are the men who kept us safe and made sure we returned home."

The Queen looks Jez up and down. Her disapproval of me is evident. Her scrutinizing gaze pierces through me, her lips pursed. I cough self-consciously, physically uncomfortable under her stare.

"I see," she says. "Well, they can wait out here."

Jez looks at me and then back to her grandmother.

"My lady, please, it has been a trying two weeks. These men saved us from many dangers, at great risk to themselves, asking for no reward in return."

A heavy sigh. "Very well then." She turns and walks through the double doors into the parlor. A butler carries in a tray of hot tea and small sandwiches. I am amazed at the display, which leaves me to marvel at the disparity between the wealth of the Royal family against the backdrop of the poverty of Hericot. The royals take seats around a small table where the butler places the tray. Tam and I remain standing.

While the twins relay the story of their capture, the death of their father, their escape into the river, an attack by bandits, and their subsequent rescue, I watch her reactions. Genuine concern registers on her face, as well as visibly restrained anger. She stops them throughout the story to ask questions, especially interested in our time at the bottom of the Great Rankin River. I can't tell, but this seems to interest her most of all until she waves it away, bored with the details, telling Jez to continue.

She takes the news of the compromised emissary protocol with alarm but asks a few questions. As they talk of the flight out of Valshannon, I notice Jes is quiet, still avoiding any discussion of what he and Tamrin encountered on their escape from Valshannon.

I really need to find out what happened there.

Jez gives her a complete account of the spiderlyches. That portion of the story causes the Queen to look in my direction. Her interest shifts toward me, observing me as Jez tells of how I killed one and injured another.

Jez leaves out the events at Rogue's Pointe and my time in the ring.

I am grateful for that.

The details of the emissary's betrayal seem to interest her greatly, especially when the subject of Krin's attempt to murder me arises. The Queen asks me several questions that I evade with half-truths rather than an outright refusal to answer. I relay my efforts to signal the emissary, Brogen's appearance at the Dead Eye Pub, and his uncanny ability to outmaneuver us. I keep the details of my history with Krin out of the discussion. She gives no indication of her thoughts as I speak, her face devoid of emotion.

When we get to our time in the Valley of Cusk, the Queen snaps her attention to me. I can't be sure, but I think I caught a hint of fear when she looked at me. It is hard to say. It happened so fast.

"You killed two Cuska, escaped one, and scared off the horde?" she says, her disbelief evident.

"Yes, your Majesty," I say. I offer no further input on the subject.

"Can you prove such a claim?" she asks.

I pull the two trophies from around my neck and show them to her. She walks over to me and lightly slides her hand under them, inspecting the symbols on the stones.

"Do you know what these are?" she asks.

I nod. "Periapts of a god I have never heard of. Cuskatana."

Again, her head snaps up to me. "How is your relationship with your god?" she asks.

"I have no god," I say. "Until recently, I did not believe they were real."

"You have no god?" she questions, surprised. I sense fear in her voice and a hint of disdain, making me uncomfortable. She won't let me be anywhere near Jesma now.

"No."

She returns to her seat but never takes her eyes off me.

The twins continue their story, but I stop listening. The Queen's gaze makes me uncomfortable, and it unsettles me. Throughout the rest of the story, she casts sideways glances my way. I turn to Tam, who periodically casts side-eye glances my way. His discomfort is evident. I can't tell if it's from standing in proximity of the Queen or if he feels as judged as I do.

The twins talk of Hericot and the undying loyalty and support of Baron Bun-Marlon. The Queen makes a point to say how she will honor him at the castle and increase the budget for the town to improve conditions there. The twins look back at me with joy at that. I smile and give an inappropriate thumbs-up.

When the story's focus turns into greater detail about Brogen, the Queen stares at me the entire time Jez and Jes relay the events. I barely listen to the conversation anymore. The Queen's gaze, intense and direct, causes me to squirm internally. It's as if a silent force threatens to press me into the earth and reduce my existence in the world. The space around me feels as if it expands in an effort to minimize my presence.

The Queen stands and finally nods in Tam's and my directions.

"Thank you, gentlemen, for taking such good care of my grandbabies."

The Queen walks over and hugs Tam, then approaches me.

"You are a man of incredible talent," she says. "How old are you, Shen?"

I'm caught off guard by the question. "Your Majesty?"

"Simple question."

"Umm… I'm fifty-three."

"Interesting. You barely look thirty. You must have good genetics."

"I, ugh, don't really know, your Majesty," I say.

"Hmm. Well, you look good for your age, young man," she says. "Thank you for putting your country over yourself. You have performed a great service. My servants have prepared rooms for you. You are filthy and in need of rest."

She leads us to the doors as they open, the butler waiting.

The End

Epilogue

We lay in bed together. Bathed, scented, and alone for the first time, Jez and I hold each other, legs intertwined. As tired as we were, I postponed sleep, caught in the passion we'd been building over the weeks. She sleeps soundly now, her hair tickling my nose. I try to brush it aside without disturbing her.

The tension of the journey finally released, our bodies relaxed, and I allowed myself to close my eyes. Jez's light purr soothes me.

I picture visions of Cuska, Grankin, and Brogen dancing, and my memories are replaced by one image.

It's of the Queen.

Her gaze made me uncomfortable. I lie here and try to sleep, but my brain bustles with activity. Insomnia sucks. At first, I thought I was worried about falling asleep in Jez's bed, not wanting to cause her problems with her grandmother, but that isn't an issue in Teshket. One of the few benefits of Teshket society is the steadfast belief that liberty of the self is paramount in our culture. The Queen, generous and welcoming once the story was complete, wouldn't blink if she found me here. She'd be more concerned with how I felt toward Jez than my lust for her.

I dismiss those thoughts only to drift into memories of the events that led to this moment. I should feel at ease, but I don't. I may have found peace, but I'm still me. A thorn pricks at my side, and I can't figure out what it is.

I haven't had a chance to speak with Tam. I'd love to get his perspective and have him talk me out of the spiraling abyss threatening the peace of this moment. I need a moment with my best friend.

I slide out of bed without disturbing the woman beside me. Pangs of disappointment almost keep me in place. But I'll never sleep if I don't talk to Tam. She's safe. Her mind resting, comfortably tucked away in a bed she'd spent many a night in, the familiar comforts of her life lulling her into a restful slumber. She doesn't stir as I untangle myself from her.

Dressed in only my pants and shirt, I wander the second-floor hall to locate Tam's room. As soon as I pass the grand staircase, I hear low, controlled voices from behind a door down the hall. I can't make out the details of the conversation. Still, being the consummate nebnose I am, I sneak to the opposite end of the hall and listen outside the set of closed double doors. A steady light, not from a flame, illuminates the marble floor under the doors. Pacing figures cast shadows across the thin sliver of light as I approach.

To my right, through a single door, Tam's snore rumbles through in a low growl. At least I know where he is.

I step to the side when I reach the set of double doors, lean against the wall, ear nearly pressed against the door to hear the Queen's voice, "He has no patron?"

"He was never one for faith," another voice says.

I freeze. I'd recognize that voice anywhere. My mouth goes dry.

"All these years, and we finally have him here? How many assassins have been sent after him? And he waltzes in here. It's almost too good to be true."

"If he hadn't rescued your grandchildren, we may never have found him," says the familiar voice.

It *can't* be.

"We haven't come across one of those since the bastard at the bottom of the river," the Queen says.

It doesn't matter what anyone says next. The voice is all I can focus on. I'd know it in an instant.

Krin.

* * *

Acknowledgments

First and most importantly, I would like to thank my wonderful, understanding, patient, and incredibly selfless wife, Jill. Not a day goes by that I am not grateful that you said "yes" to a first date, "yes" to a second, and "yes" to my proposal. Marrying you still stands as the wisest decision I've ever made. You bring out the best in me, and your encouragement and unwavering love are the pillars of my life. You are the most incredible partner anyone could ask for.

Thank you for putting up with my countless hours working in the basement office pretending to be a professional author.

Thank you for loving the nerd that I am, even though you aren't one. I still can't believe you said, "I do". Someone pinch me.

Thank you Steven Moore and the staff at Condor Publishing for all the notes, feedback, and discussions. You took a hot mess of a manuscript and turned it into something incredibly special. This book wouldn't be what it is without you, from plot lines to character arcs to prose. The decision to isolate the jumbled thoughts that were Shen's to the beginning of the chapters was the right decision. It reads so much better now. I know I still left "Dinkum", but I just couldn't get rid of it! Thank you for keeping the heart of The Growing Darkness in mind when editing. It is a much better story from where it started because of you.

To Laura Thompson and RB Michaels at Writer's Journey. Working with you on this book in its final stages was a pleasure. I'm a firm believer in a multitude of counselors. Your understanding of fantasy fiction brought the additional insight required to polish this into the best book it could be. I know I was a bit of a pain in the ass and suffer from an attitude of "I want what I want", but your patience helped me see why, so many times, you were right, and I was wrong. It's insane to me how much better this book is now. The additional character details, and countless hours show in this final version. Thank you! You tied the last bit of missing pieces together!

To my beta readers, you know who you are. Thank you for your honest feedback and the hours spent discussing everything from the origin myth of Conishant to the creation of the gods, races, and monsters. Thank you for the harsh words that improved this book and for the encouragement when something worked.

Thank you to my son, Patrick, for the long discussions on the origin myth. I think we finally got it!

Special thanks to Don Cook and DJ Cook. Good friends who listen to my ramblings over worlds, gods, magic, Shamna Rocks, and plot. Our Wednesday afternoon gaming sessions, though often devolving into histrionic shenanigans from too much drink, are always a great time and a ready source for ideas. Thank you both for letting me discuss the hidden elements that make my worlds feel real. A guy couldn't have better friends.

Thank you, Libby Mussachio, for the outstanding artwork. Your decision to hand paint the art is nothing less than shear genius. I'm so excited to work with you on the next one. So many ideas! The speed at which you sketched concepts while we spoke still leaves my jaw on the floor. I hope the final cover didn't take out too much of the details. Your canvas sits over my desk, in my constant line of sight every day. I'm frightened and thrilled by it!

Lastly, thank you, dear reader, for agreeing to go on this journey with me. Authors write for readers to read. With all of the demands on your time, the fact you chose to use some of that resource to read my book is a gift I can never repay. I hope you enjoyed the good and the bad and will join me on many more adventures. I am so glad to share this with you.

A Note From the Author

When the idea of a hero struggling with self-worth, suicidal thoughts, and fear of abandonment first hit me, I was afraid to write it. The topic is dark. The risk of creating an unlikeable, brooding character was high. I had to take care I didn't diminish the tragedy of real-life loss.

As one of the many Loss Survivors of suicide, I've struggled with making sense of everything since my loved ones first took their own lives.

I have the unfortunate experience of having to go through this twice.

Attempting to create a story honoring those who struggle with these thoughts wasn't something I entered into lightly. Creating a story with a character this heavy and forcing the reader to live inside the character's head was no easy task. The first iterations of Shen were unreadable. It was painful to write. I approached this task by only writing his inner thoughts. Fifty-thousand words of depression, anxiety, self-loathing, and fear. I cried a lot while writing them. I could hear the voices of my loved ones in my head. I was so focused on the darkest thoughts that the first five chapters became horrifically depressing. I wasn't sure I could continue.

It took several attempts to hone Shen's unique perspective and personality while still honoring those on whom he is based, giving voice to their struggles without weighing down the story. Ultimately, I had to minimize the time spent in the darker thoughts of Shen's inner monologue to create a story and character that readers would love. I can only hope I left enough to give a sense of what I believe was happening in the deepest parts of those I lost within the story's context.

Shen is an amalgamation of two of the most influential people in my life. The relationships I shared with these two beautiful souls represent some of my most cherished memories and some of my most remarkable opportunities to grow as a person.

My Aunt Bobi took her own life on January 1, 2005.

The Growing Darkness

My dear friend Nate took his life on April 7, 2019.

Aunt Bobi packed a lot of personality into a 4'11", 95 lb. frame. She was my biggest cheerleader and staunchest ally. I could do no wrong in her eyes, which is significant for those who know my history. She was readily available for every stupid adventure I wanted to go on. Barely sixteen when I was born, she inspired the boy I was. Always up for shenanigans, she would take my brother and me out of school to go ride go-carts, play at the arcade (a big thing in the 70s and 80s), and treat us to movies, McDonald's, Dairy Queen, and Disney World—something that would happen without my mother's knowledge. On one such event, Aunt Bobi took eleven-year-old me and my ten-year-old brother out of school to go to Disney World, a few hundred miles north of home, for two days without telling anyone, not even her older sister.

Her laugh was infectious and easily identifiable. Her two favorite things in the world were busting into my apartment unannounced and saying, "Who loves ya, baby?" at the end of every conversation. She'd enter a room with flare, make chocolate chip pancakes on a whim, and get into more silly bits of trouble than Lucille Ball.

Aunt Bobi was brutally honest when discussing her feelings. She was an imaginative storyteller, a horrible exaggerator, empathetically tender, terrifically clumsy, and incredibly gullible. She loved without condition and gave without expectation. She never accepted my excuses, constantly challenged my worldview, and made me a much better person than who I was when I first started out. She was the best person I ever knew.

She taught me that compassion was more important than confidence, kindness more than passion, and the journey was more important than the destination. She taught me that I was never responsible for the results, only the effort and the spirit behind that effort.

She was a graduate of the Ringling Brother's Barnum & Bailey Circus Clown College, changed religions thrice, was married thrice (one died in the line of duty, one she divorced, and one she was with to the end), and wrecked no less than four cars.

I remember when I started to see the changes in her. Most of it is hindsight now. But I tried to dig into some of them when she was still alive. Little things like not staying on the phone as long, moments of quiet sadness, or visits suddenly shortening to minutes instead of hours began to occur more frequently. I wasn't the only one that noticed. When I asked her about it at first, she'd blow it off as life getting in the way. But then I noticed she laughed less, smiled less, cried more.

I remember the day I sat with her and asked what was happening. She couldn't explain it, but she opened the door to what was inside her head, and I saw that it had all been a defense mechanism. We talked a lot that day, and then she made me promise not to say anything.

Some promises should never be kept. I should have learned then.

Like a fool, I kept it quiet. Held it inside. Kept her confidence.

She was Aunt Bobi. She was my hero. She kept my secrets my whole life. Of course, I'd keep hers.

And then she was gone.

Then came the sadness. Then, the anger. Then, the despair and then the guilt.

Self-recriminating questions come when you are a Loss Survivor.

It's a poisonous line of logic.

When he entered my life, Nate was eight years old. He lived in the neighborhood when my kids and I moved to Columbus, Ohio. Within a year, he was a regular part of the activities that went on in our home.

It pains me to say that I initially didn't like him. He was arrogant, angry, and a bit of a pain in the ass. But he had a big personality and was damn funny, and I am a big fan of big personalities with a sense of humor.

Truth is, he was too much like me, I think—belligerent, complex, and brash. But Aunt Bobi was still alive at the time, and her influence helped me become the compassionate, kind, and accepting person she expected me to be.

As a result, I chose to accept Nate for who he was. Over the next seventeen years, he became an active part of my family, spending many weekends at my house. As our friendship grew, I discovered he had the heart of a poet, a gentleness of soul, and a generosity of spirit. He was one of the greatest people I've ever had the pleasure of walking through life with. He was an irreplaceable force.

As he struggled with self-esteem in his teens, he fought hard to live a big life. He became a track star, a wrestling star, and an equestrian. He woke every morning to muck stalls on his friend's farm, then drove to track practice before school started. After school, he'd head to wrestling practice, and when everyone else was ready to call it a day, Nate hopped in his car and went to work at a pet store. Through all of that, he taught himself to work on cars, work out, have girlfriends, and goof off on weekends at my house.

When he became an adult, he became one of my closest friends, and by the time he passed, he was my best friend.

Through the years, he and I spoke frequently, went fishing, worked on cars, played video games, did yard work, and watched some of the worst B-movies together while drinking beers and laughing about stupid jokes. He was my paintball buddy, running partner, and one of the few people I let into my crazy inner world.

Fun-loving, a consummate joker, adventurous, popular, hardworking, intelligent, athletic, funny, and always up for anything anybody threw his way, he was a force of energy that touched more lives in twenty-five years than I've managed in fifty-three. Our twenty-year age difference never mattered. We became each other's "who's the first person you go to in the zombie apocalypse," a silly, indulgent conversation that I miss.

I don't know how much he told others. He had many people who felt the same about him as I do. I've never spoken to others about my conversations with Nate. I wish I had. Maybe we collectively could have done something. I should have called his mother. I'm ashamed of myself for not doing that. But fear of driving him to the very act I wished to prevent caused me to keep his confidence.

I'll always wonder if he's gone because of my fear.

I'll always wonder if my failure to learn the lesson from Aunt Bobi is the reason Nate is gone today.

I remember the last conversation we had. I remember that last

Thanksgiving. Of all the people he could have chosen to spend it with, he came to our home. I was happy he was there. It was the last time I spent a weekend with him. We had many laughs. My wife still hears his laughter in the house sometimes.

I missed the phone call. My wife was next on the list. She got the call. She wasn't home when it came. Jill was forced to drive home for thirty minutes, building the courage to deliver the news, not wanting to tell me over the phone.

Not a day goes by that I don't think about how horrible that drive had to be for you, Jill. It haunts me. I love you. I don't have words...

The year 2023 was particularly rough for some reason. The world had finally emerged from the pandemic—a three-year stint that still feels like a blur. I found myself thinking about Aunt Bobi and Nate all the time. My thoughts were consumed with these two beautiful and tortured souls. It became a cycle that I couldn't escape, almost ritualistic. I'd think about what I could have done, what I should have seen, and how I should have paid more attention. It haunted me for fourteen years after Aunt Bobi died. It became worse after Nate.

I didn't fail once. I failed twice. I must be a horrible friend.

I would think about the signs, the failed duty to tell others, the missed phone calls, and the moments when my life was too busy to take a minute to answer. It made me feel selfish, unloving, unkind. I began to doubt my vision of myself as someone who loved people.

And each night, it got worse, spiraling into self-recrimination.

For those of us who are Loss Survivors, there is a shame and guilt that we could have, should have, done more. Sadness, anger, denial, guilt, and an enduring love that will never die, never leave, cling to me, deep in my soul.

I was so angry with them for a long time.

Then I realized that it wasn't them I was mad at.

For all the love, sorrow, and pain I feel, I cannot imagine what theirs was in comparison. They didn't really know how much pain they were leaving in the wake of their choice. They were kind and gentle people who never wanted to hurt anyone.

I couldn't be mad at them. I was angry at me.

That has been the struggle.

Loss Survivor's thoughts center around culpability more often than not. I couldn't have stopped them more than I could control my thoughts. Coming to terms with that is the most critical step for us. As this realization came, my thoughts shifted from what I could have done to what it must have been like in their shoes.

For all of 2023, I obsessed over it, making myself see things from their perspective. I've come to realize that despair can take anyone, anytime. Aunt Bobi and Nate never wanted to die. They couldn't put up with the struggle anymore. I believe that deep down, they didn't realize how deeply loved and cared for they were. I began to ask myself if they struggled with these thoughts their entire lives.

I don't know the answer. But having lost two people to such tragedy, I wanted to try and see them, see the part I missed or ignored.

And out of those thoughts, Shen was born.

If you, dear reader, intend to ride this journey with me, my sincerest hope is that you walk away knowing that you are not alone, regardless of which side of this you fall.

If you identify with Shen on this journey, know that your real-life "Tamrins" care deeply for you. They will gladly carry your burdens and sit with you in the darkness until the light shines on your world again. They will mourn your loss, struggle in the future absence of your voice, and will give everything they have for one more minute with you. Others struggle with you, root for you, and stand by you.

Reach out to them and tell them you need help. They'll come like heroes and battle those monsters with you.

You Are Not Alone.

If you identify with Tamrin, hold on to those you love, cherish them, and empathize with them. Tell them, every day, without fail, you love them. Be there for them.

If you suspect something is wrong, ask them!

Don't let it go unsaid out of fear. The alternative is much worse.

And if you've already lost your loved one, I'm very sorry that the pain won't go away. Know that you will charge on, holding the flame of them in your heart forever. There are many of us out here, carrying on in the same way. Come find us. Together, we can get through this.

You Are Not Alone;

-Sean

PLEASE VISIT MY WEBSITE AND GO TO THE SECTION LABELED "SUICIDE PREVENTION" FOR RESOURCES TO HELP:

WWW.SEAN-GREGORY.COM

About the Author

Born in Ft. Lauderdale in 1971, Sean spent his childhood fascinated by *Star Trek, Star Wars, Buck Rodgers*, and *Battlestar Galactica* (the original). Introduced to J.R.R. Tolkien at a young age, he lost himself in magical worlds and all things *Dungeons & Dragons*.

A graduate from The Ohio State University, where he studied Mechanical Engineering, he works as a specialist in space flight sensors for rocket propulsion, life support, and environmental controls.

His debut novel, **The Growing Darkness**, is his first installment of The God Killers trilogy.

Sean currently lives with his wife, Jill, in Pittsburgh PA with their annoyingly cute Puggle, Sweaty Betty the Spaghetti Yeti.

Coming Soon

Also From Sean Gregory:

The God Killers Trilogy
- The Growing Darkness
- Darkness Blooms (coming Aug 2025)
- Decades of Night (coming June 2026)

The Case Files of Miles Ward
- The Ruby Rage (coming June 2025)
- The Opal Offering (coming sometime in 2026)

Stand-Alones and Anthologies
- Sierra the Cyborg Doesn't Want to Kill Anybody (and Other Oddities of the Multiverse) (2025)
- Stop to Smell the Hydrangeas (working title)
- Sex, Lies, and Cinnamon Trysts (working title)
- Everybody's Everyplace Every-bar (working title)

For updates, news on the latest releases, merchandise, and more, join our newsletter at www.sean-gregory.com

Follow me on Social Media!
Facebook: https://www.facebook.com/authorseandgregory/
Instagram: https://www.instagram.com/sean_gregory_author/
Threads: https://www.threads.net/@sean_gregory_author
YouTube: https://www.youtube.com/channel/@seangregoryauthor
Goodreads: https://www.goodreads.com/seangregoryauthor